The Devil and the Debutante

Heart of a Duke

USA TODAY BESTSELLER

CHRISTI CALDWELL

The Devil and the Debutante

Heart of a Duke Series

For more information about the author:
www.christicaldwellauthor.com
christicaldwellauthor@gmail.com
Twitter: @ChristiCaldwell
Or on Facebook at: Christi Caldwell Author

For first glimpse at covers, excerpts, and free bonus material, be sure to sign up for my monthly newsletter!

Printed in the USA.

Cover Design and Interior Format

Other Titles by
Christi Caldwell

ALL THE DUKE'S SINS
Along Came a Lady
Desperately Seeking a Duchess

ALL THE DUKE'S SIN'S PREQUEL SERIES
It Had to Be the Duke
One for My Baron

SCANDALOUS AFFAIRS
A Groom of Her Own
Taming of the Beast
My Fair Marchioness
It Happened One Winter

HEART OF A DUKE
In Need of a Duke—Prequel Novella
For Love of the Duke
More than a Duke
The Love of a Rogue
Loved by a Duke
To Love a Lord
The Heart of a Scoundrel
To Wed His Christmas Lady
To Trust a Rogue
The Lure of a Rake
To Woo a Widow
To Redeem a Rake
One Winter with a Baron
To Enchant a Wicked Duke
Beguiled by a Baron
To Tempt a Scoundrel
To Hold a Lady's Secret

DEDICATION

To Karen
There isn't a better friend in the world than you.
Thank you for accepting me as I am. Thank you for lifting me up
when I need it. Thank you for helping me solve everything from baking
dilemmas to tangles with poison ivy. Thank you for being an ear and a
shoulder to cry on. Just thank you. I love you dearly!
Faith and Rex are for you!

CHAPTER 1

London, England
Spring

AT THAT VERY MOMENT, A big, bald-headed guard escorted Lady Faith Brookfield and her friends through the narrow, darkened halls of Forbidden Pleasures.

Faith, along with Miss Anwen Kearsley, Marcia, the Viscountess Waters, and Marcia's new husband, Lord Waters, walked in a single file, putting Faith in mind of the ducks she took her young brother, Paddy, to feed at Hyde Park. That was, however, where all similarities to the bucolic image in her mind, ended.

Faith made a slow march behind her friends and the uniformed guard escorting them through the club's hidden corridors. The blood red carpets lining the halls muted their small party's footfalls.

She quickly worked her gaze over her surroundings.

Gilded frames containing portraits of naked women adorned the walls. Tapered candles within ornate crystal sconces cast eerie shadows upon crimson satin wallcoverings; shadows that would have terrified a lesser person. Sin oozed from every crevice that made up the notorious gaming hell. When it came to celebrating wickedness, no detail had been spared.

This was the place where fortunes were lost, and debaucheries of all sorts were indulged; a den of sin no *innocent* lady visited.

In fairness, Faith, and her friends, Marcia and Anwen, had not come to Forbidden Pleasures of their own free will. Abducted earlier that evening, on their way to the theatre, rescued by big, burly strangers, and whisked away to the clubs, they'd been deposited in the proprietor's offices until Lord Waters arrived to collect them.

Given all that, Faith and her friends had been fortunate to escape with not only their lives and, hopefully, their reputations, intact. As such, Faith should have only one thought in mind: getting out as quickly as she could. *Especially* since she'd been discovered snooping through the club ledgers by the head proprietor, Mr. Rex DuMond.

Faith had altogether *different* plans.

Her heart pounded. *Not* from fear.

She'd had the club's ledger in her hands. *All* the names and all the details of the members in this den of iniquity, their debt, their sins, their secrets, all at her fingertips. For all the pages she'd turned and the information she'd committed to memory, aside from Lord Waters, there'd been one gentleman whose sins she cared about. And whose information she would have had were it not for the interruption of Mr. DuMond.

Lord Somerville.

The man who'd ruined her Aunt Caroline's reputation could at last have his comeuppance.

As she continued to follow her friends through the darkened halls, Faith kept her gaze, not on her skittish friend, Anwen, moving quicker than Faith had ever seen her, or a somber Lord Waters, but that oblivious guard.

He was too predictable. Every twenty seconds, he looked to the viscount, eying him with a good deal of suspicion.

It was so very typical. A man would expect only the viscount to be one to watch.

Never did he once so much as crane his neck to catch sight of the ladies he led along the quiet passage. Another time that underestimation would have rankled. Now, she'd use it to her advantage.

Having moved ahead of Faith, Anwen paused, and looked back. Behind her wire-rimmed spectacles, horror dawned, and her eyebrows went flying up.

"What are you doing?" Anwen mouthed.

Faith touched a fingertip to her lips, compelling her friend to be quiet.

Anwen pleaded with her eyes. "*Don't,*" she silently enunciated that single syllable entreaty.

"I'm sorry," Faith mouthed. But she had to.

When they reached the end of the hall and the hulking giant finished with that predictable check, Faith bolted. Doubling back along the path he'd led them, she raced so quickly to Mr. DuMond's offices, her lungs screamed in protest. She compressed her lips tightly to keep those respirations quiet.

Pressing her left ear against the oak panel, she strained, listening for the hint of voices, footfalls, anything. Only the hum of silence greeted her.

Faith let herself back inside Mr. DuMond's offices. She swept her gaze over the room.

Empty.

Drawing the door shut quietly behind her, Faith hurried across the floor and dove under the same desk she'd pillaged a short while before. This time, she made even quicker work of the lock.

She didn't have much time.

Heart racing, Faith flipped through the pages, looking for that one name she'd spied earlier.

And there it was.

> *Lord Somerville*
> As Faith read, each sordid word burned into her mind, stamped in her memories.
> Debt to Forbidden Pleasures—twenty-thousand pounds.
> Wicked Pastimes: Dripping hot wax on his lovers
> Vices—Pays a fortune for the most experienced whores, assigns them the names of innocent young ladies of the ton, and beats his bed partners…

"Oh my God," Faith whispered. *This* is the man her Aunt Caroline had given her virtue to? She may have been brokenhearted all those years ago, but she'd dodged a proverbial bullet. No woman should ever suffer such a miserable fate as marrying such a cad as—

"Back for another look, are you?"

Faith lifted her head, cracking the top of it upon the wood drawer, and she groaned at the rush of pain. The book slipped from her fingers and landed with a damning *thump*.

Having been born partially deaf, Faith found the world often existed in a muffled hum. Speech and sounds were either quiet or distorted—especially when a room was crowded. But this room was not crowded. And there were no people present.

There was only her.

Her…and now…*him*.

Even knowing as much, Faith dipped her head out from under the desk.

None other than Rex DuMond.

At some four inches past six feet with heavily muscled shoulders and biceps that strained his coat sleeves, he conjured thoughts of that goddess Aphrodite's favored lover, Adonis. Only, the gentleman was dark as sin and menacing as Satan sauntering into sermons on Sunday. From the top of his midnight black hair to the smooth line of his Grecian nose and the wicked scar on his chiseled cheek, he'd have caused the flutter of any lady's heart—Faith's included. That was, *if* he'd not fixed a pair of unforgiving ice-blue eyes upon her.

Bloody hell.

Fear sapped the moisture from her mouth.

She'd not, however, reveal a hint of the terror he roused.

From a place she knew not where, she forced out a breezy response. "You again?"

"Me, again," he said grimly. "In my own offices. Imagine that."

With all the grace she could muster being discovered examining his books for a *second* time, Faith sailed to her feet.

"We really *must* stop meeting like this, Mr. DuMond."

"We could avoid that if you stopped snooping in my offices and availing yourself of my ledger."

"Touché." Faith forced more of that flippancy and swept across the room. "I should be go—"

He shoved the oak panel shut with one of his broad shoulders, and she stopped halfway toward him.

Mr. DuMond lounged against the door, the flat of his gleaming black boot pressed against the panel in what would be a casual repose for most. Not for this man; this man radiated an ominous energy, and his booted foot may as well have been an additional lock upon the door.

Bloody, bloody, *bloody* hell.

Well, when faced with being disarmed or doing the disarming, she'd opt for the latter.

Faith dropped her hands onto her hips. "You had me followed."

"Do you think I'm stupid? Careless?"

It was on the tip of her tongue to point out he'd been careless enough to have a lock easy for her to pick as the only thing guarding his secrets, but she thought better.

"Do you make it a habit of going through people's things?"

Given he'd found her doing that twice now, she really didn't feel an answer was required.

And then he unfurled, very much like a serpent unwinding its frame and slithering forward. He stopped a pace away. "Hmm? No answer, Honest Jack?"

Honest Jack? Faith tipped her chin back a fraction. "My name isn't Jack."

Did she imagine the smile that ghosted his lips? Surely, she did. For that firm, hard-looking mouth appeared incapable of so much as a smidgeon of warmth. He was a man toying with his prey. Toying with Faith, and that sent her spine up.

"Honest Jack was one of England's most notorious thieves."

"Oh."

"But you're a different kind of thief, aren't you?" he murmured.

Faith's heart thumped oddly in her chest, and she made herself smile in a bid to muddle him as much as he'd muddled her. Alas, his flat expression marked him as unmoved as all the other gentlemen of Polite Society had proven towards her.

In a bid for nonchalance, Faith struck out her right satin-slippered foot and struck a pose. "Are there really different kinds of thieves? Property, money, food, *people*." She looked pointedly at him on that one, and lifting a finger his way, she waggled the tip at him. "It's all bad and not at all good."

"Isn't 'all bad' and 'not all good' the same?"

She gave an energetic nod. "Precisely."

He started forward. His wasn't a walk. It was a prowl. Sleek of step, he stalked like a jungle cat she'd once been riveted by in the Royal Menagerie. *Then*, she'd been grateful for the cage between them. *Now*, she felt that same protective barrier would serve her even better in this moment, with *this* man.

She took a belated step back, but he was already upon her.

Unnerved—afraid, even—she stood her ground. She'd never been one to shrink and she wouldn't do so now.

Faith tipped up her chin another notch, daring him with her eyes, and as he leaned down and in, she promptly wished she hadn't.

With all that six feet four inches of pure heavy muscle, even as he bent close to meet her not-so-small five feet five inches, he still managed to tower over her, to make her feel tiny.

He opened his mouth to speak.

Unsettled, Faith beat him to it. "You smell."

He stilled.

"Good," she managed to finish through her muddled thoughts. Having learned early on to compensate for the sense she did not have, her others had become heightened. Always that skill had been a gift. Distracted as she was by Mr. Rex DuMond's masculine fragrance, she found herself, for the first time, regretting this heightened awareness. "You smell…good?"

"You're surprised."

"Qu–Quite. I should think you'd smell like sweat and unbathed bodies. At the very least, cheroots and brandy and—" She sniffed the air. "Though you do have a faint hint of both upon your person. But there's also a whisper of…" She sucked in through her nostrils a second time. "Orange."

His mouth twitched, and this time close as they were, she knew she'd not imagined his faintest of grins. An elusive one that teased hard lips; like he was a man who guarded his grins with the same ferocity he did the secrets of this sinful club of his.

He brought his mouth closer…to her right ear, and she abruptly turned, presenting him instead with the one she could hear fully from. So he did not have her at a greater disadvantage. So that he did not discover her greatest flaw.

"You are a thief, indeed, Faith Brookfield," he murmured, and she bristled.

"How dare—?"

"A thief of many hearts, I trust."

Faith went motionless and drew back slightly so she could better view his harshly chiseled features. And then, she promptly burst out laughing. She laughed until tears leaked from the corners of her eyes, poured down her cheeks, and her entire body shook from the force of that emotion. She doubled over clasping her knees and continued laughing.

Until she registered the otherwise stillness and silence of the room and the man opposite her.

Her smile faded, and she slowly straightened. "You…surely you aren't…serious?" she asked, because despite his deadly serious expression, he still must be jesting.

He dragged a single finger—his thumb—down the curve of her right cheek. The pad of that digit was callused and rough and yet intoxicating for the realness of it. Her body trembled.

"Do you take me for one who jests?"

"No," she blurted. "Is that a rhetorical question?" He opened his mouth. "I suspect it was."

"It was." His eyes glinted. With amusement…and desire? Surely, she imagined both. And yet, both together proved heady and distracting, and well, he was the last man she should become heady over or distracted by.

Faith forced herself to back away from him and his touch. "Either way, I'm not a thief of hearts or anything else."

A tension charged the air once more, erasing the almost playful nature of their exchange moments ago.

"Ah, but aren't you?" he whispered. "Did you not break into my desk and avail yourself of my ledgers?"

The backs of her legs collided with his desk, knocking her off her feet.

She'd not even known she'd been backing away from him, her

retreat having been primitively instinctive.

As primitive as those leopard's steps of his, the ones currently carrying him over. Closer. And then before her. Close as he was, he'd her blocked in, unable to stand unless she asked him to retreat, which she didn't bother wasting a breath on as she'd wager her fully-hearing ear he'd not relent.

"Hmm? Nothing to say?" He purred like that sleek black cat, too. "Nothing to say about helping yourself to my books, my lady?"

Ah, it had been too much to hope he'd let that matter rest.

"That…was not a rhetorical question earlier, either?" she ventured in hopeful tones.

"Not that one, either."

Drat.

Refusing to be cowed—and because to hell with him and this cat-and-mouse game he played with her—Faith angled her head farther back and met his eyes squarely. "You are, in fact, the worst sort of thief, Mr. DuMond."

"Am I?" He sounded casually bored, and that only rankled.

"Indeed. You are a thief of *people.*"

He clucked his tongue. She followed that slight but telltale movement of his lips, while only faintly making out the sound of it.

"Here I thought you should be more grateful, Faith. I, in fact, rescued you."

"I don't believe that for an instant," she shot back.

"Oh?" He folded his arms across a broad chest; that slight movement sent the black fabric of his jacket rippling over his muscles, highlighting and defining that sinew. "You must enlighten me, my lady."

His was both an order and a challenge and one she'd be wise to keep silent on. Alas, Faith had never been a master of her own silence.

"Your guards abducted me and my friends."

"My guards interrupted your abduction, brought you here, and summoned Lady Waters' husband." He scowled. "More the fool my men," he muttered under his breath.

Faith faltered. Only… "I'd be foolish and naïve to trust that you and your men operated with any real benevolence."

"You wound me." He sounded anything but.

"I think you *took* us, Mr. DuMond, so that you might leverage the funds Lord Waters now has after marrying my friend. You found a way for him to pay his debt to you. I believe you calculated— and incorrectly—that our families will not discover what you've done."

"Indeed." He sharpened menacing blue eyes on her face. A shade, very nearly aquamarine, had those irises belonged to another man, they would have mesmerized and not terrorized. "Is that all?"

There was a warning steeped within this question that this time wasn't really a question.

"It is certainly not. You see, I've gathered you aren't only a thief of people, but also of your patrons' fortunes and respectability."

In that moment, Faith knew she'd crossed a bridge too far. A gentleman would have taken offense with having his honor questioned, and yet this man...this man's eyes only sparked with an icy rage when she'd mentioned his club and his clients.

Faith dampened her lips, and unable to meet those unforgiving eyes a moment longer, she slid her gaze past him to the sealed door. "Now, if you would be so good as to excuse me?" With a toss of her head, Faith ducked around him and headed for that escape.

Mr. DuMond slid into her path, blocking her retreat. He slipped an arm around her waist and drew her close, and then lowered his mouth close to her ear.

Faith swiftly turned, presenting him with the one capable of hearing. "Never tell me you intend to say all that and just...leave?"

His voice was a soft purr, one that rumbled and resonated through her. Her body trembled and her thoughts were jumbled with disgust at his nearness. It had to be disgust.

"Nothing to say, *Faith?*"

The sound of her name falling from his hard lips brought her eyes flying open.

He laid claim and control of that single syllable as if he were the master of all. And in this universe, in this world, he was.

For the first time since she and her friends had been abducted and then separated within the gaming hell Forbidden Pleasures, the reality of her circumstances hit her. Truly hit her. The danger she faced.

A proper lady would surely worry at least some for her reputation. Not Faith. Faith was more focused on the whole living thing.

"You're afraid," he remarked, sounding so entirely pleased by that discovery, it effectively freed her from that emotion.

"Anything *but*, Mr. DuMond. I am not one who scares easily." Or she hadn't believed she was. Something about this man made her shake, when before him, she'd only believed that quavering happened on the pages of gothic novels she read.

The dark-haired proprietor smiled, a small, cold, and knowing smile. "Don't you?" he whispered. He rested a large palm on her right hip.

She felt that touch all the way through the fabric of her cloak and dress and the undergarments she wore underneath. How was it possible to feel the heat of a hand through all those layers? But God help her, she did. Her lashes fluttered. "D–Don't I, what?"

Another grin formed on his unforgiving mouth, this one slightly different than the one to precede it. This was a confident, cocksure, arrogant tip of those hard-looking lips that could only come from a man who'd gathered the effect he was, in fact, having on her.

"I'm going to commit another theft this night," he said, and she trembled once more.

"It is probably not the wisest to confess as much. A good thief would not go bandying about his intention—"

"I'm going to steal a kiss from you, Faith Brookfield," he murmured, that low baritone floating over her and doing funny things to both her heart and her belly.

Fear. It was surely fear. Only—

"What say you to that, kitten?" he teased, bringing his mouth close to hers.

"I…t-tend to prefer dogs," she stammered breathlessly. "My Uncle Leo has a dog and she's expecting pups. The dog, *not* my uncle. And he offered to give one to my sister. Though I'm sure cats are endearing too."

"Ah, but 'what say you to that, *pup*?' doesn't have quite the same feel to it."

Faith puzzled her brow. "No. I see your point there."

They conversed so easily she could almost forget that every movement of their mouths nearly brought their lips touching.

"We might opt for 'little owl'," she ventured.

"Little owl?"

"I've been told I have large eyes." Faith blinked, illustrating as much.

He slid his gaze over her face, lingering his stare on those eyes in question. "No, little owl is not beautiful enough for you, *petite chouette*."

"Little Owl in F-French does sound a good deal prettier."

"Indeed. I'm going to kiss you, *petite chouette*, and I think you are going to both want it and like it."

Faith's breath hitched, and she attempted casualness—failing tremendously the moment her words slipped forward like a whispery exhalation. "That is not…very…convincing. You *think* I am going to like it doesn't convey much confidence in your abilities."

He curled his lips up again and this was a brazen smile, a sexy one belonging to a man all too confident in his prowess. "I *know* you are going to like it."

"Th-there. That is b-better." Closing her eyes, Faith leaned up and touched her lips to his in a quick, fleeting kiss.

He stilled, bending his knees slightly, and angling back a fraction, he searched his eyes over her again. "Did you just kiss me?"

"Only to avoid having you steal it," she blurted. "The kiss. I don't like having anyone steal anything from me."

His eyes darkened. "You'd want this theft, Faith," he whispered. "It'd melt you inside and leave you hot in places you've never been, longing for more. Begging."

Her chest hitched once more. "I d-doubt that." The tremble to her voice marked her for the liar she was, and the amusement glinting in his hard eyes indicated he knew it too. "I daresay you must get on with it so that I can see for mysel—"

His mouth was on hers in an instant.

And all the saints in heaven combined, he was right, and she was as wrong as she'd suspected she'd be. His kiss was gloriously hot and hard. He laid claim to her, slanting his lips over hers. He was a man determined to possess her mouth, and Lord help her, she was more than content to surrender it to him.

And she did.

Faith whimpered, and he gripped her jaw with his left hand, firm enough that she suspected he'd leave a slight imprint of his touch, but gentle enough that she wanted him to grip her harder. "Open for me, *petite chouette*," he commanded between his kiss. Their kiss. It belonged to both of them. "Let me inside to taste you."

Faith opened for him. She was powerless to deny him. And here she'd never believed powerless could be this wickedly wonderful, just as she'd despaired of any man in London ever kissing her because not a single had expressed so much as an interest in courting her, let alone embracing her.

She'd been invisible to the men in the market for a wife.

Not that she believed Rex DuMond was in the market for a wife. Nor was she in the market for a husband—that was, a husband like Rex DuMond.

She, however, took what he gave—her first taste of passion. And she tasted of him. That citrusy sweetness of orange she'd caught a hint of before, along with cheroot and brandy, clung to him. Only those latter two didn't repulse as she'd expected. Instead, there was, if possible, an even greater aura of pure masculinity that left her warm in her belly and between her legs—just like he'd predicted.

His tongue swirled within her mouth. That hot flesh teased her, and she touched her tongue to his, tentatively at first. "Good girl," he praised, emboldening her, and then he moved his hands down her body, as if searching her, all the while enflaming her. He gripped her hips and dragged her close so she felt the long, hard ridge tenting the front of his trousers.

Suddenly he released her, and Faith stood there, dazed, hot, and her senses addled.

Rex chuckled, that guttural sound of amusement primal and filled with male satisfaction.

"Well?" he whispered against her lips, and she silently wept inside, secretly wanting more of him and his kiss.

Faith forced her lashes open and made a show of thinking. "You do smell of cheroots and brandy, after all."

"Do you mean taste of?" His was a taunting husky challenge.

"B–Both."

He chuckled. The low rumble shook his chest, and close as they were, she felt it inside. It shook her, too. In all the ways she'd not already been left shaken by him.

"I should leave."

"You should. But not without me verifying you haven't taken anything that is mine."

She dampened her mouth. "I didn't."

"Excuse me if, given the fact I've found you going through my belongings, I'm a bit hesitant to take you at your word."

Locking his gaze with hers, Mr. DuMond pressed both of his large palms under her arms, and then proceeded to run his hands along her side. There was something methodical about his search, and even so, her breath caught at the sureness of his touch.

"S–See? I-I told you." Everything she'd stolen, she'd committed to memory. "I don't have any—" Her words faded to a gasp, as he sank to a knee. "Wh–What are you doing?"

"I told you. You availed yourself to my ledgers, *petite chouette*. I'm not a stupid man, and I'm not one to underestimate anyone. I'm searching you everywhere."

Oh God. "V–Very well," she said, staring over the top of his dark hair. "Best get on with it, then."

And he did. With one hand, he slowly inched up her skirts and ran his other large hand up her leg starting at her ankle, and then shifting his search along her calf, and then higher, ever higher.

He pressed his large palm against that place between her legs that shamefully ached in a way she'd never ached before. Even as his exploration was methodical in nature, her body did not care for the distinction.

And then, he removed his hands from her and lowered her skirts. Suddenly, his features snapped alert.

"What is—?" Faith's question was interrupted a moment later by a frantic pounding on the door, a pounding loud enough for her to hear and one that both shook the panel and sent reverberations rolling along the floor.

Despite the franticness of the muffled but distinct shouts from the corridor, Rex DuMond moved with the same slow, casual grace he had through her entire brief knowing of him. Strolling across the floor, he reached for the lock.

"Your cravat," she whispered furiously.

He paused with his finger on the elaborate, carved key jutting from the keyhole, and glanced back.

Lord Waters's furious shouts reached into Mr. DuMond's— Rex's, because surely after a kiss such as that one, Christian names were permitted—offices. "Open, you bloody…"

Faith motioned frantically to his rumpled cravat.

Mr. DuMond—Rex—bent his neck forward at an awkward downward angle to examine the article in question, and then in one smooth motion, he yanked off the offending article and tossed it on the floor. "Better?"

Faith slapped a palm over her eyes. "No. That is the opposite of better. That is—"

"Worse?"

She nodded frantically.

"But eminently more comfortable." And then dismissing her outright, with his cravat lying damningly on the floor near his feet, Rex drew the panel open.

The enraged viscount all but fell forward into the room.

"Lord Waters!" Faith exclaimed.

"Are you hurt?" he demanded.

"Not at all."

The viscount eyed Rex a long moment. The proprietor offered him no assurances; he gave Marcia's husband nothing but silence.

"Come along, my lady. My wife and your other friend are with the Duke of Rothesby and Lord Landon, waiting in the carriage."

As he beckoned, Faith quit Rex DuMond's offices for a second and certainly last time.

CHAPTER 2

ꟻUCKING HELL.

Rex DuMond, the Marquess of Rutherford, set his glass down hard on his desk. The last damned thing he'd wanted or needed was to have proper, respectable ladies brought within the walls of his club. No gaming hell would survive that. His patrons—deviants and wastrels the lot of them—welcomed the sin and decadence to be found at Forbidden Pleasures. But those same men whose self-interests came first, well, even they would draw the line at attending a club where the respectable ladies of their ranks could be ruined.

In need of another drink, Rex poured himself a second brandy, raised the glass to his lips—and promptly stopped as a memory of the very lady who could see his gaming hell ruined entered his mind.

"I'm more of a dog person."

Despite himself, despite the fact Rex was hardened by life and therefore unamused by all, he felt a grin form on his mouth.

The last thing to hold his interest or tempt him in any way was a respectable lady. Even so, Rex found himself hard-pressed not to recall the little rasps of the lady's breathing as he'd made sweet love to her mouth or the ridiculously lengthy ramblings that fell from those same luscious lips.

Knock

That sharp, perfunctory rap brought him back to the present.

Rex set his glass down once more. "Enter," he called, and the door was already open as a trio of men of equal height in stature, but differing breadth of power streamed inside.

His partners at Forbidden Pleasures—the Duke of Argyll; Lord Malden, the future Duke of Craven; and Lachlan Latimer. They formed an unlikely diarchy—three of them born to dukes and one of them born to the streets. There were no other people Rex was more loyal to than the ones before him.

The moment the door closed, Latimer, head of security, provided an update. "They've taken their leave."

Rex lifted an eyebrow. "All of them *this time?*"

"All of them," the Marquess of Malden confirmed. Immaculately well-tailored, with never a crisp white cravat or blond hair out of place, he'd more the look of a strapping scholar than part-owner of a wicked gaming hell.

"Why did she return to your office?" Argyll put that obvious question to Rex.

Rex went on to explain just how he'd discovered Faith Brookfield—twice now. When he'd finished, there was a long silence.

"This isn't good," Latimer said in his raspy voice that bore the faintest hint of the rough East London streets upon it.

Rex didn't pretend to misunderstand the meaning behind the other man's words. "They aren't going to say anything."

"Are you certain of that?" Argyll asked.

"For someone who deals in the business of rotting souls of the lords and ladies of London, you're someone suddenly awfully confident and trusting that they won't breathe a word," Malden said.

Rex slid a glance the other man's way. "Need I remind you, we all deal in the business of rotting souls," he said icily, and color splotched the other marquess's cheeks.

Where Rex and Argyll had both relished the futures and fortunes they'd built off debauchery, Malden too often proved the same young boy whom Rex had once rescued from beatings at Eton. Though the other marquess wasn't frail as he'd been then, Malden still possessed the same weakness of seeking the approval of a father undeserving of that effort.

Rex put a question to the group. "What would you suggest? That we off the ladies and their powerful relatives? If abducting," – even if it were just the perception of what had happened—"is bad for business, whatever would the *ton* say to killing peers?"

"I'm not saying off them," Malden protested, his cheeks growing more flushed.

Rex stole a glance at the panel past his partners, the three barriers between Rex and ending the farcical drama brought upon him and his club. "What are you suggesting then?" he asked impatiently.

"I'm merely pointing out that there were three ladies alone in your offices," Malden said. "With the club's books unsecured."

"I keep my ledgers and business sealed under lock and key. It's a Chubb's lock," he said, pointing out they'd employed England's most skilled locksmith.

"And she picked it?" Latimer asked.

Rex nodded. The shockingly fearless minx had done just that— *twice*.

Latimer set his too-square jaw; between those slightly heavy features, and a nose bent from too many breaks he'd suffered over the years in his time fighting, it was a face of most people's nightmares—not Rex's. Rex had only ever seen the power the other man possessed and was capable of as a boon to benefit Forbidden Pleasures.

"You're the one about Town." Latimer directed his words to Argyll. Argyll was charming and affable where Rex was hardened and cold. As such, the young duke moved effortlessly between the *ton* and their den of sin. "Has the lady got a mouth on her?"

"The lady is something of a wallflower." *God, the lords in London were dolts.* "She is known to volunteer much of her time at her mother's school, the Ladies of Hope."

"And?" Latimer pressed.

"*And* it is my belief she's entirely too innocent to go about making trouble for us," Argyll finished.

The other man was decidedly wrong. Faith Brookfield was her own kind of trouble. The way the innocent had kissed him with abandon proved her interest in his books had been prompted by the lady's curious nature.

"What do you think about the chit, DuMond?" Malden asked quietly, ultimately deferring to Rex—as he invariably did and had since Rex had come to his rescue at Eton and taken him under his wing. "Do you believe she'll pose a problem?"

"She was sufficiently—" Aroused. Intrigued. Enticed. "—scared," he settled for.

"If the details of our business are bandied about, the club could be ruined," Latimer warned.

"I'm confident it won't be," Argyll vouched for Rex. "Not by Lady Faith Brookfield."

Rex hardened his jaw. "Not by anyone.

Not because he was a man who didn't believe the absolute worst things did and could happen to a person in life. He well knew it could. Nor had he given these men, his closest—his only—confidantes in the world, false assurances about Lady Faith Brookfield.

Rather, because he was experienced enough to know he'd had an innocent in his arms.

A woman who'd responded with the passion Faith had, a woman with dazed, starry owl eyes, wasn't capable of anything more than romantic thoughts and illusions of her time here.

He'd wager his very soul on it.

CHAPTER 3

FAITH SAT ON THE BENCH of the hired hackney she'd taken from her friend's household to the corner of Villiers Street long after her conveyance had arrived. She continued to peer intently at the article she'd spent weeks writing and revising and writing again since her foray inside Forbidden Pleasures.

It'd been essential that every word was right and the plan of what to do with the article be carefully thought out. More importantly, she'd known if she acted in haste after being caught going through Mr. DuMond's ledgers, that information would be easily traced back to her. So, she'd bided her time and not done anything with her work—until now.

Faith expected she should feel a greater sense of guilt giving this page over to *The Morning Chronicle*. After all, she wasn't in the business of ruining lives. No, that dubious pleasure belonged largely to greedy men in power.

On the contrary, as a rule she'd dedicated herself to being one of the helpers. Faith volunteered at her mother's school, Ladies and Gentlemen of Hope, which offered a home and schooling to girls—and more recently, boys, too—who, not unlike Faith, had different impairments. There she read to the youngest students, and when she wasn't doing that, Faith was helping look after her younger, recently adopted, brother, Paddy.

She never failed to defend the wallflowers who found themselves on the receiving end of vitriol from the ladies deemed Diamonds. Deaf in one ear and a wallflower herself, Faith knew all too well something of being an outcast. And for her friends and family who'd been hurt by love, she never failed to be that shoulder…and voice of hope for their ultimately finding more.

This would be the first time in her life that she ruined a man's life, and she didn't feel anything but a thrill of triumph.

For was it really ruining a man's life, or helping to save other, more worthy lives instead?

Alas, her friend Anwen was of an altogether different opinion.

"This is a terrible idea," Anwen muttered.

Faith knew the other woman both meant it and believed it. After all, she'd uttered the phrase no fewer than a dozen times since they'd set out at dawn.

"Men don't take well to having their lives ruined, Faith," her friend insisted. "They don't like it at all. It makes them testy, and worse, it makes them vengeful. The last thing you need is a vengeful man in your life."

The last thing she had was *any* man in her life.

"I need to do this," Faith said quietly.

Her friend quit her bench and squeezed herself onto the seat beside Faith. "Do you, Faith?" the other woman implored. She touched a hand to her shoulder; gripping lightly, and forcing Faith to look at her wide eyes, unblinking over those large, round spectacles. "*Do you?*"

"He deserves it, does he not?" she asked defensively.

"Of course, he does." Her friend paused. "But he'll eventually have his day. You being the one to carry it out? It will only make you a target for his displeasure and anger—"

"And he'll have absolutely no idea I was the one behind it," she interrupted. "I'll simply hand the article over and then take my leave, with none the wiser."

"Secrets don't stay secrets forever, Faith." Her friend spoke in cryptic tones that, despite herself, raised the gooseflesh on Faith's arms. "Inevitably someone knows something, and when someone knows something, then everyone knows everything."

That much was true.

And yet…

"Did Somerville show the same compunction when it came to

breaking my Aunt Caroline's heart?" she demanded of her friend. "I'll save you from answering. No, he did not. For years my aunt paid the price—"

"Your aunt, who is now happily married and very much in love with her husband."

"That isn't the point," she said impatiently. "My aunt was the one whose reputation suffered, whose name was ruined, and whose heart was broken." And now, he was set to marry another woman. Not just any woman, a student from Ladies and Gentlemen of Hope, partially blind and romantic and easy prey for a man still in want of a fortune.

"You believe in fate," Faith said. "Why do you think we were abducted and then locked away in the offices of the head proprietor of London's most wicked gaming hell? Why, if not to do something good with the information we learned that night?" She rested her hand on Anwen's. "Come, you of all people should be fully in support of what I intend to do."

"I believe in fate, but I'm also a realist, Faith," her friend said calmly. "I know firsthand just how men respond when women attempt to thwart their marital prospects." She was one of the founding members of the controversial Mismatch Society. An institution dedicated to helping women avoid bad marriages, it'd set society on its ear…and not in a good way. "They don't like it."

Faith beamed. "Ah, yes, but the ladies, on the other hand, being saved, do."

She reached for the door handle, but her friend stayed her hand.

"Don't do this, Faith," Anwen said quietly. "No good comes to those who spread gossip."

"This isn't about spreading gossip, Anwen," she said, willing her friend to understand. "Don't you see? It's about saving women from predators. It's about sparing ladies like my aunt from men who'd seduce them, all with the intent of getting their fortunes."

"Maybe some women don't mind? Mayhap they're more than content accepting a loveless union so that they don't become a spinster dependent upon her family's charity."

"I refuse to believe that."

"Yes, well, you're only on your first Season," her friend said flatly.

"If you're still unwed after five, six, or seven Seasons—Like Anwen, whom Faith met after her Come Out—then come speak to me."

Her heart twisted and her frustration mounted at the men who were too blind to see the real worth of women. "I don't believe you would accept those handouts, Anwen," she said quietly. "And as your friend, I wouldn't allow you to. Because you deserve to be in love and loved in return. And men like these…" She shook her pages once more. "They aren't capable of it." They were capable of far worse. "Do you believe these men," she held up the folded article she'd written, "think of the consequences of their actions? Do they think about the heartbreak they leave in their wake? You needn't answer. I'll answer for you. They don't."

Anwen closed her eyes, and Faith knew the moment she'd reached the other woman. Knew that despite her misgivings, Anwen was on board.

When she opened them, she scowled. "I still say this is a terrible idea."

Knock-Knock-Knock

The impatient driver rapped on the door.

"You coming out?"

"In a moment," Anwen called testily. She looked at Faith. "Fine," she said, in resigned tones.

Before her friend might change her mind, Faith tucked her article into her leather satchel and pushed the door open.

She held out a hand to the scowling driver and he helped her down.

"Please wait here. We'll be a moment, and if you wait there will be more coin." To demonstrate her generosity, and to keep the fellow here waiting, Faith paid him his coin, and then a small sum more.

The driver, with an impressively crop of shaggy hair that couldn't be contained by the cap atop his head, shot up equally shaggy eyebrows before pocketing Faith's money.

His disposition remarkably improved, he tipped that hat struggling to stay balanced.

Because people were a good deal kinder and better when their fortunes increased.

Fortunes had that effect on people.

It was also one of the reasons she found herself here now.

Adjusting the leather strap over her right arm, with Anwen sticking close to her side, Faith crossed the cobblestones to the narrow shopfront across the way.

She paused on the threshold and tugged forward her deep hood, using the store window to verify her identity remained concealed.

After all, a lady couldn't be caught sneaking about and certainly not here, and not with these intentions. Why her sister's chance of a match one day would be ruined if Faith were found out.

Collecting the door's handle, Faith let herself and Anwen inside.

She wasn't certain what she'd expected—perhaps a room awash with candlelight and buzzing as a small army of people within rushed about seeing to their important work.

Silence greeted them.

And darkness.

"I don't like this at all," Anwen whispered, reaching for Faith's fingers. "Let us lea—"

"What do you want?"

That blunt, loudly spoken question cut across the quiet, and the two women jumped.

Faith's heart racing, she did a quick sweep for the owner of that voice and found him framed in a doorway that connected to a back room.

Faith hastened over to meet the man. Not more than two or three years older than herself and broad like the builder who'd recently completed renovations on her family's country estate, the young man also wore an apron that looked better suited to a baker. Except ink covered the white article and marked him the man who did the important work here.

Taking care to keep her face hidden in the shadows of her hood, Faith stopped at the front counter. "I've a piece. Information I believe you'd like to print."

Folding his arms across his muscular chest, he nudged his chin her way. "Well?"

Faith reached inside her bag and drew out the page. Wordlessly, she placed the writing before him.

Absolute silence met her as the editor read.

"It is an…article," she said to fill the void. "I possess the name of a peer who is in dun territory, and details on his vast debts, many of which have been obtained through scandalous pursuits… and who is hunting a lady's fortune."

At her side she caught the way Anwen shook her head. "Bad idea."

Faith shot her a look and returned her attention to the printer.

When he'd finished reading, he raised his head. Suspicion filled his brown eyes. "Where'd you find yourself this information?"

"Ah," she whispered, wagging a finger at him. "A writer never reveals her source."

With a grunt, he considered it a second time.

For a long time.

So long, that the clock ticking became inordinately loud, and she caught the beat of her pulse in her own ears.

"I'll take it."

It was a moment before she registered those three words, begrudgingly spoken, and yet confirmation.

Faith's heart thumped harder, and she fought the urge to let out a triumphant squeal. And yet, it wasn't about the fact she'd sold the piece, or about the money. Money that she could now anonymously contribute to her mother's expanding school. At last, justice was being served.

She made herself remain still as the man pulled out a center drawer and fished out several coins. He pushed them across the table.

Collecting them, Faith tucked them in her reticule, and turned to go.

"You've got more?"

She paused and glanced back.

He nodded his head. "More stories like this?"

More stories? More gentlemen, he meant. She absolutely did. None, however, that she was willing to share with him or anyone.

Anwen was the first to find her voice. "She doesn't! At all. Not a single one. Just…that one." Her friend took Faith by the hand and gave a tug to move her along.

The editor smiled. "I'll take the lady's silence as a 'yes'."

If the stranger here could deduce her secrets, DuMond would make her his evening meal and hold onto her remains for dessert.

"I'm not looking to share anything more than that," Faith explained.

Anwen groaned and gave a shake of her head. "Too much," she whispered. "You're saying too much."

Faith turned to go but the printer stayed her with another question. "Is it revenge, then?"

She and Anwen spoke at the same time.

"Absolute not?"

"Does it matter?" Faith put to him.

"Don't suppose so." He called out again, stopping her a second time. "But if you *do* have other information like this and you're inclined to share, I'd be interested in it."

With that offer given, this time she and Anwen took their leave. As they hastily made their way down the still-quiet pavement towards the hack, she considered the printer's request…and offer.

The printer was, in fact, correct. With her ability to retain everything she read or saw, Faith did possess a good deal more details, salacious ones. Scandalous ones about some of London's most powerful men. The printer might want them. Faith, on the other hand, knew that to continue divulging details about Rex's patrons could only end badly. For her. She expected even when the Day of Judgment came, he'd be as capable of convincing the Lord he deserved not only a spot in heaven but a halo to go with it as he would talking the Devil out of his pitchfork and place in those fiery depths.

The moment they climbed in the carriage and the hack started on its way, Anwen spoke. "I have a bad feeling about this."

"It is done," she assured her. She'd ruined Somerville and that was enough.

"I suspect with a man like Mr. DuMond it is never done," Anwen said in haunting tones that raised the gooseflesh upon Faith's arms.

Her friend was right.

Sharing this particular information about the Earl of Somerville was dangerous enough. Not because that caddish fortune-hunter who'd hurt her aunt so badly was in any way a worthy adversary. He wasn't. A man so sloppy in his attempts at acquiring a fortune and ruining a lady in the process was hardly capable.

Nay, the real threat stemmed from crossing a man like Rex DuMond. The head of Forbidden Pleasures wasn't stupid. Anything but. Having not only discovered her with his club ledgers but reading them aloud, it would not take much for him to gather who was sharing that private information. Her. The last thing she wanted for herself, or her family was to acquire an enemy. Particularly an adversary as menacing as Rex DuMond.

CHAPTER 4

London, England
Several weeks later

THERE WAS NOTHING MORE PATHETIC than a man who wore his upset visibly.

And there was no one more reckless and stupid than one who challenged Rex DuMond, the owner of Forbidden Pleasures.

In that moment, Lord Ian Somerville proved to be both.

Neither was a new discovery to Rex. He was in the business of dealing in the secrets of England's peers. He knew the men better than even the poor, pathetic ladies who took their names and handed over their doweries and self-respect for the privilege of a title.

"Did you hear me, DuMond?" the lanky man all but shouted, slamming his fist against an open palm. Somerville's voice rang with desperation and terror and pealed all around the office like the mournful bells being rung at a funeral service at St. Mary's.

Rex's lips pulled in a harsh, mocking smile. More pathetic emotions there were not.

Lord Somerville stuck a finger at him. "You are responsible for this, DuMond!"

From the corner of the room, Argyll clucked his tongue. "Tsk. Tsk. Have a care, Somerville." The affable Argyll issued that warning, and the earl switched his attention briefly from Rex to the duke.

When the earl again returned his attention to Rex and spoke, there was a quieter desperation to his tones. "No one could have known the information that's been shared." With that careless charge hurled, Somerville's cheeks, already florid from both too much drink and the increasing breadth his vices had brought him, grew a mottled shade. "No one!"

Rex had tolerated the first show of temper and challenge because it amused him. Drink, he'd learned, made men do stupid, careless things. Those weaknesses served to his benefit. They'd lined his pockets. But no one challenged him.

Ever. And no one—absolutely no one—crossed him.

"Sit," he commanded in a steely, ice-laden whisper that managed to penetrate Lord Somerville's temper.

All the color washed free of the earl's cheeks. The ridiculously large Adam's apple bobbed—that exaggerated warble all the more noticeable for the absence of the man's cravat—and Somerville dropped quickly into the nearest seat. He reached up to tug at where that fabric should have been.

Malden, the most measured and eminently most respectable of the gaming hell owners and an almost invisible observer of the exchange, came forward, plucked the rumpled article from the floor, and politely handed the scrap of ivory silk over to their irate patron.

Somerville snatched the fabric from him without so much as a word of thanks.

But then the nobility didn't thank anyone for anything, not even their fellow peers to whom they were in exorbitant debt. They took the world as their due and the people in it, players on a stage, there to amuse them.

As the son of a duke, Rex had learned those truths firsthand. In fairness, he didn't deal in thank-yous, either. Those two words conferred nothing. They were empty expressions and provided no actual currency and were therefore useless to him.

Steepling his fingers, Rex flexed his fingertips, pressing them together. All the while he stared over their tops to the red-faced gentleman before him.

At last, when the man opposite him was suitably pale and

silent, Rex spoke. "First, never enter my offices and put your false accusations to me. Ever," Rex said, frostily. "Certainly not about how I operate my club and how I protect the information of my patrons. Is that understood?"

Somerville gave a wobbly nod that sent his heavily oiled Byronic curls tumbling over his eyes, putting Rex in mind of a small, pathetic child afraid of a scolding. "Y-Yes. V-Very much u-understood." The earl stretched an entreating hand, palm up. The candle's glow revealed the shimmer and sheen of sweat coating that lily white skin. "But surely you s-see...no one else could have known the information that is being bandied about. *No one.*"

"Do you truly believe no one knows of your proclivities?" Argyll drawled, with an effortless humor Rex had never managed—nor cared to attempt—in his life.

Crimson splotches bloomed on the earl's cheeks, lending them color once more. "But...this..." Somerville leaned in and spoke on a loud whisper. "This was different. These are details absolutely no one could have——"

Rex thinned his eyes into small, tiny slits and the other man instantly—wisely—fell silent. Yes, they were secrets that no one could have known. Absolutely no one, that was...except one. Only one person had gotten access to his books. An unlikely person, at that. It was a secret Rex would share with no one. Certainly not to the quaking fool before him.

"I'm not in the business of trading in my patrons' secrets," Rex said coolly. "And those in my employ wouldn't dare." They knew he'd crush them. He'd make it so no corner of this dreary, godforsaken island was safe. "Nor are my partners."

Those three, Rex would trust with his life.

Somerville's bony shoulders sagged as he slumped in his seat. "Then, who?" he whispered, more to himself. "Who could possibly know the exact sums I've spent on..."

"Paying men to whip you?" Argyll supplied. "Your habits are not a complete secret among the *ton.*"

"But not the exact amounts I've spent on my——"

"Debauchery?" Malden offered that second option.

Somerville nodded.

"If you have someone disloyal to you, someone who'd deal in your secrets, then I suggest you find that information out for yourself and settle your own business instead of coming to me." Rex lowered his previously steepled fingers and laid his palms on the table, leaning over them. Leaning forward. "But do not ever—I repeat, *ever*—leverage accusations about either me or my club…or this." He shoved the newspaper with that damning article written on Somerville's debt and reason for it back at the other man. "Am I clear?"

The earl whimpered and hunching into himself, he gave another one of those frantic bobs of his head.

Suddenly, tears appeared in the man's eyes, and if Rex had been one given to shows of emotion, he'd have openly groaned at such a pathetic display. Alas, he'd not cried even once as a child, and he'd even less tolerance for the many men who'd wept openly before him when he'd called in their debt.

"But I needed this bride." Somerville's voice trembled as badly as his unblemished hands did. "It is the only way I can pay you."

Making it a business of knowing all his clients' business, Rex wasn't the only one the earl was in debt to.

"Then I suggest you find yourself a bride who is amenable to marrying a cur like you. There are any number of ladies far more naïve and more desperate than the one you let get away."

"There isn't. Blind in an eye and sent to live at that ridiculous school by her brother, she was my best hope."

"That isn't my problem." Rex sat back in his chair and laid his arms along the sides of the seat. "Unless there is something else you wished to discuss, our meeting is concluded." He threaded a warning note through the words, one even a deaf man could have heard.

The earl shook his head.

Rex nudged his chin. "We are done here."

Somerville sprang to his feet and dropped a deep, deferential bow, then backed away quickly, only turning when he knocked into the head guard and partial proprietor, Latimer, who'd been otherwise as silent as the shadows he'd hidden within.

"Let's go," the big guard growled, and then like the rat he was,

Somerville scurried off with Latimer following.

When the door had closed behind them, Rex, Argyll, and Malden didn't speak. None of them were men given to filling voids of silence. Each was equally comfortable not lending his voice, particularly Rex and Malden who'd perfected the art of silence as children, seeking to avoid beatings at the hands of equally cruel fathers.

Latimer reappeared a handful of minutes later. "He's gone," he said, his gravelly speech containing the trace of a rough Cockney from the years he'd spent on the street. "I put him in the carriage, myself.

As if he'd been freed by that discovery, Argyll shot to his feet and began to pace. "Bloody fucking hell," the duke spat as he walked. "Bloody fucking hell."

Malden winced at that crude litany from the other gentleman.

Rex had never been so weak, either at mastering his temper or cringing at curse words.

But then, a marquess born to a vengeful duke who'd gone to great lengths to remind Rex just what his place in this world was, he'd learned early on what the world in fact was...and more, what it wasn't. It was a ruthless place, where the power a man accrued kept him safe and secure.

In order to toss their fortunes away at Rex's club, those lords and ladies needed to trust that the secrets of what went on in this place and the true nature of their wealth and proclivities were safe. If anyone learned that was no longer the case, Forbidden Pleasures would cease to exist—this club he'd purchased when it had been failing and then built up to the prosperous hell it was now.

Rex drummed the tips of his perfectly aligned fingers together in that focusing activity he'd adopted as the beaten boy in his father's luxurious nursery, the rhythm of that slight compression a distractor that channeled his attentions and energies so that he was centered only on the slight press and withdrawal.

Press. Relax.

Press. Relax.

Over and over again.

It never failed to focus him. It'd been a calming mechanism he'd adopted when the duke had backhanded him across the face and his ring had cut Rex's skin, leaving him forever scarred.

From then on, that distracted gesture had never failed to focus him. Even with the threat of doom hanging over him and his club, this time was no exception.

Argyll released his dozenth "Bloody fucking hell" before Malden looked to Rex.

"Do you have nothing to say on this, DuMond?" The younger marquess spoke in the same pleading way he had as a boy at Eton, looking to Rex to defend him against whichever bully had decided to make his life a living hell.

"What would you have me say?" he asked coolly. Rex raised a hand in Argyll's direction. "He seems to have words enough for all of us."

"I've said nothing more than 'Bloody fucking hell'," Argyll snapped.

"Ah yes. Indeed. And just how much has that helped any," Rex waved a hand over the stacks of newspapers piled atop his otherwise immaculate desk, "of this?"

The duke glared. "Well, one of us should be worried."

"I'm worried." That low growl came from the spot Latimer had availed himself to at the right corner of the front window.

Argyll jabbed a finger at the other man who'd been largely silent on the matter until now. "See. Even fucking *Latimer* is worried."

Latimer's lethal stare remained trained on the window and the patrons milling in the club, giving no indication that he was, at the moment, being discussed.

Rex had long thought if he himself had been born with a soul, the icy giant of a man responsible for the club's security would have been his kindred one. Latimer, some nobleman's discarded bastard, had worked in Forbidden Pleasures long before Rex had purchased the club and knew the hell and its patrons inside and out.

Argyll released another, 'Bloody fucking hell,' and resumed his senseless meandering over the floor.

The thing of it was, worrying didn't fix anything.

Rather, worrying rotted the brain and shriveled a man's spirit.

He'd learned early on that the worst thing invariably did happen, and the fact that he'd been alive and standing each time it did had only reinforced the fact that man could survive every single hardship, misery, and horror thrown his way.

This time was no exception.

It was a nuisance and a bloody fucking problem—and a big one at that.

But they'd encountered any number of problems in the course of their operation.

Malden cleared his throat. "If I may?" he said, raising a hand. "It does seem like someone has gleaned details only we might know."

Yes, someone had. It was a detail only he knew, and also one he'd kept from his partners because there'd been no sense in sharing it. Because he'd been certain the chit wouldn't do anything with the information she'd read. Because surely she couldn't have remembered much of what had been on those pages she'd helped herself to. And also, because he'd kissed her dizzy that day, all with the intent purpose of searching her person for a hint of evidence. There'd been none. She'd not recorded the information from his ledgers. The fault for this, however, didn't lie with Rex, but rather to the one whose folly had seen that damned debutante in his clubs.

Quitting his study of the tables below, Rex turned and looked squarely at Latimer. "Someone does know," he whispered in menacing tones. "And do you know just who that someone is?"

Latimer froze and then slowly shook his head.

Rex pressed his fingertips together once more. "A lady."

His partners reeled.

Malden found his voice first. "Surely…not," he sputtered. "Surely you aren't suggesting…who…how?"

"Oh, I don't know," Rex said. He crossed to the full liquor cabinet and availed himself to a bottle of whiskey and glass. "Perhaps if someone brought her to my offices and left her to her own devices with our ledgers."

Latimer grunted. "How was anyone to know the chit could pick a lock better than a London thief?"

How indeed?

Malden made a sound of protest. "He couldn't have just left the young lady in danger."

Despite being a partner at Forbidden Pleasures, the other marquess had never ceased conducting himself as a gentleman and thinking like a gentleman.

"Yes, we could have," Rex remarked frostily as he poured himself a drink. "*We* could have done any manner of things that night other than have her brought here. We didn't."

Latimer's cheeks grew flushed. "Creed and Tavish brought the girls here."

"As the head of club security, you are the one Tavish and Creed report to." Rex impatiently cut through the other man's useless objection. "They are an extension of you. As such, you may as well have issued a personal invitation and escort to not one, not two," as he counted, he lifted a finger on his other hand, "but *three* ladies. This," he gestured around the room at large with his glass, "is all a product of your failing."

Latimer didn't dispute the charge. Rather he lowered his head in acknowledgement of that greatest blunder made.

"Either way, blame doesn't fix the situation," said Malden, ever the moderator and peacemaker of their quartet. "The situation needs to be fixed."

And Rex would be the one to do it.

Argyll must have seen something in his eyes. "You already have a plan."

Indeed, he did. "The lady needs to be silenced. Everyone possesses sins and secrets." Things with which to use as leverage to silence them. Lady Faith Brookfield was no exception. It was just a matter of determining what secrets she sought to keep. "And when I learn hers, we can rest assured that any other information she knows about the patrons here will go unshared."

Rex smiled, a cold grin, empty of mirth. One that, had the lady seen it, would have chilled...and would have let her know the grave danger found when one crossed the devil.

CHAPTER 5

F̶AITH HAD NEVER CONSIDERED HERSELF a coward. In fact, she'd always thought of herself as brave.

And yet, following her explosive meeting with the proprietor of Forbidden Pleasures weeks earlier, and after she'd sold secrets of his club, she'd resolved to never again step foot inside his club. Or call him out. Or even think of him. In short, following the sale of that article, she'd vowed her path would never cross his.

Alas, Rex DuMond had other plans.

Faith strolled into one of the many parlors of her mother's school still in the midst of having bookshelves installed along the walls to convert it into another library for the growing student population, caught sight of the latest patron to visit and read to the children— and promptly walked out.

Her heart racing, Faith stood in the hallway. *Impossible.* She'd imagined him. That was all there was to it. She was seeing him everywhere, in her dreams, in her waking thoughts.

Only, what accounted for both seeing him *and* hearing that deep, gravelly baritone of his as he read to children of Ladies and Gentlemen of Hope?

"…Young Forester was frank, brave, and generous but he had been taught to dislike politeness so much that, the common forms of society appeared to him either odious or ridiculous; his sincerity was seldom restrained by any feelings of others."

Peeking inside, she found him. No apparition. Very real and very much here. Fully engrossed in reading to the five boys around him, he gave no outward indication that he'd noticed her.

"...*His love of independence was carried to such an extreme, that he was inclined to prefer the life of Robinson Crusoe in his desert island to that of any individual in cultivated society...*"

Heart thundering, she ducked back behind the wall. She took off running through the school halls.

Out of breath, Faith hurtled headlong into her mother's office. "What is Mr. DuMond do—oh!"

Her mother and head teacher, the Countess of Montfort, paused mid-discussion and looked up from the papers laid out upon the table.

Briefly knocked off-balance, Faith dropped a curtsy. "Lady Montfort."

The countess—a kindly woman who'd been on staff at Faith's mother's school since the earliest days of its inception—inclined her head. "Faith," she greeted warmly.

Faith cleared her throat. "I was hoping I might have a word with you, Mother?"

The two women exchanged a look, and Faith's mother said something to the countess.

Perhaps another time, any other time, Faith would have been mortified about storming her mother's office and interrupting a meeting. This, however, was not one of those times.

The moment she found herself alone with her mother, Faith rushed over. "Mr. DuMond is here," she whispered. My God, *why* was Mr. DuMond here?

Her mother looked up from her notes and glanced around the room as if the subject in question had unexpectedly joined them. "I...?" She shook her head.

Faith attempted to speak evenly, even as her heart pounded. "Mr. DuMond, the gaming hell owner," she repeated as calmly as she could manage. "Reading to the boys." His sudden appearance, though innocuous as it might seem, was too coincidental. Wasn't it?

"Faith," her mother chastised. "We are *not* snobbish. Mr. DuMond has made a sizeable donation and asked to speak with the students and learn what the funds will be used for."

Faith rocked back on her heels. Mr. DuMond who kissed like sin and tasted like temptation, wanted to become a benefactor? "Impossible." She spoke the word aloud before she realized she did so.

"Since when did you become so cynical?"

"I'm not." Faith continued to keep her tone even. "He just…" Surely he didn't know what she'd done? Surely that wasn't the reason for his sudden appearance all these weeks later? And yet, even if he hadn't…he could. It was dangerous having him around.

"I'll tell you what he just did. He just donated twenty-thousand pounds towards our expansion."

Faith strangled on her swallow. Twenty thousand pounds?

A gentle hand touched her shoulder, and Faith jumped. At some point her mother had approached, and she'd failed to hear her, this particular oversight less a product of her partial deafness and more because she'd been lost in thought.

"My understanding of what transpired that night," her mother began in a quiet voice as she took care to make sure Faith might see her lips, "was that you and your friends were abducted and that the gentlemen intervened, rescued you, and brought you to his establishment until Lord Waters arrived. Was that not true?"

Her mother couldn't know Faith's reservations stemmed from the passionate embrace she'd shared with the notorious gaming hell owner. Nor for that matter, the fact Faith had stolen information about Rex's clients and sold it to a newspaper to ruin a man. Faith had sent those funds she'd earned to Ladies and Gentlemen of Hope, so in that, she was not unlike Robin Hood. But Rex DuMond wouldn't care about that.

"Faith?" her mother urged, concern wreathing her voice. "If he hurt you in any way, if there is any reason at all I should bar Mr. DuMond from the grounds, then I will absolutely do so. But you need to tell me."

Perhaps she was more a coward than she'd ever credited because she wanted to lie. She wanted to ensure that Mr. DuMond left, so that she didn't have to risk him learning her secret.

Is it really that? a voice silently taunted. *Or is it more that you fear the way he made you feel? The kiss he gave that you still haven't been able to stop thinking about.*

"He did not hurt me," she said, grudgingly. She made one last attempt. "But I should point out, he *is* a gaming hell owner. It is one thing accepting financial support from him; it is quite another allowing him to interact with the students."

"Faith," the marchioness chided. "Your Uncle Leo was one of society's most wicked rakes," *Point*, "as was your Uncle Alex." *Another point.* "Your best friend, Marcia's, father was a notorious rogue." *Yet another.* "As was Marcia's——"

"I believe you've quite made your point."

"Good. You of all people should see all men are capable of being reformed."

"Oh, I see it," she said. "Just not this man." She added that last part under her breath.

Her mother's frown deepened. "I am disappointed. I expected you would not be so judgmental about the Marquess of Rutherford's interest in our school."

Faith opened her mouth to defend herself, and then stopped. "Who is the Marquess of Rutherford? I believed we were discussing——"

"Mr. DuMond." In a dismissive way, her mother returned to her desk and proceeded to evaluate whatever papers were spread all over the otherwise neat mahogany surface. "He is, in fact, a marquess."

Faith couldn't help it. She burst out laughing.

She laughed so hard her shoulders shook and her chest ached. She straightened, attempted to again speak, but was overcome once more. Hunching over, she laughed even harder until tears poured down her cheeks.

"Faith," her mother admonished, this time in the rarely-used-on-Faith impatient tones generally reserved for her mischievous son. "That is really quite enough."

Oh, it certainly was.

Dashing the moisture from her cheeks, Faith gasped in air, trying to get her mirth under control. "Surely you didn't believe some yarn he spun you about being a nobleman?"

"No," her mother said calmly. "I believe the yarn I know from my own knowledge of Mr. DuMond's father, the Duke of Haincourt, and the gentleman's family. The marquess himself has not said one word otherwise about being a marquess. He is more than content to be a simple Mister, which is something I'll honor, as it also says a good deal about the gentleman."

Faith rocked back once more. Rex was, in fact, a gentleman of the peerage? "Impossible."

Quitting her place at the desk once more, Faith's mother crossed over and gave her arm a light squeeze. "Sometimes there is more to a person than meets the eye."

On this particular score her mother was indeed correct. There was certainly more to not only the man but also to his intentions. That was all Faith should be focused on, getting rid of him, making her mother see reason, And yet she couldn't. Not without revealing all. Only there was more now too.

How odd to think of the all-powerful proprietor with anyone in his life. But of course, he had a mother and father, and despite herself, Faith found herself intrigued, wanting to know how a duke's son had come to be a proprietor, operating one of London's most scandalous establishments.

"What exactly do you know about Mr. DuMond's father and family?" Faith asked haltingly.

"According to your Uncle Leo,"—Uncle Leo who'd worked a lifetime in the Home Office and as such was in possession of details about everyone and anyone in England—"the duke is a notoriously ruthless man."

"Like father like son," she said.

Her mother gave her a sharp look. "The duke is notorious for bedding his household servants and for his cruel streak. I trust Mr. DuMond's wish to sever himself completely from the duke, and the young age at which he did so, speaks to the gentleman's character." There was a note of finality to that statement, one indicating her mother intended to say nothing further on Rex's family history.

Instead of satisfying any curiosity, her mother's words only further fueled Faith's questions about the man they spoke of and led to a dangerous interest in finding out how Rex DuMond had become the man he did. She opened her mouth to ask more questions, but her mother interrupted with that notorious maternal look. "We are not a family to gossip, Faith."

A knock sounded at the door, and the marchioness looked past Faith. "Enter," she called.

A footman opened the panel.

Faith's gaze slid past the servant to the towering man taking up a space behind him. Her eyes landed on the slight scar on Rex's cheek. How did a son of a duke get such a scar?

"Mr. DuMond to see you," the young man announced.

Faith's heart quickened as did that place between her legs, just like when Rex had kissed her and ran his hands over her body to search her. Shamefully, wickedly she recalled the feel of his tongue in her mouth, mating with hers.

Mr. DuMond, on the other hand, gave no indication he'd so much as noticed her standing there. That truth rankled. For reasons she really didn't care to think about.

And here she'd thought he might be here because of her. Because he'd learned what she'd shared about Lord Somerville…not for any other reason, of course. Why did that feel like a lie?

"I wanted to thank you for the opportunity to meet with your students, my lady." He spoke in that same gravelly baritone. Only unlike Faith's previous exchanges, this time, Rex's words were short of their usual cynical edge and laced with a measured calmness.

And it was a new side of him. One she'd not seen. Granted she'd only seen him once…and yet, he was different, very much the polite, respectable lord her mother had revealed him to be.

"Mr. DuMond, we are grateful for your support." The marchioness swept over, with her hands outstretched.

"I am grateful to you for the opportunity." He bowed his head, that slight gesture sending a dark curl tumbling over his eye, and Faith would have bet her entire dowry and her sister's, too, that he'd affected even that gesture as a way to soften himself before Faith's mother. "Your students are eager to learn."

Did he not see her standing there? Determined to gain his notice, Faith cleared her throat noisily.

At last, he looked her way. There was no surprise. There was no flash of recognition. Not even a smidgeon of curiosity.

Well.

"Mr. DuMond, may I introduce my daughter, Lady Faith," her mother volunteered, rushing to provide introductions. Unnecessary ones. And yet, appearances must always be kept up. The world on the whole had not discovered and could not know about Faith's visit to Forbidden Pleasures private offices.

"My lady," he murmured, bowing low at the waist, and Faith searched for even a hint of recognition. There was none.

Reluctantly, she made herself curtsy. And at last, she caught a glimmer in his eyes. Something that glinted like...amusement.

Say something. Say anything. Find your tongue. "I heard you reading," she blurted. Oh, bloody hell. "To the boys." Just stop. Admitting that she'd been listening in... "It was interesting," she finished weakly. This time she managed to control her runaway tongue.

An awkward silence fell. One Rex broke. The gentleman winged a black eyebrow up. "You take exception to morality tales, my lady?"

"Not at all," Faith rejoined, and then she registered that deepening glimmer. Why, the bounder was amused by this. By her.

"I'm quite fond of those works, Mr. DuMond. Particularly from *The Good Aunt.* I trust you are familiar with that tale?"

He inclined his head slightly. "I'm afraid I'm not."

"Faith," her mother said warningly, but Faith ignored her.

"Charles Howard was left an orphan when he was very young: his father had dissipated a large fortune, and lost his life in a duel about some debt of honor, which had been contracted at the gaming table."

From the corner of her eye, she caught the way her mother slapped a hand over her eyes. Rex DuMond, on the other hand, looked entirely too amused. Mildly. But still, amused.

"Without fortune and without friends, this boy—"

Faith's mother released a nervous laugh, cutting into the rest of Faith's recitation. "I am sure Mr. DuMond does not wish you to recite of the entire volume."

"On the contrary. It was most enlightening." His inky black lashes swept down, hooding his eyes. "It is impressive that you should remember the words upon those pages verbatim, my lady."

She went still; the breath froze in her lungs, and her feet twitched with the sudden urge to flee. And yet she searched him for some hint of knowing and blessedly found none.

"Isn't it?" Faith's mother chimed in proudly and Faith shot her a desperate look, eager for her to stop. "Faith has always been able to look at information—"

"My mama is just being proud," she said on a rush, interrupting the rest of what her mother intended to say.

"I'm certain she isn't," Rex said smoothly. "I trust you possess any number of special skills and talents, my lady."

Faith held her breath once more.

In the end, she was saved by her mother. "Faith, if you will excuse us? Mr. DuMond and I are to meet and discuss his contributions."

And just like that, like she was a girl once more, Faith was dismissed. Only this time, she was happy for it.

She sank into another curtsy. "It was a pleasure, my lord," she said, taking command of his title, taking pleasure in knowing that detail he'd kept secret from her. After all, a woman had every right to know the true identity of the man she'd been kissing.

He, however, gave no outward indication he was fazed in the least. "It was an honor," he murmured, sketching a deep, formal, and respectful bow. She'd wager it was the only respectful thing he'd done in the whole of his life, and at that, only for show. He straightened. "Sometimes people are placed in our paths, and we don't understand why at the moment…until it all makes sense," he murmured.

Her. He was talking about her.

Her heart fluttered. Her heart fluttered when, since her debut, she'd started to believe it never would. And she was truly making more out of his words than was there. Hearing what she wished—

"Faith?" her mother said awkwardly, and Faith jumped.

Her cheeks hot, she took her leave.

The moment she'd stepped into the hall, her mother closed the door behind her.

She should go.

There was no reason to remain.

Except one.

She really did need to speak with Rex DuMond alone. Because

then, and only then, could she ascertain whether or not he knew what she'd done.

CHAPTER 6

ℛEX WAS NOT DONE WITH Faith Brookfield. Not even close.

Nay, it had only just begun.

Everyone had secrets, and Rex was in the business of dealing in them. He knew the vices of most every lord and lady in London—that was, the disrespectable ones, which was also the majority of the peerage.

Everyone had a weakness. Everyone had a secret they wished to keep. Faith Brookfield was no exception.

Faith, who'd walked out of his club with information about his patrons, and who, in leaking it, threatened all he held dear.

Yes, given her flushed cheeks and habit of blurting out precisely what she was thinking, it wouldn't be difficult at all to uncover the information he could use to keep her silent.

What he'd not expected, however, was just how much he'd find himself enjoying sparring with her, both verbally and in actions.

She was spirited and fiery, unafraid of Rex—a rarity for him. As a rule, grown men of power went out of their way to avoid him. Young ladies hardly knew of his existence because he'd so severed his connection from anything and everything polite. Had they, however, they'd have run the other way from him.

Not Faith Brookfield. She was brave. Or stupid. Mayhap a bit of both.

She wasn't, however, a worthy opponent. In fairness, where his mercenary skills were concerned, none were.

His meeting with the Marchioness of Guilford concluded for the day, Rex took his leave of the proprietress's offices. The moment a servant had drawn the door shut behind his mistress and made to escort Rex from the school grounds, Rex felt her. He knew she was there long before she would have ever wished he knew.

Faith stepped into middle of the corridor. "Thank you, Jonathan. I will see Mr. DuMond out."

The dutiful servant bowed and started in the opposite direction. Careless lad.

In fact, with their heavy leaning towards trustingness, the marchioness and those on her staff proved dangerously easy marks for deception. Only Faith had proven clever enough to see him for the threat he was. It mattered not, however. Intelligent and wary as she might be, she was still an innocent.

Faith didn't speak until they were alone. "You're here, Mr. DuMond."

"I believe we ascertained as much. Just as I'd thought we had become comfortable using one another's Christian names, Faith, given how familiar we've b—"

Her gasp drowned out the rest of his words.

She grabbed Rex's hand and tugged him into the nearest room. A linen closet.

He blinked to adjust his eyes to the small, darkened space, and then shifted his mouth near her temple. "I was referring to the fact I was your savior some weeks ago."

Even in the dark he caught the telltale blush on her cheeks. "Oh. I thought you were saying…I thought you were suggesting…"

Stammering generally repelled him. Never had it amused him, before now.

He lowered his mouth close to her ear. "What did you think I was talking about, Faith?" he whispered. "Our embrace?" He placed a kiss just behind the shell of her ear, and their bodies pressed so close, he felt the tremble that moved all the way through her. "Though now that you mention it, we became even more familiar. Intimate even."

Her lashes fluttered. "I-I…do not believe I mentioned it."

She hadn't. "Not with words," he countered, sliding a hand possessively over the curve of her hip. He sank his fingers into that supple flesh and drew her close. "But with the way your chest is moving…" He brushed his spare hand along her neckline. Her breath hitched and then quickened. "The way your mouth trembles…" He grazed the pad of his thumb along the seam of her lips. "Your body tells me everything you are thinking, Faith."

He was toying with her. This was all part of a grander scheme and ultimate plan. He'd just not anticipated how much he'd enjoy it.

"What do you want?" she whispered, her voice shaking. Her lashes fluttered as he kissed a path down the long length of her neck.

"I think that should be clear, Faith."

"It's not."

"I want you."

And strangely, shockingly, he meant it. He was enflamed by her. Even as her lush mouth parted slightly in a perfect moue of surprise, his mind froze and then balked. His interest was simply the challenge she posed, because he'd never known virginal women could also be wanton and free in their desire, all fire and passion. For a man who delighted in being burned, this was a blaze he was all too happy to play with.

Then, she dampened her mouth. "I don't believe you."

Smart girl.

He winged an eyebrow up. "You find it so impossible to believe that I desire you?"

"Yes," she said, without missing a beat. "You strike me as a man who isn't moved by any overwhelming desire except as it pertains to your business and power. That is where your true passion lies."

Ordinarily, she'd be right.

Rex changed tack.

He looped an arm around her waist and drew her close. The lady went without resistance.

"Tell me, Faith. Why can't it be both?"

"Because men don't desire me, Rex," she said flatly, and with sure conviction to prove she actually believed those words she spoke. And perhaps they were true.

"The men of Polite Society are a stupid lot," he murmured.

At that defense her eyes went all soft as did her features, and it unnerved the hell out of him because the words he spoke weren't compelled by a need to seduce but rather born of an actual hungering and appreciation for the minx before him.

A hungering and appreciation? What in hell thoughts were these? Nay, his interest in the lady only stemmed from one thing—the need to gather just how much she'd ascertained about his business and keep her quiet before she did any further damage. With that in mind, Rex dipped his head and claimed her mouth in a soft, gentle kiss, one that she met with another of those innocent, breathy sighs.

She parted for him, letting Rex inside, and he kept this meeting of their mouths tender, the whispery soft sounds of desire spilling from her lips inordinately loud in the linen closet; and it fueled his hunger.

How soft and compliant she became. It was all too easy.

He forced himself to end this latest kiss.

When he did, Faith's heavy-looking lashes fluttered, and then she touched her fingers to her swollen mouth. "I…no seduction."

He flashed an uneven smile. "I wouldn't dream of it."

Disappointment sparked in her eyes.

It was oh so easy.

Her mouth opened. And then closed. She tried several times, looking a lot like the trout he used to sneak away and pluck from the duke's lake before ultimately their pathetic thirst for air had filled Rex with remorse until he'd thrown them back. Fortunately, he wasn't the same pathetic boy he'd once been. Fortunately, life had hardened him.

Faith finally found her voice.

"You're a duke's son, and a marquess by right." So, she'd gleaned the details about his parentage. He wondered just how much she'd learned.

If she'd been a score older, he'd have taken her for ruthless. But she wasn't. She was an innocent miss, who'd no idea her words were, in fact, the challenge they were. Or the dangerous waters she'd dipped her toes.

Despite himself, despite the need to charm her so he might

attain his goals, tension snapped through him. "My name is *Mr. DuMond*. Tell me," he said. "Are you really so afraid to be around me that you'd reject the funds you and your mother have been attempting to solicit from various lords all over England, Faith?" With that, he again laid claim to her name, placing a deliberate emphasis upon it, as the challenge it was.

"I'm not afraid of you, Rex."

Rex released her. "Ah, so it is just you don't think I should be here."

She spoke on a rush. "I didn't say that."

"You didn't have to."

"I…simply did not expect you of all people would be a benefactor."

"Sometimes it is possible for two things to be true: I'm a man who made a fortune dealing cards to men who have a proclivity for gaming, and I'm capable of using those funds for good…say, using them to add necessary classrooms to schools for people most in need." He saw her weakening. Caught the softening of her eyes, and the faint little sigh that slipped from her lips. "But if you don't believe I have a place here at Ladies and Gentlemen of Hope, because of our prior connection, then I can restrict my involvement to a monetary commi—"

"No!" she exclaimed.

It was all too easy.

She rested her palms along the lapels of his jacket, the gesture honest and natural and innocent. And oddly appealing. "I believe it will be good for you to learn about my mother's school, and as you are making a financial contribution, it is only right that you be here at Ladies and Gentlemen of Hope."

What a ridiculous name. There was no such thing as hope. How naïve she and her family were. "Perhaps I can even find time to show you about the school when you visit," she offered, a thread of hesitancy hanging on the end of that suggestion.

He inclined his head. "You needn't do that. I trust you are busy."

Her expression fell. "Of course."

He inclined his head.

Faith hesitated, and then let herself from the linen closet.

He waited, his ears trained on the rapid rise and fall of her delicate tread as she made her way down the hall, before the sound of her steps disappeared altogether.

Rex smiled, a cool, hard smile that, had she seen it, would have killed any doubt of his real intentions.

CHAPTER 7

THE MOMENT FAITH HAD CAUGHT her first glimpse of Rex reading to the young boys at her mother's school, she'd been suspicious. Nay, not suspicious, panicked. She'd feared his presence meant he'd uncovered the role she'd played in revealing Lord Somerville. As it turned out, she'd worried for naught.

He visited twice weekly. He was gentle and laughing as she'd never expected the gaming hell owner could be with the students, and... he barely noticed her.

Faith should only be relieved by that discovery. After all, there couldn't be a clearer signal that he hadn't deduced her role in that article.

Only, she wasn't.

Seated in the small office her mother had designated as Faith's own some years ago, Faith propped her chin atop her hand and stared out the windows overlooking the grounds outside. Down below, seven of the young boys sat in a small circle, rolling marbles upon the uneven surface of the slight patch of pavement in the gardens.

And then as if she'd conjured him, Rex was there.

Heart hammering, Faith scrambled up in her seat; willing him to look up her way.

Only, he didn't.

He walked in lock-step alongside the Countess of Montfort, his long strides more measured and modified to accommodate the woman's noticeable limp.

The lady, whom he remained completely engrossed by.

Unlike Faith, whom he barely even noticed.

Each time he visited, she made sure to place herself in the area of the school where he happened to be visiting.

At first, she'd done so to ascertain whether he'd gathered what she'd done.

But when he failed to notice her presence, it had only confirmed his lack of knowledge of the event and his complete indifference to her.

Just then, Rex said something that elicited a laugh from Lady Montfort.

And Faith proved so petty and small and pathetic because the sight of Rex, his features unguarded and a smile on his lips because of his exchange with the countess, should grate so.

Faith gave her head a hard shake and dropped her hand to the desktop. "Stop it," she muttered. She was certainly not one to ruminate about a gentleman. Given that not a single gentleman had ever noticed her, it had been all too easy not to find herself all aflutter about anyone.

So, what was it about Rex DuMond that made her want him to see her?

Because he kissed you like he was a man starving and you were his last meal.

And there was no way any young woman who'd known the power of that embrace could remain unaffected.

One of the boys noted the pair's arrival and nudged the child next to him. As the two students playing marbles grabbed their canes and stood, the rest of the group looked up, then scrambled to their feet.

Exuberant shouts went up as they greeted Rex. She angled her head toward the window in an attempt to make out what they were saying and cursed her partial hearing that made it impossible to decipher.

Her heart did another funny jump in her chest.

Liar. It wasn't just that kiss. It was this, too. It was the absolute, unabashed excitement her mother's students displayed whenever Rex came by. The boys were so eager and adoring of Rex. There could never be any doubt as to the very real joy they found in his company.

Rex and Lady Montfort exchanged a handful of words more before the lady nodded and turned to go, leaving Rex to his visit with the children.

Faith quit the spot at her desk and headed to the window, not even pretending anymore that she wasn't absolutely fascinated by him and her mother's students' reaction to him.

He dropped to his haunches so that he was eye-level with those children, and as he spoke, they grew wide-eyed and more solemn than she'd ever seen them.

Harry Simmons shot his cane to the sky, waving it frantically as the others raised their hands, waggling them to gain Rex's attention.

Rex said something that made them all cheer.

As if he'd felt her there, Rex looked up, and Faith couldn't even make herself jump out of the way to hide.

She just stood there, enrapt by the sight of him.

He flashed a crooked smile, and she discovered in that instant there was nothing more devastating than a man's uneven grin.

The distant exchange between them lasted no more than a moment. Rex had already returned his attention to the boys around him.

And Faith realized there *was* something more devastating— being enthralled with a man who was so very indifferent to her.

Faith fled, racing back to her seat, and heart hammering, she stared at the blank page.

This was really too much.

She wasn't one to have her head muddled by a gentleman.

But then, you've never known a man like Rex DuMond.

"Stop," she gritted out. She grabbed a pen, dunked it into the crystal inkpot, and proceeded to make a list.

Pro et Contra of Mr. Rex DuMond

Contra:	Pro:
Gaming Hell Owner	Kind to the children
	Generous
	Self-made man,
	despite his titles
	His kiss

Wrinkling her nose, Faith examined the not at all evenly matched columns.

There had to be more grievances against the gentleman. There had to be something else.

She added another word.

Mysterious.

Except, mysterious wasn't entirely a bad thing. Was it?

"There you are!"

Faith gasped; the pen slipped from her fingers.

At some point, her mother had entered the small office. Lost, as she'd been in her thoughts, she'd failed to hear that approach.

When she'd been a small girl, her mother would bring Faith along to her then-new school for girls and young women with various impairments. She'd established a space for Faith there, an office of her own, providing her with papers and pens and pencils so that Faith could pretend to work. Only recently had she received a real role—helping to plan events and activities for the students attending Ladies and Gentlemen of Hope.

"Mama," she greeted weakly, hurriedly flipping to empty and far less damning pages.

Her mother, however, gave no indication she'd noted Faith gawking gaga-eyed at London's most notorious gaming hell owner. Rather, she examined the empty page.

"I am out of ideas," she said weakly.

"You, unable to come up with an activity for the boys and girls to join in together?" Her mother snorted. "Now that, I don't believe. I've seen you with your brother, Paddy, and all your nieces and nephews, organizing any number of games for them."

"That is different."

"How?"

Because she'd not been woolgathering about Rex DuMond. "Because, the boys don't want to join in the activities with the girls." No truer words had not been spoken. Previously an institution devoted solely to girls and young women with various disabilities, those students had chafed at the addition of males; particularly as the boys had proven devilish towards them.

Her mother gave a gentle smile. "Well, then you must determine what activity it is that might make them forget the fact that they do not wish to engage with one another."

"My lady?"

They looked to the front of the room where one of the servants stood framed in the doorway. "The latest shipment of books is just arrived."

The marchioness's eyes lit. "Please tell them I'll be along shortly. In the meantime, see that they are escorted to the libraries."

"The latest shipment?" Faith asked, after the servant had dipped a curtsy and hurried off.

"Mr. DuMond felt the libraries required updating and donated new reading materials on top of the sizeable monetary contribution he'd already made."

Faith's heart did another little jump. "Did he?" she asked, feigning a casual attitude. *Be casual and breezy and only mildly interested.* Never more had Faith wished to discover all there was to know about the enigmatic marquess.

Alas, her disinterest worked entirely too well.

"If you'll excuse me?" her mother said, offering none of the additional details Faith so desperately craved about how that offer had come to be.

After she'd gone, Faith's gaze crept unbidden to the window, to where he visited.

He'd not only given an enormous sum, but he'd also donated books and his time to the school?

Faith made herself sit at the desk and return to work.

Or she attempted to.

She tapped the tip of her pen on the open page of her notebook.

Tap-tap-tap-tap.

Who *was* Rex DuMond? He was a man so layered…and Faith wanted to peel back those layers and discover everything there was to know about the enigmatic—

More muffled laughter met her ears, and she jumped to her feet.

Stop it. You have work to do.

Her mother had tasked her with organizing several activities the boys and girls could take part in together. The best way to ascertain as much was for her to visit with the newest members of the school and determine what might interest the boys—at least enough to abandon the usual hostility they'd shown to the female members.

Faith was not, absolutely not, making her way outside to see Rex.

And if she felt herself slightly out of breath when she did reach the gardens, it was only because of the pace she'd set, and absolutely not because Rex sat lazily upon the terrace, his back propped against the wall as if he were hiding, waiting for her.

She opened her mouth to make herself greet him, but he lifted a finger to his lips, silencing her. Then he crooked that long digit at her, beckoning her over, and she at last understood that poor plight of Eve, wanting to taste of that apple. For Faith drifted towards him, sinking to the stone floor beside him.

Rex leaned in, placing his lips so near the shell of her ear that it tickled her skin, and a soft sigh slipped out.

"Have a care, sweet," he whispered, his deep baritone making her senses run amok. "You'll give me away."

Yes, she'd give them away.

She blinked slowly.

Except, wait a moment. That isn't what he'd said.

"You'll give me away…"

Rex got onto his haunches and passed his stare out over the grounds below before sinking to the floor once more.

"What are you—?"

"Hide and seek," he whispered. He touched a finger to her lips. "Now, shh."

Now, shh.

That command alone—one that indicated his complete lack of awareness of Faith—should have perfectly grounded her, and yet the feel of his long, ink-stained, calloused digit against her mouth robbed her briefly of logical thought.

"Do you like to play, Faith?" he asked in that faint, husky murmur that continued to wreak havoc on her senses.

Faith tried to get a proper response out. "I..." Since when had she become a stammering lady? She wasn't. In fact, she'd never lost her head so.

He gave her an odd look.

"Yes," she blurted.

A little too loudly.

He pressed that same finger against her mouth. Only, unlike before, *this* time, he did not draw back. This time, he glided the tip down, gently, and caressed along her lower lip.

His eyes remained locked on his own movement, on her mouth, and she felt a wicked heat—one that should surely be shameful—build between her legs as she remembered the feel of his mouth on hers.

"Do you?" he whispered, and she managed an uneven nod.

Oh, how she remembered.

Except, wait...that hadn't been what he was asking. What *was* he asking? It was all confused in her mind. Everything was flipped upside down.

A gaze as piercing as his should be cold and yet his eyes radiated an even greater heat than his touch.

Faith knew the moment he'd forgot about the game of hide and seek and noted *her*.

It was impossible to believe, and yet even innocent as she was, she could all but see that shift as his ink black lashes swept lower and his gaze narrowed.

His thumb took the place of his forefinger, and he brushed that calloused pad against her trembling lower lip and then higher, around to her upper lip, tracing that seam in a reverse circle.

Her lashes fluttered.

He was going to kiss her.

She wanted his kiss. Ached for it.

Faith's notebook slipped from her fingers, landing between them on the stone floor.

And then his touch was gone, and that dream of a kiss she craved vanished along with it.

"What is this?" Rex murmured, helping himself to her notebook.

Disappointment. It filled every corner of her being.

Who knew it even had a taste? And it was the taste of an unrequited kiss.

He glanced up, and she made herself find words to speak. "They are my notes," she explained.

He was a man in command of any and all situations, so she braced for him to boldly flip through those pages. And yet he did not.

Rex looked at her questioningly. "May I?"

He asked for that favor, and something in that respect for her and her things sent another wave of heat unfurling within her breast.

Faith managed a nod.

With that capitulation, Rex fanned through her notebook, his keen gaze making quick work of the words she'd written on those pages.

"I work here," she explained.

He paused, glancing up from his study. "Do you?"

She nodded. "I visited since I was a girl, and I'd help my mother in her office, organizing her things, playing with the younger children, and then I eventually took on a formal role."

Her mother had offered Faith a greater responsibility. Some of that she suspected had come from the fact that Faith hadn't any suitors to occupy her attention. Which was fine. Her life was more fulfilled here. Why did it feel as though she lied—and not at all well—to herself?

She curled her toes into the soles of her slippers, expecting he knew and not wanting to see any pity from him.

Except, there was no pitying. Rather, a genuine interest. "What do you do here?"

"Whatever my mother requires of me. I've a head for recalling most anything I see. I can just look at a book and remember—" She stopped abruptly; her heart thudded in a sick way against her ribcage. She'd said too much. Or she'd almost.

He gave her a look. "And you remember...?" he asked, and there was just a plain, simple curiosity, nothing more.

"I've a head for remembering things from French and Latin and math, and as such I help at the school, providing lessons for various disciplines."

Faith was grateful when he moved his attention from her and back to reading through her notebook.

And then she froze.

Just as he stopped on a certain page.

With a gasp, Faith snatched her book back. But it was too late.

She knew he'd seen his name there, and worse the words. Even smudged as they were from when she'd slammed the pages shut when her mother had come upon Faith taking *notes*. Oh, hell. How could she have forgotten that? Mortification invaded every corner of her person, leaving no part of her untouched by embarrassment.

Please, do not say anything...do not say anything...

Alas, there was to be no reprieve for her this day.

"My kiss is like magic, is it?" he drawled, sounding entirely too smug.

The lout.

Fire burned up her cheeks. "Oh, hush."

He proved wholly unobliging.

"Don't you have a game of hide and seek to be worrying about?" she muttered.

He grinned. "Oh, no. As much as I was enjoying the game, this is far more enjoyable."

And despite the abject humiliation burning her up, butterflies danced all around her belly at his admission that he'd been enjoying his time with the children. Fighting to gain control of her dazed state, Faith cleared her throat. "There are negatives upon my list, too," she felt inclined to point out, lest his head swell any more than it likely was.

"Gaming hell owner."

She nodded.

"Given you touted my generosity in the other column, I trust the two cancel out."

Faith wrinkled her nose. Yes, well, he was right on that score too.

"And mysterious is mentioned as both a positive and negative, and as such—"

"I didn't have time to finish my list, Mr. DuMond," she interrupted the entirely-too-amused lout.

Rex reached inside his jacket and fished around.

He held out a hand.

Faith stared dumbly at his outstretched fingers. "What is that?"

He wagged it. "It's a pencil."

"I see that."

"You asked—"

"I meant, what are you doing with it, Mr. DuMond?"

"Given your list is incomplete, I'm offering you a pencil so you can finish it."

His eyes danced. Those eyes that had been hard and flinty at their first meeting but had since softened did wild things to her thoughts and pulse.

Flustered, Faith plucked the pencil from his fingers, along with her book, and set to work on her list.

Or she attempted to.

Feeling his amused stare, she looked up.

"Having trouble?"

With the negatives about Rex DuMond? She absolutely was.

"It's only because I'm not comfortable working on my list while you are here."

"Why are you working on a list, *petite chouette*?"

Why, indeed.

Her mind went blank.

For she couldn't very well say: I'm trying to compile a list of reasons why I should not be so transfixed by the mere thought of you.

Rex leaned down and in. "Is it perhaps, you think of me, as I think of you?"

He thought of her.

Oh God. It was something she'd never, ever thought any man would do.

Faith fluttered a hand about her breast. "Y-You think of me?"

CHAPTER 8

¶IT WAS TOO EASY.

In fact, Rex almost felt bad at how easy it had proven for him to slip past her defenses so he might gain her confidence and through that her secrets. Secrets with which to use her, to compel her to silence.

Why, the lady had even allowed him to collect her book and flip through those pages, free to read at will the words she'd written there.

If he were another man, he'd probably have felt a modicum of guilt.

He didn't.

He was incapable of that emotion.

Rex dusted the back of his knuckles along her cheek, and her long black lashes fluttered…shut, resting like a satiny blanket upon cream white skin.

It was altogether too easy.

"I do," he said quietly, and she opened those enormous eyes once more. "Think of you."

Her lips parted in surprise? Pleasure? Likely both.

"What do you think about?" she asked softly, taking him aback with that query, a curious blend of boldness and a total lack of artifice that should have repulsed him, but left him oddly intrigued.

Rex continued to brush his knuckles over her cheek. "I think about our kiss," he said. Nor was it a lie. There'd been any number of times the memory of the taste and feel of her had slipped in, along with the spirited abandon she'd displayed as she'd kissed him in turn.

His entire existence had seen him surrounded by people as jaded as himself. So much so that he'd come to believe the idea of innocence was an illusion used by clever manipulators as a mechanism to get what they wanted.

Her lashes fluttered open, and she stared expectantly at him.

At a loss, Rex stared back.

She gave her head a slight nod, as if she expected more "Yes?" The query tacked on the end of the word indicated she, in fact, did.

"Yes," he confirmed.

"Oh." And with that, Faith flipped open her notebook and fanned through those pages before stopping on that list.

He craned his neck to see the words she was adding to that *Positives about Mr. Rex DuMond* column, but the lady scooted, angling her shoulder so she gave him her back and cut off his ability to freely read.

Rex shifted anyway, using his greater height advantage to catch the latest addition.

Faith slapped a palm over the page and scowled at him. "Do you mind, Rex? I am taking notes."

She'd scowled and chastised him. Neither of which aided him in his seduction of Lady Faith Brookfield.

"I see that," he said, when she returned her attention to writing.

She paused a second time, gave him a little scowl, and then scooted away so he could not angle his head and look his fill.

His lips quirked up in a grin, one that felt awkward and uncomfortable as it pushed those muscles up in a movement that was foreign to them… and him.

He waited while she finished, and when she ceased writing, her eyes skimmed whatever sentences she'd added to her list. Then this time, with a pleased little nod, she snapped her book shut and placed it on the ground, well beyond his reach.

And damned if he wasn't completely intrigued. By her. By what secrets she now hid. And that desiring to know strangely had nothing to do with the plans he had to ferret out her weaknesses, and everything to do with a genuine interest. Unnerved as he'd never been in the whole of his life, Rex fought to get hold of wholly unfamiliar sentiments.

"Got you!"

They looked at the gaggle of small boys at the top of the ramp that led to the terrace. With whooping cries of triumph, the group swarmed him and Faith.

"Lady Faith," they cried. The two boys with crutches hefted them into the air in a celebratory greeting.

With a laugh, Faith returned those jubilant welcomes with a sincerity that left her cheeks flushed red and the most real smile wreathing her lips. And it occurred to him—she appeared genuinely happy to see the boys. As she spoke to them, each by name, it also hit him that she actually was.

When he'd been a small boy, just prior to his mother being sent away, she'd taken him to the Royal Museum, where there'd been an exhibit of foreign insects on display. He'd stared into the glass cases which had housed those bizarre-looking creatures, transfixed by the peculiarity of them. This instant now, observing Faith Brookfield, he felt that same sense of intrigue.

Because ladies, just like the gentlemen in London, had perverted pleasures. They were driven by the seven deadly sins. It wasn't a matter of *which* vice, but *how many* evils they enjoyed.

Yet that didn't fit with whatever very real happiness Faith exhibited as she favored each child with the attention he craved. The sight of it—of her—unnerved him. And for the first time in the whole of his life, he'd a taste of what the men and women who'd been at his mercy through the years had felt.

And he didn't like it.

In fact, he abhorred that weakness, if even just fleeting, in himself.

As if she felt his stare, Faith looked over the tops of her audience's heads, and catching his gaze, she smiled.

It was a small, slight, and strangely intimate exchange that only further befuddled him.

"Wouldn't you agree, Mr. DuMond?" Faith asked.

Wouldn't he agree about what?

The stares of seven boys swung Rex's way. As mixed up as he was in his thoughts, he'd not even heard the damned question she'd put to him. It was a new way to be for him—off his guard and at a disadvantage, and the unpleasantness of that state chased away whatever moment of weakness she'd inspired.

In the end, one of the children—Jack—proved the hero of the moment.

"Of course, he doesn't. Mr. DuMond doesn't like ladies."

Calls of consensus rang up among the group.

Yes, well, the child was right on that score. In fairness, Rex didn't like most people. Hardly anyone outside his two business partners, and even that was with reluctance.

"That is not true. Why, Mr. DuMond is quite kind towards young ladies." If he was a man capable of bursting out laughing, that statement from Faith Brookfield would have done him in. "In fact, Mr. DuMond will no doubt tell you that being polite and respectful is how all gentlemen behave." Faith urged Rex with her gaze and said with a greater insistence, "Isn't that right, Mr. DuMond?"

The idea of a polite, respectful gentleman was as mythical a concept as unicorns and pots of gold at the end of a rainbow.

"Undoubtedly," he murmured. He liked the debauched ones who turned over heavy coins to sin at his club. He liked the ones who relished throwing away their neglectful husbands' fortunes to Rex's empire. He liked the ones who warmed his bed.

Faith gave up her place amongst the circle of students and joined Rex, making it clear with her next words just what she'd been talking about when his thoughts had wandered. "The boys and girls at Ladies of Hope—"

"Ladies and Gentlemen of Hope—" ten-year-old Stewart piped in.

"That is right, Ladies and Gentlemen of Hope," Faith corrected, "are not getting on." She leaned in and whispered, "My mother's school was previously devoted to young girls and women but has since expanded to include boys."

"Hence the funds needed for renovations and expansion."

Faith nodded. "Exactly. We've recently acquired the properties next door to accommodate the growing population of girls *and* boys." She returned her focus to the group. "Unfortunately, since we've merged, the boys have proven to be antagonizing to the girls."

"Not to you, Lady Faith." Holden, a child with one arm, and the other only an empty, tucked up sleeve, spoke with the awe of a boy smitten.

Faith winked. "No, you've been entirely polite and respectful." She paused, giving the child a meaningful look. "To me."

A deep blush spilled over the boy's freckled cheeks, and he ducked his head.

"If I might add," Rex called. "It is not about just being polite and respectful…" Faith and the assembled students hung on that brief pause. "It is also about seeing women as your equals."

"They aren't our equals," Stewart called out. "We're *men*."

More cries of assent went up among the group.

It wasn't a foreign concept. In fact, it was the predominant one in the patriarchal world in which they lived. It was what had led Rex's father to exert his influence over Rex's mother. It was a principle that guided all of the reprobate lords who frequented his clubs. It was also why Rex had found a perverse satisfaction in granting membership to those women chafing at their treatment.

When the shouts had died down, Rex touched his gaze on each child present. "If a man believes women are less and deserve to be treated differently because of no other reason than that they were born female, then he is, in fact, *her* inferior in every way."

A thoroughly chastised Stewart ducked his head.

Rex glanced at Faith and froze.

Her lips were parted in that soft way they had just before he'd kissed her, and again, after. It was her weakness, then: a man who was latitudinarian in his thinking and who had a more revolutionary opinion on people's place in the world. How he could use that against her was all Rex cared about.

Someone tugged at his sleeve, and he glanced down. Ollie was the boy's name. He'd one glazed eye that bespoke his partial blindness. "Are we going to play still, sir?"

"I can't think of anything more I'd like to do," he said.

Oddly, it was true.

But only because of what he stood to gain in learning about Faith and her secret vices.

Stewart covered his eyes and pressed his forehead against a nearby Doric column, and as he began counting aloud, everyone darted down the ramp.

Faith collected her hems and headed after them, pausing to give Rex a look. "You're staying?"

"…five…six…"

"Would you rather I leave?" he asked.

"No," she exclaimed, damningly quick in her reply. "I…just expected you might have other affairs to attend. Business to see to."

He had his business to see to. In addition, as the height of his business took place in the early morn, these were the hours when Rex slept. But the time spent here, the information he gathered from Faith, was vital to his club's continued success. That's what he told himself. That's the sole reason he stayed.

Taking him by the hand, Faith pulled him along.

He'd not even played when he'd been a boy himself. He'd been shut away in his schoolrooms, with a miserably stern tutor who delighted in rapping his knuckles and taking a cane to his back.

And yet here they played.

It was a peculiar place, this school Faith's mother had established.

The moment they reached the gardens, Faith released his hand and took off running for a hiding place.

She moved like a wood sprite in the arcadian landscape, darting past hedges and bushes. Her skirts brushed along those leaves, setting them to dancing.

He followed at a more sedate pace, one that allowed him to track her flight past statues of Venus and Pan before she ultimately settled behind an enormous Canova lion which faced another. Both of those stone creatures were stretched in lazy repose; their eyes closed.

Rex dropped onto the ground beside the other statue.

Faith flared her eyes. "What are you doing?" she whispered, entirely too loudly to safely maintain their hiding spot.

He touched a finger against his lips. "Hiding."

She frowned. "But this is my spot."

He pointed to the lush emerald grass under him. "This is a different spot."

For a moment, he thought she'd challenge him further. Instead, she wrinkled her nose in that telltale way of hers, that little twitch of a button-cute appendage revealing her annoyance. "Fine."

"Twenty-five. Olly olly oxen free," Stewart shouted from where he'd been counting on the terrace.

Rex and Faith remained in silence. Both lay stretched out on their stomachs with their chins resting atop their layered hands, as alike in their repose as the stone lions who provided them with their shelter.

"Did you mean that?" she whispered.

He stared questioningly back.

"What you said to the boys," she clarified. "About women being equal to men." Her eyes conveyed the same hope as was contained upon her whispery soft voice.

"You're familiar with my club, Faith," he said. "Do you think I discriminate between men and women?" He didn't in life or business. He'd witnessed firsthand the equally mercenary nature of ladies and knew they were worthy adversaries.

"No," she murmured. She rubbed her chin back and forth in a distracted little way upon the tops of her joined hands. "My father is of a similar thinking."

She'd compare him to the notoriously honorable Marquess of Guilford? For a second time, he found himself near to laughter. "Your father is a clever man."

"Most people don't think the way you do," Faith said hesitantly, the way one might while sorting through a puzzle, speaking to themselves as they did.

You. As in he and Lord Guilford.

"I'm not most people, Faith."

She eyed him a long while. "No. No, you're not."

As one, they inched closer, each lifting on their elbows and propelling themselves nearer. They stopped, a hairsbreadth apart, their lips almost brushing.

With a sigh, Faith closed her eyes, and this time Rex didn't pretend to misunderstand what she wanted. And he gave it to her. He took her mouth in a gentle kiss—a sweet one, when he'd not believed himself capable of tender kisses. And a short one.

He drew back.

Faith's eyes fluttered. "Why did you stop?" she whispered.

Why, indeed? Why, when he wanted that kiss? Why, when he wanted her?

Don't you mean why, when continuing to kiss her weakened her and made her loose with her confidences?

A question sparked in Faith's eyes…a question, when questions were dangerous.

That was the only reason he found himself leaning in to kiss her again.

"Found you!"

They both jumped as Stewart sprang upon them.

The boy smiled wildly, looking only pleased with his discovery, too innocent to know what he'd just interrupted.

It was an interruption that Rex had needed and should be grateful for.

He leapt to his feet. "Well done. Alas, I fear I must be going."

Both Faith and Stewart wore matching crestfallen expressions.

"You must?"

"You do?"

"I must." He slid his gaze to Faith. "But you have my assurance I'll return."

Her eyes softened.

She dipped a curtsy. "Mr. DuMond."

He bowed his head. "Lady Faith."

As she covered her eyes and began counting aloud, Rex made his way through the gardens, the lyrical softness of her voice following him.

"…six…seven…eight…"

She counted quickly as if she were impatient and eager to play, and it was another detail he mentally stored away to save.

When he reached the terrace, he stopped at that place where Faith had first come upon him.

Her book lay there, closed and forgotten…and unguarded.

Swiftly dropping to his haunches, he flipped to the middle portion of the book, and stopped on that list she'd made.

Rex read that latest addition.

He only thinks about carnal thoughts where I'm concerned.

That favorable column had not grown, but rather, the negative one beside it. The previously sparse one.

"Did you have a long enough look, Rex?"

Startling, he glanced up and over.

Faith stared knowingly back, a triumphant little smile on her pillow-plush lips.

She'd startled him. It was unheard of that anyone would take him by surprise, and yet this minx had.

Faith arched a well-formed eyebrow, and he followed her gaze to the notebook he still had.

And then, it hit him. Why, the saucy chit had wanted him to read it.

Instead of walking over and returning the book to her fingers as he should, and as any proper, polite gentleman would, he remained rooted there and then held the leather journal out, daring her, challenging her, forcing her to be the one to take the steps between them.

Without so much as a wink of hesitation, Faith marched over.

Just as she reached for the notebook, Rex drew it back.

Her brows snapped together in an endearingly frustrated way.

"I do think carnal thoughts about you, Faith. But that is not all." With that, he stretched the book out, offering it back.

She gathered the leather journal, cradling it close to her breast, and as he took his leave, he felt her eyes following him until he'd gone.

CHAPTER 9

REX DUMOND BECAME A REGULAR fixture at Faith's mother's school.

He came now not just two days, but three, and in that time, he alternated between touring various wings of the establishment with the marchioness in order to determine where his funds would be best put to use and visiting with the children.

Nay, his were not simply visits. Every time Rex came, he joined them in some game or another.

In fact, where Faith and the instructors had been unable to bridge the divide between the boys and girls attending the institution, Rex had succeeded. He'd succeeded where they'd failed. With his influence among the previously recalcitrant boys, now all the children came together for daily activities and lessons.

And Faith feared she was falling a little bit in love with him.

Standing in the school's ballroom, Faith stared as he worked his magic in getting the boys to take part in a lesson none of the instructors could manage to bring them around to—dancing.

"That's DuMond." Her sister Violet's voice demonstrated a heavy amount of disappointment.

At that moment, whatever Rex had said to the seven gathered boys elicited a round of laughter, and they all collectively shot their hands up to the sky. "That's DuMond," Faith murmured.

Violet cocked her head. "I expected him to be…"

Faith glanced over. "Yes?"

"More wicked than this."

He *was* more wicked than this. Faith bit the inside of her cheek to keep from saying as much. Rex was a man whose kisses robbed a woman of thought and whose touch, forbidden and bold, left a lady longing and eager to give over her virtue without a thought of preserving her reputation.

But he was more than that, too. He was a man who saw women as equals, and also a man so very good with children. And that was proving as quixotic and heady as his touch.

Her sister gave her a queer look. "Are you all right?"

"Fi—" Faith's assurance died on her lips as Rex glanced away from his students. His gaze sliding across the room, it collided with hers.

He flashed a smile and then lifted his hand, offering her a wave.

Faith's heart jumped as it always did when he was near, and she returned his greeting.

How was it possible for a man to make her feel like she was the only person in the room? Just then, he separated himself from the group of students, leaving them in the care of Mrs. Morrow, the instructor newly hired. He headed across the ballroom. To Faith.

She felt her sister's stare and looked over.

Violet watched her with an odd expression.

"What?" Faith asked defensively.

"You're smitten," her sister whispered.

Faith strangled on her swallow. "Stop it." She stole a glance in Rex's direction. Rex, who was almost upon them.

Violet flared her eyes. "You did not even deny it."

"I...am not smitten," she said from the corner of her mouth. Yet, Faith's protestations sounded weak to her own ears.

"You paused."

"I didn't pause," she whispered frantically.

"Oh, there was a noticeable one there."

Rex reached them. "A noticeable what?"

Faith and her sister jumped. "Uh..."

"A spider," Violet blurted.

Faith resisted the urge to plant her palm against her forehead. "There was a..."

"Spider?" Rex supplied for the stammering girl.

Violet nodded frantically.

He grinned, the lopsided smile that did wild things to the tempo of Faith's heart, and then he looked to Faith. He nodded slightly, and dazed, she dipped her head in return. He gave her probing look.

He wanted something.

What did he want?

Faith shook her head.

Violet slammed an elbow into her side, hard, and Faith grunted. "Introductions," her sister whispered loudly. "He is indicating you need to make introductions."

Embarrassment scorched Faith's cheeks. "Mr. DuMond, may I present my sister, Lady Violet Brookfield. Violet, Mr. DuMond."

Rex sketched a deep, respectful bow. "My lady."

In her excitement, however, Violet did away with an answering curtsy. "You own the gaming hell!"

"Violet!" Faith exclaimed, giving her sister a slight pinch on the back side of her wrist as she'd done when they were children.

Alas, it proved no deterrent.

Rex inclined his head. "I do."

"You must tell me all about it." Violet's tone had gone faintly pleading. "Is it as wicked as they say?"

"More so," Faith muttered, and both her sister and Rex looked over. *Oh, hell.* "At least, I expect it is," she blurted. Her foray into that club was something her younger sister hadn't learned of and a secret that somehow remained one of those details the *ton* hadn't discovered. If they had, she'd be ruined. As would Violet. As would Anwen.

Violet switched her attention back to Rex. "Is it true there's a man with a rake who drags the club's winnings from the tables?"

"Violet!" she exclaimed.

Dropping his palms on his knees, Rex leaned in. "True."

Violet's eyes lit up. "I want to do that someday. It sounds like great—"

"You are not ever doing that, Violet," Faith said, dropping a hand warningly on her sister's shoulder.

Her sister released a long, frustrated sigh. "My sister is not as fun as she used to be."

Rex glanced up at Faith. "Oh, I don't know. She seems very much like a lady capable of having a good time."

From where she stood conversing with the dancing master, Mrs. Morrow clapped her hands loudly, commanding the attention of everyone present. "Boys and girls, we are to begin."

Collective groans went up among all the students as they at last ascertained something the boys and girls could agree upon.

"I don't *want* to dance," one of the students called out loudly, his declination met with a round of answering support from his peers.

"You shouldn't be made to dance," Rex said to the boy, Stewart, who nodded approvingly in return. "However, you should be warned that if you don't, you'll be missing out on some of the greatest fun."

Several boys snorted. "Touching a girl's hand?"

"Holding her," another added, and the seven girls present glared at the pair.

"Do you know the feeling you get when you're running?" Rex asked. "Imagine how that flight makes you feel, and then think of music being added to the mix." As in control as if he himself were the instructor in charge of the lesson, Rex looked commandingly to the small orchestra at the front dais. They immediately brought their instruments up into position.

Rex stretched a hand out.

Towards her?

Faith touched a trembling palm to her breast.

Violet gave her a little shove in her lower back, propelling her forward.

Placing her hand in Rex's, she allowed him to lead her onto the dance floor, and then he guided her through the steps of the waltz.

And as he'd said to the children, it was like they were flying. In great, wide, dizzying arcs, she—who hardly danced during the London Season, and when she did, found herself partnered only with family and friends of their family—circled the floor as in a dream.

"Do you enjoy dancing?" Rex murmured as he guided them through the set.

"I love it." She closed her eyes and surrendered herself to the music.

Nay, it's not just the haunting strains of the music and the steps of the waltz, but rather the feel of being in his arms.

Faith's lashes fluttered open, and she found Rex watching her. Flustered, she dipped her eyes to his cravat. "What?"

"I wondered what you were thinking."

She'd been thinking how good it felt to be in his arms.

"I was merely thinking how much I enjoy" —*your embrace*— "dancing."

"I expect you are a lady who dances every set, into the earliest hours of the morning."

He wondered, but he did not know because he didn't attend polite events. As such, she could easily lie to him, and for a long moment, she was tempted to. Because even if it was cowardly, it was also far easier than admitting the truth. "I do not dance much," she settled for.

Leading her through another wide arc, he frowned. "And why not?"

His gaze was patient as she attempted to make the humiliating admission for a second time with this man. "As I mentioned before, I'm not... sought after."

Rex snorted. "I don't believe that."

"I'm *not.*"

"Because you possess some great scandal in your past," he teased. Yet there was a hint of seriousness there, too; one that hinted at the sincerity in his question; one that also bespoke of a man who truly couldn't fathom why she was not sought after. And Lord help her, she fell in love with him just a little more then.

"There is no scandal." There was just a faulty ear that had led to unkindness from many young ladies and disinterest from men who feared a son born to her would be also partially deaf. Rex, however, knew nothing of it, and she found herself wanting to keep it so. Not because she was ashamed of herself. She wasn't. Rather, because invariably when people discovered, they treated her differently. "It is just...*because.*"

"That is the *ton,* is it not?" he asked, with a touch of hardness in his voice.

"Indeed, it is."

Rex swept her through another circle. "And yet, we all have secrets, do we not?"

She stared intently at his cravat. Was he referring to her ear? In fairness, that wasn't a secret. Not to the people who engaged in events amongst Town.

Rex lowered his head, dipping his lips close to that ear which did not hear, and said something; whispered, no doubt. But it wouldn't have mattered if he shouted, she wouldn't have made sense of it, and never more had she regretted being without hearing. Never more had she resented it. When all along, she'd believed herself completely at peace with who she was.

The music drew to a halt, and before the last chord of the tune had played out completely, she stopped.

In the haste with which she wrenched herself from his arms, she nearly upended the both of them. "I…forgive me," she said quickly, avoiding his eyes. "There is something I remember I must see to." And chicken-hearted as she was, Faith dropped a curtsy and raced off.

Faith had a secret, after all.

Just as Rex had suspected she would and did. All people possessed them. Be it innocents who'd tossed aside their virtue for the promise of love from a rake only interested in the fat dowry to be had in marrying, to the reprobate husbands and fathers who were on the surface leading pillars of society but secretly tupping the youngest servants in their employ—everyone had their vices. Ones that could be used against them. Ones that could be used as leverage to compel them to silence.

Faith's inability to meet his eyes and the speed with which she'd raced from the floor indicated there was something there for him to use.

Haste, however, made waste.

It was why he made himself return to the boys and girls who'd finally come 'round to the idea of dancing, and together with Mrs.

Morrow, moved them along through their lessons.

Carefully disentangling himself from the lesson, Rex went in search of Faith. He'd visited enough that he now knew precisely those places he could find her, the areas within the school she liked to frequent: her smallish office. The library.

The gardens, however, were her favorite. And just as he'd known he would, Rex found her there.

He paused on the terrace, studying the lady seated near the man-made pond. At some point, she'd discarded her slippers and they lay strewn beside her while she dipped her toes into those waters.

She moved them back and forth, periodically flicking droplets like one of those fabled mermaids, and Rex found himself compelled forward, no different than one of those hapless sailors steering his galleon out to sea.

The moment his shadow fell over her, Faith glanced up. "The lessons have finished?"

He dropped to his haunches. "No. The boys and girls appeared less like they'd prefer to gouge one another and more like they were enjoying one another's company, and as such, it seemed safe to take my leave."

They shared a smile, one that came far more easily than it had days ago, one that didn't strain his facial muscles and proved something worse, more dangerous—*sincere.*

Nonsense. You're merely elated at finding her here alone so you can probe her for secrets you can use against her. That was all it was.

"I offended you," he murmured.

She shook her head. "It wasn't that."

"What was it?"

"It is my circumstances."

This was interesting. "And what circumstances are those, Faith?" he murmured.

"That I am unmarried and likely to remain so."

A black curl fell over her brow, and he tucked that tendril behind her ear. Or he intended to. The moment he held that silken lock between his fingers he froze, rubbing at that satiny soft strand.

Faith's lips parted; her mouth trembled.

He made himself release the curl. "I want to know about you,

Faith." Those were the truest words he'd given her and likely the only true ones he ever would.

She scrunched up her nose. "There is nothing to know. I'm eminently boring."

Respectable. Innocent. Romantic. Given she was all of those things he'd long despised, he should be in agreement with her. And yet oddly, he was not. Unnerved by that realization, he shifted. "I don't believe that."

Faith proceeded to tick off on her fingers. "I've devoted, loving parents, a role at my mother's school which brings me greater responsibilities than most any other woman will ever know."—Had he asked her to compile a list he might use to further his own goals, it couldn't have been easier than securing this enumeration.— "I've a large also loving family." She paused. "With the exception of a villainous grandmother. I have a sizeable dowry that will pass to me if I don't wed."

In short, she'd just described a woman who didn't have a single sin to use against her.

There had to be something.

Everyone had *something*.

"I should want for nothing more," she said softly, distractedly to herself.

"And yet, you do?"

She hesitated, then nodded. "My parents are in love. My uncles and their wives are in love. My aunts love their husbands. Marcia is in love."

Marcia, as in the Viscountess Waters, who'd fallen for Andrew Barrett, a viscount and rake in dun territory.

"And you want that?"

She nodded. "I do."

"And why do you believe you can't have it?"

"I…" She warred with herself. He saw the battle she fought playing out in eyes that were a convenient window into her soul. "I cannot hear," she said.

And of everything he expected she might say, that hadn't been it. He opened his mouth to repeat his question, but Faith shook her head.

She pointed to her right ear. "I can't hear out of this ear."

This is what she saw as her weakness?

As if unable to meet his eyes, Faith shifted her gaze back to the pond.

Rex took her chin gently between his thumb and forefinger and angled her so they looked at one another. "That's no failing, Faith," he said. Unlike every lie he'd fed her before, this was actually a truth. He caressed the lobe of that ear she'd spoken of. "That's no weakness." It was nothing he could or would ever use against her. "It's no vice. It's not evil. It is just…part of who you are." Just one of many interesting things that made her, her. "And if you let other people's opinions of it any of your energies, you give them more power than they deserve."

Her lips parted. Her eyes went soft, and she'd the look of one who'd just had a star placed in her hand.

Rex abruptly released her. Dropping his hand to his side, he jumped to his feet.

Disappointment lit her expressive eyes. "You're leaving."

"I have to." Which was true. He had to get away from her. He needed to regroup and refocus himself on a plan forward with her.

Faith drew her toes from the water and stood. "I'll see you again?"

"You will."

She had to. Because he required information about her. About sins or scandals in her past that he might use to ensure her silence against other members of his club. Then he'd be done with her. Free of all the jumbled confusion that came from simply being around Faith Brookfield.

Faith smiled. "Do you know what I believe, Rex?"

He shook his head. "What?"

She took a step closer, wafting the whispery hint of rosewater that clung to her skin. Despite himself, he shut his eyes a moment, taking in the heady, evocative scent of her. "I believe there is far more to you than the world sees or knows."

As Rex took his leave, her words followed him.

She wasn't completely wrong in her thinking.

That fact was true about all. There were layers to everyone and secrets within. It certainly must hold true about Faith. She couldn't be this good. All people had scandals in their armoires. He, on the other hand? He was precisely what the world took him for—cold, hard, ruthless, mercenary. And he'd have it no other way.

CHAPTER 10

THE FOLLOWING MORNING, CLOSETED AWAY in her family's library, Faith sat with her most recent memories of Rex DuMond.

There'd been any number of times when she'd found her thoughts all higgledy-piggledy because of the notorious gaming hell proprietor. There'd been his stolen kisses—though in fairness, they'd been kisses she'd freely given. There'd been the time they'd played hide and seek and took shelter and found privacy amongst the gardens at Ladies and Gentlemen of Hope. That day when they'd rested in a like repose, with their gazes locked and their foreheads near touching.

Not a single one of those intimate moments, however, could compare to yesterday when he'd caressed the shell of her ear and spoken so sincerely, so naturally, about her partial deafness. Because even as he was correct, that it was just a part of who she was, the world on the whole did not view it in that same light. To strangers, even members of her family, she was, if not to be pitied, then treated differently. And to at last find not only a person but a man who viewed Faith as simply Faith was heady, powerful stuff.

Footfalls echoed in the hall, intruding on her thoughts, and she looked up just as her family's butler Cranston appeared with a friend in tow. "Lady Anwen," he announced, and then backed out of the room.

The moment he'd gone, Anwen pushed the panel shut, and hurried into the room. "We've a problem."

Yes, they certainly did. She was falling further and further under

Rex's—

Anwen dropped a newspaper on the mahogany tea table. *Thwack.*

"What?" she asked, dread formed a pit in her belly, and she reached for those sheets.

Oh, hell.

"It is Cressida," Anwen said. She sank quickly onto the sofa beside Faith. "Cressida Alby." Even being as close as they were next to each other, Anwen spoke in a whisper-soft voice. "As you know, she is one of the earliest members of the Mismatch Society. Her brother is Baron Newhart. He is a contemptible, detestable fiend."

From behind the round frames of her spectacles, fire blazed in Anwen's pretty eyes. "He inherited a bankrupt title and to support his licentious existence, he's attempted to use his sister as a pawn. He's been deterred in the past, but he's desperate now and won't be for long. He intends to marry her off this time, for good."

Hearing something in her friend's voice, Faith glanced up from the pages she'd been reading, and registered the seriousness of Anwen's gaze.

"To whom?"

"Lord Bourchier. Cressida is suspicious of his sudden interest, an interest that came only after her aunt fixed a sizeable dowry upon her. Her brother insists that Cressida is fortunate to have a respectable, charming man such as Bourchier. Her aunt has already approved the match. And I was wondering…hoping…if you'd happened to discover anything that supports Cressida's fears?"

Lord Bourchier. The earl whom the whole world believed to be charming and respectable and rich because he'd inherited a loaded gold mine in one of the Carolinas. And yet, those mines had not been prosperous—for him. The illusion of wealth was nothing more than that—an illusion that he used to maintain his excessive gaming habits and his proclivity for whipping his bedmates.

All those details Faith knew from the words she'd committed to memory in Rex's ledger.

Cressida Alby's marriage to the earl would see the young lady tied for all time to a lecherous reprobate without a farthing to his name, who in turn would run through her inheritance.

And on the surface, the whole world believed Lord Bourchier to be an upstanding fellow, no different from any of the other also-respectable gents who visited their clubs.

Anwen continued. "Cressida suspects her brother learned the truth about Lord Bourchier and the two men struck up an arrangement, one that will see them split her dowry."

In other words, "If the world were to discover that Lord Bourchier isn't really as respectable...."

"Then Cressida's aunt will not support the union."

Unlike Faith and Anwen, however, who each had large, loving families, Cressida Alby was alone, at the mercy of only a merciless brother for support and a well-meaning aunt, who'd also inadvertently set Cressida up for harm. The young woman would find herself trading one cruel cage for another, even crueler, one.

Faith shivered, recalling those vices inked in Rex's book. No young lady should be subject to such pain. No person should.

"Faith?" Anwen said, insistently. "Faith? Are you listening to me?"

She opened her eyes to find the other woman's worried gaze on her, and her stomach sank.

For she knew.

Faith knew what her friend was asking even as she'd not asked it yet. She knew because it was what she herself knew to be the right thing to do.

"I know I said I did not approve and that it was dangerous," Anwen said on a whispered rush. "And I don't want you to earn *his* wrath."

Earn his wrath.

Was a man like Rex even truly capable of wrath? She knew what the papers said, but she'd also witnessed firsthand a man who played hide-and-seek with her mother's students and who read to those children and who used his persuasiveness to bring the boys around to dancing with the girls.

Following her visit to the *The Morning Chronicle*, she'd waited with bated breath for fear of the moment Rex called Faith out for her involvement in disseminating that precious information about one of the members of his club. Only that moment had not come. Instead, something else had—a friendship.

Nay, this time, it was not fear of him that gave her pause. This time, it was that relationship which held her back.

Though it wasn't really just a friendship. After all, one didn't dream of a friend's embrace the way thoughts of Rex haunted her. A friend didn't cause one's whole body to tremble during a dance-set—a delicious, dizzying tremble, that was.

Faith dropped her head along the scalloped back of the sofa and stared at the ceiling. Whether she liked it or not, for good or for bad, that night she'd scrummaged through Rex's books, she'd found herself in possession of useful information that could help other ladies, women like her Aunt Caroline, who found themselves prey for heartless men.

Also, information that, coming from Rex's clubs, could threaten his business. His business, though wicked, still provided valuable resources and support to institutions like her mother's school.

Faith jammed her fingertips against her temple.

The leather squeaked as Anwen shifted closer. "You don't have to," she said quietly.—Faith didn't want to. But she didn't want to for all the wrong reasons. Because of how much Rex had come to mean to her. And she couldn't have Rex in her life as anything more than they were while simultaneously using his business against him.—"In fact, I more than understand if you do not. It would be wrong of me to expect that you would."

"No, it wouldn't," she said tiredly. "It *would* be wrong of me to allow Cressida to marry such a cad."

Anwen searched her gaze over Faith's face. "You'll do it."

"I will." She didn't have a choice. Not really.

She would do it, and hope that once more, Rex remained oblivious to Faith's involvement in ruining the reputation of another of his clients.

CHAPTER 11

Ⅎaith didn't hate balls.

On the contrary, she rather enjoyed them.

She loved the room being awash in so very many candles that one oft couldn't tell where day ended and night began. She loved the strains of the orchestra's music that swelled above even the noise made by the many guests always in attendance. And the dancing. She loved that the most.

Of course, she'd love it even more if she'd had more opportunities to partake in it. That was, partake in it with those who were not her male relatives, or male friends of her relatives who'd put them up to dancing with her.

She'd not resented her circumstances. She was really quite practical. Some ladies were Diamonds—like her friend Marcia had been. Some were not. *She* was not.

Even if she had been, however, it wasn't that she'd wished for very many dance partners. Just one would do.

A specific someone.

Seated on a Louis XVI ballroom chair, Faith stared wistfully at the couples sweeping through the steps of the latest waltz to be played by her aunt and uncle, the Marquess and Marchioness of Waverly's, orchestra. The blissfully happy couple were always asking for more waltzes to be played than was fashionable. Where most balls had two, they would always have a third and sometimes a fourth, and dance every single set together. And every time they twirled past, the earl holding his wife close, their audience of every other lady present secretly pined for romance of their own. Faith included herself among those ranks.

While couples waltzed, she'd sit with thoughts rolling through her head of some dashing gentleman who might fall fully and completely under her spell—a spell she discovered she possessed only because of him.

In those imaginings the figure was always amorphous, his face unclear and undefined in her mind. Until now.

Now, she saw someone there.

Rex DuMond. The Marquess of Rutherford, who didn't go by his title, but rather who shunned it, displaying a pride in being a self-made man.

It was not every day—in fact, it was not *any* day—when the nobility rebuffed their lavish lifestyle and the privileges that came along with their like, elevating the accomplishments they'd achieved on their own, instead.

Yet even as his business catered to the nobility, Rex didn't otherwise enter the world that Faith inhabited and so there'd never be a glorious waltz in his arms—that was, outside of the schoolroom of Ladies and Gentlemen of Hope. There'd not be the thrill of a full orchestra and a candlelit room, and… *would there be anything at all, if he discovered you were the one behind this morning's latest gossip about one of his best patrons?*

Guilt licked at her insides. She'd told herself Lord Somerville would be the only one of Rex's patrons whose information she'd spill, and she'd done it quite freely, too, with hardly a guilty conscience. Her aunt's reputation had been forever destroyed by a cad who'd skated quite blithely free of all deserved censure.

Then there'd been Anwen's request on behalf of Cressida Alby. Cressida who, were she forced to marry Lord Bourchier, would face a horrific fate as his wife. Faith couldn't have very well let her suffer, no more than she could have let any other young lady. In a world where women were regarded as nothing more than chattel or property, the fortunate few like Faith who had stable, happy families and secure situations had a responsibility to save others who were not quite so lucky.

She'd visited the printer that morning and traded those salacious details for a handful of coin. It was done. That would be the absolute last time she revealed the proclivities of Rex's patrons.

That, however, didn't make the feeling that she'd betrayed Rex simply go away. For these two things, helping innocent ladies and hurting Rex's business, were not compatible.

"Pansy for your thoughts."

Faith gasped and she blinked up at the smiling figure who now obstructed her view of the dancefloor.

"Aunt Caroline," she blurted. Unlike the seeming perpetual sadness which had cloaked her father's sister for so long, a genuine, wide smile wreathed the older woman's cheeks flush with color that only happiness could bring.

Her aunt gestured to the available chair beside Faith. "May I join you?"

"Of course."

Caroline settled onto the matching oyster white chair on the right of Faith, a considerate gesture her family never failed to remember when speaking with her.

The moment she'd seated herself, Caroline spoke. "There is something we need to discuss," she said without preamble.

Faith's mind went blank, and her heart thudded sickeningly against her rib cage.

She knows.

She'd deduced that Faith had been, in fact, the one to ruin Lord Somerville and all his hopes of marriage. Surely, she'd not be upset, and yet that was certainly the lesser worry. For if Aunt Caroline had figured it out, then anyone might. Say, a certain gaming hell owner whose company and presence she found herself increasingly welcoming entirely too much.

"I thought I should return this to you." Caroline took Faith's hand and rested something in it.

Even through her satin gloves, Faith felt the cool, solid press of metal. She glanced down.

"Someone once told me some women need magic," her aunt murmured. "Some don't. It only seemed right that you wear it now." With that, she draped the thin gold chain upon Faith's neck.

The moment the clasp had been slid into place, Faith's fingers came up reflexively to touch that cherished piece handed down from her mother. She'd oft told the tale of all the happy women who'd donned the necklace and found true love. Faith's friend Marcia, and now Aunt Caroline, recently married to the Marquess of Exmoor who loved her so very much, were both included among those lucky ranks.

"There," Aunt Caroline said, with another smile.

How much more real that smile had become too since she'd fallen in love.

"Well?" the other woman went on. "Do you feel any different?"

Again, Faith fingered the pendant a moment, then shook her head. "No." When she'd first been regaled with the legend behind the piece, Faith had expected that the moment the wearer donned it, something would happen. In a bid to study the gift her aunt had conferred Faith tipped her chin down awkwardly. "I feel very much the same."

"Yes, what I've learned," Aunt Caroline said, "is that it does feel that way." She paused and Faith looked up. The other woman's voice grew faraway. "Until your path first crosses with the one who makes up the other part of your soul. Then there is an energizing heat. It is like…" She hung on the long beat of silence leaning in, waiting for her aunt to finish that thought. "Magic."

"Magic," Faith whispered, echoing that thrilling word.

A buzz went up around the ballroom, a din noisy enough to briefly drown out the strains of the orchestra's latest set.

As one, Faith and her aunt looked to see what accounted for the crowd's reaction. Seated as they were, however, they could not make out the source of the guests' interest. Lords and ladies alike, both strained up on tip-toe to catch sight of whatever it was that had snagged their attention.

And then…she felt it.

A charge went through her as the heart pendant throbbed against her chest, radiating… "An energizing heat," she whispered.

Her aunt slid a curious look her way. "Faith?"

Faith opened her mouth, but then words failed, as did her thoughts. For her gaze caught and landed on the very person responsible for the flurry of interest from Lord and Lady Montfort's guests.

Rex.

Her heart picked up a steadily quickening tempo. Everyone knew that aside from his clubs, Rex DuMond did not mingle with the peerage. Everyone knew he didn't dip his toes into polite events. It was why she'd only allowed herself the dream of waltzing in his arms.

But he was here.

Dressed in midnight black from his jacket, to the expertly folded cravat at his throat, to his breeches and boots—boots when all the other man had buckled shoeware for dancing—he wore the look of sin.

Faith's breath caught.

He strode through the ballroom with a commanding presence, one of those Greek gods of lore who elicited fear among the mere mortals under them. And those mere mortals stepped out of his way, making a wide path for him, each person craning their neck to follow where he went, each lord and lady trying determine who it was that had beckoned him from his world of debauchery and into this polite-on-the-surface one he now inhabited.

She willed him to see her.

I am here, she longed to call. Because surely he was here for—

Rex stopped.

Before Faith's…father and mother.

Her mother, who met him with palms outstretched, a friend greeting an old friend, and her father, smiling and speaking so casually as if they'd been expecting him. As if he were a special guest they'd invited, and their business dealings together alone accounted for Rex's presence.

Disappointment.

Who knew it had a taste? It was sour like vinegar and hot like pepper and, mixed together, really quite awful.

Faith felt her aunt's gaze on her and made herself look away from the sight of her parents conversing with Rex.

"Faith? Faith? Are you all right?"

Faith whipped her attention back to a concerned Aunt Caroline. "Fine," she said quickly, and it was the biggest, fattest lie she'd ever uttered, which given the fact she'd snuck off any number of times with Marcia this past Season was saying a good deal indeed. "I… was just…" she searched and searched. "…hot." And unsettled.

Flipping her fan open, she proceeded to flutter the silk frame in front of her face.

"Would you like some air?" Caroline was already rising to help her up, but Faith waved her off.

"No, I'm fine. The fan has already…" From the corner of her eye, she caught a movement. A trio of people headed her way, and those latest lies she'd given her aunt died on her lips.

He was coming.

They were coming. Her parents and Rex.

And then they were before her.

Aunt Caroline came to her feet.

Belatedly, Faith stood.

Even as her parents made introductions between Aunt Caroline and Rex, it was as though there were just Faith and Rex; all the world melted away, so that it was only they two in it.

And then, the focus shifted to Faith.

They went through the motions of pretend; the four of them privy to Faith's already existing connection, with Rex maintaining that important pretense.

"Lady Faith," he murmured; that silken, low baritone that never failed to cause her belly to flutter. "It is an honor."

"Mr. DuMond," she returned. Her voice sounded faintly breathless to her own ears, and she prayed the resumption of activity and noise in the ballroom drowned out some of that breathy response.

His long, inky black lashes swept low. An enigmatic glint in his eyes indicated he'd heard and that he recalled the secret only they two shared of passionate kisses and heated touches.

"As you know, Mr. DuMond has become the leading patrons of Ladies and Gentlemen of Hope," Faith's father shared.

"And," Faith's mother added, "to convey our gratitude, we invited Mr. DuMond to join us for the upcoming ceremony commemorating the momentous moment. However, he's proven entirely too modest and wishes to remain anonymous in his contributions."

"You won't come?" Faith asked, unable to quash her regret that he'd not join her and her family.

"I'd not have my presence detract in any way from what the day is truly about," Rex murmured, and then adroitly steered away from her parents' request. "I would, however, be honored to request a set with you this evening, my lady."

Her soul screamed in delight as her head spun in a dizzying way that only came from being waltzed too fast. Faith managed a nod and held forth the card dangling at her wrist.

A waltz.

She glanced at his bent head as he scratched his initials onto her embarrassingly empty dance card.

She would, at last, have her—"*Quadrille?*" she blurted.

Her aunt, parents, and Rex all collectively looked at her.

That was, he'd not claimed the most intimate dance, that forbidden one that would see her in his arms for an extended time, but rather…a quadrille.

And then to cover up that exclamation, she raised a fist to her mouth. *Cough-cough.*

"Are you all right, Faith?" her father asked, that seemingly most popular question of the night.

"Perhaps she needs a glass of lemonade," her mother answered, already availing herself of one from a passing servant's tray. She pressed it into Faith's hand.

As Faith made herself sip from that drink, she felt Rex's heated gaze upon her, hot like a physical touch, warm like the charmed pendant she wore about her neck.

Standing on the sidelines of the Marquess and Marchioness of Waverly's ballroom, Rex waited, biding his time.

Every move he made in life was measured, calculated. Everything this night from his late arrival to the set he'd requested from Faith Brookfield had been carefully orchestrated.

The guests present went out of their way to avoid his gaze.

Unlike Faith.

Faith, who sat on that chair beside her aunt, the woman who'd been ruined years earlier by Lord Somerville, who was subsequently ruined in turn by Faith. The pair spoke animatedly but it wasn't the older woman who commanded Rex's attention, but rather the young lady with long black curls and a heart-shaped face and a smile that went on for days.

Rex didn't even bother to hide his interest.

In the weeks he'd spent with Faith Brookfield, Rex had discovered any number of things about the lady. She snorted when she laughed. She fluttered a hand about her heart when she was unnerved.

He'd also learned the lady wore her feelings and emotions like an open book. There wasn't a scrap of artifice to her. Unlike he and the people whom he dealt with, who excelled in donning a mask and keeping those facades in place, Faith revealed her every thought.

It was how he'd known she'd been disappointed—disappointed the set he'd requested hadn't been a waltz, but rather a quadrille. Just as he'd known she'd have longed for that dance that placed her in his arms.

Rex tensed, looking over just as the Duke of Argyll joined him.

"My god, hell hath surely froze over," the other man drawled. "*You* attending a ball."

"My reasons for doing so are business in nature." As one, they looked to where Faith still conversed with her aunt. The two women laughed uproariously at something one had said.

Argyll's expression grew serious, and he stirred the contents of his glass. When the other man spoke next, his mouth barely moved. "All anyone is talking about still is Somerville."

He tensed. "I am aware of that."

"You've been in her company for more than a fortnight now." The duke spoke in hushed tones. "I trust you've ascertained there's some secret that might prove useful to us."

Actually, he hadn't. As he and Argyll sipped champagne, Rex considered the other man's erroneous assumption. Rex's dealings were with mature women, unhappily married wives, very-happy-with-their-circumstances widows. Mayhap it was only after they were corrupted that they were forever changed, and Faith had simply not been altered.

But a person could not be as pure as Faith Brookfield. It just wasn't a possibility. Everyone had secrets. Everyone had vices. Even young ladies. There were innocents who stole pin money from their fathers and ones who met clandestinely with strapping male servants. There were young ladies who secretly bandied gossip about their supposed friends.

Or that's what he'd believed. Where Faith was concerned, however, there were none of those helpful-to-him sins. Faith, who, in the time he'd spent with her and observing her, did not even seem to visit shops but rather donated all her time to working with children at her mother's school, and who kept a remarkably small circle of friends. Just Lady Anwen and the Viscountess Waters.

Which would also mean there is absolutely nothing you can gather about her that you can in turn use as leverage against her.

It would also mean he and his time together with her were done, and he required another strategy to compel her to silence.

"Do we know how much information she is in possession of?" Argyll said from around the rim of his glass, that flute cleverly placed in a way to conceal his mouth's movements. "Is it possible she wrote that information down?"

"She did not." Having embraced her and had his hands all over her, he'd searched her for sign of concealed documents that night she'd been brought to his offices.

"She couldn't very well have remembered much more than that," Argyll ventured, with an optimism that bespoke one who'd lived a charmed life. For she had.

Whatever my mother requires of me. I've a head for recalling most anything I see...

In one of his earlier meetings with Faith, she had inadvertently and helpfully revealed she'd a penchant for seeing something and remembering it. As such, he couldn't be certain just how much she had recalled, only that she was in possession of some of his information.

"Perhaps she is done," Argyll ventured.

Rex slid a hard look the other man's way. "Do you want to stake the success of our business on that assumption?" Because it would be a faulty misstep.

His properly chastised partner went silent.

From across the way, Rex continued to study Faith.

As if she felt his gaze, the lady glanced over.

Their eyes met.

Rex inclined his head in the slightest of acknowledgements.

Faith smiled.

She was always smiling. A big, wide, generous, and foreign-to-Rex sincere tilt of her lips. She made no attempt to hide that reaction. And it unnerved the hell out of him. The effects of her ease and happiness around him proved as dangerous as the information the chit was in possession of.

The orchestra concluded their latest set, and without a parting word for Argyll, Rex headed across the room to where Faith sat. The moment he reached her, she hopped up, and placing her fingers atop his sleeve, he escorted her towards the dance floor.

"I'm cross with you," she declared, as they took up their position alongside the other couples.

"Indeed?" They brought their arms up into position. "And here, I thought you were eager to see me, *petite chouette*."

The set required they chasé away from one another.

When they again met, Faith spoke. "You requested a *quadrille*."

Rex quirked an eyebrow. "And there is something wrong with a quadrille?"

He and Faith traded partners, making their way through the mincing steps of a dance he really quite despised. In fairness, he despised all dancing. Oddly, however, he found himself enjoying this particular set.

"I'd thought, given the scandalous nature of the waltz, someone like you would prefer to dance that set," she declared, as they came together.

"A waltz is not scandalous." When they met once more in the middle, he whispered, "Meeting a man alone in her host's library is."

Faith's lush lips parted. "Was that…an invitation?" She searched her gaze over his face.

"Do you want it to be, *petite chouette*?"

She did.

Even as they found themselves switching off with other partners and his question going unanswered, Rex knew. Just as he knew he intended to meet her alone this night and once and for all find out exactly how much information she was in possession of.

The music faded to a stop, and the dancers came to a rest.

Faith stood before him, and he before her. Their eyes locked. Positioned as they were with the chandelier directly overhead, the glow of a hundred candles bathed her face in an almost ethereal light, momentarily stripping him of his thoughts.

Rex gave his head a slight shake, and then finding his footing, held an arm out.

Without a word exchanged, he escorted her back to the chairs she'd occupied earlier. He bent over her hand, pausing for an infinitesimal second as he straightened, and their stares met once more. "The library," he mouthed. "In two sets."

Faith's lips moved as if she were trying to make words, and then she nodded.

Releasing her, Rex took his leave and headed for Lord Waverly's library, where he waited for a woman who, even without any secrets or vices or sins to her credit, was proving far more dangerous to him than the blackest souls he'd ever had dealings with.

CHAPTER 12

FAITH HAD NEVER BEEN SCANDALOUS.

The closest she'd come to it had been when she'd arrived in London at the start of the Season, donned a pair of breeches she'd borrowed from one of the stableboys, and ridden astride in Hyde Park at dawn.

It seemed though since she, Marcia, and Anwen had been abducted and brought to Forbidden Pleasures, Faith's jejune existence had changed.

It had all changed because of Rex. Everything about him, everything about just being with him, left her feeling things she'd never before felt. Each moment since him, had been thrilling… and scandalous too. From their shared embraces to the times they'd stolen away together, Faith at last had a taste of what wicked really was. And she feared now that she'd tasted of it, she'd forever crave this feeling that only came in being with Rex.

Faith paused outside her aunt and uncle's library, and stared at the pretty, robin's egg blue panel.

Nothing good could come from continuing to meet him alone this way.

Only what if it could? a voice whispered in her mind. What if there could somehow be more between her and Rex? What if that dream she'd carried for herself, of a grand romance and even grander love such as the one that was shared by her parents, could come true…with him.

His interests in her had baffled her from the start. But mayhap, just mayhap, he'd been bit by the same magic.

Faith let herself inside her uncle's library.

She blinked, adjusting her eyes to the dim lighting and then found him.

He'd availed himself of a brandy from Uncle Gabriel's Chippendale sideboard and sat perched on the rolled arm of the leather sofa, his gaze on hers.

"Shut the door, Faith," he said quietly, and she managed to move at last.

Her trembling fingers struggled to do as he ordered.

There was something so very commanding in his words and his ways that should offend her, and yet, strangely, left her weak inside.

"Now, lock it."

Suddenly, the piercing heat of his gaze, so powerful and potent that it ran all the way through her, was too much. Giving him her back as she saw to this latest order, she struggled to breathe properly.

And then, even as she'd not heard his approach, she felt it. She felt him so close, her back brushed the hard wall of his chest. Faith's eyes slid shut.

"The moment I saw you behind my desk, Faith," he murmured against the shell of her ear, "I knew you were going to be trouble for me. I just never expected how much."

"I'm n-not really trouble, you kn–know," she whispered.

"Actually, I don't know any such thing."

For a moment, she froze; for a moment she thought she heard something more in his words, a harshness in his tone that had only ever been there the first time he'd come upon her under his desk and reading his ledgers.

She angled her head back to look him in the eyes. Whatever she'd thought she heard was gone for his stare was heated, glinting with passion—a passion she'd discovered only because of this man.

"You've ensnared me, *petite chouette*," he said huskily, and pressed a kiss against her shoulder.

Her lashes fluttered as she fought to keep them open. "H–Have I? B–Because I've n–never had that effect on anyone."

"I'm not just anyone, Faith." He continued to kiss away at her neck.

"N–No. Th–that is true."

Rex pressed his lips to her nape, and then reaching around, he cupped her breasts in his palms; the muslin fabric of her ballgown crunched noisily, in a forbidden, wicked way.

Oh, goodness.

Faith's legs trembled, and her eyes slid shut.

"Do you like that, Faith?"

"I suspect you know I do," she said, her voice weak, her limbs even weaker.

"Yes, but I like hearing you say it more." She heard the smile in his voice.

"Very w–well. I very m–much enjoy the feel of your hands on me." She should be mortified at the lewd admission she'd spoken aloud. Instead, it only further enflamed her senses.

Between each kiss, his breath fanned her skin, eliciting the most delicious, distracting tingles. "I'm intrigued by you, *petite chouette*."

"I'm really not that intriguing."

Rex licked at her earlobe and then suckled lightly on the oversensitive shell. "That modesty only adds to your appeal."

She had appeal? That was a heady thought, indeed. Faith turned in his arms.

"Why?" she asked, with unabashed curiosity and honesty.

He paused in his seduction, and just stared at her, as if she'd taken him aback.

"It's just, I expect a gentleman such as yourself—"

He tweaked her nose. "Mysterious?"

Faith ignored his teasing interruption. "Worldly," she corrected. "Would have altogether different interests."

His expression grew serious, his gaze shadowed, and his lashes swept low, obscuring those dark irises but not before she caught the raw emotion there. "The women I've had dealings with are singular. Mercenary. They have vices. You have none." There was a question hanging there.

"I midnight snack," she blurted.

He stared at her.

"I wake up in the dead of night and wander the house while

everyone is sleeping and make my way to the kitchens, and I'm only vaguely aware of doing so. But I avail myself to the prior night's desserts and leave crumbs on the table."

His lips twitched.

Then the mood in the room shifted once more.

Rex sank to his knees.

"Wh-What are you doing?" she whispered, as he pushed her skirts up.

He paused. "Kissing you in the most intimate way." He breathed against the inside of her thigh. "Would you like that? Will you allow my kiss?"

Without a scrap of hesitation, she nodded.

"I'd have you say the words." His was another sure command.

"I would like you to kiss me in that way." In a way she didn't understand or know, beyond his having spoken of it, but she wanted this. Needed this.

"Very good, *petite chouette*. Now, spread your legs for me," he ordered harshly, even as he gently but firmly parted her, and brought her right leg over his shoulder, exposing her all the more.

Then he hovered, his mouth near the thatch of curls between her legs, and Faith quivered.

Surely he wasn't going to… "Surely you aren't—"

Only, he was. Rex kissed her. His mouth covered her, and it was in that most intimate of ways, and she understood, God, how she understood. A shuddery gasp slipped from her lips, as he slipped a tongue between the folds of her womanhood and stroked her there.

Faith collapsed against the door, the panel knocking loudly, and she couldn't care. The townhouse could have caught fire with this library the only way out and the guests bearing down on them, and Faith couldn't have made herself stop from giving in to this. She rocked herself forward, her body urging him on.

"You are so wet," he praised, as he laved her channel.

His words were forbidden. Indecent. And she must be naughty too because she felt herself grow shamefully wetter between her legs.

"You like that naughty talk, don't you," he teased, and then he cupped her buttocks in his hand, bringing her closer to his mouth. She whimpered.

"Ah, there's no shame, *petite chouette*. Not in this."

Faith Brookfield's greatest sin was that she liked to steal down to the kitchens and snack on decadent treats while the whole world slept.

It was patently Faith.

And that admission on her part marked the moment Rex had realized this needed to end.

At some point, *something* had shifted. At some point, he'd forgotten the real reason of his being here with her and the information he'd sought, and somehow it had morphed into simply a need for her.

He wanted to taste of her.

He wanted to consume her.

This hungering to do so had nothing to do with uncovering her secrets or silencing her or even about saving his gaming hell from the ruin she could bring down upon it were patrons to discover their secrets were no longer their own.

Rather, it only had to do with a need *for* her.

And that terrified the everlasting hell out of him.

And for that reason alone, he needed to be done with her. Once he had her in this way, he'd cease feeling anything.

There wasn't going to be anything gained to silence Faith because she was as pure as they came. Purer than he knew anyone could be. She was an innocent who dreamed of romance and magic and love, and yet none of that could be used to ensure her silence. None of that solved the problem.

And worse, it was dangerous.

If he were the true dastard he'd taken himself for, he'd have seduced her and then leveraged that information against her, ensuring her silence. Only, this seduction of her now had nothing to do with any scheme he'd crafted, and everything to do with having her in this way, before putting her from his life and his mind for good. One night would be enough. The only need he'd had for women in his life had been for sex. That was the only raw and real emotion between a man and woman. This hungering for her would go away once he rid himself of the veneer of innocence that had so ensnared him these past weeks.

Rex laved her center, sliding his tongue inside the satiny folds of her channel. She was drenched, swollen, and he was a man starving for her.

"Rex," she moaned, thrusting her hips with an unbridled enthusiasm.

He sank his fingers into her buttocks and urged her closer, urged her on. There wasn't a single spot of artifice to this woman, and he who'd avoided innocents and scoffed at the men who'd wanted even the illusion of that virtue among the whores at Forbidden Pleasures, at last understood that sin they'd sought. This was why Adam had fallen. Rex, however, was not a man to fall or falter in any way. He'd give her this, and then set her free.

He increased his strokes, and Faith's hips rocked, her movement jerkier. The door thumped loudly and her body tensed, indicating how very close she was to release. "Come for me," he urged harshly, and then suckled her nub hard.

Faith stiffened, froze, and then with a soft scream that echoed deliciously and damningly around their host's offices, she ground herself against his mouth. The sounds of her desire melded with the thumping of the door. She bucked, pushing herself against his mouth and his ministrations. And then, with a low, keening moan, she collapsed.

Rex placed one final, tender kiss atop her damp curls, and patting her once, he lowered her skirts back into place. The light lilac muslin fabric slid noisily, covering and concealing those long, slender limbs still a'tremble from the force of her climax.

Collecting the kerchief in his pocket, he opened the crisp black monogrammed fabric with a snap and wiped the remnants of her from his face—regretfully. Though the musky taste of her remained seared in his mind.

He looked up.

Faith's shoulders moved up and down quickly, her breathing, noisy and fast, and her eyes remained closed. "Look at me," he commanded.

Faith's lashes fluttered, and she complied with that directive, revealing those enormous, owl-wide brown eyes of hers that were a window to her every thought and feeling. "There is no shame in finding pleasure, Faith. This is the truest, the realest emotion there will ever be. In matters of sex, there are no falsities, no complications, no doubts. There is just a satiation of one's greatest wants."

Her lips parted. "What of... *love?*"

Love?

Love, on the other hand, was the fakest, falsest emotion there was. It was nothing more than a weakness that chipped away at a person's strength and left them weak and hollow and empty as his mother had been upon her husband's continued betrayals and cruelty. "You don't need love, Faith," he said. If there was one lesson he could leave her, it would be that. "You only need this."

Her eyes grew sad, and she caressed her fingers through his hair. "I liked this, but I rather believe I need love."

Rex narrowed his eyes.

He slid a hand under her skirts and caressed her still swollen and throbbing mound. She moaned. "You only *liked* this?" he purred.

The cadence of Faith's breathing increased once more. "I-I, perhaps I rather loved it."

Love. There it was again.

Only this time, correctly applied to the animalistic urges that ultimately compelled them all. Rex dropped the hem of her gown, reveling in the frustrated little groan that spilled so very revealingly from her untried lips. Rex stood.

They looked at one another, their gazes each moving over the other's face.

This was the end. At least of this. For this was not working. Not in the sense that he'd gathered anything of value he'd needed from her. The pull of her was too much. No good could come of it. Not that would leave him better off and unscathed.

This would be goodbye.

Rex looped an arm around her waist, and she was already melting against him, offering her mouth to his, and he took it. He took her lips as he took anything and everything else he wanted in life. Even as she freely gave, and her latest surrender left him throbbing, aching even more.

His shaft begged for release, but he didn't need it.

Because he didn't need anything or anyone.

But you do want *to experience your own physical release with her, and in her?* the devil inside, taunted.

Rex broke the kiss. Faith's chest continued to heave, and her eyes remained shut before she opened them once more to reveal the dazed state he'd roused.

Go. Leave. You're done here. You're done with her. At least in this way.

Why, then, couldn't he compel his feet to move?

Rex looked at the tangle of curls that had escaped her voluminous chignon. He caught one of those midnight black tresses between his thumb and forefinger, feeling it for a final time, and then tucked the strand back into its proper place.

He made to go but stopped, his gaze locked on her mouth, and the hungering to drink of that mouth once more won out.

Rex took her lips, ravaging that flesh, and Faith whimpered. Gripping him by the lapels of his jacket, she pressed herself against him, leaning up and into that violent kiss.

He wrenched away.

Without another word, he continued tidying her hair. All the while he worked, he felt her gaze upon him until all but a lone lock remained, dangling at her shoulder. Rex dropped a kiss upon that delicate flesh.

"Goodbye, Faith," he said quietly.

And then he left.

CHAPTER 13

WHAT HAD HAPPENED? *Everything* HAD happened. And only one thing was certain; Faith was never, ever going to be the same.

She waited several minutes after Rex left before quitting the library. Drawing the door shut, she leaned back against it, borrowing support from that sturdy oak panel. A giddy sensation suffused every corner of her being, and she surrendered to that breathless laugh.

Her heart still raced from all the magic he'd opened her mind, body, and soul to this night, and she rather suspected they always would remain open. Because a woman never, ever forgot that level of magic. It was a manner of wonderment seared forever upon her.

Faith's breath grew raspy and quick once more as she recalled the feel of his mouth on her most private, most secret place. He'd laid possession to it, to her, like he'd wanted to consume her. Another ache built between her legs, an ache that she now understood and needed fulfilled.

Only this feeling she carried inside for him…it was not purely sexual, as he'd insisted was the only truest of emotions a person could feel. She cared about him.

The necklace her aunt had returned to Faith's care felt hot against her chest. She brought her fingers up to the heart-shaped pendant that fairly burned to the touch.

Nay, that wasn't wholly true, either. She didn't just care about Rex DuMond. She'd fallen in love with him.

She knew that now.

Rex, a man of mystery whom society saw as the worst sort of scoundrel, who earned his coin dealing in the business of sin. But who'd also proven to be so much more than that. With every moment they'd spent together, she'd discovered layer upon layer of the complex marquess who shunned his title and embraced the wicked reputation he'd earned. He was a man who gave away those funds to worthwhile causes like her mother's school. And a man who gave of his time, visiting the boys and girls at Ladies and Gentlemen of Hope.

And Faith was never, ever going to be the same.

With a giddy little laugh, Faith touched a hand to her chest.

There'd been an explosiveness in their latest exchange. There'd also been something different about his kiss too. It had felt almost desperate. Like he'd been trying to commit her to memory for all time. It'd born the hint of a good—

"Enjoying yourself this evening, are you?"

Gasping, Faith dropped her arm facing the man whose approach she'd failed to hear. The tall stranger, near in age to her father, stared back.

Her mind went blank. "Who—?"

And for the first time through the magic that had been every part of her exchange this night with Rex there came a remembrance—about her reputation and the risk of discovery she and Rex had flirted with. "Forgive me," she said quickly, dipping a curtsy, and made to step around him; eager to be free of this man's company.

He slid himself into her path, blocking her retreat.

"Running off only now, are you? Now that you've had your itch scratched?"

Shock lanced through her—at the man's crudeness, and more. At his accuracy.

His dark hair contained just the hint of gray specks at his temples. His eyes were harsh, and...familiar. And yet, one surely never forgot a figure this cold.

Faith found her voice. "How dare you? This is my aunt and uncle's household, and I'm merely—"

"I know whose household this is, just as I know who you are, and I also know what you were doing. It wouldn't take much to deduce what any woman meeting my son was, in fact, doing even if I hadn't happened to hear the door thump-thump-thumping."

Oh God. He'd heard that. Which meant he'd heard all of that intimate, most special of exchanges with Rex. It felt wrong and filthy and—

His son.

And then the significance of the words he'd spoken hit her.

This man was the Duke of Haincourt. The man her mother had spoken of, hinting at his cruelness and speaking to the implications that living with once such as the duke would have on Rex.

"I'd have a word with you, *Lady* Faith."

He wrapped a whole other level world of disdain and mockery into that overemphasized word.

Faith tipped her chin up. "There is hardly anything I care to speak with you about."

"Oh, I suspect that much is true; however, I will have my piece said." He paused. "Or we could, of course, have this discussion here." As if on a damning cue, there came the echo of approaching voices and footfalls. His Grace glanced pointedly in the direction of those nearing footfalls.

Faith scrambled back deeper into the room.

With a chuckle, the duke entered after her. He closed the door firmly behind them.

He was a devastatingly handsome man and in many ways the image of his son. From his impressive height to his broad shoulders and powerful chest, she'd a glimpse of what Rex would look like in the future.

She recalled the words her mother had spoken about Rex's father. Cruel. Hard. Unfeeling. Nay, Rex looked nothing like this man.

The duke's gaze locked with hers, and a chill went through her. The resemblance lay on the surface. In every other way that mattered most, however, Rex was nothing like the soulless figure standing now before her.

"What do you want, Your Grace?"

Surprise lit his flinty eyes, and he caught his chin in his hand, rubbing that clefted, hard flesh contemplatively. "I will get right to the reason for my being here." Only, he didn't. He stared at her a long while. "I expected mousy. You are not mousy, Lady Faith."

"Thank you," she said coolly, even as his didn't sound like a compliment, even as she expected he was a man incapable of giving out compliments.

"See, I keep a keen eye on my son's comings and goings and was confused when I learned of his interest in you." He began to circle her as he spoke. "Everything I read about you and know about you does not fit with everything I know about my son."

She made herself remain still as he walked a path around her, his steps purposeful, like the lion she'd once observed at the Royal Menagerie who'd cornered a mouse at the center of his cage and toyed with his tiny prey before devouring the smaller creature whole.

"My son favors beautiful women, and while you are pretty enough, you're not his usual appetite." Those crude, casually spoken words struck like a barb. "And you're flawed. My son doesn't bed flawed ladies, and he certainly will not marry them, either."

Oh God. All these years, she'd believed herself at peace with the fact she was partially deaf, all this time thinking herself immune to such cruelty and ignorance about her hearing, only to find she'd been wrong. Only to learn she'd never been fully exposed to the depth of cruelty this sharp, that it cut like a knife and shredded away at her self-confidence and self-esteem.

He stopped before her. His hard, unflinching gaze threatened to sear all the way through her. "I'd realized there had to be some reason for my son's different tastes, this time. And there was."

And there was.

It took a moment for those three words to penetrate the hurt and fury roiling in her brain. She stared dumbly at him. What was he saying?

"The truth is, Faith…" With that use of her Christian name, he abandoned all pretense of politeness and respect. "My son? He doesn't love anyone." The duke smiled, the first real smile she'd seen from him, an expression she recognized as that of a proud papa. Only unlike her father, who wore that look when Faith had learned to ride or when he fenced with her, this man found joy in that which marked his son cold and unfeeling.

Hurt cleaved away at her insides, at the life Rex had lived. No wonder he'd become the hardened, cynical man he had. "Perhaps that is true," she began.

"It is."

Faith continued over that interruption. "Because he's not been exposed to that emotion for so long." She wondered at the story of his mother and hoped there'd been some warmth, some regard from one of his parents. "But it does not mean he is incapable of loving someone or being loved in return."

He snorted. "And what do you think? That you might be that woman? That of all the sophisticated, exquisite beauties he's taken to his bed, he'd fall under your spell."

Her entire body went flush with white-hot humiliation.

The duke wasn't done with her.

"No, Faith. My son doesn't love you. He doesn't like you, and he certainly couldn't respect someone as naïve and stupid as you." Each word he hurled struck like pins being jammed into her heart. "Which led me to wonder why would he pursue you of all women? And do you know what I found?"

She didn't want to know. She didn't want to have him speak whatever his discovery had been. And yet, neither could she stop herself from shaking her head; urging him to share those findings.

"I found out you'd had a foray into my son's club…and also that you have had some dealings with a printer."

Oh God.

A dull humming filled her left ear leaving her completely deaf, and she watched his lips move, making out most of the words he was speaking.

"…selling information…my son's patrons…he knows what you've done…"

He knows what you've done…he knows what you've done…

His harsh words and sharper voice came whirring back into clearer focus.

And yet, if he did, would he have treated her with such goodness, a voice at the back of her mind, silently pleaded.

As if he'd heard those pathetic, desperate thoughts, Rex's father chuckled, the sound empty and cold and so very twisted it was hardly recognizable as a laugh. "The sole reason he's been revealing an interest in you is because he's determined to keep you silent, which relieved me greatly, of course." He flicked an imagined speck of lint from his sapphire coat sleeve.

"Why are you telling me this?" Her voice emerged fuzzy and distant, as if she were speaking down a long hall and the echo filtering back had grown all distorted.

The duke stared down the bridge of his hawkish nose at her. "Because I don't trust that my son, out of his hatred of me, wouldn't marry you and stick the dukedom with a deaf heir for spite alone. Good evening, Faith." He politely inclined his head.

Just as Faith had stared after the son who'd departed her life this evening, now she watched as the father turned and marched away.

Unmoving, unblinking, Faith stared at the doorway. The ticking of the bronzed Boule bracket clock filled the room.

Good evening?

That bizarre show of deference on the heels of all the insults and ugly truths he'd hurled pulled a panicky laugh from her chest. It climbed her throat, lodging there so it emerged as nothing more than an odd gurgling sound.

Oh God.

Everything hurt. Her lungs, stomach, heart, soul, and mind. Faith wanted to curl up in a ball so tightly the pain stopped and she ceased to feel anything. Only there was no escaping this greatest of betrayals, and the duke's harshest of words.

Everything with Rex had been a ruse, a clever lie contrived so that he might somehow silence her.

And this night, panting and moaning and thumping away at the door as he'd brought her pleasure, she'd given him just the information needed to ruin her if he so wished. Which he would. Because if his father was correct, and Rex had deduced she'd been the one spilling secrets about his patrons to the newspaper, there'd be no doubting he'd do anything to destroy her. Nor was there a doubt that Rex knew what she'd done. His father had ascertained the details of her dealings with *The Morning Chronicle*. It wouldn't matter to Rex the reasons she'd shared what she'd shared. Ensuring that she stopped would be his sole and primary motivation.

Faith finally knew why one such as Rex would be interested in someone like her. Pain the likes of which she'd never known battered her heart, and she almost preferred to be pummeled by her anguish, so she wasn't capable of feeling anything, ever again. Because this? This hurt so bloody much.

She'd been right about one thing this night.

She was never, ever going to be the same.

CHAPTER 14

HE'D HAD A TASTE OF her and had been haunted by the memory of her since.

She'd proven a distraction he didn't need.

Never had that fact proven truer than now, with Lord Bourchier railing before Rex, while Rex's head remained stuck on thoughts of last evening's ball when he'd brought Faith her first release.

And what was more, he didn't like it. He didn't like it one bloody bit.

Not unlike when Somerville had come calling, Bourchier paced the same path the other man had taken before Rex's desk. "I am ruined," he said sharply. "Ruined." *Because of you.*

Those three words hung, unspoken but clear.

Argyll and Latimer were stationed in opposite corners of Rex's office. The latter proprietor cracked his knuckles menacingly.

Bourchier paused and glanced over at the stony-faced pair.

Finding no mercy in that corner, he looked to Malden, positioned near Rex's shoulder. "Surely you understand the reason for my upset?" he implored.

"Of c—"

"Let us be clear," Rex warned, cutting off those assurances the peacemaker among the partners sought to provide. If the other man thought he'd find comfort from any of them, he was vastly mistaken. "You are ruined because of you."

Lord Bourchier rested his palms upon Rex's desk and leaned forward. His eyes flashed. "*No one* could have known these details except you."

"You expect me to believe we're the only ones to know your mines aren't, in fact, the rich ones in the Carolinas but empty ones in Georgia?" Rex winged an eyebrow up. "In fact, if I'm not mistaken, the entire reason you were in the position of marrying Cressida Alby is because her brother deduced your secrets and was coercing you into wedding her so that you might divide up her dowry."

High color flooded the earl's cheeks. "But my standing amongst the *ton* has been damaged beyond repair. Newland needed the funds as much I did! He wouldn't have destroyed both our fortunes.

The baron hadn't been responsible for revealing the information. Rex knew as much. The gentleman before him, however, did not, and if he had his way, never would.

"Why wouldn't he, Bourchier?" Argyll put to the other man.

A handful of creases formed in the earl's high forehead as he mulled the duke's question.

Rex wasn't above letting blame for this mistake fall on one such as the lecherous Baron Newland. Newland, who'd attempted to sell his sister numerous times to Rex. Rex might be a black-hearted monster who didn't blanch at much, but selling virgins against their will was a sin too dark for even him.

Seeing the other man wavering, Rex continued planting further seeds of doubt. "Perhaps Newland found a real purse, a fatter one than your empty pockets, and the only way to sever the agreement and save his sister's reputation was by revealing the true nature of your circumstances."

Under that logic, Bourchier faltered, and Rex knew the moment the earl had bought the yarn.

"I'm not going to be able to pay off," the gentleman said, glancing down at his feet. "It is my hope that there will be another scandal that will replace this one, and that the mothers and fathers looking for a match for their daughters will forget." –They wouldn't.— "And then I'll wed and secure a fortune. But until that happens, I—" Bourchier lifted his empty palms signaling the sorry state of his fortune and future.

Rex steepled his fingers and made a show of studying the earl from over the top of them, feigning contemplation.

After three minutes of silence, Rex dropped his palms to the arms of his chair and spoke. "I do not take well to men coming into my office and throwing accusations my way, Bourchier. Nor do I doubt your charges today stem from desperation over the debt you owe. This," he swirled a hand, "situation? It changes nothing. We expect our payment."

The earl's face fell, and his eyes slid shut.

"But," Rex went on, and at that syllable of hope Bourchier's eyes flew open, "this time, and this time only, I'll excuse it as part of your desperation. After your behavior this day, I'm inclined to tell you to go hang." The earl's expression sank once more. "However…"

Bourchier brightened.

How pathetic these people were who wore their every thought on their proverbial sleeve.

Only…Faith Brookfield did, and you didn't find it pathetic. You found yourself entranced as you've never been before by that sincerity and innocence.

The earl bowed his head slowly. "However," he ventured, desperation making him impatient enough to urge Rex on.

From across the room, he felt the probing stares of his partners.

Bloody hell. You can't clear your head of her even now? This was too much. Too damned much.

Rex forcibly thrust thoughts of Faith and worse, his obsession with her, aside. "However," he repeated. "It does not serve my interests to exact my monies in another way, and you? Your settled future means I secure my money."

"Yes! Yes, it does."

"I'll grant you an extension through the end of the London Season, Bourchier."

The earl cleared his throat nervously. "M–Might you consider *next* Season?"

"The summer. Nothing more."

Bourchier firmed his lips; his eyes proved glacial. "Thank you, Mr. DuMond."

Rex gave a dismissive wave of his hand. "We are done here." He directed that to Latimer who immediately took his cue.

The head of club security drew the door open.

Not even bothering with a bow, Bourchier spun on his heel and stalked across the room.

Rex stayed him before he crossed the threshold. "Bourchier?"

Glaring at Rex, the earl turned back.

"You'd do well to remember," Rex warned, "if you think to come in here ever again and challenge me and disrespect me here or anywhere, I will not be so forgiving in the future, Bourchier. Are we clear?"

That icy threat managed to penetrate Bourchier's earlier confidence. "A-Abundantly, Mr. Du-M-Mond."

Rex looked to his partners again and gave a final nod.

They escorted Bourchier from the office to Hinkley, the waiting guard who stood just outside. After the earl had gone, no one said anything. Rex's partners certainly knew better.

Instead, they headed over to the sideboard and each made himself a drink.

Bloody hell, if ever he'd been one for outward displays of frustration, this was that moment.

After more than a fortnight spent in her company, he'd begun to believe she'd intended to not act a second time, and it had made it easier to walk away from her. This latest article in *The Morning Chronicle* about his patron's proclivities, along with the sorry state of that gentleman's finances, spelled trouble.

Bourchier hadn't been assuaged by Rex's assurances. If the earl and Somerville spoke to other patrons from Forbidden Pleasures, it would leave enough people questioning if their secrets were safe here. And then... it all went away. All of it.

The hell it would.

Argyll was the first to speak. "This isn't good," he said. Carrying his drink over, he claimed one of the two open leather armchairs. The duke tossed back a long swallow and then grimaced.

No, it certainly wasn't.

He'd spent more time with Faith Brookfield than he'd ever spent with another woman. *And you enjoyed every goddamned minute of it, too*, a voice taunted, He thrust back that mocking thought. It'd been purely sexual. Just as he'd told her last evening before he'd lifted her skirts and buried his face between her legs. Ultimately, it was the only emotion that mattered because it was the only emotion that was real.

"You have an idea, don't you?" Malden murmured.

He certainly did. "One of you will marry the lady."

Argyll choked on his swallow and hacking away, struggled to get control of himself.

"I certainly can't marry the lady," Malden protested over the other man's paroxysm.

Rex narrowed his eyes. "And why not?" Not a rogue, and one who conducted himself in a respectable way, the strait-laced man would be a perfect husband for Faith.

"Because she's not suitable," the other man said on a furious whisper. "There was a scandal around her mother's second marriage to Lord Guilford who'd come to blows with some gentleman or another, fighting for the lady's affections. The trio was discovered by an audience. The lady's never borne the marquess an heir, and furthermore, Lady Faith volunteers at a *school*, owned and operated by her *mother* and she cannot…" He gestured weakly to his ear.

Anger whipped through him. "And?" Rex infused a lethal edge and warning into that single syllable.

Malden wrestled with his cravat. "There is the future duke to consider, DuMond."

And in that way, Rex couldn't be more different than the other ducal heir. Where Rex reveled in making decisions that would rankle his sire, Malden still engaged in a futile bid to win his father's affections and approval.

Which meant…

Rex slowly turned his focus on the only other feasible option, the one gentleman who made sense. Faith was a romantic, a romantic who needed to be silenced. Argyll was the charmer among them, the rogue. With younger sisters, the other man knew precisely how to treat ladies. The two would be a perfect pair.

Something uncomfortable settled in his belly, and he shifted in his chair, forcing whatever that sentiment was aside.

There wasn't time for reservations. Not when the wealth and future of Forbidden Pleasures was on the line.

"You," Rex said in dead tones.

"Me?" Argyll stared at Rex in a way that unnerved, and he made himself remain still under that probing stare. "You're suggesting *I* marry the lady?"

Rex narrowed his eyes. "And why can't you marry her?" Because if another one of his partners so much as alluded to Faith's damned ear as though that somehow made her inferior, he was going to bloody the lot of them.

"It is just..." Argyll hesitated and briefly looked to Latimer as if for help.

The stony-faced proprietor shrugged.

Argyll returned his focus to Rex. The other man weighed his words as he spoke. "I expected given the time *you've* spent with the lady, and the interest *you've* shown her that mayhap..." The duke nodded pointedly.

Rex frowned. What in hell was Argyll suggesting? And then Rex froze, as his meaning registered. He was implying Rex cared about Faith Brookfield? He didn't. He felt nothing about anyone. "The interest I've shown her was solely business in nature," he said icily. "It was a ruse to ferret out anything we could use to stop her. That's all it was."

It had been business in nature, but he'd also enjoyed his time with her more than was good or safe. He'd sooner jab a pen through his eye, however, than admit as much.

His obstinate partner looked as though he wished to press the point, but Rex narrowed his eyes again, sharply, warningly. They might be partners and the closest Rex had to friends, but he'd be damned if he put up with Argyll or anyone questioning his strength. Faith would be far better served with a charmer like Argyll. Rex would have ultimately broken her spirit and crushed her soul as his father had done to Rex's mother. And strangely, he found he didn't have the stomach for that level of evil. "It will be you who marries her," he said, the matter already settled.

Not unlike the patron who'd had an audience with them a short while ago, Argyll stammered. "*I'll* marry her?"

Argyll shot a desperate look Latimer's way, but the other man hardly proved help on that score. He lifted his big, bear-sized shoulders in a shrug. "Can't be me."

No, it couldn't. Bastard born and a London street dweller and thief longer than he'd been a prosperous part owner of Forbidden Pleasures, Latimer would never be a match for Lady Faith Brookfield.

But then, in those ways and many ways, Rex had far more in common with the head muscle of his club than with Argyll or any of the other lofty patrons tossing fortunes their way.

The duke switched his focus back to Rex. "Need I remind you that you were the one who allowed her and her friends to be brought to your offices? By Polite Society's standards, you may as well have lifted her skirts that day and tupped her on your damned desk." The other man paused and narrowed his eyes on Rex. "Did you?"

Rex let his silence stand.

He'd made love to her in other ways, but her virginity was intact. His desire for her was...had been...an incongruity, but then the lady herself had been one too.

Young and innocent and yet not simpering and scared. Rather, she possessed a bigger and braver spirit than most of his most powerful male clients.

She'd be one who tore up the sheets and rutted like a cat in heat.

Argyll took a step forward. "Because if you did, you would easily be the one who should marry the lady. You've spent time with her and become friendly."

"Do you truly believe with the complete lack of experience he has with innocent ladies, DuMond is going to marry the chit?" Latimer muttered. "Not that any sane lady would want to tie herself to one with his reputation and proclivities."

Only, do you think Latimer was right, and that Faith wouldn't marry you? A lady who'd been as hot as she'd been last night in his arms would have given him her virtue, name, and anything else he'd sought.

"This is goddamned impossible," Argyle muttered, increasing his pacing.

"I could threaten her real good," Latimer said as casually as if he'd suggested inviting an innocent young lady to tea and biscuits.

The hint of a rough cockney still hung on the other man's

imperfect tones, a forever reminder of just where—and how—the other man had lived before coming into this place.

Argyll looked between them. "That could work."

"It could," Rex agreed. With any and every other lady. "It won't." Not this one.

If Rex had believed a threat might move the needle either way, he'd have entered her chambers weeks ago and laid out a warning in no uncertain terms.

"What the lady needs is to be charmed," Rex said, and as one he and Latimer glanced across the room to a still restlessly pacing Argyll.

The duke drew to a slow stop and looked back and forth between the two men. Bright crimson color splotched the other man's cheeks. "You really are suggesting I marry her?" He choked on the remainder of his words.

But then, such would be the effect for one of London's most notorious rogues and scoundrels.

"*Saying*," Rex said coolly. "I don't suggest things. The lady is a romantic." Rex ticked off on his fingers as he went. "She's young. Impressionable. More importantly, she can be molded, and you are the man to do that."

"I'm not the one who wants to do that," Argyll snapped.

"You need an heir."

"I could give as much as a shite less about my lineage then you do about yours," the other man shot back.

Rex scoffed. "Come, you and I both know that is not true."

"The hell it isn't!" Deeper color flared on the duke's cheeks. He balled and unballed his hands, that visible sign of his upset just one more indication of how dissimilar he and Rex were.

Rex winged a single eyebrow up in a coolly mocking manner meant to infuriate. "Isn't it?"

Argyll snapped his focus over to the window but not before Rex caught the flash of frustrated annoyance.

With two younger sisters reliant upon his protection, Argyll *did* have people he cared about, and therein marked yet another significant difference between he and Rex. The biggest one of all. Rex, on the other hand? There wasn't a single person he gave so much as a damn about. People all served a purpose. His partners, and the closest thing he had to friends, were no exception.

Just as Faith didn't matter to him, either. No matter how much he'd enjoyed—

"What are you even proposing I do exactly?" Argyll asked in terse tones, ones that hinted at a man who'd already capitulated—even if he didn't yet realize he had.

"The lady is smearing the club and spreading our patrons' information. You court her, woo her, and set her up as the head of your household." A memory slipped in of her keening moan and the thumping of the door as she'd rocked against his mouth. His body hardened at the memory of her unrestrained release. Only an insidious thought slid in…of Faith, with her legs parted and Argyll kneeling between them as she panted and moaned."

Argyll stared at him. "You've really thought all of this out."

Rex unclenched the fists he'd not realized he'd tightened. "I have."

Argyll released a long and lengthy black curse. "Very well."

"Take heart, it isn't all bad," Rex said, grabbing the bottle of brandy near the newspaper piles and filled his empty glass. "You'll find yourself someone to watch your sisters, and then she can see to your care. In fact, she is the answer to all your prayers. Her fortunes would be tied to the club. Offer her, as your wife, early donations for her mother's school." He reminded himself of that because that thought should be enough to replace that thought of Faith coming undone in another man's arms. It was. It had to be.

"My prayers?" the duke snapped. "What about yours?"

"Mine?" Rex curled his mouth in a smile that felt cold and hard to his own lips. "I don't have them."

If he did, he'd have spared one for the young woman who was about to find herself charmed and wed to his business partner.

Alas, he didn't. And unfortunately, she was to pay the price, one she'd likely be more than happy to pay for the pleasure of being a duchess and landing herself a husband.

"To your bride," Rex said, and lifting his glass he saluted his poor friend about to land himself a hellion bride.

CHAPTER 15

ꟻAITH HAD SPENT TWO NIGHTS weeping. She'd cried until her body hurt inside and out. And then when she finished sobbing and was sure there wasn't another tear left to shed, she found there appeared to be a limitless amount of those drops, created by grief at Rex's betrayal. Worse, she'd not been free to give into those feelings because she'd told her family she'd been suffering a megrim and wished to remain alone. So, she'd let her misery loose into her pillow, and then in her wardrobe with her door shut and that same pillow used to muffle the sounds of her grief.

On the third day, she woke up from another restless, hard-fought sleep, looked in the beveled mirror at her swollen cheeks and even more swollen eyes, and vowed she was done crying over Rex DuMond. Just as she was done hiding herself away from the world and her responsibilities at Ladies and Gentlemen of Hope. So she'd taken a cool bath and pressed cool compresses over her face and resolved not to hide herself away anymore. Or weep anymore.

Only, later that afternoon, on the outskirts of London, Faith wanted to cry all over again. This time, however, it had nothing to do with Rex DuMond and his deception.

She'd gone and lost her brother...and on this most important day; with their mother seeking a sizeable donation and sponsorship for the expansion of her school.

Her family sought the patronage of their host, Lord Chevening, as well as financial support from the earl's other influential guests. Given, any donations would directly benefit the children at her mother's school, Lord Chevening had decided to make the event a family affair at his grand estate. Paddy proved mischievous every day, but *today*, they needed him to be well-behaved.

"Paddy?" she whispered loudly, marching through their host's notoriously famous high-hedge garden maze.

Her sister reached Faith's side and looked around. Then placing her two middle fingers in her mouth, she let out a piercing whistle.

Faith whipped her gaze around. "Violet," she chided on a furious whisper, yanking Violet's hand back to her side.

"What?" the younger girl asked defensively. "We have to find him, and he always responds to the whistle."

Him as in their younger brother. Adopted by their parents when he'd been a boy begging on the streets, he'd proven a master at making mischief from the moment he'd entered their family. It'd always been endearing. Except today.

"Mama and Papa are meeting with the earl," she reminded her sister.

Violet shrugged. "I know that."

"If you know that, then you understand how important that meeting is and how the last thing that would prove helpful to Mama would be for us to raise a hue and cry because our troublesome brother has gone missing."

Faith resumed her march, calling out quietly once more for her brother as she did.

When she'd yearned for a distraction from thoughts of Rex DuMond, hunting down her misbehaving brother had absolutely not been what she'd had in mind.

Trying to squelch the panic in her breast, Faith strained up on tiptoes and attempted to peer around the enormous hedge.

To no avail.

"Do you wish to talk about it?" her sister asked quietly.

Faith sank back on her heels and held a palm above her brow to shield her eyes from the sun's glare. "There's hardly anything to talk about. We arrived, and were told to watch Paddy while Mama met alone with his lordship and—"

"I meant the fact you've been crying for several days in your rooms," Violet interrupted softly.

Faith stared blankly at her sister.

"Faith, you are my sister." Violet gave her a gentle smile. "You haven't liked being alone in your room *ever*, and you've never suffered megrims." She paused. "I visited your chambers and heard you."

Panic built in her breast. If her sister had heard her…

"No one else did," Violet rushed to assure her. "I stationed myself outside and whenever mother or father or a maid came to visit, I intercepted them."

Tears pricked Faith's lashes, this time for different reasons than the pain of Rex's betrayal. "Thank you."

Her younger sister looped her arm through Faith's, and giving it a light squeeze, she leaned in. "I am your sister. That is what sisters do." Violet's eyes grew more serious, and she moved her gaze over Faith's features. "Are you and Mr. DuMond no more?"

A blush immediately slapped her cheeks. How did her sister know that? "Mr. DuMond and I never were." And how could that very true admission still hurt, even after he'd betrayed her in this terrible way?

Violet snorted. "I might be younger than you, Faith, but I'm not a dolt. I saw you with him at Mama's school, how you lit up, and I read about how he even showed up to his first London ball in longer than the *ton* can remember, all to dance with you."

All to betray her, more like. She bit the inside of her cheek. Even with her sister's devotion, she found herself unable to speak about the fool she'd become where Rex was concerned.

Alas, there'd be no reprieve from her sister's doggedness. "Did he break it off with you that night?" She'd always been tenacious. Since they were small girls and would go off fishing at their father's lake where she'd insist on standing at the shore until she caught a fish…even if it was from sunup to sundown.

"I broke it off with him," Faith made herself say.

Her sister's gaze grew stormy. "There must have been a reason for you to do so."

"I am fine now, Violet. Truly." Faith took in a deep breath and glanced about. "We really do need to find Paddy."

Violet opened her mouth as if she wished to continue challenging her, but then stopped. Faith was so very grateful when moments later her sister called out for their younger brother, this time in a quieter voice than her earlier shouts.

Frustration mounting, Faith stopped once more. "Paddy?" she called on a furious whisper. "This has gone on long enough. Mother and Father need you to be a good boy today." She carefully turned her head, angling the ear she was able to hear from, searching for a hint of sound.

Only more silence met her quiet plea.

"You can always put me on your shoulders," Violet suggested helpfully.

Incredulously, Faith paused in her search and looked at her younger sister. "I do think the days of that are at an end," she muttered, and cupped her hands around her mouth. "Paddy," she called out, with a firmer edge to his name. This had really gone on quite long enough.

"I thought we weren't yelling."

"Desperate times and all that."

Faith opened her mouth to call out loudly.

"Faith?" her sister called her attention over, and Faith looked questioningly at the younger girl. "I just wanted to say you don't have to tell me what happened with Mr. DuMond, but…you've stopped wearing the Heart of a Duke necklace."

Reflexively, Faith touched her deliberately bare neck.

"It's just…" Violet's expression grew earnest. "I'd not have you stop believing in romance and love all because one man proved undeserving of you." And then, much the same way she'd always done when they'd been small girls, she launched herself at Faith and held tight.

Faith's arms came up immediately to encircle her younger sister as she accepted that much-needed hug. "Thank you," she said, when they broke their embrace.

"Don't thank me." Violet shrugged. "I'm your sister."

She ruffled the top of Violet's curls. "Now, let us resume finding our brother."

"Boys," Violet muttered. "They're trouble at any age."

If Rex DuMond wasn't proof of that, Faith didn't know what

was. "Except Papa." She felt inclined to defend the good.

"Except Papa. And Uncle Gabriel and Uncle Alex…" Violet tacked on.

"And let us not forget the Earl of Montfort, or Lord Tennyson and—"

"And it seems like they aren't all so bad, after all," Violet said, giving her a knowing wink.

Faith's lips twitched. "I see what you did there."

"Make you point out that not all men are rotters? Yes, yes, I did." Violet raised her palms about her mouth, and matched Faith's calls. "Paddy?"

"We can just make our way out and fetch help," Violet suggested as they reached another dead end.

"Can we, though?" she muttered. "Can we?"

Violet nodded. "I dropped peppermints marking our way." She held up the reticule dangling from her right wrist and gave it a little shake.

Faith paused and glanced back the path they'd recently crossed. Sure enough, a small circular peppermint rested stark upon the lush green grass. "Rather clever, don't you think?" Violet asked, puffing her shoulders out and patting the back of her curls.

"Quite," she praised. They need just circle back and retrace their footsteps to the point they'd last traveled with their six-year-old scamp of a brother.

And yet as they made their way back, each calling out intermittently for the troublesome boy, the mint trail disappeared.

Her sister came up short. "I…why…I believe he's eaten them!" she exclaimed.

Sure enough, there came an answering little giggle.

Faith whipped her head in the direction of that noisy expression of mirth. "You little scamp," she muttered, and yanking her skirts up around her ankles, she set off in swift pursuit. Violet came close at her heels.

"Paddy," she whispered frantically, and then dropping to her knees, Faith flattened herself onto her stomach and squinted, attempting to look under the greenery. Sure enough, her gaze snagged on a gleaming pair of small boots. Triumph brought her shooting upright. "Got you, you scamp," she muttered, and paused only long enough to grab her sister's hand before she took off racing.

"You do know you'll be meeting with the earl shortly too," Violet reminded as they sprinted along a narrow corridor constructed of greenery. "You arriving in grass stains will be met with even more shock and questions than Paddy."

Yes, well, she'd worry about that, later.

Faith tugged Violet around the next row, her gaze alighting on the small, familiar form. "Got you," she exclaimed. "You are..." Her words trailed off, as her gaze landed on a tall, also familiar figure. One she'd seen whilst at Forbidden Pleasures when Faith and Anwen had been deposited in a parlor and made to wait while Rex spoke to Marcia. That night when another had commanded all Faith's thoughts, this man had proven a paler shadow which, given his halo of loose golden curls, was saying a good deal, indeed. Rex's partner, the Duke of Argyll. Tension snapped through her. Three days ago, she may have believed this meeting to be nothing more than a coincidence. A person grew and changed a lot in three days, however.

"Faith," her brother cried, as he jumped to his feet and quit the side of the man he'd been keeping company with.

She immediately clasped the boy close and glared over the top of his head. "You," she muttered.

The Duke of Argyll straightened. "Lady Faith," he greeted, bending low at the waist in a respectful bow.

Faith felt her sister's stare moving between them. "Do you know one another?" she whispered loudly.

"No."

"Yes," he supplied at the same time.

The lines of confusion creasing Violet's brow deepened.

Faith cleared her throat. "What the duke meant was we've briefly met at a social gathering. One time."

He flashed a wide, knowing smile, but let her lie stand.

Or it would have been a winning one, if she didn't know his connection to that scandalous club or the company he kept...and the fact that she'd discovered him alone with her brother. All over, her fury with Rex boiled to the top. "What do you think you are doing with my—"

Her prepared diatribe was cut short by the sudden appearance of a small girl, near in age to her brother. "Gregory, I've found…" With her equally blonde curls, there could be no doubting the little stranger's identity. "Girls," she cried happily.

Her mouth moving but no words coming out, Faith looked on as the small sprite sprinted over.

"We were taking a turn about the maze," the duke explained, "when we stumbled upon a peppermint trail, and it led us directly to this young fellow."

They all looked to Paddy.

He gave a happy wave of his fingers. "Gregory and Millie found me, and I meant to come back but then we got to talking and Gregory here—"

"Gregory," Violet silently mouthed to Faith.

"Well, he knows card tricks," Paddy exclaimed happily.

Faith finally took note of the detail that had escaped her, the deck of cards set out. She narrowed her eyes on the gaming hell proprietor. "I expect he does."

Violet shoved an elbow into her side, and she grunted.

Paddy, however, remained oblivious to the tension. "Not just card tricks, magic tricks, Faith. Magic!" Not allowing her a word edgewise, her brother turned to the duke. "Show her. You must show her."

"If you insist," His Grace said.

The duke held an empty hand close to Violet's ear, and then closed his palm quick into a tight fist, opening it a moment later to reveal a missing coin.

Violet laughed and clapped excitedly.

"Isn't it splendorous?" Paddy cried.

"Most so."

"You must tell me how you did it, Your Grace," Violet pleaded.

The gentleman swept a deep flourishing bow. "Alas, I fear a magician does not reveal the secrets of his tricks." Neither did a scoundrel like Rex and clearly his partner here.

As the three children of varying ages pleaded with him, Faith watched.

He was tall and by way of looks, perfectly handsome.

He'd golden curls that glimmered in the sunlight, that halo giving him the look of the archangel Michael as rendered in paintings she'd taken in at the Royal Museum some years ago. The gentleman had an honest—enough—smile.

Watching after his sister and playing with her and Paddy, he was dashing and charming.

And she didn't trust him or this chance meeting for a moment.

As if he felt her stare, the duke glanced over. He lingered a heated gaze on her face, and then ever so slowly winked before his attention was reclaimed by his sister.

Faith hadn't known firsthand before this moment the charm he possessed *per se*, only what the papers had written of him. After all, he'd never noticed her, which was simply the way of gentlemen in Polite Society. Those predictable men with their even more predictable wants in a wife—golden-haired, docile. Possessed of the use of both of her ears.

In short, everything Faith was not.

"Isn't he magnificent?" Paddy called, interrupting her musings.

"Indeed," she drawled.

Still too young to detect sarcasm, her brother took Faith by the hand and pulled her closer to that quartet.

The duke dropped a bow. "A pleasure to meet again, Lady Faith."

"I don't want you teaching my brother your card games," she said tightly.

A little voice piped in, taking the teeth out of Faith's intended lecture. "Oh, he wasn't teaching card games," the girl said. "Though he does know those, too, and can teach him."

"By the way, this is Millie," Paddy explained, looking stunningly awe-struck by the girl, not disgusted and annoyed as he was with the young girls who were taught at their mother's school. "She knows card tricks, too."

"Does she?" Faith asked her brother who nodded eagerly in return before turning his besotted gaze back to the girl a year or so older than him.

"But peppermints are ever so much better than card tricks,"

Millie explained. "Do you know what is even better?" She left the ominous query hanging there. "Hiding." And then taking Paddy by the hand, the two children bolted off.

Faith's heart sank. Not again. Violet, swifter to act, hiked up her hems and bolted after the giggling pair, leaving Faith and the duke alone.

She made to hasten after the trio, but Argyll slipped into her path. "It is unexpected, meeting you here, Faith," he murmured, and catching a curl that had come loose he tucked it behind her ear. He paused before turning it loose, pressing it between his thumb and forefinger in a way Rex had done. In a way she now knew was contrived, nothing more than the rulebook of a rogue.

Her heart hurt all over again.

She waited until the duke released that lock. "You must think me addlepated."

He blinked slowly. "Lady Faith?"

"Do you think I'm naïve enough to believe this was a chance encounter, Your Grace?" she asked coolly.

"Hardly," he murmured. "I believe you're entirely too clever to be so duped."

She'd thought the same thing too. Though in fairness, she'd been too innocent to ever consider someone would want to dupe her. "You don't know me at all, Your Grace." He knew her no more than she knew Rex DuMond.

"That's hardly true. We had a chance to meet before," he said in a soft, silken baritone that she expected had charmed any number of women from their virtue and reservations. "And I've found myself unable to think of anyone but you since that day."

She snorted and folded her arms at her chest.

"You find that so hard to believe, dear heart?" he whispered, sliding closer.

Dear heart... Her mind briefly drifted back, to another time and place, another man.

Petite chouette.

Oh God. It would never stop hurting. It couldn't. It was still fresh three days later.

"Petite Chouette it is. I'm going to kiss you, petite chouette, and I think

you are going to both want it and like it."

Her heart raced and triumph flared in the eyes of the arrogant man before her, a man who believed she'd been roused by him and not the memory of another.

"I do find it certainly coincidental, your being here and your sudden bewitchment, Your Grace." With that, she started on once more, heading back the way she and her sister had come.

"But isn't that the nature of being bewitched?" he asked, easily catching up to her.

"Indeed," she said softly, unable to keep the sadness from creeping in. She knew exactly what it was to be so bewitched. She also knew it had been a lie. Now she knew the truth Rex's father had informed her of; Rex had deduced the fact she was sharing secrets of his club with the gossip pages, feared for his business, and thought by befriending and then seducing her, she could be effectively silenced. And it appeared it mattered naught which one of the proprietors saw to the distasteful task.

As she made to turn the corner of the maze, the duke caught her lightly, gently by the arm. "It is a travesty, Faith," he said in husky tones.

Yes, it was. So much of this was. "What?" She winged an eyebrow up. "That I'm completely unmoved by your rather poor showing at seduction, Your Grace?"

A host of emotion flared in his eyes—shock, amusement…and interest. This time real, and unfeigned, and she expected if she'd been most any other lady, her heart would have stirred at that hint of genuine desire.

"Gregory," he murmured. "You should call me Gregory."

The duke brushed a gloveless palm down the curve of her cheek. His caress was deliberate, his touch sure and she allowed that touch. She considered it the same way she had the science experiments she'd so loved as a child. Handsome as he was, the glide of his long, strong fingers should have stirred even the smallest spark inside.

It didn't.

At her lack of resistance, the duke cupped her by the nape. "I fear you've left me with no recourse except to redeem myself, dear heart," he said huskily, and then he kissed her.

He was the second man who'd ever kissed her. And he did so with the skill of a man who'd kissed any number of women before her. His lips were firm and by the glide of them over hers, clearly experienced.

And yet, it did not move her at all. It did not set fire to her inside and leave her aching. And she found herself regretting that, because it meant that Rex's touch had indeed meant more.

Agony cleaved her breast. Faith turned her head, and the duke's kiss landed on her cheek.

"Are you done?" Faith said, her voice perfectly even.

He appeared dazed by her unaffectedness. Good. It would serve these overconfident louts right.

She started to leave, heading after her siblings, and then stopped. "Oh, and Your Grace?"

He looked at her.

"Clean your finger. You still have wax on your hand from that little *magic* trick you performed."

His eyes widened.

"Good day, Your Grace." She turned to go for a second time.

"I can give you anything, Faith," he called.

She didn't even look back. "There is nothing I want or need from you."

"Marry me."

Faith stopped in her tracks and whipped around to face him. These men were really so desperate to silence her. First Rex and the game he'd played, and now this notorious rogue would offer marriage?

"Become my duchess," he said, his voice a husky purr.

The duke glided over with those languid steps all London's scoundrels must be schooled in, the way ladies were in curtsies. He stopped before her. "I will drape you in diamonds. Yearly donations for your mother's school, the size of which you'll never have to go begging other lords for their paltry contributions." He placed his mouth close to the place her neck and shoulder met, and the sough of his faintly brandy-and-chocolate-tinged breath brushed her skin.

"And then," he dropped a kiss upon her right shoulder, "I'll give you what you really want."

"A-And what is that?" she asked, her voice trembling slightly at this harder, more lethal side to the always-charming rogue.

The duke hooded his lashes. "I'll bring you pleasure the likes of which you've never known."

Given the heights she'd soared with Rex, she rather doubted that.

He moved to claim her mouth a second time.

Faith pressed her fingers against his lips, stopping that kiss. "My family does require funds for the school. There are more students than rooms, and each day more and more foundlings are arriving."

Triumph glinted in his hard gaze.

"Except, I'm no whore to be bought."

With that, Faith steeled her features and left the duke on a whir.

If Rex DuMond believed he could send the charming, roguish duke to silence her, then he'd another think coming.

CHAPTER 16

STANDING ON THE CROWDED FLOORS of Forbidden Pleasures, his hands clasped behind his back, Rex assessed the noisy room of mostly drunken patrons as they lost handily at his club.

It was a familiar sight: the thick cloud of cheroot and cigarillo smoke hanging over the hell like a tobacco-scented fog. The teardrop crystals of the chandeliers glimmered brightly from the glow cast by the wax tapers. Foxed lords dangled whores on their laps while tossing away their futures and fortunes on a hand of vingt-et-un and faro.

The tableau of debauchery had always been a satisfying sight. It'd meant Rex's pockets were getting richer as his club thrived.

Oddly, this night there wasn't the usual calm to be found here.

Because everything this day, the future and fate of his club, hinged upon the actions taking place outside Forbidden Pleasures. The revised plan for Faith Brookfield had been set into motion early that morn when Argyll had headed for the Earl of Chevening's estates.

Latimer caught his eye and wound his way over.

"Is he returned?" Rex asked the moment his partner reached his side.

The lead for security shook his head. "Not yet."

Rex tugged out his timepiece.

Nine o'clock.

"I have a man stationed outside with orders to report to you the moment Argyll's carriage arrives," Latimer said.

"A carriage," he growled. Of course, Argyll had needed to take a goddamned carriage because he'd had his sisters, Millie and Meredith, along with him. But couldn't his partner have returned by a bloody horse and left his siblings in the care of a companion? But then, it was the most ducal thing the other man did—he looked after the ladies who were his sisters.

As he and Latimer continued to study the gaming hell floor, Rex's stare landed on a young beauty with dark curls, that hue similar to another woman's. Only her curls were slightly tighter than the loose, natural ones of another woman, who was fresher in face, with owl-wide eyes. The serving girl had abandoned her silver tray of drinks on a nearby table and straddled a flamboyant dandy's lap. While the young man placed sloppy kisses upon her neck, she moved against him, setting those corkscrew tresses bouncing.

Lady Faith Brookfield was young, impressionable, naïve, and romantic. Tentative but bold. Passionate and given to whispery soft sighs, she'd be an easy mark for one of Argyll's prowess.

The night had just started. As was undoubtedly Argyll's seduction of Faith. Even now, she'd be well on her way to being the next Duchess of Argyll.

Rex's belly twisted in a weird way.

Impatience. That's all it was. He wasn't a man who liked waiting or being in the dark, and he'd been doing just that for the whole of the day.

And in his mind, Lucy, the dark-haired woman rubbing herself passionately against the patron, again shifted and took the form of the woman who would not leave his thoughts. And it was not the eager prostitute riding the gent fresh from university, but Faith atop Argyll as the more experienced man guided her hips, urging her on to her release.

A growl climbed his throat.

"You all right?" Latimer gave him an odd look.

"Fine," Rex gritted out. He was beyond fine. Better than it, really. Or he would be, when he'd confirmation that all had gone to plan where Faith was concerned. "Send Argyll to me the moment he arrives," he ordered, and stalked from the floors of his club. Rex made his way above stairs to his offices that overlooked the gaming hell and let himself inside.

He headed straight for his desk, drew the top center drawer out, and fished out a cheroot. He held the tip of the tightly rolled scrap against a sconce candle, and then sitting back heavily in the folds of his deep leather chair, he sucked in a deep, cleansing breath of the smoke, and he welcomed the sensation as it filled his lungs.

Rex slowly released a cloud of white from the corner of his mouth, and he stared through that slight haze cast by the smoke, in his mind seeing another moment not so very long ago.

"...We'd be foolish and naïve to trust you and your men operated with any real benevolence. I think you took us. I believe you calculated—and incorrectly—that our families will not discover what you've done...I've gathered you aren't only a thief of people, but also of your patron's fortunes and respectability..."

Rex shook his head and took another pull from his cheroot.

He'd known from the moment he'd stepped into this very room and found the minx rummaging through his ledgers again that she was going to be trouble for him. He'd never imagined just how much trouble she'd be. Because in his mind, innocent ladies, debutantes new on the market, weren't complicated. Unlike the seasoned women who patronized his clubs and sought a place in his bed, virgins lacked artifice and experience. Where they were concerned, what one saw was precisely what one got. Faith, however, who'd challenged him from the start, and who possessed an uncanny ability of recalling exact details about his patron's proclivities and the specific numbers of the debt they owed, had flipped everything he'd once believed on its ear.

He'd underestimated her, and he wasn't one to make such a mistake.

A growl worked up his chest, and he jammed his fob back into his pocket. Stamping out his half-finished cheroot on a crystal tray, he abandoned the scrap and headed for his sideboard.

Rex absolutely did not care how Argyll's time with Faith had played out today. He grabbed a decanter and poured himself a snifter. That was, aside from the fact that he wanted answers as to whether Argyll had been successful in securing the future of Forbidden Pleasures.

He took a long drink, and as the spirits slid warmly down his throat, he slipped his restless gaze around the room until it landed on the wall clock.

The gathering at Chevening's estate was long past over, with all the guests having surely taken their leave and returned to their homes.

If all had gone to plan—and there was no reason to expect it wouldn't—Argyll's seduction of Faith was at an end. The duke would have whispered sweet words the lady desired that Rex had never and *would* never have been able to give her. She'd likely been halfway to falling in love with him. Now, she was likely more than halfway in the other direction to falling for Argyll.

Good. It was perfect. It was what he'd planned.

A romantic like Faith who'd so freely trusted a rough-around-the-edges scoundrel like him would be powerless against a charmer like Argyll.

Perhaps the reason Argyll hasn't returned was because his seduction had gone so well, he'd gotten Faith to agree to meet him somewhere else. Why, even now, given everything he knew about both Faith and Argyll, the duke likely had her in some alcove with his hand up her skirts. She'd be sodden as she'd been when Rex had tasted of her wet channel, pleading and moaning—this time for Argyll.

A red haze of fury blackened his vision, momentarily blinding him.

Rex's fingers tightened around his glass, and he squeezed it hard—too tight.

The snifter exploded in a spray of glass and amber liquid. A crimson speck bubbled on the fleshy pad of his palm, followed by another and another. He welcomed the sting left by the tiny crystal fragments.

A knock sounded, loud and incessant.

Argyll had returned.

That sick feeling in his gut grew. *Because you want to verify that the other man had succeeded in the plan you put forth.* That's all it was.

Only, if that much was true, why did an animalistic rage threaten to consume Rex; this when he'd always prided himself on being even and unaffected.

Knock-Knock-Knock

This pounding came more frantically.

Reining in his emotion, he tucked his injured hand behind his back and called out, "Enter."

Flynn stepped in. "You've got a visitor."

A visitor?

Not Argyll, then.

Odd, that realization brought with it an unexpected surge of relief.

"I'm not taking visitors," he said curtly. "Not tonight." And certainly not for any damned desperate patron.

"This one was sneaking around back. Henke was on guard outside and found her." The other man grunted. "Not really found her. Walked up bold as brass she did and started knocking away at the back door."

"I don't care if it's goddamned Joan of Arc risen from the ashes," he seethed.

"That's what I said, but the lady said she didn't intend to leave. That she'd want a meeting with you and that you owed her one."

"I owe nobody anything." He issued that icy reminder to the other man.

"Said that, too, but…" Flynn coughed uneasily into a large fist and shrugged.

"But?" Rex barked.

A small figure slid out from behind Flynn's larger, broader frame. "But I wouldn't be deterred."

Every muscle of Rex's person went taut, on alert. And even concealed as she was under the shield of that outrageously large cloak and even larger hood, there could be absolutely no doubting the identity of his mystery visitor.

Of course. Given Flynn's reporting of the meddlesome person found lurking outside his clubs, Rex should have ascertained as much.

God, the chit was brazen and fearless. Or stupid. Perhaps, she was a blend of all three. A respectable young miss with marriage on her mind would sooner be caught dead than risk being discovered at the most wicked gaming hell in London, and yet, here she was…a second time.

He narrowed his eyes. "Get out."

As the guard rushed to close the door, Faith stepped fully inside and then meandered as casually as if she were on a stroll through Hyde Park rather than entering the offices of London's most ruthless businessman.

She tugged off a pair of stark white gloves trimmed with even whiter lace.

"You seem to be in a foul mood," the lady remarked. "What's the matter, Mr. DuMond? Cat's got your tongue?"

Insolent. Let him add insolent to the mix of all things this woman was. "It's an owl," he purred in a silken whisper. "An owl does."

The lady trembled; the slight quaver of her body set the noisy fabric of her muslin rustling.

He smiled coolly. Good. She wasn't as unaffected as she'd let on.

Lady Faith backed up several steps and turned the lock of the door his partner had closed.

He sharpened his gaze on her. "You are the first person to willingly lock yourself in a room with me, *petite chouette*," he said in a steeling whisper he infused with an ominousness edge.

The big-eyed lady didn't so much as bat one of her inky-black, forever-long eyelashes. "Never tell me," she drawled. "Because people fear you?"

Her droll tone contained a level of mockery not a single man had dared use with him. And yet, this woman did.

Rex strolled over, infusing a lethality to his steps that managed to at last freeze her in her frenetic tracks. "That is it exactly, *petite chouette*. They fear me, and you would be wise to, as well." He strolled a path around her, and the lady tipped her chin up a notch, the defiant movement knocking her deep hood back slightly.

Rex caught the edges of that ridiculous fabric and lowered the material.

The lady's dark curls were in disarray, as though immediately following her family's long carriage ride from Kent, she'd forgone sleep and set out to see him. Her cream-white cheeks were tinged with a rose-red color that had suffused every corner of her pixie-like face and freckled nose. Her rosebud mouth trembled slightly, and he shifted his focus on that tempting crimson flesh.

Rex lingered his attention there.

Did she recall the last kiss they'd shared? The one he'd given her while he'd knelt between her legs.

Or perhaps the reason for her flushed cheeks and untidy hair was because she was a woman who'd been well-loved that day.

A different image slithered forward of Argyll guiding Faith to some pretty sofa while he kissed her mouth and pulled breathy moans from her, those desirous sounds that he swallowed.

Rex felt another growl rumbling low in his chest.

She jutted out her chin, mutinously.

"A proper lady would fear being seen here, Faith, and yet you've risked that not once," he touched a finger to her lower lip, and her breath hitched, "but *twice* now."

"I'm good at sneaking."

His lips twitched and his mouth, untrained and untried in a genuine smile, strained with actual mirth.

She bristled. "What? I am."

"This from the same woman who just this Season was abducted and saved by my guards?"

At her mutinous silence, Rex continued needling her. "There's also the matter of me having found you sneaking under my desk twice." And his life hadn't been the same since.

Giving him an arch look, the minx folded her arms at her small chest. "Yes, well, I won't have my sneaking skills called into question because of all that."

Won't. Not can't. As in, she wouldn't allow it.

Rex rested against the sofa. "*This* I have to hear." And oddly, he meant it. He meant it when ordinarily the last thing he ever wanted to hear or cared to hear were the nonsensical ramblings of a virginal miss.

Faith gave a little toss of her head, sending those curls bounding about her shoulders. "*That* time, I was not sneaking. The night you are referring to, I was out with my two friends, headed to the theatre."

"Otherwise, you have extensive experience sneaking about."

She gave him a mysterious look. "I have…some."

This had gone on long enough.

"What do you want, Faith?"

"I think that should be clear, Rex."

"What do you want, Faith?" he repeated, refusing to take the bait she set and follow her down a path to whatever latest verbal sparring she attempted to engage him in.

"Given your aversion for a waltz, I didn't take you as a dancer, Rex, and yet here you are." She spread her arms, gesturing to him. "Dancing all around the reason for my being here."

"Which is?"

"Oh, come." She made a clucking sound with her tongue, putting him in mind of the chicks he used to sneak away and hide with when he'd been a boy evading the duke's wrath. "I happen to be visiting with the Earl of Chevening's estate and in the garden maze stumble across your partner, the Duke of Argyll, who suddenly finds himself with an interest in philanthropy."

The garden maze. It would be a perfect spot for seduction: secluded, away from polite eyes. Away from all eyes.

"And?" he asked, his voice graveled and harsh.

"I trust, given you pride yourself on knowing everything, you also know your partner came to seduce me."

Rex knew precisely what Argyll had been up to. Rex himself had put him up to it, and yet something in hearing Faith speak those words aloud made real all those darkest, insidious thoughts that had been tormenting him this evening. He made himself say something, forcing out another guttural single syllable. "And?"

"And?" Faith repeated. She winged an eyebrow up. "Do you want to know if he was successful?"

He did. And being truthful in this instant with himself, he admitted the need to know had nothing to do with the damned plan to ensure Faith's silence, and everything to do with finding out whether Argyll had kissed that mouth as Rex had. Whether the other man had worshipped the downy curls between her legs with both fingers and tongue.

Faith moved her gaze over his face. She sought an answer from him.

This time, Rex said nothing. This time, he couldn't even manage to get out that same syllable as before, one that would bring answers to questions he suddenly no longer had a stomach for.

Only, Faith proved more in control and stronger than Rex in this moment.

"Do you want to know if Gregory seduced me, Rex?" she asked again, quietly.

That question would have been easier had it emerged taunting like before, and not this solemn query she put to him now.

Gregory.

She referred to Argyll by his Christian name; it bespoke an intimacy. It bespoke an exchange that had occurred where Rex's partner had offered her the use of his given name and she'd accepted.

Rex couldn't speak. He needn't have bothered even trying. She'd words enough for both of them.

"Do you want me to say that unlike you, he tasted of brandy and chocolate?"

A dark curtain of fury fell across Rex's eyes, briefly blinding him, searing him with the image she painted of her with Argyll.

She was unrelenting.

"Or would you have me tell you how he kissed my shoulder, Rex, and promised to show me pleasure the likes of which I've never—"

"Stop!" he roared, and she remained calm in the face of that explosion. Still, where he was ravaged. Unaffected, where he'd descended into a place of madness.

His lungs were filled with fire and rage wrapped around those organs like a vise, making his breath emerge a harsh, raspy exhale. So, this was that emotion of jealousy he'd so mocked, a visceral rage that caused his gut to clench.

He curled his hand so tightly, his fingers bit into the palm, bleeding.

"Did he?" That query ripped from his throat, harsh and furious. "Seduce you?"

CHAPTER 17

ℱAITH'S GAZE REMAINED LOCKED ON Rex's hands, those powerful palms that had once stroked her and caressed her now crimson from blood. She took in the shards of glass scattered throughout the floor that indicated there'd been a struggle of some sort and hated she should wonder and worry about this hateful, hurtful gaming hell owner.

Faith forced her eyes back to his.

Rex stared furiously back as if he were a child who'd been caught with his hand in the biscuit jar and resented the one who'd discovered his secret.

Rex DuMond had made a fool of her. What was worse than that, however, was he'd broken Faith's heart. He'd made her fall in love with him when all along he'd been making her fall for an illusion, the dream of someone she'd yearned for in every way. A man who gave of his time to her mother's school and who made her laugh and treated her as an equal.

He'd made her body sing. Only when she'd been weak-kneed from his most intimate loving, her senses addled, she'd been doused with the truth of what he'd done. By his father, at that.

As such, she should hate him. And she did. Or that was what she'd told herself the whole carriage ride home from the Earl of Chevening's, when she'd been forced to sit in a carriage with her family, acting as if everything was all right. Pretending that she'd not been shattered in the most painful of ways again.

But if she did hate him, she should relish the sight of any pain he might suffer. So why didn't she? Why did the sight of that ravaged, blood-covered hand cause a like pain in her breast?

"You're hurt." Her voice sounded faintly accusatory to her own ears.

"I'm fine," he said gruffly. "I don't give a damned about my hand." He fixed a hard stare on her face. "What I want is an answer about you and Argyll." His gravelly demand bordered on a growl. "Did. He. Seduce. You?"

She should tell him to go to hell with his arrogance. What gave him the right to think he was entitled to any answers from her about what had transpired—or not transpired—with the Duke of Argyll or, for that matter, any man? Only…Faith angled her head. With the fury radiating from his eyes and the harsh set to his features, it almost appeared as if he were jealous.

Which was preposterous. Absolutely ludicrous. A ruthless man did not send another man—his business partner at that—to seduce a woman and then feel any way about it.

Faith drew her hood back into place, and she caught the way his eyes flared as she headed over to the door and unlocked it.

"You're leaving," he taunted. "I never took you for a coward, Faith Brookfield."

Ignoring that mockery from the cocksure man who'd upended her world, she drew the panel open and spoke quietly to the guard stationed there.

She waited.

And while she did, Rex said nothing. He didn't press her for any more answers about the time she'd spent with the duke. But she felt his piercing gaze upon her, searing a spot in her back.

Several minutes later, a young servant came. The small boy, near in age to students at her Ladies and Gentlemen of Hope, handed over a small pitcher of water that Faith took with her left hand, as with her right, she accepted a small bowl with a cloth and tweezers inside.

"Thank you," she said to the child, and Faith closed the door.

Turning back, she headed over to his desk, that same desk she'd twice pillaged and earned herself not a suitor but an enemy in the man before her. She set her things down.

"Sit," she muttered, pointing to one of the chairs positioned at the foot of his desk.

His eyes grew adorably confused. It was the most vulnerable she'd ever seen him, and she'd wager her soul the most vulnerable he'd ever been. "What are you doing?"

"I said, sit," she said impatiently, and surprisingly, he complied with that command.

Faith removed her cloak, tugged free her gloves, and sank to the floor. She took Rex's hand in hers with a far greater gentleness than he deserved. Blood trickled from the injury he'd sustained. Her heart twisted, and she hated herself for caring about his pain. And yet, she did. God help her for being a pathetic, weak fool, she cared about him still. At the very least, she didn't want to see him hurt. *You wouldn't want to see anyone hurt*, a voice in her head reminded her. *It is totally normal to be upset by the sight of him bleeding so.*

"It looks worse than it is," he said gruffly, proving again how in tune he was with even her silent thoughts. "The hands always bleed copiously when cut."

Unnerved, she glanced away and looked back at the mess littering his office floor. "Were you in a fight?"

"I was."

Faith looked at him.

"With a glass."

She puzzled her brow. With a *glass*?

He grunted. "I didn't realize my own strength."

He'd squeezed the snifter, then. That was the source of his injury? Faith waited for him to explain, to say more, but he remained tight-lipped, and she went back to examining the bloody palm.

Tiny shards protruded from his hand. She brushed away the remnants of glass resting on the surface then reached for the tweezers. Working in silence, Faith diligently extracted each fragment.

He winced.

"Good," she muttered, not lifting her head from her task. "It serves you right."

"And just why is—" His breath ended on a sharp hiss as she

applied a none-too-gentle pressure.

"Careful," she warned.

Rex grunted. "You did that on purpose."

"Indeed." Removing the last bit of crystal chips from his hand, she grabbed one of the small, folded towels the servant had brought and applied pressure to the still bleeding wound.

"Well, then?" he said.

"You'll live."

"I'm going to live forever." His lips quirked in a cold, mocking smile. "Only the good die young."

Had she seen that frosty grin before, it would have been all she'd needed to know to run as far and as fast from Rex DuMond as possible.

Yes, and he was as bad as they came, blackhearted to the core. And none of that did anything to ease the loss of what she'd dreamed of with this man.

"That isn't, however, what I was asking, *petite chouette*," he murmured, stroking the curve of her cheek with his uninjured index finger. "I was wondering—"

"How I discovered the fact you've been pretending to care about me?"

He didn't deny it, and a vicious hurt lanced her foolish heart.

"Your father," she said, as she finished bandaging his hand, the fight going out of her.

Rex's body recoiled like he'd taken a bullet to the chest, and like a terrible, menacing beast with a taste for blood, he growled. "The duke sought you out." The dark slashes of his eyebrows came together quick.

Faith shivered. Never, not even the time she'd been under his desk, examining his ledgers, had she seen this lethal look from him. "He did." She paused, and tipping her chin up willfully, she held his gaze. "Immediately after you left. He was listening at the door."

"What did he say?" Any other man, nay, any other person, would have been utterly horrified by that admission. Rex remained immobile, wholly unaffected by a revelation that left Faith cringing still.

"He informed me that your interest in me and my mother's

school was anything but real. That a man such as you couldn't possibly desire me, and that you merely sought to silence me."

What a pathetic fool she was for wanting him to deny the earlier words she'd spoken and hurting all over again when he didn't.

"So, you see, Rex, I was more than a tad suspicious when your business partner all of a sudden finds me irresistible. I'm a daft ninny for falling for your scheme." She glared at him. "But I won't be fooled again."

Of course, his father would be the one to alert Faith about Rex's true intentions.

And yet, the tingling of fury licking away at his insides, a sparkling fuse about to fully combust, came not from the fact that she'd found out, but in the idea of the duke with her.

His Grace even standing in her shadow was a perversion of good and innocence.

Faith flashed a small, mocking smile. It was a cynical smile, the likes of which he'd never before seen her wear, and something in it shattered him, in ways he didn't think he could shatter because he was unbreakable. Only, if he was unbreakable, why did he feel this hollow emptiness at this transformation—a transformation he'd wrought?

Rex had always known precisely what he was. A blackhearted bastard. One couldn't be born to a devil like the Duke of Haincourt and somehow enter the world pure or good in any way. For all the ways in which Rex was ruthless, his father was soulless, crafted in the image of Satan by that dark lord himself.

Her shoulders heaved, and she glared fire at him. "You are a cad."

"Absolutely."

"And a scoundrel."

"That's never been in question."

"And a terrible, horrible man."

He curved his lips into a hard smile. "Not a single soul would disagree with you."

"Of course, they wouldn't," her voice climbed, "because you are—"

"A terrible, horrible man?" he supplied.

If looks could kill, he'd have been smote with that single fiery glance she gave him.

Rex made himself ask again that question she was determined to not answer. "Did Argyll make love to you?"

"That was the goal, was it not?" she rejoined.

Vicious tentacles wrapped about him, burying spikes in different corners of his being and unleashing a hot poison within. It was a seething, burning rage the likes of which he'd never before known.

"He is quite skilled at seduction," she said. Unlike before, when her tone had been cold and made to taunt, now she spoke with a quiet sincerity that made this moment all the worse. "He is a man clearly with much experience kissing a woman."

Argyll now knew Faith's kiss. It was what Rex had all but ordered the other man to do, and more.

In the course of Rex's life and career, he'd wished to see any number of people dead—his father, the brutes who'd dared put their hands in violence on the prostitutes in Forbidden Pleasures. It was, however, the first he'd wanted to see Argyll, dead.

He felt Faith's stare on him, and the inquisitive little glimmer there penetrated that momentary lapse into insanity. For what in hell madness was this that he should focus on Argyll's seduction of her and not the outcome of the meeting, and more, the ramifications it now had for Rex and his club? He'd had enough.

He got to the heart of it. "You are bandying around information about my patrons, Faith."

Her expression briefly fell, as if she'd sought different words than the statement he'd made.

When she remained stubbornly silent, he steepled his fingers and studied her from over the top of them. "You won't deny it."

Faith scoffed. "What would be the point of that? You aren't a stupid man. However, I now know, you *are* mercenary enough to deduce what I've done."

He inclined his head. "I'm honored."

"That wasn't a compliment," she mumbled.

If he were a man given to smiling, Rex would have managed one of those expressions in this instant.

Faith continued. "The only reason you've been coming to my mother's school and," her cheeks went red, "feigning an interest in me is because of what I learned. Your father spelled it all out for me."

His pursuit of Faith had been prompted by a singular intent, but the interest she now spoke of—his desire for her—had only ever been real. It was an admission he'd not breathe aloud because it was a mark of his weakness for her.

The time for games with her were at an end. "I want your silence, Faith."

She lifted an eyebrow. "Or what?"

My God, not a single man with a fortune and power handed him by the king himself had ever been so brave before Rex.

"I want the papers you've made on my business, Faith." That day she'd first left Forbidden Pleasures, he'd known she'd not carried anything on her person, but he did however, suspect that when she'd left, she'd written down enough information to do irreparable harm and damage to his club. "And I want them destroyed."

She chewed at her lower lip. "I'm afraid I can't do that."

God, she was obstinate. He narrowed his eyes. "And why is that?"

"Because I'd have to give you myself. I don't have notes."

He stared at her.

Faith touched a finger to her temple. "It's all in here."

"You expect me to believe you recalled verbatim the details of Somerville's and Bourchier's habits and debt?"

"Not just them. Several pages of—" The lady abruptly stopped speaking, going close-lipped, she peered intently at the window over his shoulder where his patrons were on full display.

He thinned his eyes.

"I…have a head for recalling information," she muttered.

God, the chit with her ability to ramble off too much was an innocent, that innocence proving helpful to him and damning to her.

"Do you?" he murmured, and she finally went close-lipped. But not before the damage was done.

For it meant she was in possession of even more information than he'd originally suspected or feared. Another time he would have been impressed with that mental acuity, one that could serve all number of purposes for his club. Christ, this was bad.

He made a tsking sound and walked a slow circle around her. Through it, the lady remained locked to her spot on the floor and kept her unswerving gaze straight and center. "What am I going to do with you, Faith?"

"Nothing?"

On the contrary. *On the contrary.*

Unlike many of his patrons who had an affinity for debauching innocents, Rex had never been one who dabbled with virginal misses. And yet, with this woman, with this spitfire scowling up at him, he truly understood the appeal in that pastime.

Rex looped an arm around the lady's waist, and she emitted a small breathless squeak. "Wh–what are you doing?" Her voice trembled…with desire. This time, there was no question about the emotion that had set both her words and body a'quiver.

He placed his lips alongside the shell of her left ear. "Afraid, *petite chouette?*" he whispered.

She edged back and met his gaze. "No."

He believed she meant that.

And it proved she was a damned fool. Because if she'd a lick of sense she would have known to steer clear of his club, and not involve herself with his patrons and certainly not with him.

Rex drew her close, giving her leave to pull away. Only she melted against him as she always did when he held her close, and there was a thrill of triumph.

He covered her mouth with his, consuming her lips, in his mind seeking to banish thoughts of Argyll worshipping this flesh as Rex now did.

Clutching at the folds of his jacket, Faith whimpered and pressed herself closer.

And there came a thrill of triumph. She wanted him still. No matter what had come to pass between her and Argyll, it was still Rex's embrace she hungered for. The thought enflamed him, and not breaking their kiss, Rex filled his hands with her buttocks, drawing her nearer so that she could feel the hard length of him.

Had he ever wanted a woman as he yearned for the one before

him? He'd told himself that having tasted of her as he'd done in Lord and Lady Waverly's library would be enough to satiate him. But it had been a bloody lie he'd fed himself. The scent and taste of her lived on in his mind and had only deepened a hungering to know her in every way.

Faith kissed with a greater confidence than she had at their first meeting, her tongue meeting his in a bold parry. She managed to steal his thoughts and fill them instead with only thoughts of possessing her in the most primitive of ways. He who was always a master of control at everything, including his passion. This unfamiliar hungering shook him, leaving him at sea in ways that he'd never been, unnerving the hell out of him.

He wanted—

Faith turned her head, and his questing mouth landed smack on her cheek.

His breath came hard and fast as he sought to make sense of that abrupt cessation.

As if the earth hadn't been completely knocked off its axis, Faith stepped out of Rex's arms.

"He did not seduce me," she said quietly, and through the haze of passion clogging his head, it was a moment before he registered those words.

He froze.

"He didn't," he repeated carefully.

Faith shook her head.

Rex's heart thumped in an odd way. Relief. He recognized the sentiment from years earlier when he'd evaded beatings at his father's hands. Never in any of those instances had he felt this manner of relief. It washed over him. Filled him up. And left him dizzy in a different way.

"I confess to being incredibly disappointed in you. If there was something you wished to discuss with me, I took you as one who'd confront me directly himself. Not as a coward who'd send his inept friend." She gave her chin another one of those wayward tilts. "A word of warning, Mr. DuMond? In the future, if you're intent on seeing me seduced to get something you want, then do it yourself instead of sending others."

With that bold challenge, Faith scraped a derisive glance up and down his person, donned her cloak, drew the hood into place, gathered up her gloves, and swept from the room.

He stared at the door long after she'd gone.

His father had told Faith that Rex wasn't one who could ever desire a woman such as her, but just as he'd been wrong in every way in his miserable ducal life, his father also proved completely off in this regard, too. With her spirit, courage, and innocence, she was a veritable Peitho—goddess of seduction, and she'd enflamed Rex from the start.

A short while later, there came a rush of heavy footfalls and a hard knock on his office door.

Rex headed behind his desk, taking care to keep his injured, wrapped hand out of sight. "Enter," he called.

A dusty, wrinkled Argyll stormed inside with Malden and Latimer following at a more measured pace.

Rex consulted the ticking clock across the room. "You've been gone all day," he said without preamble. The other man had been beat back to London by a young lady.

"Yes, well, my time was not my own there," Argyll muttered, the moment Latimer closed the door. Not breaking stride, his ducal partner headed directly for the well-stocked sideboard and poured himself a glass of whiskey and then another. "Following an early dinner, the earl was engaged in a discussion with my sister on botany, and even after the other guests took their leave, my sister had us stuck there." With a tumbler in each hand, he turned back to Rex. "You're going to want a drink for—" He stopped abruptly and blinked slowly at the mess of glass on the floor. "What happened here?"

Rex felt color climb his neck. "Get on with it," he said with a flick of his uninjured hand. The last thing he'd ever speak to anyone about was his own weakness.

"She was…suspicious." Argyll tossed back one tumbler, and grimacing, he downed the other.

"Oh?" Rex said, leaning back in his chair.

"The lady…was…skeptical." High color filled the other man's cheeks.

Latimer eyed the other man incredulously. "She's just eighteen years old, on her first Season, and who likely hasn't left the comforts of her family's country home or London, and you are telling us she is skeptical of *you*?"

The other man nodded, his face flooded with another rush of color. "She was," he said defensively.

Folding his arms, Latimer leaned against the door panel and snorted.

Setting his tumblers down, Argyll flashed an annoyed glance at the head guard. "I'll have you know, she's not really as innocent as you'd both make her out to be. She's quite ruthless and devious and cynical."

Latimer proved unrelenting in his ribbing. "A lady who'd never so much as kissed a man is devious and cynical?" With that, he erupted into another guffaw of amusement.

The duke shot him a dark glare. "What?" Argyll snapped. "She is," he repeated for good measure. "You don't know her. She's not like normal debutantes. Tell him," he issued that directive to Malden.

"She isn't." Malden's mouth tensed. "I said as much before this latest problem with the lady."

Rex felt a ghost of a grin fight for a place on his lips. No, indeed she was not. For the title of duchess and the pleasure of being seduced by the skilled gentleman, any other young woman would have fallen hard and fast and freely into Argyll's arms.

"Did you try to seduce her?" Latimer's question for Argyll instantly killed Rex's silent humor.

The duke's color deepened. "Of course, I did. Used tender words, stroked her cheek, kissed her good."

Kissed her good…

"Not good enough, apparently," Latimer ribbed.

And as both men sparred about Argyll's prowess—or lack thereof—despite himself, despite knowing the outcome of that attempted seduction, the duke had painted a real picture of what had transpired between Argyll and Faith. With words, he'd given more life to an image of Faith in Argyll's arms while he devoured her mouth, and that slithering serpent of jealousy twisted and turned insidiously within Rex.

He bunched his hands into fists, welcoming the sting of pain that came from his injured palm.

Faith had kissed a man and done far more than that—with Rex. Even now, lust bolted through him as he recalled Faith as she'd been, with her skirts rucked about her waist while he knelt between her legs and drank of her nectar.

"DuMond? DuMond?" Argyll's insistent voice cut through those lustful musings. "Are you listening to me?"

Rex gave his head a slight, clearing shake. What the hell was it about this imp that so consumed his every thought? "And...?"

With his spare hand, Argyll tugged at his already rumpled cravat and muttered something under his breath.

Rex angled his head, shifting an ear in the other man's direction. "What was that?"

"I said the lady laughed in my face," the duke exploded.

While Latimer exploded in another fit of amusement, Rex stared at his partner, as another wave of relief riddled his chest.

It is only because you are possessive of all that is yours: your club, your fortune, your power. This singular focus of Faith Brookfield was no different.

"It was hardly the ideal situation for a seduction," Argyll said defensively. "We were in a hedge maze."

"Tucked away in a labyrinth of greenery seems like the optimal place for seduction," Malden remarked.

"Yes, well...we weren't alone," the other man mumbled. "I'd it on authority that her younger siblings would be there and thought it wise to bring my youngest sister into the maze so that she might engage the lady's siblings while I engaged with Lady Faith. I also trusted she'd be charmed by witnessing me with the younger ones."

"But she wasn't," Rex said quietly.

"She wasn't," the other man confirmed.

"Bringing children to a seduction," Latimer said. This time, the other man kept his expression deadpan. "Whatever could go wrong there?"

Because Faith had witnessed him with the children at her

mother's school and had since gathered his reasons for being there had been disingenuous. It had made her suspicious of Argyll who'd shown up with one of his sisters. That evidence of a new cynicism in Faith Brookfield left him feeling...*something*. Something that felt very much like regret.

Rex released a curse. This here was exactly why a person didn't let anyone close, and yet for better or for worse, he had. Only...

He stilled. Why could he not have everything he wanted and needed? He desired Faith more than he'd desired any woman, and she also happened to be a lady in possession of his club's secrets. On top of all that, his father despised her.

She would make him the perfect wife.

"What happens now?" Malden asked with his usual somberness.

"Now?" Rex grinned coolly. "Now, I settle it."

CHAPTER 18

ℱAITH HATED THE THEATRE.

It wasn't that she didn't enjoy the productions or operas. She very much did.

She enjoyed the swell of the orchestra and the dramatic gesturing and expressions of the performers upon the Theatre Royal stage.

She enjoyed it despite the fact that the only reason most people attended the theatre was so they might lift their glasses and peer around the room in search of gossip and that buzz of chatter invariably made it nigh impossible for Faith to hear the actions unfolding below.

This night, however, proved the exception. With her dramatic rendering of *La Vestale*, Guiditta Pasta had accomplished what Faith had previously believed to be an impossible feat—the great soprano had rendered an entire Covent Garden crowd silent.

As such, Faith should be happily and completely lost in the haunting performance, and yet, this night, Faith also proved to be the one patron not wholly and thoroughly immersed in the performance.

As Senorina Pasta launched into the haunting aria Tu Che Invoco, Faith absently scanned the packed theatre house.

Tu che invoco con orrore,
dea tremenda, alfin m'ascolta:
questo misero mio core
fa che possa respirar.
Thou whom I call upon in terror,

fearful goddess, now hear me at last.
Grant that my abject heart
may breathe again.

Nay, her distractedness this night had nothing to do with frustration over underappreciative peers who made it nigh impossible to adequately hear the performers, and everything to with…him.

Rex.

Or che vedi il mio tormento,
le mie smanie, i miei contrasti,
deh! Ti basti. In me l'ardore
puoi tu sola dissipar.
Now that thou see'st my anguish,
my madness, my torment,
ah, let all that suffice. Only thou
can'st lessen my ardor.

And his betrayal hurt so much more…here.

Unbidden, her gaze went to the other occupants of the opera box. Anwen sat, nearly perched on the edge of her velvet-upholstered chair. As wide-eyed as all the other patrons, she stared on riveted at the performance. The couple on the other side of Anwen, Lord and Lady Waters, however, remained as oblivious as Faith herself.

Only her friend Marcia's absorption was with that of her new husband, the Viscount Waters.

The enrapt pair, who sat with their fingers twined and tangled, only had eyes for one another.

Su questo sacro altare,
che oltraggia il mio dolor, fremendo io porto
la sacrilega mano. L'odioso
aspetto mio pallida rende tal
fiamma immortal:
To this sacred altar,
outraged by my sorrow, trembling I bring
my blasphemous hand. My hated face
makes the immortal flame
grow faint:

The dashing viscount ran the pad of his thumb along the seam of his wife's wrist, and Faith knew he caressed that spot where the other woman's pulse pounded because Faith's body had responded in a like way because of another man.

And feeling like the worst sort of voyeur on that most intimate of moments between husband and wife, Faith proved petty and small. She should only be happy for Marcia's happiness, but sitting beside that happy couple, seeing the not-so-secret longing glances they stole in one another's direction, Faith found she desperately wanted that for herself.

She always had. Even after knowing the sting of Rex's betrayal.

Absently, she touched the heart pendant she'd donned once more.

Ever since her mother had regaled her and Violet with the legend of the necklace that had passed among ladies throughout London, bringing all its wearers the hearts of their true loves, Faith had yearned for the day she herself wore it and found that grand love for herself.

The thing of it was? She had. She'd gone and fallen completely head over heels in every way for Rex DuMonnd. Only to discover, his seeming desire for her, the interest he'd shown, had all been a ruse. A game of pretend in the cruelest of deceptions. She'd gone and fallen in love with nothing more than a romantic illusion; and yet, her heart didn't care about those important details. She knew she'd enjoyed every moment spent with him. And she knew that never, as long as she lived, no matter which man she'd one day marry, would she ever forget the taste of his kiss and the passion she'd discovered in his arms.

E qual delirio, ohimè!
miei sensi invade?
Invincibil potere
a' danni miei cospira;
mi stringe, mi trasporta…
What madness, alas,
invades my senses?
An invincible power
conspires against me —
Presses upon me, carries me away —

She felt a stare and glanced over.

Marcia had shifted her focus from her husband to Faith. "Are you all right?" she mouthed silently, but slowly and clearly.

Faith managed a smile. "I am." How singularly odd that her dearest friend in the whole world should know absolutely nothing about the fact that she'd both fallen in love and had her heart broken.

"You're sure?" Marcia pressed.

Faith nodded. "I'm enjoying the show," she whispered, reassuring her friend. To lend truth to the lie, she raised her opera glasses and directed them across the theatre—and froze.

Ma Licinio è colà...

But Licinius is there

Her heart hammered as her gaze remained locked on the gentleman seated directly across the room with his glasses lifted in a like-way as hers—staring at her.

posso mirarlo...favellargli, ascoltarlo,

e il timor mi trattiene?...

I can look at him ... speak to him, listen to him,

and fear holds me back? ...

She dropped her hands to her lap.

Both Marcia and Anwen looked over with concern-filled gazes.

"Fine," she assured them, even as they hadn't asked a question, because she saw it there in their like expressions.

This time she more measuredly lifted her glasses and made a show of staring at the great soprano on the stage below. Stealing a peak from the corner of her eye, she made sure her friends had returned their focus elsewhere before moving her opera glasses once more...sliding them slightly to the right.

As bold as the London Season was interminable, Rex remained with his opera glasses fixed on her.

Why is he here?

And then, even across the length of the way, she caught the crooked grin on his lips, that devil may care turn that did wild things to her pulse's beat.

e il timor mi trattiene?...

yet fear holds me back?

She chewed at the inside of her lip. Everything about him and them was false. She knew that now. So, what was this latest game he played?

No, non più; del mio delitto
furore, amor, la pena han già prescritto.
No, no more. Love and madness
have already prescribed my punishment.

She intended to find out.

As the mezzo-soprano's husky song concluded, the crowd erupted into applause, and taking advantage of that distraction, Faith set her glasses down and stood.

Marcia looked over questioningly.

"I am going to speak to my mother a moment," she said loudly enough to make herself heard over the din.

Marcia and Andrew made to rise, but she waved them back. "They are only a box away. I'm quite capable."

And before they could object, she stood and took her leave; the thick velvet curtains snapped closed in her wake.

The moment her slippers hit the candlelit-lined corridor, Faith took flight. Between Anwen and Marcia, she could not be certain they wouldn't have noted something was amiss and followed her anyway. Stealing a glance over her shoulder, Faith quickened her stride.

A powerful arm snaked out, catching her by the waist.

Faith gasped as she was drawn into a darkened alcove.

Drawing her fist back, she struck her captor on the cheek, her knuckles smarting as they collided with flesh.

Only, her efforts were met with nothing more than a chuckle.

A familiar chuckle.

Her body tensed and she registered the scent of citrus and cheroot smoke.

Rex placed his lips close to her ear and frustratingly delicious shivers radiated in that spot his breath caressed her skin.

"You," she muttered.

"Looking for someone, *petite chouette?*" There was a smile in his smug voice and in his question, and she hated that her heart should flutter.

The arrogant lout knew she'd been seeking him out. "Why, as a matter of fact, I was looking for someone," she remarked with as much casualness as she could muster. "I noted the Duke of Argyll is in attendance and had thought we might renew our acquaintance."

Rex's grin instantly died. "Meeting Argyll in his box would be quite the scandal, indeed. A surefire way to find yourself the duchess." He traced the pad of his thumb along her lower lip. "Though it would leave one to wonder. If that was your ultimate goal, why didn't you just succumb to his seduction at Lord Chevening's?"

A seduction this man had planned because he was so heartless as to be unmoved by the idea of his partner bedding her and wedding her. Her chest tightened in an agonizing way.

Damn him for being astute and indifferent.

Faith tipped her chin up a fraction. "Perhaps that *was* the case," she acknowledged. "But perhaps since our meeting in the maze, I've had time to remember his kiss and longed to know more."

Rage flared in Rex's eyes. A less than human growl rumbled in his chest, and Faith felt it resonate through her person.

Why, he wasn't as unaffected as he'd have her believe.

Sliding a hand to her hip, he dug his fingers deep into the folds of her dress, and Faith sank her teeth into her lower lip as she felt the press of his fingers. His was a possessive grip and Faith's breath quickened.

She trembled with a dangerous longing for him and the magic she knew his hands were capable of.

Another one of those scoundrel's smiles curved the right corner of his mouth in the laziest of grins. "You don't want Argyll," he whispered, with an arrogant knowing that could only come from a man so very competent in his skills and in her body's response to him. "Do you know what I think, *petite chouette*?"

Incapable of words, Faith shook her head.

"I believe you want me."

God forgive her weakness, she did. And tipping her face up, she lifted her mouth to receive his kiss.

A kiss that didn't come.

Rex chuckled and her eyes flew open.

Frustration—with him, with herself, and with the feelings she could not help herself from experiencing where he was concerned—all boiled to the surface. "Would you—"

He touched his lips to her neck, that most sensitive place where her neck met her shoulder, and Faith's lashes fluttered close. The feel of his breath, the scratch of his slightly roughened cheek, and there was an immediate rush of desire that stole all reason.

"Would I…what, *petite chouette*?" He lowered one of her puffed sleeves, exposing her skin to the cooler air in a heady juxtaposition to the warm sough of his breath upon her. "Kiss you here?"

And then he did.

He touched his lips to her shoulder, and Faith's breath shuddered noisily.

Rex followed a path along her collarbone, and then lower, caressing each swath of skin with tender kisses that left her dizzy.

"Or," he whispered, as he continued that questing journey with his mouth, "would you like for me to kiss you…" He stopped, hovering his mouth just above the neckline of her gown. "Here."

Faith's breath caught and she braced, waiting for him to lower that fabric, wanting him to. Needing him to.

"Ah-ah, *petite chouette*," he murmured, stroking a finger along the lace trim. "You must say the words."

"I want you to kiss me there," she whispered, her voice throaty and thick to her own ears.

Rex proved unrelenting. "Where?" he urged. "Say the words?" To entice her along, he flicked his tongue along the top swells of her breasts aching for his attention.

Her breath's cadence increased, and she made herself look him in the eyes. "My breasts," she said, her voice an unwavering command. "I want you to kiss my breasts." And before she closed her eyes, she caught the purely male triumphant grin on his hard lips.

Lowering her bodice, he did as she asked.

He filled his hands with her breasts, palming the flesh, bringing the mounds together. Then, lowering his mouth, he drew one of those tips deep into his mouth.

A hiss exploded from between her teeth as a bolt of delicious longing shot between her legs. And as he suckled and worshipped at first one nipple and then the next, her hands came up reflexively and she curled her fingers in his hair, holding him close, anchoring him in place as he suckled.

The life drained from Faith's limps and her entire body slumped.

Rex caught her, guiding her back against the wall, and she took the support there, happily pinned by his powerful frame.

His mouth found hers, devouring her. Gripping the front of his jacket, she met each angry slash of his lips, tangling her tongue with his in a passionate dance.

He was wrong for her in every way. He'd hurt her. Yet, her body didn't care about those betrayals. In this instant, all she cared about was him and this moment.

Every sensation was heightened by him. Everything was sharper, more acute, because of him. Light and noise all filled her senses and—

Gasps.

And curses.

Faith stilled.

Wait…

Rex hastily drew the neckline of her gown back into place.

She angled her head and froze. Her heart stilled. Her stomach somehow sank, clenched, and churned all at the same time.

"You bloody bastard," someone hissed.

Marcia's husband, Andrew, Lord Waters.

The viscount had Rex by the sleeve and had a fist in his face in a moment.

Rex kept his feet, the blow nothing more than a midge fly.

Only there was another man there—her father. His gaze was locked not on Rex, but rather Faith. Faith and her disheveled gown. Mortification snaking through her, Faith hurried to set her dress to rights.

With fury the likes of which she'd never even known him capable of burning from his eyes and the promise of death in that hard, lethal stare, her father turned his attention back on a coolly silent Rex.

Without a word, the marquess let his fist fly. Flesh connected with flesh in a sickening strike that again didn't so much as cause

Rex to sway.

"Please stop, Papa!" she begged; for even as Rex remained standing, that blow her father landed could only bring pain.

Her father ignored her pleas and on a second fist to the face, at last he brought Rex to his knees. Even so, only a small grunt escaped him.

Faith cried out.

Gasps went up, those quick, noisy inhalations all capturing varying degrees of shock, horror, glee…and pain. Gasps from the audience that had left one show for Faith's more private, humiliating one.

Numb, Faith looked over Rex's sprawled form to where her mother, Marcia, Anwen, and some several dozen others bore witness to her ruin.

CHAPTER 19

THIS MEETING HAD BEEN EXPECTED. The timing of it, however, proved swifter than Rex had anticipated.

"Should I show him in?" Latimer asked. "He's in quite a fierce temper."

Yes, such would be the response of a man and father who'd witnessed his daughter half-undressed in Rex's arms.

He inclined his head. "Show him in."

Latimer hesitated, then quitting Rex's offices, he returned a moment later.

His partner looked to Rex, and he gave a nod.

The two guards flanking the Marquess of Guilford's sides immediately let the older man enter.

Seated behind his desk, Rex didn't even bother to feign politeness. With a flick of his hand, he urged the guards off, to allow Rex's guest the audience he sought.

Marquess sized up marquess.

Lord Guilford stalked over, availed himself to the chair across from Rex, and stared at him with a somber gaze.

Rex'd hand it to Guilford; the man had greater gumption than any other fellow who'd set foot inside his office.

They locked in a silent battle, one that Faith's father broke.

"Do you know which book was Faith's favorite as a girl?"

He didn't. But knowing her, Rex suspected it would be some grand fairytale, a story of love and happily-ever-afters.

At his silence, Guilford went on. "Of course, you don't," he said quietly. "Because you don't really know my daughter. You don't really care about her."

Faith's father was flat out right. Rex didn't care about anyone. Yet even as he silently acknowledged that, he thought about the time he'd spent with Faith. When they'd lay face to face on the ground in the midst of a game of hiding seek. Her smile. Her laugh. *All of which you effectively killed,* a jeering voice taunted. His gut clenched, and Rex made himself breathe slowly and evenly to sort out suddenly disordered thoughts.

He looked away from an impressively stoic Lord Guilford. For the first time in his entire existence as a grown man, he felt completely unmatched. It was a foreign feeling. And he quite abhorred it.

Alas, Faith's father pressed his advantage. "Let me enlighten you, Mr. DuMond. Her favorite story was *The Little Glass Slipper.* Are you familiar with it?"

Impatience built in his chest. "I trust you're not here to discuss—"

"It is a fairytale about a little girl who'd been so very cherished and loved by her father. In the tale, Cinderella's father is dead, and she finds herself left at the mercy of cruel people until a prince comes along and rescues her."

It was as Rex had suspected, then. Faith's favorite had been a fairytale. And damned if he, the most blackhearted bastard in London, didn't find himself fighting a wistful smile.

Guilford caught the underside of his chair and dragged it closer to Rex's desk. "But you see, DuMond," he said, leaning forward, "unlike the cinder girl, without a father to protect her, I am very much here, and unlike the father who bore that storybook girl, I will take care of my daughter and see she's happy for the rest of time."

Rex contemplated the other man.

Rex himself had been born to a hateful duke who'd made everyone's life a living hell. During the misery of his childhood, Rex had yearned for a good father, a devoted, loving one who'd teach him to fish and ride and wipe his tears.

Between both the boys he'd known in his time at school and the eventual patrons of his club, he'd had confirmation that there was no such thing as a loving father. All peers were rotted fathers who cared not at all for their offspring, children whose only purpose they saw as an extension of their power, influence, and lineage. The idea of doting, loving fathers was no more a myth than the tales of the great, all-powerful Zeus, and the even greater myth of a God above.

And yet here sat Faith's father, a man who spoke of her happiness, and not only wanting his daughter around, wanting her around for all time. Unnerved by that discovery, Rex made a show of climbing to his feet, crossing the room, and making himself a drink.

All the while, he felt Lord Guilford following his movements.

After he'd taken a sip, Rex returned to his seat and cradled his drink. He didn't want to hear any more stories about Faith when she'd been a young, trusting girl, or witness any further evidence of this closeness she had with her family. Determined to move this exchange along, once and for all, Rex got to the heart of it. "I'm going to marry Faith."

The marquess smiled frostily. "The hell you will."

"Her reputation is ruined," Rex said matter-of-factly, sipping casually from his snifter as he spoke. "There is no gentleman who will marry her."

And because he'd always been a bastard of the worst kind, that realization left Rex oddly relieved.

Faith's father peered at Rex in an unswerving search. "How easily you speak about her ruin," Guilford said gravelly. "As if hurting her and her *being* hurt mean absolutely nothing to you."

It didn't. Rex told himself as much. He opened his mouth to confirm that assumption for the marquess. Only the words, for some reason did not come.

Guilford rested his palms on his knees and leaned forward. "If you were to wed my daughter, which you *won't*, but if you were, where exactly is she going to live?"

"Not with you, if that is what you're suggesting." Rex smiled coldly. "Faith will live with me." And she'd belong to him in every way.

The other man's face grew taut with a palpable fury, and then he drew in a slow, audible breath. "Do you truly believe London's wickedest gaming hell, where desperate men, scoundrels with black hearts and even blacker reputations, is a place where Faith will be safe? A place where a child would be safe."

A child. Rex went completely motionless. Lord Guilford's query conjured an image of a tiny babe cradled in Faith's arms with Rex watching over that pair. For that was the manner of mother Faith would be, a devoted one. A loving one.

He felt the marquess's stare and blinked several times to clear away those imaginings that had briefly clouded logic and sanity.

Lord Guilford must have seen something, however, for he spoke with a greater earnestness. "A man such as you possesses powerful enemies. Those enemies will find in Faith an all too easy target to get to you, and in the end," the emotional lord thumped a fist against his chest, "my daughter is the one who will pay the price. Not you. *Her*."

He'd gone too far. Rex leveled a glare on him. "I keep my people safe. My wife will be no exception."

"The manner of business you operate, and the people whose fates and future you control, will ensure that is a promise you have no place making.

Rex took another sip of his brandy.

Frustration tightened the other man's mouth. He made another attempt. "You're right. There is no man who will marry her. Not right now," Guilford conceded, and he spoke in solemn, somber tones. "But someday there will be a man—a good, loyal, honorable man who still won't be deserving of her because no one is. That gentleman will love her and care for her and dedicate his every day to simply making her smile. And you, Mr. DuMond, are not that man. You never were. You never will be." With that impressive takedown, Lord Guilford stood. "Name your second."

Rex stiffened. He should have suspected that would be the outcome of this. And yet he'd not. The thought of facing Faith's father across a dueling field left him oddly sick inside. *It's only because he stands in the way of my marrying her and silencing her. That is all it is.*

There came a commotion outside, and he and Lord Guilford tensed.

Jumping to his feet, Rex yanked a pistol from his drawer and was around the desk just as the door opened, revealing two of his guards flanking either side of a small, cloaked figure. It was a moment reminiscent to one not so very long ago when she'd arrived at his clubs for the first time. Since then, she had upended him and his life in every way.

"She insisted on seeing you, Mr. DuMond," Tavish said. "Said she wouldn't be turned away."

Of course, she wouldn't be turned away. Rex knew that cloak. Just as he knew the spirited woman concealed by that garment.

Just as Faith's father knew it too.

Rex nodded. "Leave us," he directed.

After she'd entered, the guard drew the door shut behind them.

Lord Guilford stormed to his feet so quickly, the legs of his chair screeched along the floor as he upended that seat and raced to her side. "What are you doing here?" the marquess implored. Desperation brought the other man's voice up an octave.

"You were discussing my future, Papa," she said softly, her voice steady. "How could I not be?"

Faith pushed her hood back. At some point her chignon had come loose, leaving her glorious black curls in a riotous tangle about her shoulders.

The sight of her—that pugnacious, slightly-too-square chin and freckle-kissed nose—stole the breath from Rex's lungs. It was a foreign way to find himself—completely, entirely, and hopelessly enthralled by a woman—and yet Faith Brookfield had captivated him.

"Shall we sit?" she asked quietly, in that lilting, almost musical voice.

And Rex, unsteadied by her presence here, found himself grateful she'd taken command of this moment. When his hands had never been unsteady, now they shook, and to give them a purpose, he tucked the pistol in his center desk drawer.

Rex grabbed the upended chair, righting it for the marquess, and by the time he'd come around his desk and reclaimed his own seat, he'd managed to focus himself.

Faith looked back and forth between Rex and her father. "Well? Do either of you intend to tell me what was discussed in my absence?"

"Faith, I'm settling—"

"Your father challenged me to a duel," Rex drawled, earning a glare from Lord Guilford.

The color leeched from Faith's cheeks, turning her natural pallor to white and leaving the dusting of freckles along her nose vivid on that pale canvas. "What?" she whispered.

"Faith," the marquess said entreatingly. "You have to understand, I must defend—"

"No."

"—your honor," Lord Guilford continued over Faith's reputation.

"I will not have you do this," she insisted, adamant in her denial.

The marquess took one of her hands in his. "Some women are worth fighting for," he said, gently.

"Are they worth dying over?" she snapped.

Lord Guilford flashed a sad, resigned smile. "You and your sisters and mother? Absolutely, Faith."

Fire flashed in her eyes. "Well, I don't want you to die for me."

Faith knew. Because she was clever and wise, she knew the same thing Rex did—if he faced off against Guilford in a duel, the older man would never emerge triumphant. That was unless Rex aimed his gun to the sky. *But can you truly kill Faith's father?* Rex shifted in his seat, afraid he couldn't speak in an absolute about whether he would, even if it meant saving his own skin.

Faith slid her gaze over to him.

They stared at one another.

He'd expected following her public ruination at Rex's hands, her eyes would be swollen from weeping and her features pale.

He should have expected differently.

"I forbid you from killing my father."

Rex inclined his head. "Then it would be a good time for me to share that I offered to marry you." He quirked his lips in a wry grin. "I suspect that offer prompted the challenge of a duel more than..." Guilford tensed, and Faith gave him a fiery glare, "*other* reasons," he substituted. toasting her with his half-empty snifter and opting not to bait the marquess and move them all beyond a point of no return.

"You're not marrying him, Faith," Lord Guilford said flatly. "I won't give my permission."

She folded her arms. "That isn't really your decision to make, Papa."

A muscle jumped at the corner of the marquess's right eye, a telling tic. "You aren't of age."

Faith returned her attention to Rex. "Gretna Green, then?"

"Faith," her father begged. "Do not do this."

"Papa," she spoke with a gentle affection for the older man that Rex had never witnessed once in his miserable life. "I know you feel badly for not having called out Lord Somerville. But this situation…it is not that."

Rex's ears pricked up.

"This isn't about her," Lord Guilford said between gritted teeth.

"No." Faith paused. "It is about *me*."

Father and daughter locked in a silent battle.

So that was why Faith had bandied Somerville's sins about; the cad hurt her aunt. That act was the most patently Faith-act ever.

The marquess quit his chair and dropped to a knee beside Faith.

"All I want is for you to be happy and loved," Lord Guilford said, his voice thick and wobbly with emotion. "And this man…" He didn't even look at Rex when he gestured to him; neither did Faith. For all intents and purposes Rex had been forgotten. "He is not the one to do it because he is incapable of such emotion."

Yes, the other marquess wasn't wrong on that score.

Faith captured her father's hands in her own. "It is *my* decision, Papa."

"But it would be the wrong one, Faith," Guilford said, desperation creeping back in his tone. "You wanted a loving husband who will steal to the kitchens with you in the dead of night and snack on the leftover desserts…and…and you want a hundred babes so you two can play the grandest game of hide and seek."

Years ago, when Rex's now-dead mother had been banished, he'd sobbed until his whole body hurt. To break his heir of that weakness, the duke had dragged Rex along to a public hanging and forced him to watch from the front row as a young thief, near in age to his own then, had been strung up and then had flailed and twisted until drawing his last breath. Rex found himself staring at the tender tableau between Faith and her father with that same sickening inability to look away.

Tears filled Faith's eyes. "Papa, I was six when I said that."

The marquess bent lower so that his forehead nearly touched Faith's. "But be it a hundred babes or just one, you still want a husband who is a partner and a playmate to your children. One who'll play those games of hide and seek and charades, because your dream of a loving, devoted husband and father to your children hasn't gone away. Just the number of how many babes you'd have."

The marquess had offered a glimpse into the girl Faith had once been, the dreams she'd carried, the hope she'd had for love and a big family, and…it was too much.

"Well, Faith?" Rex said, infusing a hardness that came all too easily for him. "The decision is yours."

She and her father looked Rex's way, her expression now unreadable when it'd never been before. Before his betrayal, that was.

"Why would you marry him?" Lord Guilford pressed.

Rex swirled the contents of his drink.

Why, indeed?

Faith contemplated him a long while, her opaque gaze locked with his. She stood. "May I speak to Mr. DuMond alone?" she asked quietly.

"Absolutely not," the other man said before the question had fully left her lips.

"Given my circumstances and the fact I'm no longer a child but a woman, I believe I merit that time with Mr. DuMond."

God, she was breathtaking in her confidence, courage, and strength. Any other lady would have been content to let her father handle the entire exchange. Faith had not only stormed the offices, and directly inserted herself into the discussion about her future, she'd also demanded an audience alone with Rex.

Lord Guilford's features twisted and then the gentleman climbed to his feet. "Five minutes, Faith."

Without so much as a look for Rex, the other marquess let

himself from the office, leaving Rex and Faith alone.

She looked at Rex, searching his face for a long while.

Rex remained motionless, keeping his expression carefully guarded.

"You were only at the theatre to ruin me," she said quietly.

Yes, that had been his intention. "Is that a question?"

Faith took a step closer and continued coming until she reached the other side of the desk. "You wish to silence me," she remarked. "That is all this was ever about. The visits to my mother's school. The sweet words. The p-passion." That slight warble hinted at her grief, and she yanked her stare away from him but not before he caught a glimpse of her watery eyes, and the sight of those crystal pool struck somewhere painfully in his chest.

Rex flexed and unflexed his fingers, attempting to rid himself of feeling…anything. Because he *didn't* feel anything. He was hard and cold and ruthless, and hard, cold, and ruthless men didn't feel this gripping pain that now squeezed like a vice about his lungs.

When she looked back, she'd managed to blink away that evidence of her suffering. "Do you have nothing to say?" she whispered.

Rex turned up his palms. "What is there to say? You've deduced my intentions."

"Yes." Her lips twisted in a sad little smile. "Yes, I did."

He tried a different approach. "Answer me this, *petite chouette.* Why did you break into my desk? What business was it ever of yours what my patrons' proclivities are?"

"I don't care what they are," she said with such a calmness, he actually believed her. "I care that they're men who've squandered fortunes at your tables and that once their pockets are empty, they turn their focus and energies upon some poor unsuspecting woman, in turn stealing first her heart, then her virtue, and ultimately her good name so that he might then in turn rob her of her fortune." Her voice shook from the force of her emotion.

That was very specific. This was what she and her father had discussed without details. "He hurt someone you cared about."

It wasn't a question, but she answered anyway. "My Aunt Caroline."

Ah. Of course. She was a regular warrior woman avenging those who'd been wronged. She'd still not gathered that her affection for others was nothing more than a weakness of hers and left her all too easy to be toppled.

"And did your airing Lord Somerville's sins to the world undo her hurts?" he asked, infusing a gentleness to his tone he'd never before employed as a tactic.

She hesitated then shook her head. "It is not about vengeance. Not *just* vengeance," she conceded.

"What is it about then, Faith?" he asked quietly.

"To save another young woman from making the same mistake. I've ensured she and every other lady in London know him for precisely what he is."

"Mayhap she already knew. Mayhap she didn't care that he's to let in the pockets or weak for the tables because she loves him."

She eyed him with a proper modicum of incredulity. "*You* believe in love."

"No." He believed people thought they were in love, but that the emotion was as empty as promises and the fairytale of goodness in the world.

"And what of Lord Bourchier?" he asked.

"One of Anwen's dearest friends was being forced to marry him. I ensured that match did not happen."

"You proved you'd do anything for your family and friends."

"I would."

She had.

"Does that surprise you?"

"It does. People don't do anything for another person unless it serves them."

Faith drew back. "Is there no one you would do anything for, Rex?" she spoke like a woman who desperately wished for an affirmation on his part.

"I'd do anything for my club, and that's about it, Faith," he said bluntly.

"Is there no one you care about?" she ventured softly, pressing him. "No one whose happiness matters most and for whom you'd do anything and be anything?"

Rex's gaze locked with hers. He didn't understand this woman, and perhaps that explained his inexplicable draw to her.

"I can't afford to have people in my life, Faith, and I've had enough dealings with people to understand it is better that way. They aren't honest in their feelings, as you are."

He struggled to remain still under that sad, pitying gaze she ran over him.

"How cynical you are and how very lonely you must be, Rex."

She brought them back to the reason for her being here.

"You think in marrying me, you'll possess me, and in turn ensure my silence and control my actions, and yet," she tipped her pugnacious chin up, "I will never be controlled by anyone."

With that, Faith headed for the door.

She wasn't going to marry him.

And why should she? He was rich as God, but she didn't need money, and oddity that she was, proved to be the one woman who didn't care about the fortune he possessed.

It also meant he was about to lose her, and when he did, she'd be gone from his life forever. That thought left him oddly panicky.

"Faith," he called out, just as she reached for the door handle.

She stopped but did not look back, and he proved a coward for he was grateful she didn't, that she couldn't witness this utter powerlessness gripping him. "I would have you know," he said quietly, "not all of it was a ruse." He paused. "It may have started out as such, but I…" Oh God, every word spoke left him feeling exposed, left him further at sea. "I came to enjoy being with you." Restless, he pushed back his chair, and stood. "When you talk about love and emotion, I don't know these things you're talking about. I don't have those feelings." His father had exceeded in ridding Rex of the ability to feel. "I can promise, however, that if you marry me, I will take care of you. You'll have the protection of my power. You'll never want for anything. I'll never seek to control you or your movements." As his father had done to Rex's mother. "I will never hurt you."

He finished, and Faith stood there so long, silent and motionless, he almost wondered if she'd failed to hear what he'd vowed.

And then she turned slowly, looking back. Only, she remained silent, still.

Rex made his way across the office, stopping when he reached her. "You were right in all the charges you leveled against my character." He teased his fingers along the gold necklace draped around her slender throat and trailed his touch lower before capturing the small gold heart that dangled from the chain, weighting it in his palm.

Her chest hitched.

"I'm a scoundrel, a blackhearted bastard." He continued to toy with the heart-shaped bauble and then suddenly stopped, dropping his arm back to his side. "But you were also wrong about one thing more...."

She stiffened.

He lowered his lips close to her left ear. "The passion...it was never feigned." He parted her cloak and kissed the hollow of her neck. "This was always real," he whispered.

Faith trembled and Rex had moved to claim her lips when she spoke. "I believe you," she said, her voice tinged with more of that soul-wrenching sadness. "Because I believe that is all you are capable of." She turned her head, handing him the first rejection of his life.

And for the first time in his life as well, he found himself unable to look someone in the eyes. This time he proved a coward, for he beat a retreat back to the throne of his office.

Knock-Knock-Knock

Time was up.

As was his time with her. Why should that leave him feeling panicky?

She let Lord Guilford in, and as she closed the door behind them, the marquess moved his gaze over his daughter, as if needing to verify with his own eyes that she was untouched and unhurt.

"I'm going to marry him, Papa," she said quietly.

Shock brought Rex's spine erect.

"No!" That denial came ripped from her father's chest like the growl of a wounded beast.

Relief swelled strong within Rex, leaving him oddly buoyant. Ignoring the other man, Rex held Faith's eyes. "I'll secure a special license. We wed tomorrow."

"Faith," her father begged.

"We won't be able to secure a license," Faith said, ignoring her father.

"Don't you yet know, Faith? I can do anything." No matter how, he *always* got what he wanted.

She nodded once. "Tomorrow, then."

And taking her father by the hand, Faith quit Rex's offices.

She'd said…yes.

The moment they'd gone, the tension suddenly seeped from Rex's frame, leaving him with more of that unfamiliar, heady, light sensation.

Because at last he'd bind himself to the woman who possessed his club's secrets, and he'd also be able to finish what they'd started in Lord Waverly's library. That was all it was.

Wasn't it?

What else would it be?

CHAPTER 20

GIVEN THE HASTINESS OF THINGS, Faith had expected her marriage to Rex would take place in her father's offices at home and be a somber, sad affair.

Knowing her family and friends as she did, Faith should have known better.

Standing outside the music room with Marcia, Anwen, and Violet close, and her father even closer, Faith paused and took in the scene before her.

Gilded chairs had been carefully arranged on either side of the makeshift aisle made by a pretty pink runner. Faith's family and friends had packed themselves into the dozens of seats, while the chairs reserved for Rex's guests comprised just two. They were filled by the big, broad gentleman she recognized as a guard from Forbidden Pleasures and the Marquess of Malden.

Only the Brookfield family could manage to throw together an elaborate, heavily attended wedding on less than a day's notice.

Alongside a rector, Rex stood conversing with the Duke of Argyll. Faith's bridegroom and his friend were absorbed in whatever business it was they discussed.

Faith took in the sight of Rex. Dressed in all black from his cravat to his gleaming boots, he may as well have been attending his own funeral. And yet…mayhap that is how he viewed it. *Because he doesn't really want to marry me.*

She briefly pressed her eyes shut.

She hated that should hurt so.

Faith opened her eyes once more, and her gaze landed on the magnificent floral arrangements, meticulously done in what could only be the hand of her Aunt Caroline who so excelled at creating masterpieces from flowers. They were a vibrant array of myrtle, daffodils, camellia, and chrysanthemum, a cheerful explosion of color in direct opposition to the hard look worn by the man who'd be her husband.

Faith stared at those flowers a long while recalling the words spoken not so very long ago by another gentleman, who'd come begging for her Aunt Caroline's hand.

"I couldn't just bring any flowers …The daffodil…Because I hold you in the highest of regards. Because my love for you, Caroline…it is unequalled…Chrysanthemum, because I love you most ardently. The camellia because I long for you…Myrtle, for it represents love in a marriage, and I want that with you. Marriage, and there will be love in it…"

And suddenly breathing, that reflexive, life sustaining movement, became a physical chore.

"Are you all right, Faith?" Marcia's worried voice drew her back from a precipice of misery.

Faith managed a nod. Except tears pricked her lashes, and it should happen to be that moment when Rex looked across the room and found her there.

He took her in with a sweeping glance, his gaze revealing nothing.

What should it reveal?

There is no affection. No real love. Not on his part. And on yours? Your feelings were forged of fakery and lies. So why did her heart not realize that? Why did she mourn still what could have been and what she'd wanted: love. A joy-filled marriage.

It was too much.

Faith squeezed around her friends, father, and sister and hastened several steps down the hall to a place where she was out of sight from him and the party all assembled as if it were a ceremony steeped in joy and a match made in love.

Her father started towards her, but Violet said something, staying him, then she, along with Marcia and Anwen, joined Faith.

"Would you like for me to kill him?" Violet asked as casually as if she offered up the last chocolate biscuit for breakfast. "I can grab Sir Cheever's sword and take care of it all immediately," she offered, referring to the coat of arms they'd played with together.

Marcia shot a hand up. "I can dispose of the body."

Anwen gave an enthusiastic nod that sent her spectacles tumbling to the bridge of her nose. She pushed them back into place. "I can help."

Faith attempted a smile. "No. I must do this."

"Kill him?" Violet piped in hopefully. "Yes, yes, you do. *We* do," she swiftly amended.

Marcia and Anwen's lips twitched with smiles.

"I meant marry Mr. DuMond."

Her sister's expression fell. "Drat. Murdering him would be better."

In the immediacy of discovering his betrayal, Faith had certainly felt that way too. She'd come to quickly learn, however, that hurting him or seeing him hurt in return wouldn't undo the agony he'd wrought on her heart. *Because I care about him still...*

You foolish, foolish woman, that voice inside silently jeered.

Anwen caught her hands and squeezed. "Must you, though, Faith?"

Marcia remained silent. Having also been ruined, her now-married friend knew once one made those decisions, one couldn't simply be selfish. Not when there were people who relied upon them. "I do."

"Because of me." Faith's sister spoke with a solemnity greater than her years.

Faith stared at the younger girl.

"You're doing it because of me," Violet repeated.

In large part, yes. In some smaller part...in some smaller part, for other reasons. Reasons she did not understand. "The decision is mine."

"I don't want you marrying some heartless scoundrel for my future," Violet said, insistently. "I'll only wed an honorable gentleman who's quite content with our scandalous family."

"There wouldn't be one because honorable men do not marry

into scandalous families."

"I should mention I believe my brother is honorable and he married into a scandalous family," Anwen volunteered.

Yes, the Viscount St. James's sister-in-law had run a fighting club out of her parlor, where she instructed ladies on how to box and defend themselves.

"And Wynn married Aunt Caroline," her sister pointed out.

Marcia nodded. "There you, go. There's two."

Yes, their recently wedded aunt, who after years of heartbreak had finally found love with a good, kind, honorable, respectable man. One who brought flowers and got down on his knee and pledged his love for all time and—Oh God, it was too much.

Faith took a deep breath. "I'm marrying him," she said, and her sister looked as though she wished to fight Faith on her decision, but then a resigned glimmer lit her innocent eyes.

Violet nodded, and as the younger girl and Anwen headed back toward where Faith and Violet's father waited, Faith turned to go. Marcia put a staying hand upon her shoulder.

"You are missing something on your wedding day."

Faith looked questioningly at her friend.

Marcia opened her other palm revealing a beloved, familiar chain and pendant. One Faith had once longed to wear on this very day; that talisman of hope and love and happily-ever-afters. She struggled to breathe through the pain cleaving away at her breast.

"Violet told me you'd stopped wearing it, and thought you should on this day," Marcia murmured.

Before Faith could protest, Marcia draping the cherished piece around Faith's neck.

The chain and pendant were warm against her skin, pulsing slightly, and she touched her fingers to the Heart of a Duke. "There won't be love," Faith whispered, her voice catching, and this time she didn't try to conceal the agony that admission wrought.

Marcia caught her lightly by the shoulders. "My husband married me because he needed a fortune, and...well, if we hadn't been discovered as we were, I suspect Andrew would have never offered for me. But he did, and because of that, Faith, he fell in love with me, and I fell in love with him again."

"It is different." She'd confided in Marcia and Anwen just last evening, everything that had transpired between her and Rex. A tear streaked down Faith's cheek, followed by another and another. Marcia caught each, wiping them away. "You and Andrew were always friends. Rex and I? We don't even have that. What I did briefly have with him was all because of a lie."

"Do you know what I think, Faith?"

Faith shook her head.

"Rex DuMond is a man who doesn't have to do anything he doesn't want to. If Rex DuMond wanted you to be silent, he wouldn't tie himself through marriage to a woman he didn't... Well, he'd have found some other devious way to compel you. I believe he wanted to marry you, but he just couldn't admit that to himself."

A sentiment that felt very much like hope stirred to life in Faith's breast. Perhaps it was because she was still a silly romantic. Perhaps it was because against all better judgment she'd fallen in love with a man who was nothing more than a lie. But somewhere deep inside she longed for the words Marcia spoke to be true. Perhaps Rex was as seductive as Lucifer with his deceptions and lies. But one thing could even destroy Lucifer, and that was hope.

Mayhap, she could have more with Rex. Nay, there'd never be the grand love her friend or mother or aunts knew, but he desired her, and mayhap they could have, at the very least, a friendship.

Her father came over. "Should I show him out?" he asked in a hope-filled voice.

Faith's father, friends, and sister all looked to her. "I'm ready," she said softly, and then, laying her fingers on her father's sleeve, she allowed him to escort her to her bridegroom.

Faith was late.

Some eighteen and a half minutes late, a fact Rex knew not because he'd yanked out the timepiece as he'd wanted to countless times this morning, but rather he'd ascertained by the clock at the far back corner, inconveniently placed and impossible to see whenever the taller guests shifted into his line of focus.

"As betting men, what are we wagering that you aren't about to be jilted?" Argyll drawled, with entirely too much humor.

Rex shot the other man a look, one that went unheeded, and then as if their business didn't hang in the balance of whatever happened this day, Argyll whistled.

The odds were high.

Faith was clever, courageous, and possessed something Rex himself didn't. A heart. As such, it had been only a matter of time before she came to her senses and realized he was the last man she should marry. That there was some less cynical, less miserable bastard than himself to tie herself to for all time. Some fop who'd read her poems—because he knew, with her romantic nature, she'd likely yearned for that. And some fellow to bring her flowers—because when she had almost entered the room, Rex had caught the sad little look in her eyes as she'd stared at those mockingly cheerful urns overflowing with too many blossoms.

And Rex wanted to reach in his own imaginings, drag the nameless blighter from his thoughts, and beat him to a bloody pulp.

There was a certainty neither Rex nor that amorphous fellow deserved her, but Rex deserved her far less.

He was selfish enough to want her anyway.

With a growl, he fished the chain of his watch fob from his pocket and consulted the time. Twenty-one minutes.

She was not coming. She was…

Here.

He felt her.

He sensed her presence, long before the crowd of guests turned and craned their necks to the front of the room. And Rex was grateful that every eye went deservedly to her, so that no one could see the way a mere glimpse of her left him unsteady.

She was a vision in ivory satin, that color he'd previously mockingly associated with innocence and purity. He'd never again see that shade without thinking of her in this moment. The luxuriant fabric gloriously bright, shimmered in the sunlight that streamed through the endless row of windows. A pair of diamond hair combs glinted amongst those luxuriant midnight tresses.

Something moved in his chest.

Some seismic shift that robbed his lungs of air and the thoughts from his head.

And then on the arm of her father, she was coming towards Rex, moving closer and closer still…to him…to a future with him. Nay, he sure as hell didn't deserve her. But he was determined to possess her, anyway.

Faith reached him.

Her eyes were red. Her cheeks still wore a slight sheen from tears that had recently fallen.

She'd been crying.

Of course, she had. Why *wouldn't* she?

Still, that evidence of her misery hit him like a kick to the gut, and he'd have preferred a good pummeling to this. For at least a fight he could ultimately prevail in; pain from a blow was something he could countenance. But this? This he could not control, and it terrified him out of his bloody mind.

He looked over to Lord Guilford and found the man glowering at him. "Hurt her and I *will* kill you."

Faith's father couldn't. He might want to. But he didn't have the necessary evil in him to see that deed done. Pitying that other man and his complete lack of power, Rex proved himself more generous than he'd ever credited, for he inclined his head slightly in acknowledgment of that almost plea.

"*Dearly beloved, we are gathered together here in the sight of God, to join together this Man and this Woman in holy Matrimony…*"

"I thought you weren't coming," Rex whispered, as the vicar ran through the solemnization of matrimony.

"I almost didn't," she confessed.

He'd known as much before she'd even spoken that admission aloud. So why did hearing her voice it aloud, land another lance in his chest?

"You would have been wise not to, *petite chouette.*"

"*…to be honourable among all men: and therefore is not by any to be enterprised, nor taken in hand, unadvisedly, lightly, or wantonly, to satisfy men's carnal lusts and appetites, like brute beasts that have no understanding…*"

Faith lifted a midnight eyebrow. "Are you attempting to persuade me to change my mind?"

Perhaps that was what he was doing. Perhaps she was more clever than he, after all. Because it was suddenly occurring to him that he might be no match for Faith Brookfield. It was preposterous to think this innocent lady, a virgin who'd never been kissed before him, should have the upper hand over him. Yet, he'd no experience in dealing with women such as her, and as such, she had him at a disadvantage. One that terrified the everlasting hell out of him.

"...First, It was ordained for the procreation of children, to be brought up in the fear and nurture of the Lord, and to the praise of his holy Name..."

Even as the answer didn't really matter, he wanted to know anyway. "Why did you decide to come, Faith?"

She stared directly at the vicar. "I have a sister to think about, Rex. My ruin means her ruin too."

Of course.

She would be that selfless, and suddenly her decision to accept his offer made sense.

Her response was a level of logic and reason, not grounded in emotion. As such, he should understand. That discovery certainly shouldn't leave this hollowed-out feeling inside his chest.

When it came time for Faith to speak her portion of the vows, her voice rang out sure and steady, and without any of the hesitation and regret he'd expected to hear from her.

And then, it was done. Most of the guests streamed from the music room, with Faith's family and their closest friends lingering behind while the signings were completed.

His portion finished, Rex headed over to his partners. "It's done," he said.

"Yes, well, let us hope you make it out of here alive," Argyll drawled.

As one, they looked to Faith's friends. The new Viscountess Waters and Miss Anwen Kearsley stood shoulder to shoulder, their arms folded at their chests, each throwing impressive glares his way. None, however, wore quite the lethal look as her sister, Violet.

The girl pointed slowly to her throat, and holding Rex's gaze, she made a menacing slashing motion.

"Yikes. She's as ruthless as the elder sister," Malden whispered. Horror wreathed the other man's tones.

"I'll need to hire more guards," Latimer said, a laugh in his voice.

"I'd like a word with you," someone declared, and it was a moment before Rex found the owner of that small, child's voice.

Rex and his partners glanced down.

It would have been easier had the child wore the same hate-filled stare of all the other Brookfield guests present.

The child puffed his tiny chest out. "I'm Faith's brother, Paddy. I'd like a word with you, sir."

His partners took that as their cue to quit the music room, leaving Rex alone with the boy.

Aside from the times he'd spent visiting Ladies and Gentlemen of Hope, Rex hadn't had any experience with children. They were as foreign to him as those feelings he'd spoken with Faith about just yesterday evening.

The boy's eyes were as somber as Rex's had been when he'd been a child. There was a level of innocence, but also a wariness that only living life's cruelties could instill, and something Rex recognized all too well.

Rex dropped to his haunches. "How may I be of assistance?"

"I think that should be clear, my lord," he spoke with a directness Rex could appreciate. "Are you going to care for my sister?"

He touched a hand to his heart. "I'll protect her with my life."

"You won't hurt her?"

He'd already hurt her more than she would ever forgive. Pain knotted his chest, in that space where his hand still rested and where his heart beat. Rex silently railed at the fact that he felt. Because feeling was bloody awful and miserable, and yet, for reasons he couldn't understand, Faith had wrought this change within him.

Paddy narrowed his eyes. "I asked you a question, my lord. I'd suggest you answer and wisely, or I shall grab Sir Cheevers's sword and run you through."

"Sir Cheevers?"

"He's the knight that stands in one of our halls. Faith and Violet and I play with him frequently. He has an impressive broadsword."

And even spoken in his child's voice, there was an impressive warning contained within that hinted at the powerful man Paddy Brookfield would one day become.

"I will do everything in my power to never hurt her." That was, more than he already had.

Paddy assessed him a long moment and then must have seen something that assured him. "She loves the dahlia, especially the purple one but she also likes the pink, peach, and two-color dahlia. Do you know those ones?"

"I don't, but I expect I can learn."

Faith's brother gave a big nod of approval.

As the child continued, he imparted intimate details, ones that offered a greater window into memories and thoughts of the woman Rex had married. Faith would surely hate knowing her brother had revealed those pieces to him. And yet Rex found himself grateful for that glimpse, inexplicably wanting to know everything there was to know about Faith Brookfield.

DuMond.

She now bears your name, as will her children.

Their children.

That thought should bring with it horror. Only…Rex's gaze slid to the front of the room, over to where Faith and her friends conversed. Whatever the viscountess said just then earned a robust laugh from Faith, chasing away the sadness she'd worn since she'd walked down that makeshift aisle to become his wife. That winsome smile transformed her, and he was helpless to do anything but stare as an image flitted in of an impish girl—a child that looked just like her—with a patch of freckles along her cheeks and enormous black curls and even bigger eyes, and lightness filled every corner of his chest.

The girl would be spirited and stubborn and clever as her mother, and for the first time in the whole of his miserable existence, Rex found himself…relishing the thought of a child he'd previously been determined to never have.

And he was grateful he'd already sunk to the floor, for that discovery rocked the world under him.

Faith's brother tugged at his sleeve. "Are you getting all of this, my lord?"

No. "Yes." He had been. Everything had gotten all disordered in his mind though.

"Are you sure?" Paddy asked skeptically.

"Her favorite flower is the purple dahlia," Rex said, reciting every detail he could recall the boy having shared. "She enjoys shortbread, and especially enjoys sneaking downstairs to eat the ones left over from the evening dessert. She hates bullies but loves people who stand up to them. She hates eating fish but loves to catch them and release them."

Paddy gave an approving nod. "Very good. But do not forget—"

"She has a taste for dishes made of fowl, and loves all marzipan, though she prefers them most when they are shaped as miniature fruits."

Paddy beamed. "Bravo, my lord."

Rex bowed his head under that high praise. "Given we are now brothers by marriage, might I allow you the use of my Christian name, Rex."

"Rex. That means "king". I learned that in my Latin class."

"Yes, it does." Because even when siring a child, the duke's ultimate concern had been on highlighting the thing most important to him—power.

Paddy's eyes lit up. "Which means that Faith is now your queen."

"And you are her knight and protector," Rex said, admiring the child for wanting to protect his sister, while also finding himself grateful the boy wasn't a dozen or so years older, for he'd have already grabbed that familial sword he'd spoken of and run Rex through—deservedly so, of course.

"We shall both be her protectors," Paddy vowed. "You may call me Paddy." He extended a small, fragile hand.

Rex stared at the tiny palm a moment and then placed his hand in the child's. Had there ever been a hand smaller, more fragile, than this one? Once again, it surfaced thoughts of a child created by him and Faith, and his throat closed up and his mouth went dry with the fear of how not repulsive the idea of a child between them, in fact, was.

His skin prickled and he looked over.

Faith remained conversing with her friends, but her gaze was squarely on Rex and Paddy. Even with the length of the room between them, she radiated a tenderness he'd not seen since prior to her discovery of his treachery.

And a buoyant lightness suffused his chest.

"Are you all right, Rex?" Paddy asked, concern filling his query.

"Yes," he lied. Faith Brookfield had wrought madness over him, and Rex wasn't sure he'd ever be fine again. He was sinking. Drowning. Struggling to breathe. Everything within him screamed run, but his limbs were made of lead.

After the wedding breakfast, the guests adjoined to a parlor. The furniture had been arranged in a circle about the cheerful Aubusson carpet, leaving a wide opening at the center of the room Faith's friends swept her away and Rex found himself alone in the corner amidst a houseful of smiling, laughing strangers.

Not all strangers.

A number of them were former patrons: Lords Rutland, Tennsyon, Brookfield. Edgerton.

The lot of them, reformed rakes who wore entirely too-easy grins and joined in that mirth as if it were the most natural thing in the world, and not as though they were the same men who'd relished some of the wickedest pleasures at Rex's club.

Though, in fairness, they weren't all smiles.

Periodically, those four leveled dark, impressively menacing glances Rex's way.

Those he welcomed. That hostility Rex knew what to do with. The other lighthearted business, he'd not a bloody clue.

Latimer joined him. "What in hell are we doing now?" he asked under his breath.

Never had he been more grateful for the arrival of anyone.

"I have no bloody idea." Rex continued to take in the scene, feeling lost at sea, still. Suspecting that was to be a familiar fate now.

Argyll, on the other hand, appeared entirely at ease among the revelry, but then he'd always been the charmer and rogue among them. Rex observed his partner conversing with Faith's father and mother, neither of whom looked as though they wished to slice him open and serve him up for breakfast as Faith's father had looked at Rex. Rex froze. Argyll was the manner of man whom Faith had deserved. One who wasn't hate-filled and hateful but rather a gentleman who belonged in her world and knew how to make her smile and—Rex growled.

A happy cry went up from Lord Tennyson's young daughter. The wedding guests began rushing to various spaces throughout the room, some claiming spots upon sofas and armchairs. Others remained conversing in the corner. Nay, just his wife. His wife spoke with her sister and Lady Waters, the three seeming oblivious to whatever was afoot. An inexplicable urge to join her filled him.

As if she would want you there…

"What in bloody blazes are they doing?" The head guard put that to the one partner among them who could answer that.

Except Malden shook his head, eying the peculiar lot with the same abject confusion as Rex and Latimer. "I don't—"

"It's charades."

Rex and his partner started. He, Latimer, and Malden swung their focus down to the small boy whose tiny presence they'd failed to note.

The boy smiled widely and waved. "Hullo, Rex."

And surprisingly, it felt natural returning that little wave.

"What are you, a pickpocket?" Latimer growled.

"Not anymore," Paddy said with too much matter-of-factness to be anything except the truth.

Rex and Latimer burst out laughing.

"Come on with yourself," Latimer said between great, big guffaws.

"He is telling the truth," Malden explained. "It's well-known."

And yet, Rex hadn't.

Paddy yanked at his lapels. "I was the best at it too." He lifted his left hand. "Until a gent broke my finger." He pointed to the noticeably curved index finger in question, and Rex's amusement instantly died. "I can't use it. Had to learn to use my right hand instead. My ma made me the first boy at her school, and now they have more. Like me."

As in people the *ton* tended to ignore or disdain for not being perfect by societal standards.

Rex sank to his haunches and spoke in an exaggerated whisper. "So then," he said, tipping his head back in the direction of the flurry of activity going on, "what are they up to?"

"Charades. It's a tradition whenever a Brookfield marries. We play games." Paddy tugged Rex's sleeve. "You'll play, too."

Rex's mouth went dry, his skin grew hot, and he'd a sudden urge to rip the buttons of his jacket off, yank open his jacket, and then tug free his cravat. "I'm afraid I don't know the game." Games hadn't ever been allowed. Only when his mother had been alive and for the short time she'd been part of his life.

Paddy flashed a big, trusting smile. "Worry not. I'll help you with the clues."

Oh, Rex was worried. It wasn't a child's game that had him panicky but rather the dangerous hungering to be part of whatever this was.

CHAPTER 21

¶IT WAS GOING TO BE so easy for Faith to hate her husband. He'd deceived her. Made a fool of her. And worse, he'd broken her heart. She and Rex were destined to be left with a cold, emotionless union forged of deceit and necessity.

Or she'd thought so.

Only, it wasn't proving so very easy, after all.

Faith would forever remember Rex as he'd been in her family's music room, on a bent knee, speaking so easily, so comfortably, with her brother. And mayhap it would have been easy to dismiss that moment as a chance one between an unlikely pair.

If Paddy weren't now secluded in a different corner, speaking rapidly, his hands flying as he did, to Rex.

Framed between Marcia and Violet, Faith watched her new husband and brother, the two of them joined by two of Rex's business partners.

Something Paddy said drew hoots of laughter from the boy's unlikeliest of audiences.

Violet shifted closer. "Whatever are they speaking about?"

Unable to take her gaze from her husband and younger brother, Faith could only manage to shake her head. She couldn't even begin to imagine what a man like Rex would find as common ground to speak to her young brother about.

Another chorus of guffaws went up.

Marcia nodded towards the group in question. "Whatever it is appears to be of the amusing sort."

"Perhaps he isn't so very bad, after all?" Violet ventured, sounding almost fearful of making that admission. "I'm not saying he *isn't*," she rushed to assure. "Just..." Faith's younger sister discreetly gestured to Rex and Paddy. "Nasty, horrible, evil men don't talk to children. They eat them up or snarl them away."

Faith cocked her head. Rex wasn't doing either of those things.

At that moment, he and Paddy stole a look at her Uncle Alex's latest attempt at charades.

Rex and her brother lifted their thumbs up, while Mr. Latimer and Lord Malden pointed their thumbs down, and into a clenched fist.

The oddest of quartets erupted into another round of laughter and this time as they did, Faith's new husband affectionately ruffled the top of Paddy's golden curls.

Faith's heart stirred.

"Perhaps he isn't all bad," Marcia murmured. "Perhaps his intentions were, but mayhap that is not all there is to him."

Before, at her mother's school, he'd had every reason to feign interest and kindness towards the students there. Now? Now, he'd everything he wanted—her as his wife and a flimsy belief in her silence. No, behaving kindly to her brother benefited neither Rex nor his goals. And it left her mind all mixed up.

"You should join him, Faith," Marcia said quietly.

"He does look lonely."

Faith and Marcia glanced at Violet.

"What?" the younger girl bristled. "He may be with his friends, but it's only his friends and Paddy he's with. No one else is speaking to him."

Why should they? Faith's family and friends all knew the circumstances behind her marriage to Rex. She should delight in his being excluded. Only, she did not. Faith sighed. She was the biggest fool around.

She started across the room.

Absorbed in their discussion, Rex, his friends, and Faith's brother didn't even note her approach.

"There was once a small boy who'd oft been praised for quickness of reply. One day, a gentleman remarked to the boy that children sensible in their youth oft became stupid and dull as they grew older. The child looked up and said: 'You must have been a very sensible boy then, my lord'."

The gathering erupted into another chorus of laughter. Until Mr. Latimer registered Faith's presence. He nudged Rex in the arm. Their earlier brevity immediately cut off, as each man looked her way.

Faith stood there a moment, fighting the urge to squirm, feeling like the biggest arse for thinking she was either needed or wanted.

"Faith," her brother greeted, coming over to join her. "I was telling them some of the jests you told me. Rex said you must be very clever and witty."

She met her husband's cryptic gaze. "Did he?" she murmured, her eyes locked with Rex's.

"Oh, yes," Paddy answered.

A piercing whistle went up over the din in the room.

They looked to the opposite corner of the room, still occupied by Violet and Marcia.

"Paddy," Violet called loudly. "It is your turn next."

Paddy's blue eyes grew even brighter. "Huzzah! Prepare to watch a master at work, gentlemen." With that boastful invitation, he swaggered off.

"Given there's a master at work, we should get a closer seat." Mr. Latimer touched the brim of an imagined hat and moved to join the other guests, with Lord Malden following close behind, leaving Faith and Rex alone.

She and her new husband watched as Paddy took his place at the center of the room.

"Do you enjoy charades, Faith?" Rex asked when her brother had begun his pantomime.

Puzzled by that peculiar question, she glanced over briefly at Rex. "I do." Did he really care either way? "I trust given your acting skills, my lord, you are quite adept at charades."

"I've never played."

Startled, she looked over. "You've never played. Not even when you were a child?"

"I was never a child," he said impassively. "The duke...my father, didn't allow games."

The brief bit her mother had shared about Rex's father coupled with that which Faith had gleaned during her one meeting with him had all spoken to the man's cruelty. Was it a wonder Rex had become the man he'd become.

Only she slid her gaze his way, once more, finding his focus trained on Paddy's efforts. A blackhearted man like the duke wasn't one who'd ever engage a child as Rex had her brother. And mayhap she was the biggest fool wanting to see good in him where there wasn't. But he'd nothing to gain in being kind to her brother, and yet he was.

"My father is terrible at them," she said.

Rex looked over in surprise, searching about for a moment as if to verify he was the person she spoke to.

"Charades," she clarified. She slid closer, taking up a place directly beside him. "Violet is very good," she said, pointing over at her younger sister enthusiastically clapping and cheering Paddy on. "But my father?" she repeated. "He is the worst. But he does try, and we all love him even more for that."

Love. That emotion he didn't believe in. But then, what reasons did he have to believe in it? One who'd never known the warmth and love of a parent or sibling could never grow in that emotion.

Her husband remained guarded for a long moment more before some of the tension eased from his harshly set features. "The groom preparing for the wedding."

She furrowed her brow.

Rex nodded towards Paddy. "He is quite good."

Faith lifted her eyebrows. He'd already solved Paddy's clue. Her husband had been playing along in silence. Something dangerous shifted and moved within her breast. Something she recognized all too well and feared so much because of how this same man had hurt her. "He used to hate games," she shared. "My father and his dear friend, the Duke of Bainbridge," she discreetly gestured over to where the duke and his duchess spoke with Faith's parents. "Every Christmastide Season they attend a fair where they pick gifts for their wives. Paddy was caught picking a gentleman's pocket, and had his finger broken—"

"Paddy shared with me."

Faith started. "Did he?" she asked, unable to keep the surprise from creeping into her voice.

Rex nodded.

"My brother doesn't speak of that with anyone. Not even Violet or me."

"Perhaps he saw in Latimer someone he could relate to."

Perhaps in Rex he had seen someone he could speak freely to. To say as much would only lead him to spring those walls back between them.

"When Paddy came to live with us, he was frail and even smaller than he is now. We can't even say for sure how hold he is. He was so very angry. Not that anyone would ever blame him. He mocked our family for playing games and wrought havoc upon the household in every way he could. Throwing food at every meal. Dumping his water on the floor. Until one morning he came into the breakfast room, sat down, placed a napkin on his lap, and began to quietly eat. Do you know what he said?"

Rex folded his arms and again glanced over. He shook his head.

Faith slid closer to this man who'd hurt her but also a man who was hurting, even as he'd likely never admit as much to her, himself, or anyone. "He said, 'No one ever wanted me, because I'm such a miserable bastard. But anyone who's seen the worst of me and didn't throw me out on the curb doesn't seem to be going anywhere.'"

Rex's features shifted, his jaw worked. "I'm…not a small boy, Faith," he said, his voice slightly garbled.

Of course, he'd have understood what she'd been saying.

"I'm not someone who can be changed."

"Perhaps." He'd lived a lifetime in coldness, and not just the few years Paddy had. "But I have to believe we're all capable of learning, and if not changing completely, growing in some way."

She was supposed to hate him.

Why wouldn't she?

Aside from his partners, no one liked him. Everyone feared him.

Yet this woman, this young lady with every reason to despise him, did not. The grace she showed him was grace he didn't deserve.

Cheers went up around the room as Argyll solved Paddy's charade. The duke dropped a deep bow, then with a flourish took his spot at the center of the parlor, commanding the silence and attention only he'd ever been able to. Argyll lifted a gloved hand, and the Marchioness of Tennyson called out mid-movement from the duke.

"Giving a toast!"

Pressing that same palm against his chest, Argyll staggered back. "Only a fellow so good at charades could have managed such a feat."

"Or a lady so good at guessing clues," Faith's mother shouted back, raising another round of laughter among the wedding guests.

Argyll pointed a finger her way. "Indeed. You have me there, my lady."

How damned easy the other man made it look. Rex had never resented the duke. But he found himself feeling a sense of annoyance at how naturally it came to him, charming Faith's family.

Not that I want to charm Faith or her family. I don't. Why would I?

"You know, you can play," Faith remarked.

He glanced over. "Me?"

"Yes, you." Faith's eyes twinkled.

When was the last time her eyes had sparkled that way, without the wariness and mistrust he'd roused with his betrayal. Nay, he knew the precise moment when. In her uncle's library, when he'd made love to her with his mouth. Before she'd known about his deception. They couldn't go back to that. Once trust was lost, it was lost forever.

He shook his head. "I couldn't."

She waggled her eyebrows. "Are you afraid of not being the best at something, husband?"

Husband. Warmth crept into the darkest corners of his heart. He caught Faith's fingers in his and drew her closer so that their bodies touched "I never doubt my abilities, Faith," he murmured, layering a promise within that silken vow.

Her lips parted.

Rex eyed her mouth, wanting to take it, and he'd never been one to deny himself.

"Rex," a little voice called out, shattering the moment. "You must join me."

He glanced across a room that had gone silent and found every set of eyes trained on him and Faith.

Rex instantly released his wife's hand and took a step back from her.

Paddy jumped up and down, waving his arms wildly back and forth as he did. "Be my partner," the boy urged a second time.

Lord Guilford put a hand on his son's shoulder, saying something, no doubt warning the child off his summons. But Paddy shrugged free of that touch, ran across the room, and taking Rex by the hand, attempted to drag him towards the center of the room.

"Paddy," he said gruffly.

Faith's brother, however, wasn't taking no for an answer. "Oh, come, Rex. You aren't scared of charades. We'll make quite a team."

Yanking hard on Rex's hand, the child forced Rex to a knee, and he gladly dropped to the floor because it brought him a reprieve for being on display before Faith's closest friends and family.

"We've been doing a wedding theme all day, Rex," the boy whispered into his ear.

Rex nodded. "And?"

A devilish grin tugged at the boy's lips. "*And* we are going to confuse them all by doing something completely different, something they shall never suspect because they're too busy thinking we're acting out something about the wedding."

"Isn't...the purpose of the game to perform so well, people guess your action?" Rex asked, completely puzzled.

"Yes." The mischievous twinkle in his eyes grew brighter. "For some. I enjoy confusing everyone."

Feeling Faith's gaze taking in their exchange, he glanced over.

She wore a smile, that glorious one that stretched near ear to ear and that radiated a joy he'd never known in his miserable existence. Until her. A smile he'd thought to never again see, at least because of him. And there was no way he could resist that adoration spilling from her eyes.

Oh, bloody hell.

Rex forced his focus back to an expectant Paddy. "Very well. What is our clue?"

Paddy leaned in and whispered in his ear.

No. Absolutely not. There was no way. "Not that—"

"Yes, this one. Let's go."

Determined to get this humiliation over and done with Rex climbed to his feet and allowed the boy to tug him into the center of a silent room.

Cursing under his breath he dropped onto the Aubusson carpet, onto all fours. Paddy instantly scrambled onto his back.

From the stillness started a rumble as the guests erupted into jollity.

Faith's brother gave him a kick on his arse. "Off with you!" the boy shouted, earning more cries of gaiety from those present.

Out the corner of his eye, he caught Argyll and Latimer bent over beating their knees, while Malden reflected Rex's own horror at the situation.

"Yah-Yah!" Paddy shouted over the crowd's hilarity. Faith's brother leaned down and whispered, "You're *supposed* to be a horse."

"I know." God did he know.

"Do you also happen to know of any horses that *don't* move when kicked, Rex?"

Touché. Biting wit appeared to be a Brookfield trait.

With that challenge, Rex proceeded to tromp around the floor. He made four loops around a rose-inlaid table before his frustration boiled over. Paddy drew on the imagined reins bringing Rex to a stop directly in front of the ivory upholstered walnut settee occupied by none other than the Marquess and Marchioness of Rutland and a passel of their children.

For the love of God.

"Surely one of you supposedly skilled players of charades has some inkling of what we're doing?" Rex snapped at London's notoriously reformed scoundrel.

"Oh, we do," Rutland drawled. "This is entirely more enjoyable."

The marchioness pinched her husband's arm. "Behave," she

whispered.

Lord Rutland only grinned in return.

As if Rex should have expected mercy from *that* one.

He looked to his partners, the trio lined all in a row near the doorway out, and for a moment, he briefly contemplated riding on past them with Paddy on his back to escape. "Help," Rex mouthed.

Argyll flashed a smile. "Sorry, chum. I'm with Rutland on this one."

As the guests' amusement swelled to deafening, it proved contagious, and Rex found himself shaking from the force of the absolute ludicrousness of it all. Paddy wrapped his arms around Rex's neck and held on tight.

When had he last enjoyed himself this way? Had he ever? For the first time he had a glimpse of just why the Tennysons and Rutlands and Edgertons of the world forsook a life of sin in favor of a different way of living. Because this was altogether different than the merely existing Rex had done before Faith and her Brookfield family.

As he took Paddy on a turn around a side table, his gaze collided with Faith's. Faith, whose cheeks brimmed with color and her slender body trembled with happiness.

The earth ceased to spin on its access and the heavens collided and a commotion sounded in Rex's mind.

Wait, no, that wasn't the game of charades.

He registered the guest framed in the doorway and froze. All Rex's previous mirth shattered, tinkling around in his mind like the shards of joy falling.

"The Duke of Haincourt," the Brookfield butler announced, and the room went quiet. Even the many children didn't so much as stir.

But then, he'd always had that effect on people—Rex's *father*.

The duke pulled off his white leather gloves and managed to peer down the length of his hawkish nose at the entire room. The austere duke took in the scene before him, sliding an all-to-brief glance at Faith, that cursory look intended to show all present that he'd found her wanting. He at last trained that glacial stare on Rex, conveying all the disdain he'd always carried for him.

"Not even an invitation to a wedding from my own son," His Grace said icily.

Rex gritted his teeth. Of course, he'd ruin this day. He ruined everything he touched—including Rex himself. And God help him, for in that moment, Rex found himself transported back to the pitiable, pathetic boy who'd cowered in terror because of this loathsome figure before him.

Lord and Lady Guilford exchanged a look with one another and then started forward to greet the duke, but Faith was there, stopping them. She said something, and then gave a slight shake of her head.

Rex carefully set Faith's brother from him, and as Rex came to his feet, the duke sharpened his focus on him. "My God, look at you. On the floor, playing games like a bloody, stupid child." The duke peeled his lip back in a sneer filled with loathing. "But then, I should have expected nothing less than such an uncouth display from your pitiable bride and her fam—"

Rex was across the room in an instant, with an arm at his father's throat. He propelled him through the door, into the hall, and shoved him hard against the wall.

"Never insult my wife," he whispered, his chest heaving with the force of rage pumping through his veins.

The duke's eyes bulged, and he scrambled to remove Rex's hand, but Rex tightened his grip, relishing the rage, feeding it. "If you so much as mention her name, if you speak another ill word about her or her family, I will *end* you." With that, he released him, flexing his fingers.

The duke collapsed upon the pretty pink carpet; he choked and gasped; laboring for breath.

Emotionlessly, Rex glanced over at Latimer and Argyll who'd joined him the moment he'd shoved the duke from the parlor. "Get him out of here."

"On your feet, Your Grace." Latimer yanked the duke up and proceeded to steer him through Lord and Lady Guilford's corridors.

In the course of his life, Rex had alone borne the misery of his father's abuse with only the duke's staff there to bear witness to his shame. Never, had there been an audience. And now it was this one. His wife. Her family. Her friends. Humiliation poured through him, and he wanted to drown in that pitiable sentiment so that he didn't have to face any of them.

Soft fingers twined with his, and stiffening, Rex glanced down. *Faith.*

The feel of her hand in his caused a great swell of emotion in his throat, and he attempted to swallow or breathe or say something. *Anything.*

Concern and tenderness brimmed for him in her expressive eyes. "Are you——?"

"It's time to leave," he ordered harshly, knowing he was a bastard, but hopeless to help it. He let her hand go, instantly cold at the loss.

Faith's parents came forward, protesting, but Faith interrupted them.

"It has been a full day," she said softly, holding her mother's gaze.

Tears glimmered in the marchioness's pretty brown eyes, Faith's eyes, and then on a whir, he and Faith made their way through the halls to the foyer and then at last, the carriage, where the door was shut and he and Faith were alone. Unlike the parlor, when there'd been a room full of guests. And this was its own kind of uncomfortable.

To give his fingers a purpose, Rex tugged the curtain open and stared at the passing Mayfair townhouses. He fixed on the steady clip-clop of the team and the rattle of the wheels to keep from thinking about the horror that had just unfolded.

"I'm so sorry, Rex," she said softly.

He should have expected she'd not let it rest.

"I'm also sorry your fun was ruined," he said tersely. In his inability to meet her eyes, he proved himself a coward he'd never thought he was.

The springs squeaked as Faith moved, joining him on his bench. "That isn't what I'm sorry about." She paused. "Not that I wasn't sorry for you. You were enjoying yourself."

Yes, he had been.

"I'm sorry your father is so cruel, Rex."

He shrugged a shoulder. "What he did back there? It doesn't bother me."

"I don't believe that," she said instantly.

She wouldn't, because someone as pure and good as she—a lady who'd been a cherished daughter, beloved—couldn't imagine how a man such as Rex became jaded as he had. "When I was four, he banished my mother to one of his many country properties where she eventually died alone," he said flatly. "I wasn't even permitted to attend her burial." Out the window, Rex caught a glimpse of a handsome, smartly-dressed young couple linked arm in arm. He watched them until the carriage rolled past, and they were distant like the memories he now spoke of.

"When I was five, he caught me playing with a cup and ball, and backhanded me. Caught me with his ring here." He motioned to the scar upon his cheek. "From that moment on, I promised I'd never play games again." He continued ruthlessly. "When I was thirteen, he put my horse down because in naming my mount, I'd shown myself to be too affectionate for a creature whose only purpose should be a functional one." He hardened his jaw. "So, if you think a handful of words hurled at me can hurt? They don't. I'm quite accustomed to it."

The window reflected Faith's features twisted with sorrow. Her eyes glittered with grief as if she'd been physically hurt by nothing more than the stories he'd recounted about his youth. "Oh, Rex."

He tensed. Oh God.

"I didn't tell you this because I want your pity," he gritted out. He'd only done so that she might understand he'd been unaffected by today's latest display from his father.

"No one can become accustomed to that, Rex," she whispered.

"I did."

"Because you had to," she said, smoothing her fingers along the sleeve of his jacket. "But you don't have to be accustomed to it anymore. Life, family, it doesn't have to be this way. You saw my family and our friends."

Yes, and he'd never seen anything like it in the whole of his miserable existence. But that was her world, a world of light and good to which she'd been born and belonged.

"It is this way for me, Faith," he said quietly. The sooner she realized that the better off she'd be. The better off they'd both be. For a brief sliver of time today, he'd believed an illusion. "You wouldn't understand."

She arched an eyebrow. "Because you see my family is a happy one and assume I've only ever known kindness?"

Precisely.

"Rex, my late father, the one who birthed me, didn't have time for a daughter. He never failed to remind me that I'd failed him in being born female. He railed at me, berated me, and lamented the fact that, being born with a broken ear, I'd likely always be his responsibility."

Rage tightened every muscle in his body. It was a good thing the bastard was dead in the grave, for if he weren't, Rex would have happily killed him.

"I didn't know," he said. "I just assumed…"

"After he died and my mother fell in love with Lord Guilford and they married," Faith said, "I discovered not all fathers were like the one who despised me for circumstances beyond my control."

He looked away.

"I have something for you," Faith said softly, pulling his attention back over. "A gift."

Rex just stared at her. He'd wronged her in every way, and she had every right to hate him and she had still gotten him a gift.

"I'd intended to give it to you before," she explained.

Before he'd betrayed her. That made far more sense. One didn't give gifts to those who deceived you.

Faith cleared her throat. "And so now it is a wedding gift."

If she'd hated him as she should, as he deserved, she would have burned—in the hottest hearth fire—whatever gift she'd once picked out in fondness. But she hadn't.

"Faith," he said thickly. The last person to ever gift him anything had been his mother. It'd been a set of marbles that the duke had ultimately confiscated. "I…" He didn't know what to say. Many times he'd been deliberately laconic with people, but he'd never been without proper words.

Faith pressed something into his hand, and he glanced down at the thick little leather book she'd placed there.

A memory slipped in of a day not so very long ago when he'd first heard of that title from the woman who now sat beside him.

"Moral Tales for Young People by Miss Edgeworth," he read the title aloud.

"…I'm quite fond of those works. Particularly from The Good Aunt. I trust you are familiar with that tale?"

He lifted his gaze.

Faith's eyes twinkled with humor.

Somehow, despite the havoc wrought by the duke that day, Rex found a grin tugging at his lips, and then a low rumble started slowly in his chest, and he found himself laughing, and damned if it didn't feel good.

Coming up on her knees, Faith placed her fingers on Rex's chin and forced him to look at her. She moved her gaze over his face. "You think the world can only be a cruel, ugly place, because you've known so much ugliness and cruelty, but it can be better if you let it be." With that, she settled back on the bench and rested her head against his arm.

Rex stared at the top of her dark curls, a pink dahlia tucked within those tight coils.

She was wrong. The world was this way. He'd lived an entire lifetime with evidence of just how cruel people n were—himself included among those ranks.

But…what if she were right? What if he could have more? And have it with her?

CHAPTER 22

FAITH'S WEDDING DAY HAD PASSED in a whir. For all the scandal and sadness that had surrounded the reason for Faith's nuptials to Rex, the day had been filled with jubilant laughter and the sounds of her family and friends joining in charades.

At first, he'd worn an almost befuddled look, and he'd taken in each exchange the same way she'd examined the auguries of the planets with her unconventionally wonderful governess, Miss Allen.

The rooms had brimmed with such joy, it had been contagious, and Faith had found herself laughing alongside Rex, and everything had been so very wonderful and natural. He'd bonded with her brother. He'd played charades.

Then his father had arrived, and it had all come to an end. In an instant, the duke had killed the day's joy. Her husband's smile and laughter had died, and he'd become guarded, all humor gone.

She'd found herself thinking of what her mother had revealed about Rex's father, the duke, and Faith's own singular experience with that hateful man, and what she'd witnessed on her wedding day. At last, she'd understood how Rex had grown to be hardened, and understood how the loving tableau he'd witnessed that day had surely been foreign to him.

After they'd arrived at the grand mansion that housed Forbidden Pleasures, he'd introduced her to the head housekeeper in charge of the private suites. Rex had taken his leave of Faith, and she had not seen him since.

They'd shared no intimate wedding dinner…or any other intimate thing, for that matter.

There'd been no wedding night.

At that moment, Faith stared morosely at yet another single tray brought to her rooms for the latest evening meal. Just one platter, and one place serving, and one glass, all of which signified her new husband had no intention of joining her—*again*.

Why would there have been? Everything with Rex had been feigned and fake.

Faith propped an elbow on the white lace tablecloth, dropped her chin atop her palm, and stared miserably at the la fricassee de poulet aux champignons.

Rex may have said he desired her. He ran a gaming hell where all manner of wicked things went on between men and women. What he'd done with her, he'd no doubt shared with any number of women before her. The night he'd brought her to her first release, he'd shaken her world, but it had been just any other encounter for him.

Faith hated that realization should ravage her so.

Grabbing a fork, she pushed the buttered carrots around the fricassee of chicken.

Buttered carrots, always her favorite, and yet she didn't have a taste for them.

At least, it wasn't fish. "There is that," she muttered, just so she could hear herself, because it was so quiet, and she wasn't accustomed to quiet. The Brookfield gatherings, be it breakfast or dinner or when they assembled afterward in a parlor, were always boisterous, noisy affairs. There was laughter and discourse and jests, just as there'd been immediately following Faith's wedding. And she wanted that again with her husband.

Tears pricked her lashes, and she blinked them back angrily. "You are not a weeper, Faith Brookfield," she said firmly.

Only she was a Brookfield no longer.

"DuMond," Faith murmured, testing the name on her lips. His name and now hers. "Faith DuMond."

It fit. It sounded right.

Even if it wasn't right. Even if *they* weren't right.

For there could be no doubting there was nothing healthy about this start to her marriage.

She tightened her mouth.

Well, she wasn't alone.

She lived in a blasted gaming hell, bloody brimming with people.

Setting her fork down hard, Faith shoved back her seat. The legs of the ebonized open armchair scratched loudly upon the floor, and coming to her feet, Faith marched across the room, tugged the door open and—

She froze.

"You," she blurted.

The big burly man smiled. "You again too. Though sporting a new name, you are." And then, as if remembering himself, he bowed. "*Mrs.* DuMond."

"Mr. Tavish," she exclaimed. For drat if there wasn't something comforting in seeing anyone familiar. Even if that someone was, in fact the man who'd rescued her and her friends when they'd been abducted and then brought here. That day had upended her world in every way and put Faith on the path to this very moment in her lonely, miserable marriage. "It is so very good to see you again, good sir."

He preened like she'd handed him a dozen stars.

"Felicitations are in order, I understand." He touched his brow. "Felicitations, Mrs. DuMond."

She was a bride, married to a man who'd rather handle his club's business than join her.

Felicitations, indeed.

The big guard drew his shoulders up and tugged at his lapels. "One might even call me a matchmaker."

And Faith managed her first smile since the game of charades on her wedding day. "You would set any London mama to shame."

If possible, he grew several inches under that praise.

"It appears you've got me under lock and key again, Mr. Tavish."

Tavish's face dropped. "I'm no captor." He smiled again. "Not this time, anyway. Mr. DuMond assigned me to stay close to you and make sure you're safe while he sees to business."

A memory slipped forward of the day he'd made her that promise.

"I can promise that if you marry me, I will take care of you. You'll have the protection of my power."

Warmth filled her breast. He'd vowed to look after her, and that was precisely what—

He'd had another man do.

I am pathetic. The only reason he has one of his men looking after me is because he can't be bothered to see to the onerous task himself.

He'd no intention of joining her.

Should she be surprised, though? He'd been clear that the only reason he'd pursued her had been because of the secrets she harbored about his club.

"Will you join me for the evening meal."

He flushed. "Can't step in your chambers, Mrs. DuMond. That wouldn't be appropriate. I take my meals with the rest of the men. In the kitchens, anyway."

She straightened. "Now?"

And so it was, Faith found herself in the kitchens a short while later greeted by the aroma of fresh baked bread blended with the smells of cooked onions, bacon, and garlic. She took in the jovial scene, identifying the Duke of Argyll and another gentleman Faith recognized from *ton* events and her wedding as Lord Malden. Rex wasn't among the some dozen or so big, broad men who sat around an enormous oak table, each vying to make himself heard over the person beside him. At the end of the bench, with a cut crystal glass in his hand, the Duke of Argyll gestured as he spoke.

Whatever he'd said earned a hearty round of laughter from all.

The din in the cheerful kitchen rivaled the noisiest, merriest, of her family's affairs.

Faith smiled. For suddenly, she didn't feel so very alone, at all.

The feeling lasted but a moment.

"Ahem," Mr. Tavish said loudly. When that failed to penetrate the clamor, he repeated; "I said *ahhhhem.*"

A heavily scarred fellow next to Lord Malden caught a glimpse of Tavish, and then the stranger's gaze landed on Faith. He nudged the gentleman beside him.

The marquess whipped his head upright.

Then a dozen or so men looked her way.

The merry din came to a screeching halt, leaving only a resounding echo of an awkward silence.

Faith cleared her throat. "May I join you?"

She may as well have demanded they name her a fifth partner of the gaming hell for the walleyed way they looked at her.

Argyll surged to his feet first with each other man standing, one behind the other, like moles popping up from the earth. As Faith made her way to the table, more of that godawful silence met her.

A serving boy rushed over with a wood chair and plopped it down at the end of the table between the duke and another familiar face. And even as that face proved familiar because he'd been the other guard at Forbidden Pleasures to bring her and her friends here all those weeks ago, a swell of relief at seeing anyone who wasn't a stranger built within her.

"Hullo. You're the friend of Mr. Red's," she greeted him, as she took her seat. "We meet again."

Beaming, he dropped a bow. "Fancy meeting again, and with you the mistress of the club no-*oww*," The fellow scowled at Lord Malden. "What was that for?"

Only silence and a glare from the tall, wiry fellow who'd shoved his elbow less than discreetly into Tavish's arm met that query.

A serving girl placed a bowl of white soup down before Faith, along with a spoon and a plate containing a hunk of bread. The clank of the silver spoons striking porcelain proved inordinately loud.

Faith resisted the urge to sigh, and picking up the flaky bread, she tore a piece from the corner, dunked it in the soup, and took a bite.

All the while no one said anything.

The men just slurped.

Silence and slurps. It appeared to be what was on the menu for the evening meal.

As she popped a piece of bread into her mouth, Faith stole a sideways glance at Rex's partner on her right—the duke. Even the affable, glib rogue had found himself with a sudden, inordinate interest in the hunks of chicken within his creamy soup.

Faith swallowed and exchanging the bread for a napkin left by another servant, she dabbed at the corner of her lips.

"A long, long time ago," she began, and every set of eyes swung her way. "Emperor Augustus launched a tour of his realm. One day, he came across a man with whom he bore a striking resemblance. The emperor? He was intrigued. He searched his mind desperately for how he recalled him. Unable to place just how he knew him, Augustus asked: 'Did your mother, perchance, once serve at the palace?' The man did not hesitate: 'No, Your Highness.'" Faith paused. "'But my father did.'"

There came a pause, and then the table erupted into loud, bellowing guffaws of hilarity.

With a grin, Faith ripped off another bite of bread, this time with her teeth, earning another round of laughter.

And with that, the table resumed its prior, easy course.

The Duke of Argyll dropped his elbows on the table, framing his nearly empty bowl of soup. "Brava, my lady."

"Yes, well, every lady has her talents." She winked, pulling another laugh from Rex's partner.

He leaned close, and that slight movement sent a golden curl tumbling across his brow. And it occurred to her. He was a very handsome man, and sitting here bantering with him should have vanquished all thoughts of the husband who didn't wish to be with her. Alas, it didn't.

"Some more than others," he murmured.

Faith snorted. "Are you complimenting me, Your Grace?"

"If you cannot tell, I fear I'm doing a deuced bad job of it."

"Yes. We've already deduced seduction is not your strong suit."

He flushed. "I'm not trying to seduce DuMond's bride."

"As in me?" Faith set her features in a grave mask. "Not this time, perhaps."

His color deepened, and he opened his mouth to say something but must have at last noted the teasing glimmer in her eyes. The tension left his broad shoulders, and a lazy grin formed on his lips. "I've not improved, then?"

"Since three days ago?" She shook her head. "I'm afraid it will take a good deal more than that."

Argyll laughed. Faith joined in and it felt so good to not feel sad, if even for just a moment.

Feeling eyes upon her, she looked for the source of that focus.

The Marquess of Malden eyed her and the duke with a disapproving look. He swiftly averted his attention, directing it to the fellow at his right.

Given the scandals in her family's history, Faith's path had rarely caused with the illustrious marquess before now. He'd been one of only three guests who'd joined Rex at their wedding, and she wondered at that relationship.

"How do my husband and Lord Malden know one another?" she asked curiously.

"Malden? He is a partner."

Faith started. She'd not even known there'd been another. It just highlighted one more way in which she didn't know anything about her husband—not his business, nor him, the man. "Malden?" she repeated.

He nodded.

And as the duke proved more willing to share those details than Rex, Faith sought out all she could about the man she married and his business. "Lord Malden hardly strikes me as one who'd pursue business dealings, let alone a venture of such a scandalous nature."

Argyll waggled his blond brows. "Unlike me?"

She grinned. "Precisely." Her smile dipped and picking up her spoon, she distractedly stirred a circle in the white broth. *And my husband.*

"Yes," Argyll said, confirming she'd spoken those thoughts aloud. "Malden, on the other hand, is equally committed to his current title and his future one," he explained, picking up a glass of claret, he took a sip. "Although it is well-known he's a part owner of the hell, neither is it something he speaks of, and enough people fear his father. They also know better than to discuss that aspect of his life."

Her meal forgotten, Faith dragged her kitchen chair closer to the duke. "If he's ashamed of his investment, then why be part of it?"

Cradling his glass between his fingers, he gave a shrug of his broad shoulders. "Because of DuMond, of course."

She stole a glance down at the meticulous gentleman seated at the center of the table. His chestnut hair perfectly groomed without so much as a strand out of place, his white silk cravat immaculately folded, he may as well have been the righteous angel to Rex's iniquitous one. "They seem so…"

"Different?" he supplied for her. "They are."

How had such a friendship or partnership ever been formed then?

"The two met at Eton," Argyll expounded. "Malden' and DuMond's fathers were both miserable bast—men," he hastily corrected himself.

Though the former certainly suited the heartless monster who'd confronted Faith and hurt Rex on his wedding day.

"DuMond was bigger than most boys. Malden was the smallest of almost all the students. Quiet. Stammered when he was nervous. And people were unkind to him, for it."

Faith took in the tall, heavily muscled gentleman silently eating his soup. Some three or so inches past six feet, it was hard to imagine he'd ever been the frail child the duke spoke of now.

"DuMond came upon several of the older boys who had Malden on his knees between them and his face in a chamber pot."

Her heart seized at that level of cruelty. "How terrible," she whispered.

"Rex beat them both handily, concluding that fight by shoving each of their faces in that same pot and vowing to do worse if they ever so much as looked at Malden again. From that moment on, a friendship was born, and Malden's loyalty earned." The duke took another drink, and after he'd set it down, collected his spoon. "Malden would walk through hell for Rex."

While he ate, Faith considered that long-ago memory of her husband.

Since she'd discovered all the lies surrounding Rex's interest in her, in her mind, she'd come to see the man she married as only ruthless and incapable of warmth or kindness, and yet everything the duke had shared flew in the face of that assumption. As did the side she'd seen of him with her family.

The duke had painted an altogether different portrait, one of a boy who'd challenged cruelty and championed another child so desperately in need of that grace. Even as a part of her mind mocked her as trying to find good where there was not, she couldn't neglect the other truths to be gleaned from the story the duke had shared. Rex hadn't just saved the other marquess, he'd become a friend for life.

Mr. Red shouted from the opposite end of the table; cutting into her musings. "You got any others jokes, Mrs. DuMond?"

Lord Malden glared at the guard. "She is a marchioness. She—"

Faith waved off the gentleman's scolding. "I have a good many of them more, Mr. Red," she called over.

The other diners proceeded to pound the table with their forks in a rolling wave of clattering metal that grew and grew.

At her side, the duke motioned to the table, signaling the audience was hers.

"All right, I'll share another," she shouted to be heard over the clamor.

Faith waited until the approving hollers died down, and she had their full attention.

"How do you entertain a bored pharaoh?" she asked the room at large.

The men throughout the table either shook their heads or called out. "How?"

Faith flashed a mischievous smile. "Why, you sail a boatload of young women dressed only in fishing nets down the Nile and urge the pharaoh to go catch a fish."

Silence.

More of it.

Thick and heavy and tense.

She frowned. It had been going so well. "And here I thought that one was a good deal funnier than my earlier one," she said. Alas, not a single man present spoke, laughed, or so much as looked her way. Rather, they each had their gazes trained behind her.

Faith followed their stares and froze.

The buttons of his midnight black jacket unfastened and his waistcoat hanging open, Rex stood there with a day's growth upon his cheeks and his black hair wet and drawn back as if he'd just climbed from a tub and hastily dressed.

Her husband passed a narrow-eyed gaze upon the previously merry diners.

And she hated that her heart should race so at the mere sight of him, even as he should remain so oblivious to her that he would abandon her on their wedding day and go see to his usual gaming hell business.

As one, his men came to their feet and filed past him, servants and serving girls following, until only Faith and Rex remained.

Faith stood and tipped her chin up. "Mr. DuMond," she said stiffly. "It appears you are one to clear a room."

He folded his arms and leaned against the now-closed the door. "And it appears you are one to be the center of it, Mrs. DuMond," he said, in cool tones she could make nothing out of.

Mrs. DuMond.

Again, her heart did a funny little leap. She was his wife. And he, her husband.

That also served to remind her that they'd spent the better part of their first day as Mr. and Mrs. DuMond apart, and not for the first time that day, Faith fought the urge to cry.

Rex had intended to go about his club's business as usual. After all, there was nothing more important than Forbidden Pleasures. As such, he'd returned with Faith in tow, turned her over to the head housekeeper, and headed to the gaming hell floors.

Only, as he'd assessed the crowded tables and the latest drunken guests tossing away their fortunes, he'd not been able to think about business expenses and profits or the patrons seeking their credit extended or the markers he needed to call in.

Instead, his mind had been lost on thoughts of Faith.

Faith, the cherished, beloved daughter, sister, and niece of the Brookfield family, who'd left behind their loving folds for a new life, one with him and inside a scandalous gaming hell. He'd been so hell-bent on possessing her that he'd not stopped to think about what that would mean for her because bloody hell, he didn't think about other people's desires and interests before his own.

The moment he'd left her in the care of his housekeeper he'd headed out to Willenhall. Because Faith had deserved something from him, some sign that he cared about her, as much as a beast like him was capable of the emotion.

He'd ridden like hell, trading out tired mount after tired mount at the stations he'd horses kept at from here to West Midlands. After he'd seen to business, he'd returned at the same breakneck speed, stinking of horseflesh and sweat. He'd taken a break only long enough to bathe the stench from his person before setting out to find her.

He'd expected to find her alone in her rooms, sad, and sulking. He'd imagined her teary-eyed at being away from her family for the first time, and thrust into this new, foreign, and wicked world. The thought of her miserable in that way had left him miserable in ways he'd never before felt, and certainly in ways that he didn't understand and in ways that he liked even less.

Only she'd been none of those things. Her cheeks had been flushed with happiness, a smile had wreathed her cheeks, and that joy had nothing to do with Rex but rather to do with the company of a dozen or so other men she kept company with. And a visceral rage pulsed within him.

She'd been so easily conversing with his partners and the staff of Forbidden Pleasures. She'd been telling jokes. And yet, for him, she'd only greet him with stiff silence.

He winged a black brow up and broke that impasse. "So then, are we to be the polite couple who refer to one another by my surname, *Mrs.* DuMond?"

"When we're cross," she said testily.

He stared at her.

"I intend to refer to you by our surname, because it is mine now, too."—God, she was breathtaking.—"When I'm cross."

Rex pushed away from the door and strolled towards her. "You're cross with me."

"How did you know?"

"Because you said—"

"I was being sarcastic, Rex."

His lips twitched. "Don't you mean, Mr. DuMond?"

Faith gritted her teeth loud enough for him to hear them clank together. "You are insufferable."

"What are you doing in the kitchens, Faith?"

"Where should I be on my second day as a married woman? Locked up inside the rooms of a home you couldn't even bother to have shown me?"

She'd call a gaming hell a home? If ever there'd been a woman for him, she was the one.

In retrospect, he could certainly see how she must have surely felt when he'd left.

Rex reached inside his jacket, withdrew a gold chain, and held the gift out.

Faith stilled and then took that necklace, fingering the elaborate key at the end.

He should have wrapped it. But he'd been so consumed by the need to see her.

She lifted confused eyes to his. "What is this?"

"A key," he said. When she only continued to stare at him, he clarified, because she didn't understand. Once she did, his departure would make sense. And…more. The things he couldn't say because he didn't know how…because he didn't understand. "After our wedding night, I journeyed to Willenhall and saw Mr. Jeremiah Chubb of Chubb Locks. Chubb is responsible for all the locks and keys within my club."

"You went to your locksmith?"

She didn't understand.

Rex tried again. "Not just any locksmith. The best, perhaps, in the world. That key is yours, Faith," he said quietly. "It will open both my offices and the compartments within my desk." All that he held dear dwelled in that room.

Her gaze went to the key, and then back to Rex. "The lock I already picked?"

Precisely. That was why he'd been so captivated by her the first time he'd discovered her hiding under his desk. "No one can pick a Chubb lock, Faith."

Her endearingly freckled nose scrunched up in abject

puzzlement. "I did."

"Exactly."

"So why do I need a key?" she asked hesitantly as if she hated to ask because she feared offending him, but who had done so because the need to know had won out.

Of course, she'd not understand the significance of that offering. He'd never let anyone into either his office or his life this way. The innocent lady whom her younger brother had shared her likes and dislikes with wouldn't see the world in the same way as Rex had. "I just thought you should have it," he said weakly.

Faith fiddled with the chain for several long moments. "Do you know what I did these past two days?"

He shook his head. Since he'd ridden off, leaving her behind, he'd wondered just that and only that. He'd sooner gnaw his own hand off than admit as much.

"I sat by myself in my rooms and then a servant brought me trays for each of my meals."

Befuddled, he stared at her. "And you had a problem with them?"

"I did."

"Indeed?" Her brother had assured Rex that Faith preferred fowl for her main course.

She set her jaw. "Because I was alone. And so, you asked what I am doing here." She pointed a finger at the kitchen floor, and the gleaming key hung forlornly down from the chain Faith still held. "I *was* eating, but you scared everyone away."

He smirked. "I have that effect on people."

"I can't imagine why," she muttered.

Another smile pulled at his lips.

Exasperated, Faith stuffed the key inside a clever pocket sewn along the front of her gown. "I'll have you know, you are the only man, the absolute single one in the whole world, who'd be happy and proud about being able to drive people away, *Mr. DuMond.*"

"Being able to run people off does serve its purposes," he murmured, and then slipped an arm around her. "Especially now."

"O-Oh." That long syllable emerged quavering and breathless.

"Oh," he echoed, filling his hands with her buttocks and bringing her body flush to his, so that she could feel the hard ridge of his shaft against her belly. Rex touched his lips to her shoulder, and Faith drew in a shaky breath, reflexively tipping her head to allow him access. He continued his quest, dropping a kiss upon each swath of skin he exposed. "You pick locks." He kissed the hollow of her throat. "You tell lewd jokes." He touched his lips to the sensitive spot where her pulse now pounded. Slowly, Rex pushed her puff sleeves down, exposing her skin to the night air, and then with his mouth, he caressed that part of her he'd bared to his eyes. "You like naughty talk. What other wonderful secrets do you hide, dear wife?"

"Mayhap if you were around, you'd find out."

He kissed the hollow of her throat. "I'm here now." And damned glad for it.

Faith's eyes slid shut. "You know, m–most men w–would not find such behaviors favorable in their wives."

"You've not figured out already, Faith? I'm not most men." He placed a kiss at the point where her neck met her shoulder. "So, you wanted a tour of your new *home*," he said, placing an extra, mocking emphasis on that word.

"I would." She edged her chin up a notch. "That is, unless, you'd otherwise send the Duke of Argyll in your stead."

Touché, and yet… He froze, his lips pressed against her neck. Her words sent a visceral response through him, her taunt a reminder that Argyll had attempted—and failed—to seduce her. It was the reason Rex even now found himself married to her. That thought should grate; the last thing he'd wanted or ever intended was to marry. And yet in this moment, he no longer denied himself the truth. He wanted this fiery-spirited minx staring back with a boldness only an innocent could manage, and he found himself eager.

It is just sexual, a voice reminded. That was the purest emotion. The only true emotion. Why did it feel as though he lied to himself?

"You don't know what you are saying, Faith. This isn't your usual Mayfair townhouse. This isn't some pretty theatre. You don't want to see what really happens in this place, Faith," he murmured and cupped her neck to take her mouth as he longed, but she shifted her head, and then ducked out of his arms.

"Oh, but I do." Her chest still heaved with the force of her passion, and her eyes still bore the glazed sheen of desire.

Frustration at being denied that which he really wanted gripped him. "I will gladly show you, myself, *petite chouette*." Then sweeping his arm forward, he motioned for Faith to move.

She hesitated a moment.

But he already knew. She'd go. She couldn't help herself. She was afraid and yet, not unlike him, she wasn't one to lose a challenge.

Rex guided her from the kitchens and led her down the dark labyrinth of candlelit halls and corridors. The glow of the ornate gilded sconce candles sent shadows dancing upon the bloodred silk wallpaper and matching red carpets. That carnal shade of sin a tantalizing juxtaposition against the white silk worn by his innocent wife.

Rex led her inside a generous bedroom, motioning for her to enter, daring her with his gaze to do so.

She didn't even hesitate, as bold as brass and spirited as Zenobia, she merely swept inside, and *then* stopped.

The chambers would have given *anyone* pause. An enormous bed rested against the right wall and jutted out into the middle of the floor; the red silk bedding put a person in mind of a sacrificial slab. Manacles and whips of varying sizes and textures hung within a case on the left side of the enormous four-poster bed. Black satin restraints hung from the ornate, gilded headboard.

"Second thoughts, Faith?" he whispered. "Would you like to turn back?"

This time, she did pause and then shook her head.

And he was the depraved beast the world proclaimed him to be for the rush of lust and relief that declination wrought.

Rex closed the door and with slow, deliberate steps headed over to the gold satin curtains. Never taking his gaze from Faith, he stopped before that covered window and motioned to the fastenings. "Look, *petite chouette*," he murmured. "Unless you're afraid?"

She hesitated a moment more, a long moment, and he expected her to ignore his dare. But then she came forward and drew the fabric back and revealed the tableau unfolding in that other room.

Faith inhaled noisily; her words emerged breathless. "What are they doing?"

Was she really this innocent? Somehow her question, that realization, only fueled his desire.

He placed his lips near her ear. "They're making love," he whispered, and close as he was, he felt the little shudder that moved through her.

The gentleman bent the voluptuous woman over so that her pendulous breasts hung over the side of that table and her buttocks were tilted up, a lush offering for him. Then he sank his fingertips into her hips the way Rex so loved gripping Faith.

His own breathing grew labored, shallower, and he recalled the taste and scent of her.

The masked fellow on the other side of that window plunged himself high inside his partner. The woman released a long, high-pitched scream, her entire body convulsing.

In the glass panel, he caught the way Faith bit her lower lip, troubling that plump flesh, and he ached to cover her mouth with his. "Is he hurting her?"

"Does it look like she is hurt?" he countered, as the woman pushed herself back against the man fucking her, meeting his determined thrusts.

"I...I'm not sure."

As Faith stared with a directness that belied her innocence, Rex whispered against her ear. "It is a different kind of pain. The most wondrous agony, a little death, like you experienced when you came in my mouth."

And he watched that couple with her. The man withdrew his long rod and his partner writhed, angling her head back and pleading with him. Her lover, however, merely teased her hunger, granting each inch by inch, slowly, until the lush beauty was incoherent with her need.

Scoundrel that Rex was, he didn't seek to deny himself that which he truly wanted in this moment—the woman before him.

Rex touched his lips to Faith's neck, and she angled her head, allowing him better access to her. "Do you see how he teases her," he breathed, nipping her lightly. "Do you see how she wants him?"

In the reflection of the double mirror, he caught the way Faith again bit her lower lip, and he shifted her slightly, enough so that they could both see the trysting couple, but also faced so he could take her lips as he hungered to.

"Would you like to be watched, Faith?"

"No," she said quickly. Too quickly.

Voyeurism was as common as rain in England. And yet, the idea of another man watching Faith as she reached her pleasure... He growled and yanked the curtains closed, wanting no one in this moment with him and Faith.

Sinking to his knees, he shoved Faith's skirts up. "Open for me," he ordered, needlessly; she'd already sagged against the curtain-covered window and parted her thighs for him.

Holding her skirts up with his left hand, he searched his other up the expanse of creamy white flesh exposed to him. "So beautiful," he breathed, kissing a path up her leg until he reached that place between her legs. She was drenched, her dark curls already damp with her want. He placed his lips there, close.

Faith's limbs trembled.

"Do you want my kiss again, Faith?" he whispered, teasing her opening with a finger.

She moaned and shifted her hips.

"Ah, ah. You must say the words. I'd have you *tell* me you want this." She did. He already knew. The musky scent of her desire flooded his nostrils.

"I want th–this," she said, her voice throaty, her voice breaking.

"Very good, *petite chouette*." With that, he rewarded her response with the kiss she craved.

Rex tasted of her in the way he'd longed to since the last time he'd had her this way, in a way he'd thought to never again to know. He'd thought that one time with her would be enough. He'd been wrong. He'd never tire of her. He slid his tongue within her folds, stroking her, until Faith's speech dissolved to nothing more than a quiet, desperate keening.

"Rex," she begged, tangling her fingers in his hair and holding him at that place where she wanted him most.

Fueled by the evidence of her longing and the freedom with which she gave herself over to her body's yearning, Rex deepened his ministrations, laving her. Licking her. Nipping lightly at her bud.

Faith's thrusting grew jerky. Urgent. Her body stiffened.

And then he stopped.

"No," she cried, her entire frame buckling as she spasmed at the release he'd denied her.

He swept her up and carried her to the bed, depositing her upon the center of the mattress. With her kneeling there, he came behind her and set to work undoing the many pearl fastenings down the back of her gown. The dress she'd worn the day he'd made her his in name. Now, he'd possess her in every other way. He pushed the fine article below her waist and then helped free her of that lace trimmed gown. Next, he removed her chemise until she was bare of all but her silk stockings.

He passed a heated gaze over her naked frame, taking in her nipped waist, wide hips, and rose-tipped breasts. A bolt of lust shot through him. With her cream-white skin draped upon that blood red fabric she was that supple apple from which to sin.

"Lie down, *petite chouette*," he commanded, guiding her back. Then lifting her arms, he reached for the satin ties.

Faith's lashes fluttered, and she followed his movements. "Wh-what are you doing?"

"Do you trust me?"

She nodded. She didn't even hesitate. She should. But she hadn't. She merely entrusted herself to him, and the evidence of her faith enflamed him.

Rex fastened her arms on either side of her head so that she was bound before him, a sprawled, carnal offering; his for the taking.

Her chest heaved.

Shrugging out of his jacket, he tossed it aside, and then, with her gaze upon him, he slowly discarded his shirt and trousers, adding them to the pile of the garments behind them so that he was naked.

Faith's throat moved wildly, and her big eyes grew bigger as she dipped her gaze to his enormous erection.

She dampened her plump mouth, still swollen from his earlier kiss. "I…that," a blush filled her cheeks, "is entirely too big for this to work." She tugged at her restraints.

Rex chuckled. "Oh, it will work, love," he said huskily, running a hand along her sleek thigh, lingering on her hip. "Your body was made for this." Made for him. "Do you want me to untie you?" He palmed the thatch of black curls between her legs. "Say the word and I will stop."

She moaned and splayed her thighs in complete surrender. "Noooo."

Toying with her center, Rex leaned forward and captured the pebbled tip of one breast between his lips, suckling deep. With his other hand, he tweaked her other previously neglected peak.

Faith arched her hips, pushing herself against his touch, writhing in a bid to bring her body closer.

He periodically ceased caressing her channel and then resumed stroking her in a game he knew would drive her to the brink of madness. He used his fingers inside her to stretch her channel, to prepare her for him.

Faith bucked and twisted, writhing against the silken bonds. "Please," she begged, panting. "I need to feel you."

Rex paused long enough to release the knots he'd made around her delicate wrists, and she gasped the moment she'd been freed and wrapped her arms about him, clinging tightly.

Rex devoured her mouth. He plundered it delving his tongue inside to tangle with hers, tasting the sweet hint of claret upon her. Wedging a knee between her soft, silken thighs, he parted her and rested the tip of his shaft against her entrance.

Sweat beaded his brow.

Fuck, he wanted her, wanted her with the same impatience he'd shown as a youth, but this, this was a need far greater and inexplicable, for he was a man in full control of everything. Only, in this instant, with this woman, the innocent lady he'd taken as his wife, he didn't feel very much in control of anything.

He moved himself slowly inside her tight, hot, sodden channel. Rex groaned. his body screaming to surge forward and plunge into her over and over again as he longed to do. But he made himself go slow; exercised an even greater restraint than he'd known he possessed. He didn't want to tear into her like his cock demanded.

Faith moaned, and he paused, searching his gaze over her features, tensed not in agony but on that point of pleasure very near to pain. Her chest heaved from the force of her breathing, and he leaned forward, taking a nipple into his mouth.

Faith cried out. Folding her arms around him, she sank her nails into his back. "Rex," she pleaded.

"Tell me what you want," he ordered harshly, sliding in another fraction, giving her only an inch of what she yearned for.

She moaned. "I don't know."

"You do." He retreated, slowly withdrawing, and she cried out.

"Please," she rasped, sinking her fingers into his shoulders, and anchoring him close. "I want to feel what I felt before."

He rewarded her obedience by gliding his length forward and then stopped.

She whimpered, tipping her hips up to take what he denied, but he withdrew, denying her both that which she sought and control. Her frustrated cries echoed through the room and their echo pealed in his mind.

"Say it, Faith," he commanded, rocking gently. "I want to hear you share it all."

Faith's lashes fluttered open, and her eyes, glazed with unrestrained passion, met his. "I want to feel that same feeling when you kissed me."

"Where did I kiss you?" he asked sharply.

"Between my legs," she cried out, and he rewarded that honesty with that which she craved.

"You want my cock in your cunny, making you come. You want to come, Faith. Say it."

"I want to come."

"Good girl," he praised, sliding another inch inside of her.

A low moan spilled from her lips, and she clenched her eyes tightly. "Please, Rex."

Ending the game he played with her, Rex gave her what she wanted most. He plunged slow and deep; her cry melded with his groan. Never had he felt a channel such as hers.

All he wanted was to grab her hips and leverage himself inside of her, over and over again, but he forced himself to stop. "Do you need me to stop?"

That would be the act in his miserable existence that ultimately did him in.

She shook her head frantically and several damp curls fell over her brow. "I'd die if you did."

That made two of them.

Rex brushed those loose strands behind her ear, feeling her eyes upon him as he did. He began to move. Slowly at first, giving her virginal channel an opportunity to grow accustomed to his size and length. Then as she began to keen softly and jerk her hips impatiently, he increased his movements.

She lifted to meet each thrust, their bodies moving in perfect tandem.

"You are so wet." He rasped those words of praise. Soaked as she was for him, it was a smooth glide. Never in his life had it been like this, as it was with this woman. Afterward, he'd worry about that. For now, all he wanted was to lose himself within her.

"Ohh," she panted. Her slender body grew more and more tense in his arms, signaling she was close to surrender.

Rex took the tip of her right breast in his mouth, suckled deep, and rocked.

Her body began to shake, signaling her surrender was close and he lunged deep once more.

Faith came on a piercing scream, writhing and twisting and pushing her hips to meet his.

Rex continued thrusting until she collapsed on a gasp, replete, her body sated. He denied himself that same surrender, wanting to prolong the moment. It was so good with her. She was so good. He gritted his teeth and continued to fuck her. Slow. And then harder. Faster.

Until it was too much.

With a guttural groan, he stiffened and came in long, rippling waves within her, blinded by a bliss so bright, it shoved out all thought and left in its place only the feel of Faith, and the sensation of being buried deep within her.

He gasped and then collapsed over her. It was a moment before his breath slowed and his heart ceased pounding. As it did, and Rex came slowly back to earth, he stared at Faith, her eyes closed, her smile dreamy, her features soft. Had there ever been anyone like her before?

And yet, he knew the answer to that. He knew there was no one like Faith Brookfield. Whether he liked it or not, for better or worse, he was completely and thoroughly besotted by his wife.

CHAPTER 23

AFTER THE FORBIDDEN EXCHANGE SHE'D had with Rex in a library in her aunt and uncle's house, Faith had been so very certain she'd never feel anything more magnificent, more splendorous than the glorious feel of his mouth upon her, as she'd found pleasure for the first time.

She'd been wrong.

And this time she'd been wrong in the worst ways.

For last night in Rex's arms had been pure magic. He'd been a sorcerer weaving a spell, one whose hold she'd be forever under. After he'd made love to her in that scandalous bedroom, he'd tenderly cleaned that sensitive place between her legs, scooped her up, and carried her through a maze of hidden corridors to her rooms, where he'd then proceeded to make love to her again.

All night.

He'd made her body sing over and over, and then as exhaustion had won out, she'd fallen asleep, curled against him, his arms wrapped about her, enveloping her in such warmth.

Only to wake up...cold. Finding nothing more than the indentation made upon the silk sheets where he'd lain beside her. Smiling like the cats in the kitchen did when Cook presented them with a bowl of cream, Faith stretched. With a giddy laugh, she rolled onto the place where Rex had lain.

Hopping out of bed, she winced at the twinge between her legs from all the times she'd made love with Rex. Not finding him in the connecting sitting room either, Faith did manage to locate her maid and a tray of food.

A short while later, after she'd bathed and dressed, Faith went in search of her husband.

"Husband," she murmured aloud, as she used the same hidden halls Rex had carried her the evening prior. He was her husband. She grinned again.

Faith managed to find her way to the hall leading to Rex's offices. Only her path forward was blocked by a mountain of a man.

The uniformed guard had to be nearly seven feet tall. His muscles strained the fabric of his trousers and jacket, a jacket pulled even more taut with the way he'd clasped his arms behind him.

"Wot ye want?" he asked in a thick, nearly indecipherable Cockney.

The man might be bigger than most small trees, but by damn, she refused to be treated as a stranger in her own home. "My name is Mrs. DuMond," she said coolly.

His implacable, sun-bronzed features conveyed none of the respect her rank in this household commanded.

"And I don't answer to anyone,...?" She placed a question at the end of her words.

He grunted, reluctantly handing over his identifier. "Gruffton."

Yes, well that suited him.

"I don't answer to anyone, Mr. Gruffton. Now, if you will allow me to pass?"

A greenish-blue vein pulsed at his temple.

"Ye need 'elp with anything?" he muttered, as if it had pained him to be polite in even the smallest way.

"I do not, Mr. Gruffton," she said, appreciating the effort he clearly made.

"Oi can get ye a maid? Or—"

"I don't require anything, at all." She paused. "Except to pass."

For a moment, she expected he'd deny her request that wasn't a request, but then reluctantly, he stepped out of the way.

She hastened on, eager to see Rex.

Faith caught the door handle and attempted to open it.

Locked.

Furrowing her brow, she stared at the locked panel a moment

more, then, raising her hand, made to knock, but stopped.

Faith smiled.

Removing the chain from around her neck, that gift given her by her husband now making so very much sense, Faith inserted it into the lock and let herself inside.

"Now I understand the reason for the k—Oh," she blurted, that droll greeting for her husband dying as she faced not Rex but rather another man.

Standing near Rex's immaculate desk, the Marquess of Malden stared at Faith with an opaque gaze. "What are you doing in here?" he demanded, and the ice in that question briefly froze her.

First Gruffton and now Rex's childhood friend. Only the marquess's challenge proved far different from the surly guard's. Malden looked at her and spoke to her with an almost icy disdain.

Finding her voice, Faith entered her husband's offices. "I intended to ask you that same question, Lord Malden."

He tightened his mouth. "I'll remind you I am a partner here. You, on the other hand, are a woman hellbent on destroying everything your husband built."

She winced. The marquess knew she'd shared secrets about their patrons with the world. No wonder he loathed her.

The suspicion in his gaze deepened, and he looked over her shoulder. "Where is your guard?"

Her guard. Because as kind as Red had been and was, the real reason he'd been assigned her had been not for protection but to monitor her movements. "That is not your business, my lord," she said, matching him ice for ice.

"Isn't it?" he asked coolly. "Do you truly believe it's not in my interest to know why you're skulking about your husband's offices?"

He was not wrong for the fury he felt, and he was also a friend who mattered very much to her husband. Because of that, Faith reigned in her annoyance and attempted to start again with the surly marquess. "My husband understands my reasons for—"

"Attempting and nearly succeeding in destroying the one thing he actually loves?"

She wrinkled her nose. "I was going to say doing what I did. I'll not, however, speak to you about what those reasons were."

Lord Malden quit his place behind Rex's desk and headed across the office.

Unnerved by his approach, Faith forced herself to remain still and confront whatever additional accusations he'd hurl.

"When DuMond purchased Forbidden Pleasures, it was a failing venture, in greater debt than most of the degenerate members of the peers combined. The carpets were frayed. The drinks watered down. The place was on the cusp of shuttering. I couldn't understand why he'd want to sink any funds into such an establishment."

"And yet, you became a partner," she remarked.

"Because I knew the manner of man DuMond was." He locked his gaze with hers. "He'd the devil's own luck, but he'd more than that. He'd an ability to come out first in everything he ever did at Eton and Oxford. I knew his success in transforming the nearly bankrupt venture was a certainty."

The marquess might resent her and be surly in his recounting of Rex, but he also offered a window into her guarded husband's life and for that Faith was grateful.

"How many noblemen—at that, a future duke—would commit themselves to a business venture that required them to do actual work?"

"Not very many," she allowed. And yet her husband had, and it spoke volumes about his character.

"Not very many," he concurred. "He loves this place in ways he will never love anything." He pinned another hard stare on her. "Or anyone."

Her heart twisted at that blunt and all-too-clear statement.

His blue irises seared her. "A word of advice, my lady. In the future, do not enter a single room in this establishment and call out me on my loyalty or my right to be here. I have far greater right than you ever will."

With that, he stared pointedly at her. Waiting for her leave. Urging her to get the hell out.

And she wanted to. Unable to meet that hate-filled stare, she directed her focus to the floor. Even as she'd shared Lord Somerville's and Lord Bourchier's information with the world, she'd done so for reasons that were good. They were each hateful, terrible men who would have brought misery to whatever poor woman they wed. Yet none of that negated the fact that she'd risked something Rex cared very much about. Nay, something he loved.

Faith made herself lift her gaze and look at Rex's friend, once more. "You are neither wrong in your charges against me nor in the reason for your upset. But my husband," she placed a deliberate emphasis upon that word. "He trusts me."

The steely marquess looked her up and down. "He doesn't trust you, my lady," he said coolly. "If that was the case, he wouldn't have married you."

His words ran her through more effectively than Sir Cheevers's ancient steel saber ever could have. For it was one more unnecessary but still agonizing reminder that the sole reason Rex had ever feigned an interest in her was to keep her quiet and protect his club. "Perhaps," she made herself say, her voice thin to her own ears. "But he did give me a key to his offices and desk."

Shock brought his chestnut eyebrows shooting up to his hairline.

"I expect he wouldn't have done so if he didn't trust me," she said.

The marquess's expression grew harder. "Are you very sure of that, my lady? Or do you think perhaps it's a test on DuMond's part?"

Faith touched the key her husband had given her, a peculiar gift he'd left on their wedding day to procure. Which made more sense, after all? That Rex's present had contained some deeply intimate meaning? Or that it had been something he'd handed over to gauge her loyalty?

Feeling the marquess's harsh eyes upon her, she made herself release that golden chain and let her hands fall to her side. "I understand you are a loyal friend of my husband's and that you clearly resent me for…for…things I've done."

"Things you've done to hurt him," he said flatly.

She'd not allowed herself to think of it precisely in those terms. She'd been so very fixed on the ways in which he'd hurt her, she'd failed to properly consider just how much her actions had hurt something so very dear to him. "But I do want to promise you, my lord...my husband? He has nothing to worry about where my loyalty is concerned," she said quietly. "You have my word on that."

"The word of a woman who sold the secrets of several gentlemen for a handful of coin, my lady?"

She bit her tongue so hard she tasted the metallic hint of blood. For she could go toe-to-toe with him in all the ways those *gentlemen* had been anything but, and had either ruined women, or would have brought heartache to others. "In time, I expect you will discover that I will never do anything to hurt my husband or his business." Not anymore.

His expression grew shuttered. "I certainly hope that is true for both of your sakes, Lady Rutherford," he said cryptically.

Faith found herself at an impasse, in the company of a man with whom she could speak until her face turned blue and she passed out cold from trying but who would never believe her. Only her future actions would prove the truth in the promises she made. "One thing, my lord," she made herself say.

He thinned his eyes.

"My name is Mrs. DuMond." If her husband didn't go by a title he hated, then she certainly didn't intend to, either.

With that, Faith let herself quietly from her husband's offices, and as she drew the door shut behind her, she felt the marquess's piercing gaze following her every movement.

She'd not allow him to steal her joy. She wanted so much more than a marriage of convenience. She wanted what her parents had, and what her aunts and uncles and Marcia did. She wanted a husband who was both a partner and friend. Someone who trusted her and laughed with her and who wanted her in his life. And she could have those things with Rex. She believed that now. A man who'd entrusted her the key to that which he valued and guarded most.

Faith arrived at her private suites...to a noisy commotion.

"Where in hell is she?" her husband's thunderous roar spilled from her rooms and billowed out into the corridor.

Red rang his big hands together. "I–I never saw her come out."

"Because I didn't," she called, and never more had anyone look as relieved to see her as Mr. Red did.

His entire face lit up at the mere sight of her, and he jabbed a finger her way.

"Found her, Mr. DuMond," he cried happily. "Found her I did."

She smiled at the older man, so very grateful that someone should look—

Her husband tore from her chambers, his expression dark and furious as she'd never before seen.

His ink black lashes swept low, and his eyes disappeared behind hard, impenetrable slits.

"Leave us," he growled.

Red hesitated a single moment, giving Faith a regretful look.

"Now," Rex snapped.

The guard instantly snapped to attention, dropped a bow, and beat a hasty retreat in the opposite direction.

There came the click of the doorway to the private apartment's doorway being closed and then Faith and Rex were alone.

"Rex! I'm so—"

"Where the hell were you?" he asked, his voice sharp.

She wrinkled her nose. Well, then. "Good morning. It is so very good to see you, too, dear husband."

Rex's chiseled cheeks grew mottled. "You still reside in a gaming hell, Faith. If you are to leave, you are to do so with a guard at all times."

What was this? She dropped her hands on her hips. "Given the gift you shared with me last evening, I'd expected I'd some freedom of movement in my new home. Now, you're indicating I'm a prisoner?"

"These areas are private but that doesn't mean you cannot stumble upon someone unsavory in a corridor. The guard is to ensure your safety." He spoke through gritted, perfectly even, pearl white teeth. "I protect what is mine."

"What is yours?"

Rex gave a tight nod. "Yes. You belong to me now."

Like a physical possession. Such as his club. Only as Lord Malden had pointed out, Forbidden Pleasures, Rex loved. How was it possible to so despise an inanimate object?

The earlier joy she'd felt when waking that morning popped

like a big soap bubble. "I belong to you?" she repeated.

Only a man with the boatloads of arrogance her husband possessed could so readily confirm that with another one of those infuriating nods.

"Let me be clear, Mr. DuMond, I don't belong to anyone." Faith took a furious step forward, finding comfort in her rage. It was safer, more comfortable, easier than the agony of an empty marriage to a man who, despite her better judgement and past hurts inflicted, she still cared about and yearned for. "And that includes you."

Rex stood opposite his wife, the barrier between her and her bedchambers—he and Faith, locked in battle.

He'd found himself in this same state nearly the whole of his life. He didn't bow to people. He battled them. It was a way that was familiar and comfortable, and yet…with this woman, with Faith, his wife, he didn't want to battle her.

She is here.

It was a mantra in his mind, a reminder he gave to himself, over and over.

When he'd returned that morning and entered her rooms to find her missing, and the guard he'd assigned to look after Faith singularly unaware of where she'd gone and how she'd gotten out and equally frantic, Rex had nearly gone mad.

Panic the likes of which he'd never before felt in the whole of his miserable existence had gripped him. The pure terror in discovering her gone wrapped about his brain still and leant his heart that same, quickening beat.

"Now, if you will excuse me, Mr. DuMond? I have plans."

He was again Mr. DuMond and she had plans, plans that didn't include him. Rex was hard-pressed to say which of those chafed more.

She gave him an impressively commanding look, urging him out of her path, and he proved as helpless as the team of warriors Joan of Arc had singlehandedly defeated. He stepped aside to let Faith pass, hating that he'd made her into this cold woman, aching to have things the way they'd been with her before. As they'd been last evening when he'd made love with her.

Faith started forward and he moved into her path once more.

"What n—"

"I was worried!" That confession ripped from his chest, and it was harder to say who was stunned by that admission.

Faith's lips parted and her big, owl eyes formed perfect circles.

Rex's neck heated, and he resisted the urge to snatch at his suddenly too tight cravat.

"I came back and found you gone and didn't know where you were." His voice grew raspy as he spoke. "You could come to great harm here." And it would destroy him. That realization terrified him out of his bloody mind, but there it was, and there it would forever be.

Her features softened. "You have guards at every corridor, Rex." She spoke his name gently. Not: *Mr. DuMond* because she was cross. "And I'm very capable of taking care of myself."

Rex dragged a shaky hand through his hair. "Not against men who are bigger, meaner, and evil in ways that you will never be, Faith."

He'd brought her to live in this hell, and yet, he'd failed to properly consider the implications of Faith, his innocent, trusting wife dwelling within a house of sin and evil.

Sending her away would ravage him. She was a siren, and he was beating himself against a rock every time she was near. "You don't belong here," he said, his voice oddly flat. Keeping her here with him, however, would only further destroy him.

"Yes," she drawled. "Well, I guess we are a little late for going back now."

"No." He held her stare. "I mean you should not be living here, Faith."

Confusion slowly clouded her eyes, and then understanding dawned within their clever depths "What are you saying exactly?" she ventured in hesitant tones he'd never before heard from her.

"Perhaps it is best if you live somewhere else." That separation would save both of them. Himself from this helpless descent into weakness, and Faith from potential harm at the club. He made himself speak before he could talk himself out of keeping her here.

"I've several properties."

"You are sending me away?" Her voice climbed.

"I have a townhouse in London. In fact, I have several. You can reside there, and I'll assign Red and Tavish to your security." She got on well with them. She'd like having the two big guards about. "It is in Grosvenor Square. It is perfectly respectable, and I will visit you there." The more he voiced that idea aloud, the more sense it made.

"Visit me there?" she echoed, incredulity ringing in her hurt tones.

Perhaps only to him.

He nodded. "Yes."

"Like a mistress."

Heat slapped his cheeks. Is that what she thought of him and how he viewed her? *But then, you've never given her much reason to think anything different.* "Like my wife whom I'm protecting."

"Like the wife you never wanted," she cried. The tinkling echo of her despair pealed around the halls.

She was right to her assumption, and he should let her continue to carry it.

Her hands on her hips, Faith swept over. "You speak about protecting me." Her lips curled in a sneer around that word. "But it's not that. If you were worried about my safety, you'd secure the private areas of your club. But that would be too much trouble, me being here in your precious club. It's really that you don't want me close." Tears filled her eyes, and those drops hit him harder than any physical blow had or ever could. "You don't want me at all. You were only worried about keeping me silent and maintaining your p-patrons' secrets."

Dumbly, Rex stepped aside, allowing her to leave the sitting room. Faith entered her rooms and closed the door behind her.

Click.

Rex stared blankly at the ivory French panels.

Go in there. Say something.

Only, he couldn't make himself make that move. He sank onto the floor, resting his back against the matching pair of doors opposite the room Faith just entered.

Yes, that was precisely what it had been—about silencing her while also assuaging the powerful hungering he had for her.

Now everything was all twisted, confused in his mind. Because he'd lied, and he'd believed that lie. He'd told himself he'd wanted to possess her. He'd convinced himself he'd lusted after Faith Brookdale and nothing more, only to find, he wanted her in every way. Her smile. Her laughter. Her naughty jokes. The tales of her past. Her dreams for the future.

Squeezing his eyes shut, Rex silently beat the back of his head against the door. He'd spent a lifetime feeling nothing. Having been separated as a boy from his mother and then enduring a wretched existence with a hate-filled duke for a father, it'd been all too easy to become the cynical, life-hardened man he'd become. There'd been no affectionate governesses or tutors or servants. His Grace's staff had known better than to gainsay their employer and treat Rex as something different than the heir to the dukedom he'd one day inherit. By the time he'd met Malden, his first friend, Rex had been as hollowed out as the other boy, beaten down by life.

And then he'd met Faith.

Rex opened his eyes, his gaze fixed on the curvy portion at the center of Faith's door panels.

If caring about someone other than himself and his own wants wrought this manner of misery, he wanted no bloody part of it, and yet it was too late. He'd fallen completely under his innocent wife's spell, and there was no going back.

Faith was breaking apart into a thousand million pieces.

Every step was a chore, every breath was a struggle. Even the beat of her heart protested its natural rhythm.

Silence hummed in the room, now awash in a bright sunlight from curtains that appeared hastily yanked open. Unable to get air into her lungs, she pressed a hand to her chest. And the fight went out of her.

Closing her eyes, Faith leaned back against the door, and borrowed support from the solid panel. For ten minutes. Ten hours.

Time didn't have much meaning at all. When she opened her eyes, her gaze landed on the silk sheets still twisted from when she and Rex had made love. And she wanted to go back to the moment just prior to waking, when she'd believed anything was possible for her and Rex. That there could be a future and a joyous one at that. For surely one who'd made love to her as he had, felt...something.

Faith folded her arms around her middle and squeezed tightly.

She'd deluded herself once more. Really, all along, where Rex was concerned. She'd wanted to believe there could be love with him, and so she'd seen what she'd wished to see. The charming man who'd read stories to the boys at her mother's school, and who'd raced around playing hide and seek. The same man who, after his and Faith's wedding ceremony, had dropped to a knee and spoke to Faith's young brother as if he were an equal.

She turned her head, and then froze, her gaze locking on a vibrant array of blooms. Of their own volition, her legs moved, and she stopped before the vanity and just stared at the mounted vase upon a gilded base. With fingers that trembled, she brushed her fingers over the white owl painted at the center of the porcelain piece. That snowy white, wide-eyed creature stared back. From within the chiseled bronzed vase sprung an array of dahlias from perfect tiny circles to enormous plate-sized blooms in a beautiful explosion of color—amethyst, pink, peach, and one that melded shades of purple and fuchsia.

"Oh, my heart," Faith whispered.

Faith pulled free one of the two dozen or so purple dahlias and held it to her breast.

She angled a look over her shoulder at the door she'd shut.

What a dunderhead she was. She'd been so consumed in her own hurt that she'd failed to see the panic and fear in her husband's eyes.

The lone stalk in hand, Faith headed for the adjoining sitting room. As she flung open the door, she almost stumbled over Rex seated on the floor, unblinking, staring at the entrance of her chambers.

Tenderness filled her heart, and Faith joined him on the crimson carpet.

Rex didn't say anything as she did, just continued staring in that distant way.

She spoke softly. "You brought me flowers."

"The key...it didn't make sense. I realized that...after."—Faith's fingers flew to that first gift he'd ever given her.—"To me it did. It was something I understood, but it wasn't a gesture you did."

Her chest tightened, and she pressed her palm firmly against the ornate metal. At last understanding. "It is perfect," she whispered. "And the vase. It is so very lovely."

"It is an owl," he said needlessly.

"I saw that."

"Because I call you *'petite chouette'*."

The sight of him at sea in his emotions and in this exchange made her heart turn over painfully in her breast. She willed him to look at her, and when he did, she continued, "The flowers, they are beautiful." Tears made her voice husky.

"Paddy informed me of your preference for the dahlia." And then, bashful as she'd never seen him, uncertain as she'd not known he could be, Rex stared intently at his lap and directed his words there. "He said you love the dahlia, especially the purple one and that you also like the pink, peach, and two-color ones." He abruptly stopped; an endearing blush filled his cheeks.

Oh God. In that moment, she fell in love with him. Not for the first time. But all over again. She'd never stopped loving him. Even when he'd hurt her. Even when she should have stopped, she'd not, because the heart knew what it wanted, and she wanted him. She always had. She always would. From the moment she'd popped her head up from behind the desk and found him there, his gaze only on her, Faith's heart had been forever his.

Lifting his head, he spoke on a rush. "Unless he was wrong and there is another flower—"

"No!" She brushed back the tears that had fallen. "Paddy was right. *You* are right," she hurried to assure him. "They are perfect, Rex," she said, her voice thick.

They were silent for a while.

Faith rested her head against his shoulder. "You don't *seem* like someone who wants to send me away."

"Because I don't." He shifted, and she felt him looking down at her. "I find...I...rather...like you."

Her lips twitched. "La, you're going to turn my head with such romantic talk."

Rex moved swiftly, scooting around so that he faced her. "That's just it. I'm *not* romantic, Faith. I operate a bloody gaming hell. A wicked one, at that. And I don't understand feelings or warmth or affection." His words tumbled out quickly, each one spilling into the next. "I thought I could marry you and making love to you would be enough, but it isn't because you make me feel things I didn't know I could feel.

"Just because you don't understand, doesn't mean you can't ever. You just never had anyone show you how." Faith waited until his gaze met hers. "I love you."

He stilled. "Faith." His voice was strained, hoarse. "I don't...that word...that emotion? I can't imagine you would feel that way for me, and no one ever has, but I can't—I'm not—"

"Shh." She pressed her fingertips against his lips, halting that panicky flow. "You don't have to say anything. I don't expect anything. Love isn't *about* expecting anything. Love is just...*love*."

Faith rested her hands atop his and his larger ones tensed. She held her breath, bracing for him to pull away, and then he did, and she felt that rejection like a physical loss.

Only...

Rex slowly twined his fingers with hers, joining them together. "I want to try...at this," he said, thickly. "At us."

She squeezed his hand. "We'll try together."

He might not love her yet, because as he'd said, the emotion was too new, too foreign for him. But as they leaned against one another, Faith rather thought someday soon he might.

CHAPTER 24

ℛEX HADN'T EVER TRULY BELIEVED rakes, rogues, and scoundrels could reform.

The patrons who'd quit his clubs after they'd married and who'd sought out more respectable establishments had likely deluded themselves into believing they loved those women who'd changed them. All the while he expected the bloom would fade from that which was new, and then the old vices would call. Those reformed rogues would return to a life of sin, but they'd do so discreetly.

For who could ever truly give up the thrill of sinning for the pedantic misery of marriage?

There'd been a time Rex had thought he'd rather slit his wrists with a dull letter opener than suffer through a respectable event. Standing outside his wife's bedchambers not only prepared—but eager—to join her and her family at a respectable event, at last he understood.

Slipping through the panel that joined their dressing rooms, Rex entered his wife's chambers, and he took that moment with her unaware of his presence to drink in the sight of her as her maid fluttered about putting the finishing touches to Faith's luxuriant black tresses. He devoured Faith with his gaze, eating her up with his eyes, wanting to consume her in every way. Draped in a diaphanous gown, Faith was a seductive vision of elegance and beauty. The translucent puff lavender sleeves and festoon flounce along her bodice begged a man to stare. Her slightest movement lent a rippling quality to the fabric, creating an otherworldly iridescent effect.

His body hardened as it invariably did at the mere sight of her.

Folding his arms, Rex dropped the bottom of his foot against the door panel, deliberately commanding his wife's attention.

In the mirror, their eyes met.

"Leave us," he ordered, and the lady's maid dipped a shallow curtsy and bowed out.

The moment he reached her, Faith turned her mouth up to his for a kiss.

Opening her lips, she let him inside, and he drank of her as he longed to, tasting the sweet citrusy hint of lemon upon her. "We're going to be late," she panted between each glide of his lips over hers.

"Do you care, *petite chouette?*" he whispered, placing a kiss on the creamy swell challenging the neckline of her dress.

She whimpered. "I sh-should."

"You should," he agreed, licking a path along her flesh. "But you don't."

"No, I don't." Faith's head fell back, allowing him greater access to that long, graceful column.

He perched her on the edge of the vanity and slowly drew her skirts up.

Faith bit her lower lip, troubling that plump flesh. "You're g-going to wr-wrinkle my gown."

Rex nipped her throat. "You don't care about that, either."

"No. Th-that is *truuue.*" Her admission ended on a moan as his fingers found her moist and hot as she always was for him. "But we shouldn't—" He quickened his strokes within her.

Reaching down between them, Rex freed himself from his trousers and guided himself to that place he needed to be. With a hiss, he plunged inside her.

Faith cried out, wrapping her legs about him; she gripped the edge of the vanity and lifted her hips to meet each downward lunge.

Panting, sweat beading at his brow, Rex caught a glimpse of them in the mirror, their bodies straining, and the sight of them in the throes of fucking drove him to the brink of madness. Gritting his teeth, he sank his hands into her hips and leveraged his thrusts. Fragrance bottles and mirrors tumbled to the floor; the tinkling sound of breaking glass melded with the rasp of his wife's breathing, and a prettier symphony there wasn't.

Faith keened softly, biting at his shoulder like a feral cat, and he felt her teeth all the way through the fabric of his evening jacket.

He withdrew, pulling out of her with a deliberate slowness.

Faith released a pained moan. "*Nooo*. Don't stop. Please."

Her pleas sent another bolt of fire through him. "Be a good girl," he growled. "Tell me you want to come." He slid within her, inch by slow inch. "Say it and I'll give you what you need."

She whimpered. "I want to come, Rex."

"You'd skip this evening's festivities and let me make love to you until your body is weak with pleasure?"

"Anything," she cried, writhing against him.

With an animalistic grunt drawn from that most primitive part deep inside, Rex pulled back and slammed into her. Again and again. Until Faith stiffened, and her shrill scream rent the chamber, filling every corner of the room and his mind. Faith wept; the force of her climax sent tears streaming down her cheeks. Still, he continued stroking her long and hard until she came a second time. And then Rex allowed himself to join her over that precipice where pleasure became confused with pain. "Fuck yes," he hissed, and then burying his head in the curve of her neck, Rex spent within her.

Her body went lax, and the tension left him on a rush. Sinking onto the bench, he drew Faith atop his lap and nuzzled her throat.

"You are shameful, husband."

"We are shameful." He grinned, nipping at a heart-shaped birthmark along her collarbone. How had he never noted that clever little marking? How was there always something new to discover about his wife?

Faith edged back and looked at him. The passion had receded from her eyes, replaced with an uneasiness. How openly she wore her emotions. One time he'd have considered that a display of vulnerability and been repulsed by that weakness. What magic did she weave that she'd changed him in even this way?

"What is it, love?" he asked, smoothing his hands over the small of her back in that way he'd come to learn these past weeks she so very dearly loved.

"You don't want to go."

"Leave this chamber and your arms? I'm a hot-blooded man who cannot get enough of his wife." Rex attempted to take her lips in another kiss, but she shifted out of his reach, denying him that meeting.

"Rex," she chided.

Surrendering his attempt at seduction, he met her overly somber owl-eyes. "Faith, the idea of joining polite functions like the charitable event hosted by your parents is one I'd rather have traded my club than willingly attend. Until you. Now, I find...I don't really mind it so much, as long as you are there with me."

Faith's eyes watered. "Truly?"

"Truly. It's madness, but there you have it. I've something for you." He reached inside his jacket and withdrew a narrow velvet case.

She glanced down at the package. "What is this?"

"Open it."

Faith lifted the lid, revealing the piece he'd had commissioned for her, an intricately crafted gold, diamond and ruby key hanging from a gold chain. A gold heart setting held a large blood-red ruby and the shaft of the key was sparkling diamonds.

"Rex," she breathed. "It is beautiful."

"I know you used to wear a heart pendant and you no longer do."

"I no longer had a need for it," she murmured.

Rex made to remove the simpler chain, but Faith pressed her fingers to the key there, stopping him. "I *love* my necklace."

"That one is a key to rooms and locks. This key is more."

"Yes. I didn't understand at first the significance, but when you explained to me, well, now I'll never remove it."

She was the only woman in the kingdom who'd prefer a bronze key to the fortune in gemstones he'd gifted her this night.

"How about," he murmured, placing a kiss against the corner of her mouth, "you wear my key when we are out, and at night, when I'm making love to you, you wear nothing more than the brass key?"

"What if I wear the key *and* the heart when you make love to me?"

He smiled. "That is a compromise, love."

Rex slid a hand between her legs, but Faith laughed breathlessly and moved from his arms. "Not now. We are going to be late as it is."

He flashed a wolfish grin. "Ah, but it will be worth it."

"Yes, it will, but my gown is wrinkled and my hair disheveled as it is; it will take but one look for everyone to know why we're late. I must fetch my maid."

As she started for the bell–pull, Rex tucked himself in his breeches. He caught up to her, taking her lightly by the arm and drawing her close.

"Ah, but I'm perfectly capable of taking care of my wife."

After Rex had tenderly cleaned Faith between her legs, he'd urged her back to the vanity where they'd made love.

As Faith sat there, she stared at her husband as he set to work righting the chignon that had come loose while they'd made love. With an infinite tenderness, Rex proceeded to gather the tendrils that had come lose from her heart-shaped hair combs, tucking them back into place with a greater skill and competency than any lady's maid Faith had ever had.

How she loved him. And how she longed to hear him utter those words in return. And yet, though he'd never spoken aloud of his feelings for her, with every day that passed, he'd shown Faith in every other way that he cared about her. From Paddy he'd gathered her favorite desserts, meals, and treats, and ensured there was never a day she went without one or all of them. She read in his offices while he worked at his ledgers. They exchanged dirty jests, until they both laughed uproariously, and then made love afterwards. Every day, he made her body sing and took her soaring to new and undiscovered heights of bliss.

Rex, seeming to feel her gaze, looked up from his task. Their eyes met in the mirror. "What is it, love?"

Love. Her heart danced as it always did at the effortless way in which that endearment now fell from his lips. "I love you," she said softly, "is all."

Color flooded his cheeks, and Rex hastily returned to his task of straightening her curls. With as many times as she'd uttered those three words, he'd proven endearingly shy still. Faith didn't doubt he cared for her and mayhap even loved her. But she also knew that after a lifetime of the cruelty he'd suffered at his father's hands and the guards Rex had put into place to protect himself, the process of believing he was deserving of love and freely showing it in return was one that would not come overnight. Or as the case may be, over a fortnight.

"Done," Rex said, and she looked at his completed work.

Faith's fingers immediately went to the lone, long curl he'd left to dangle about her shoulder. The corkscrew bounced at that crevice between her breasts.

"This one is for us," he murmured, drawing Faith to her feet. He placed a kiss on the place where that coiled tress touched her skin. "Our secret to remember what we did this night. And then," he moved his lips in a slow path to along her collarbone, kissing his way to her shoulder, "when we return this evening, I'm going to make love to you ten more times, Faith."

She trembled, her lashes fluttering, and only when he'd left her breathless once more did he stop.

A small mewl of protest escaped her. "Come along, *petite chouette*." Taking her by the hand, he led her from the room. "We have your family and friends to scandalize."

They reached the hall and Faith forced him to stop. "*Our* family and friends."

He stared questioningly at her.

Faith rested her palms upon the black fabric of his beautifully tailored wool evening coat. "They are our family and friends now, too, Rex. You aren't alone. Not anymore."

Some powerful emotion glinted in his eyes, and he drew her into his arms, covering her mouth with his.

A swell of shouts went up, breaking the moment, and she and

Rex apart.

The doors to the private suites exploded open, and Rex pushed her behind him just as his partners, along with Mr. Tavish and Mr. Red, poured through speaking loudly over one another in a swell of chaotic words that blended in a discordant cacophony.

Rex spoke over the din. "What in hell is—?"

Malden slapped a newspaper at her husband's chest. "*This* is what is going on." He turned a hate-filled glare upon Faith.

Faith had never been one to hide, but in this instant, with so much hate gleaming from within those hard, blue eyes, she reflexively moved closer to Rex, pressing herself to his back.

"She's done it again," Malden said icily, as her husband read.

She?

"Whose done what again?" she asked while her husband's eyes raced over that front page.

"That isn't all," Argyll spoke, more measured and calmly than Lord Malden. He held a note out for Rex. "Bourchier requested a meeting. He refuses to come here and demands we see him on his terms."

"All of us," Latimer added.

"He's pieced together what is going on and demands an audience, or he'll bring the information he's in possession of to all the papers."

Bourchier…as in the other nobleman whose information she'd shared with the papers, which also meant…which also suggested…

When he glanced up and his eyes finally met hers, Rex's gaze proved inscrutable and impenetrable as it had been before they'd found happiness in their marriage, and she wanted to weep with the loss. And then, in an instant, she was forgotten as he and his partners spoke.

To give her shaking hands purpose, she took the pages from Rex's hands, and he made no attempt to stop her.

Faith read.

MORE SECRETS SPILLED

The secrets of London's scandalous set continue to fall. This time, not only the finances of the Earl of Denbigh have been served up for public consumption, but also the famously straightlaced gentleman's peccadillos and wicked vices. Though it's secret to none that Lord D is plump in the pockets, it has been shared with this esteemed writer that Lord D—

Faith stopped reading and looked up at her husband still embroiled in a heated discussion with his partners. "I didn't do this," she whispered. Rex didn't so much as look at her, and she tugged his sleeve, demanding his attention.

His harsh gaze seared her. But he said nothing, still.

She made herself say it again. "I did not do this, Rex. Surely you believe that." *Please say you believe that.*

"What reason would he have to believe it?" Malden snapped.

"Lord Denbigh is a good man. He is the best friend of Aunt Caroline's husband. I would never—"

"Spill the secrets of the friends and family you deem worthy of protecting?" Malden glared.

"No. That isn't what I'm saying—"

"Enough," Rex ordered, his tone cold and impatient. He looked to Malden. "We'll meet Bourchier. My wife is to join her fam—"

"You won't be coming," she said, even as she knew he couldn't.

"You expect him to dance attendance and sip champagne while his business is crumbling?" Malden tossed at her.

"Hey, now," Argyll chided. Not her husband. His friend and partner.

Faith winced. "No, that isn't what I'm saying. I—"

"I'll send word to your father," Rex interrupted her.

So that her family could discover she'd been abandoned by a husband who had so little faith in her? "The only word you'll send is that we will not be attending. If you aren't coming," she spoke calmly, "if you are dealing with this, then I will stay here."

"Very well." With that dismissive reply, Rex turned to Latimer. "He can request all of us be there, but I'll be damned if I allow you to abandon your post here." He looked to Mr. Red. "You are to remain on duty with Mrs. DuMond—"

"Are you making me a prisoner?" Faith demanded.

"Malden, see that word is sent with my and my wife's regrets."

As the marquess hastened to do her husband's bidding, Rex gave their audience a look. They filed from the corridor.

"You are not a prisoner, madam," he said, the moment he and Faith were alone.

"*Madam?*"

"I offered to send you to your family's gathering. You declined, madam. Now, if you'll excuse me, I have bloody crisis to contend with, Faith."

She grabbed his hands and drew them close to her breast, to that place where his key rested. "You do believe me when I say I did not do this." Not this time.

"It does not matter—"

"It matters to me, Rex."

"Who else could it have been, Faith?" he asked. It would have been easier had there been frost in his tones and not this quiet, calm acceptance. "It was someone in possession of exact numbers from my club."

She reeled.

"I'm not saying it was you," he said.

"You all but did." And through the shock of hurt and a fresh betrayal, she froze as a memory slipped in. "Lord Malden," she whispered, losing her grip on his hands.

Rex stared at her a moment then glanced around as if expecting his partner had returned.

Her mind raced. "I went to find you several weeks ago, and I discovered him in your offices."

"I've known Malden since we were boys. He's been a partner at the club from the beginning. He is loyal—"

"And I'm not?" she shot back.

Her husband dragged a hand through his hair. "That isn't what I'm saying."

"Then, what are you saying?"

There came a firm rapping on the door. "Your mount is readied," Mr. Gruffton called through the heavy oak panels.

Rex continued speaking to Faith. "I'm saying, I don't know who is responsible for it, but I cannot stay here and discuss the possibilities at this time. I have to put this to rights."

Faith stared after him and then at the doors he drew shut behind him. It hadn't escaped her notice that her husband hadn't given her any assurances he, in fact, believed or trusted Faith in this. Her heart ripped open.

Faith had never known happiness like she had these past weeks as Rex's wife. She'd been so very certain it would never end. She'd been wrong. So wrong.

Wrapping her arms around her middle, Faith hugged herself tightly.

As she sat watching the clock tick the minutes by, there came a loud thump on the other side of the panel. With a frown, Faith drew the door open and froze. His eyes cold, his heart even colder, a tall, handsome gentleman stood over Mr. Red's inert body.

Lord Somerville grinned. "If it is not *the* Mrs. DuMond."

She opened her mouth to scream but he lifted a pistol, pointing the barrel of that gleaming weapon at her breast.

"Uh-uh." He made a clicking sound with his tongue. "I would not do that if I were you. Thanks to a certain peer, I know it was you who have made things very bad for me. Now there is something you are going to help me with."

CHAPTER 25

A TALL, PAINFULLY THIN BUTLER ESCORTED Rex, Malden, and Argyll down the darkened hallways of Lord Bourchier's crumbling townhouse. Not a word was spoken among them.

Had anyone looked carefully enough over the years and noted the earl's frayed carpets and wax candles near nubs failing to properly light the profligate gambler's household, they'd have gathered the true state of the man's finances long before Faith had shared that evidence with the world.

If anyone discovered the information was being shared by someone residing within the club, Forbidden Pleasures would cease to be. A gaming empire built on sin could only survive and flourish if its patrons had assurances their secrets would remain just that—secrets. As such, his mind should be solely on this upcoming meeting, and yet he could not shake the thought of Faith as she'd been: stricken and hurt.

Even as he now realized she'd not lie to him, in the moment he'd not possessed the same certainty. He should have given the assurances she'd sought. He should have told her that he believed her, but explained he needed to focus on working through the latest crisis to hit Forbidden Pleasures.

The butler brought them to a stop before a paint-chipped panel that didn't quite fit the frame, indicating that at some point the actual door had been replaced by this cheaper oak board. As the servant scratched at the door, Rex shoved aside thoughts of Faith; he'd make it right with her later. He'd explain that he'd been an utter ass doubting for even an instant and spend the rest of his days and nights earning her forgiveness.

"Enter," Bourchier called out almost cheerfully, and Rex and his partners were shown inside.

But then, having the upper hand had that effect on a man.

"Gentlemen, so good of you to join me." Bourchier sat behind a sloppy desk covered with hastily-opened ledgers and papers. Several decanters littered various spaces upon the surface. He paused and assessed his audience. "I requested all of you be here."

"And leave my club unattended?" Rex said coolly. "Then you don't know me."

The earl cleared his throat. "Won't you sit?"

"We'll stand," Rex said coolly, and with that refusal, he briefly cracked Bourchier's bravado.

The other man's grin slipped a moment, before he found his footing. "Oh, I insist you take a seat."

Rex narrowed his eyes, and then grabbing the Rosewood Bergère armchair, he sat.

Setting his drink down, Bourchier dropped his arms to his desk and abandoned all pretense of pleasantries. "You've been lax with your patrons' secrets. I'd expected more from you, DuMond."

"What do you want?" Argyll asked quietly.

"I don't need anything from *you*," Bourchier said.

Which suggested he needed something from someone else.

"I don't need anything from you, DuMond, as I've already received what I need from someone else."

At Rex's side, Malden stiffened. The pallor of his skin grew noticeably worse, and Rex caught that slight but telltale gesture. Warning bells went off, as Faith's earlier suggestion slipped forward.

No. Malden wouldn't. It wasn't possible. It—

"One of your partners has proven very helpful. Isn't that right, Malden?"

"You bastard," Malden hissed, taking a step forward.

The earl, however, only smirked.

"What is he talking about?" Rex demanded.

"You see," Bourchier answered when Malden only remained stubbornly, damningly silent, "it was one thing when it was just

Somerville. Everyone knows Somerville is a wastrel and that he's in dun territory. Me, on the other hand? Only your club possessed that secret about my mines in the Americas. After Somerville and I spoke and with a little help from your father, it didn't take much for us to gather that someone within your club was sharing our secrets."

His goddamned father.

"I want more names." Bourchier jabbed a finger into an open ledger, punctuating his point. "And I intend to have them."

"By God, you said you wanted one." Malden surged forward but Argyll caught him by his arms.

"I *gave* you what you sought."

"So he could blackmail one of our patrons?" Argyll asked incredulously. "*Jesus*, Malden."

Stunned and grateful he'd taken the damned chair after all, Rex looked to his oldest friend. What exactly was Malden saying? What was he admitting? Only, he knew. The warning Faith had issued before he'd set out reared its head. She'd been on the mark, and he'd been so blinded by his long history with his partners that he'd failed to even hear her out.

The man whom he'd considered a friend turned his palms up in supplication. "They vowed to reveal your wife was the one behind those articles. If I shared this with you, they said they'd tell the world. They'd ruin her reputation, and with society knowing she now lives at Forbidden Pleasures, the club's future was at stake."

Rex sharpened his gaze on Lord Bourchier. In having visibly reacted, they'd already given the man before them an upper hand.

"Your father, the duke, was so very good to let us know what your wife has been up to." The earl sipped away at his brandy, smug as he'd never been at Rex's gaming hell tables.

God rot his father's blackhearted soul.

"Is this why you insisted on an audience with all of us?" he asked coolly. "If you think for a moment I intend to give you the name of another patron, you're mistaken." Rex stood. "You may have gotten that one name; however, I'll be goddamned if you get anything else from me or my club." He'd deal with the fallout, but he'd be damned if he gave bastards like Bourchier or Somerville another thing more.

Bourchier's eyes bulged. "W–Wait!"

Rex arched an eyebrow.

"D–Didn't you hear what I said? I will tell the world!" Bourchier exclaimed.

"Tell them what you will." Rex headed for the door. "No one will believe you. Not with their now knowing the truth about you."

"Y–You can't leave!"

The panicky thread of desperation halted Rex in his tracks. Warning bells chimed in his mind. Rex went motionless, and then slowly turned back. There was something there. "Why?"

Bourchier's mouth moved several times before any words came out. "B–Because…" He shook his head. "I…I just…thought we'd c–continue to discuss the matter further."

Sweat slicked his palms and a shiver of apprehension raced up his back. Oh God.

"What is it, DuMond?" Argyll asked.

"He is attempting to stall us," Rex whispered.

Faith.

Dread swirled low in his belly, rising higher and higher until it spread to his chest and climbed into his throat, stealing his ability to breathe, to talk. He tried to will his legs to move, but they remained immobile; he was paralyzed.

"This meeting…it was a diversion," Rex said, his voice peculiarly flat to his own ears, distorted all the more by the odd buzz that had begun there.

"No." The earl yanked at his cravat. "I–I don't know what you're talking about."

With a growl, Rex stormed across the room and snatched Bourchier by the shirtfront. The earl cried out as Rex dragged him across the desk, sending papers and books and crystal bottles flying to the floor.

He wrapped a hand around his throat. "What have you done?" he snarled.

His cheeks a mottled red, Bourchier writhed and scrabbled beneath Rex's fingers.

Rex tightened his grip. "I'll snap it." He squeezed.

The earl's bulging eyes went to Argyll and Malden; both men remained impassive against that silent plea.

Bourchier managed a jerky nod.

Rex loosened his hold enough to allow him to speak.

"It was S-Somerville's idea." He gasped for breath.

Rex growled and squeezed again. "*What* was?"

"I-I don't know. H-He told me all I n-needed to do was call a m-meeting and he'd handle the rest."

Rex released the earl, and the sniveling coward collapsed face down on his desk, coughing as he attempted to get air into his lungs.

"You had better hope for the sake of living that my wife is unharmed," he seethed. He sucked in a breath then continued in a silken whisper "Because if so much as a hair on her head is out of place, I will return and happily rip the limbs from your cowardly body and feed upon them while you watch." With that, he dragged Bourchier up and shoved his fist hard into the other man's face, shattering his nose and relishing the scream of agony that spilled from his lips.

Rex set off at a run; his breath came hard and fast, and he was dimly aware of Argyll and Malden racing to keep up.

"Latimer is there," the duke reminded him.

That assurance didn't help. Because Rex, the one man who should be there looking after his wife, seeing her safe from harm, wasn't. He groaned.

"I'm so sorry," Malden rasped. "They threatened to reveal the fact your wife was behind those articles. And with her now living there, were that information to come out, the club would never recover. DuMond, I was trying to save the club. I thought if I gave them the wealthiest patron, they'd leave her and Forbidden Pleasures be."

He didn't give a damn about the club. All the power and money to be had from that establishment meant nothing. There was nothing if there was not Faith in his life. Reaching the foyer, Rex shoved the front doors open and headed for the beggar boy holding his horse.

Malden tried again. "Please," he begged, as Rex pulled himself onto his mount. "When we were younger, you always saved me, and then you taught me how to solve my own bloody problems. I was trying to help."

Rex glared down at the man he'd called friend. "Your intentions may have been to spare her name and save the reputation, but when that failed, you attempted to shift blame onto my wife. You put her life in danger." He set his jaw. "You had better hope she is unharmed, or you'll pay the same price as Somerville and Bourchier."

Without a backward look, Rex wheeled his mount around and headed at a breakneck speed for his wife. He fixed his gaze forward; the ride proved interminable. His panicky thoughts were incapable of thinking of anything but one person—*Faith*.

Faith, who'd shown him more happiness than he'd certainly ever deserved. Faith, who'd made him laugh and who loved him, even as he'd hurt her in a way that might have forever killed her feeling for him. His chest grew tight. And how had he repaid her love? By doubting her. By shutting her out. He'd not even managed to give her those three words she so deserved, words that he now knew were true.

Not having said them hadn't kept him safe from hurting. Loving her hadn't made him weaker; she'd made him stronger in every way that mattered. She'd made him a better man, one who didn't want to live a life relishing in people's weaknesses, but existing to do good and be good—for her and those people he now knew as family and friends.

If anything happened to her, he wouldn't survive. He wouldn't *want* to survive. The only world he wanted to live in was one where Faith was smiling and happy and as thoroughly in love with him as he was her.

At last he arrived outside the front of his club. Servants came forward to claim the reins of his mount while the guards stationed at the doors drew the panels open so he could pass. Rex skimmed his gaze over the floor, not knowing what he'd expected—perhaps some hint or sign that the world had been turned upside down. But men and women tossed down coins, serving girls filled glasses to the brim. Everything looked normal.

He raced through the busy gaming hell floors.

Once he'd only ever cared that the tables were packed and the room brimming with patrons. Now he cursed the crowd as he shouldered his way to the lone entrance leading upstairs. The two guards, Creed and Bathgate, remained stationed there. "Have you left this entrance once since I've been gone?" he demanded.

"Not once," Creed assured him.

Malden hung off to the side, staying close, this time wise enough to say nothing.

Argyll appeared with Latimer. "I came around the back entrance. Stewart and Stonely are there."

Relief so strong swarmed Rex, it threatened to take him down. He'd not be content until he saw her. He bolted for Faith's rooms. *I am never leaving her again. Ever.* The moment he saw her, he was going to beg her forgiveness and at last tell her how desperately he loved her, and then after that, he was going to make love to her and escort her to her family's gathering. And he was going to enjoy every damned moment of it because he loved her world, one that she'd welcomed him into. He loved that there was light and love and laughter in it, and not sins and evil and darkness.

Rex reached the lone door at the center of the hall that connected the private suites to the main corridors and stopped.

His heart thudded sickeningly against his ribcage.

"Where is Gruftton?" he asked dumbly of his partners. Fear made that question garbled and thick.

Latimer shouted for Creed.

"Oh God," Malden whispered. "I...he was helping me with... the situation."

"A situation that with your handling has been fucked up in every way," Rex barked.

Creed arrived. "You called?"

"Where is Gruffton?" Latimer put that question Rex couldn't manage a second time.

Creed frowned. "Was here the last time I swept this hall."

"When was that?" Latimer demanded.

"I...ten—fifteen minutes ago?"

Rex took flight. "Faith!" he thundered, barreling ahead, and then he staggered to a stop.

Red lay sprawled on the floor; a vicious gash upon his head had spilled blood upon the floor. The sanguine stain had turned the pink carpet black.

As Argyll dropped to a knee to check for a pulse, Rex stepped over the prone guard's body.

"He's alive," Argyll confirmed, and Rex dimly registered those words as he did a sweep of Faith's rooms. It didn't take him long to discover her chambers were empty, the mess made when they'd made love still littering the floors.

A tortured moan spilled from his lips, and then throwing back his head, he roared. "*Faith.*"

There came the delicate footfalls of a woman, and another rush of relief coursed through him only to die a moment later.

Faith's maid widened her eyes on the prone form between them, and then with the deference only a servant of the peerage could manage, the girl dipped a curtsy. "Mr. DuMond."

"My wife—" he rasped.

"I…" The maid seemed to register all at once the tension. "Mr. Gruffton said she was in the kitchens."

Rex cursed blackly, and the girl blushed and stammered over that interruption.

"B–but Lord Guilford arrived a short while a–ago, to c–collect her. Mr. Cressley showed him to one of the parlors and asked me to collect her."

"I'll handle the meeting with Guilford," Argyll said quietly, and then headed off to meet Faith's father.

Faith's father who would and *should* take Rex apart at the seams for having failed to protect her.

It was just as the other man had predicted, but then you were arrogant, and you wanted her at any and all costs.

And Rex set off at a sprint for the one place he knew Faith and Somerville would be.

CHAPTER 26

Faith had gotten herself into it now. Though in fairness, she'd really gotten herself into it the moment she'd sold Lord Somerville's scandal to the papers and secured herself an enemy.

And yet, even as that same enemy now marched her through the halls to her husband's club, she couldn't bring herself to regret what she'd done. Not just because she'd saved another young lady a miserable fate as his wife—though there was that, too. Nay, if she'd not done what she'd done, then Faith would not even now be married to Rex, and that was something she would never, could never, regret. Even if it meant dying.

Of course, she'd so very much rather *live* with him than *have lived* with him for the small time they'd spent together.

Faith wanted more time with him. It wasn't enough. She suspected it never would be.

Lord Somerville prodded her between her shoulders, urging her onward through the darkened corridors. "You are stalling."

"I'm not." She was. Because with every fiber of her being she trusted Rex would somehow piece together that something was afoot, and he'd come here, and when he did—she shivered, thinking of the fate that surely awaited Lord Somerville when he did. "I'm not accustomed to using these corridors."

"How easily lying comes to you, my lady. I have it on authority from one of DuMond's guards that you frequently sneak through these halls."

Fury filled her at thinking of those who'd betrayed her husband.

"Who?"

"Gruffton."

Of course. Now his halting her while Lord Malden did whatever he did in Rex's offices made sense. Faith wasn't naïve. She knew incriminating information he shared with her meant there was no other way of this ending for her except death. That realization didn't make her sad as much as enrage her.

Faith made to lead him down another wrong way, but he gripped her by the arm, squeezing hard enough to surely raise bruises, and tears sprung to her eyes.

"I am done with your games, my lady," he whispered. "Now you have one more opportunity to take me where I need to go, and if you don't…" He slipped a finger along the bodice of her neckline; her stomach revolted at that bold touch.

She made to slap his fingers, but he caught her wrist, gripping it with the same intensity he had her arm. He propelled her against the wall, pressing her body hard against hers.

Faith gasped and squirmed, fighting to push him out of reach.

"You're going to take me exactly where I want, because if you don't," he repeated, "I'm going to enjoy tupping you within these hidden halls. I had your aunt. She was rubbish. Something tells me you'll be fire."

"You were never fit to so much as lick my aunt's riding boots," she hissed. Her chest heaving with panic and repulsion, Faith brought her knee up to catch him between the legs, but he evaded her efforts.

Lord Somerville laughed softly, his breath stinking of spirits, and an overwhelming hint of marjoram wafted over her face. She gagged.

"As I expected. You are fiery, my lady, and I'd quite enjoy rutting on you if you don't give me exactly what I want."

Faith glared. "My husband is going to kill you."

"Perhaps." He spoke with the arrogance of a man who'd only confidence in how his mad plan would play out. Somerville pressed the barrel of his pistol against the spot where her heart thumped.

Despite herself, despite the desire not to show him her fear, Faith whimpered.

"Not so very feisty now, are you," he crowed. "Now, move." He grabbed her by the arm and shoved her forward hard enough that she fell to her knees.

She cried out, making no attempt to disguise that sound, using it as any attempt to raise a hue and cry from one of the guards stationed outside. All the while knowing—

"They can't hear you," Somerville said happily. "DuMond is notorious for having constructed thick walls that mask all manner of screams. Usually, those sounds are of pleasure or pleasure-pain, but it comes in handy for circumstances such as this." His smile turned dark. "I won't ask you again. One more delay and I'll shoot you and find the way there myself."

Faith struggled to her feet. He'd make good on his threats, and she'd rather take her chances with Somerville outside this labyrinth than within it.

She stopped before the doorway nearest her husband's offices.

"Very good, sweet," he praised, and motioned with the gun for her to open the panel.

Faith complied, and as she entered ahead of the earl, reminiscent of a scene not so very long ago she found Gruffton in wait. She glowered at him as she passed. "My husband will kill you if you continue with this, but if you help me, he, despite what you've done, will likely spare you."

The guard appeared unswayed. "Your husband isn't much known for his forgiving ways."

"Don't waste your energies on Gruffton. He is being paid quite handsomely for his help." Somerville gave her another less than gentle shove. "Now open it."

Faith drew the chain off and made a show of inserting it into the lock.

"Faster, my dear."

Click.

And then he propelled her in.

Faith stumbled and fell to her knees; pain radiated up her legs, and she opened her mouth to cry out—

The earl leveled the pistol at her head, and that scream died on her lips as dread tightened in her belly. "You're far cleverer than that." His expression hardened. "Now, the ledgers."

"I don't know where he stores them."

"My sources say you do know." He cocked the pistol. "I trust this will help you remember."

She scrambled around the desk. "You really are a pathetic man."

"You dumb twit. I've got a gun trained on you."

Faith stole a peek at the closed door, willing her husband to come. She made a show of rummaging through her husband's drawers. Every second more was a second closer to his deducing there'd been something more at play this evening.

Somerville took a step closer. "You didn't find those books in his drawers, and you know it. You picked the damned lock." He launched into a heated diatribe and Faith found herself staring at his mouth as it moved; it was as though she were watching a scene play out of another person's life.

He was going to kill her. She knew that now. She'd known it from the moment she'd discovered him in the private suites, but the look in his eyes erased the fledgling hope she'd allowed herself. Faith wanted to rail and weep at the unfairness of it. She'd wanted tiny babes with Rex, sons and daughters who'd hop on his back and be ridden about the room during games of charades and make-believe. She wanted to picnic with him and fall asleep in his arms because these two weeks doing so as his wife hadn't been enough. And yet, a calm stole through her. An acceptance of her fate.

The world came whirring back to the present.

"Did you hear me?" he demanded, wagging his weapon at her.

"I won't," she said softly.

His eyebrows climbed. "You won't?"

Faith shook her head.

There came a commotion in the hall and a large thump, and as the door exploded open, relief threatened to bring her to her knees.

"Rex," she whispered.

Only Rex as she'd never seen him. Not like this. White-hot fury poured from his powerful frame, his chiseled features etched in rage.

He did a sweep of the office, his flinty gaze landing briefly on her, and she saw the unspoken question.

She mouthed, "I am fine."

He studied her a moment longer before sliding his gaze slowly to Lord Somerville.

The earl paled. "N–Not another step," he warned in a trembling voice. Backing up several steps, he raised his pistol at Rex, but Rex continued coming. Faith bit the inside of her cheek hard enough that the metallic hint of blood filled her mouth.

Somerville abruptly shifted the head of his weapon to Faith.

Rex stopped fast.

He hadn't known fear since he'd been a small boy. After the abuse he'd suffered at his father's hands, he vowed he'd never feel that puling emotion again. And he hadn't. Until this very moment. With Lord Somerville pointing his pistol at Faith's chest, he knew an even greater terror than all the miserable sufferings combined during the course of his childhood.

The earl had a panicky glint in his eyes. He'd the look of a caged beast trapped in a corner—which he was. And Rex knew all too well how dangerous those creatures could be. Desperation stripped a person of their usual restraints and left them volatile, unpredictable.

"Put your weapon down, Somerville," he spoke with a calm he didn't feel, but required.

"S–So you can kill me? I think not, DuMond."

"It is not too late to turn back from this."

"Do you think I'm stupid?" the other man snapped, his voice climbing, and his weapon trembling as did the finger Somerville had upon the trigger.

"Of course not," he made himself say. Bile climbed Rex's throat, and he choked it back. Losing control of his thoughts and actions wouldn't help Faith. Faith who was so very still, pale but unshaken, a veritable queen of her castle, brave in the face of her keep being stormed. And he loved her more than ever.

"I'll have you know, this is all your fault. You were the one who told me to do this."

Rex stared at the madman before him.

"If you have someone disloyal to you, someone who'd deal in your secrets, then I suggest you find that information out for yourself and settle your own business instead of coming to me."

Oh God. His stomach churned. Those long-ago words he'd uttered came back to haunt him.

"Sound familiar?"

"What do you want to go away, Somerville?"

"I want my and Bourchier's notes, along with the ledger."

"You can have it. Just put your weapon down. You can have the book." The other man could take anything—his ledgers, his club, all his patrons. Just so long as he didn't hurt Faith. Faith, who was all that was good and pure and fiery and clever.

Rex turned his head slowly, looking to his wife. So still, and yet so very strong. "Faith, give him the ledger."

She shook her head. "I won't, Rex."

God, she was breathtakingly stubborn and foolish, all at once.

"It doesn't matter, Faith. Let him take it. Let him take it all." He looked her in the eyes, hating that he'd waited until this very moment to speak the words she'd deserved long before now, deserved in a way that had been so much more special. "None of this matters, Faith. This club, my patrons, all the money and the power in the world. Not if I don't have you." He held her gaze. "I love you."

"You love me?" she whispered.

He touched a hand to the place where his heart beat; it beat for her. "With all I am."

Her eyes shimmered with tears. "I love you."

"All very touching," Somerville snapped. "You don't live unless I have it."

She could only live. There was no world without her in it. "She has to," Rex said, his voice oddly calm, when inside, panic ravaged his chest.

Faith blinked back those drops and then shook her head. "No."

Rex's eyes slid shut and he cursed.

"No?" Somerville squawked.

"I don't live either way. Because the moment you have the information you seek, you will kill me." She spoke so simply of her end. How, when the mere thought of it shredded Rex's mind, soul, and spirit? "If my husband lives, you can try and place blame on him. Mayhap you'll say ours was a marital quarrel, and he reacted in rage after I disseminated information about his club to the gossip pages."

By the way, Somerville paled, Rex's clever wife had hit the nail on the mark.

Faith tipped up her chin. "I'll be damned if I allow you to frame my husband for your crimes."

The earl cursed, and his fingers tightened about his pistol.

"You have one bullet," Rex said. "And it had better be for me. Because if you are foolish enough to use it on her and let me live…" The rumbling in his chest became a full bestial growl. "The moment that bullet leaves your pistol, if it strikes her, if it so much as brushes past the air she breathes, I will rip you open and pull your still-beating heart from your chest and choke your dying body with it."

The earl wavered, his pistol trembling.

A commotion sounded in the hall, briefly pulling Somerville's attention to the door.

Rex moved. He sprung forward, launching himself in front of Faith, registering the report of the pistol, the force of the bullet knocking him back, Faith's cry, and the burn of smoke from the earl's fired pistol. Dazed, Rex lay sprawled on his wife's lap, dimly aware of Argyll and Latimer dragging a screaming Somerville from the room.

Faith's father thundered for a doctor, and Malden went running.

"Rex." She wept, her tears streaming onto his face. "Why did you *do* that, you silly, stupid man?"

He smiled and reaching up, caressed her cherished cheek with his fingers. He looked briefly at her father standing over them. "A wise man once said some women are worth dying over."

The marquess's features twisted in pain.

Faith cried all the harder.

"You, Faith, are one of them," Rex murmured. "But having

finally found you and loving you as I do," he brushed her damp cheeks, his efforts futile as there were only more to replace it, "today will not be that day." He reached a hand inside his jacket and withdrew a small, thick leather volume that bore the mark of a bullet.

Faith froze. *The Moral Tales*. Her eyes flew to his.

"Since you gifted me with it, I always carry it close. It seems, dear wife, you've, in fact, saved me. In every way."

Faith scrambled from under him and then launched herself atop him. "I thought you were going to die," she sobbed.

Rex folded her close. "I'm not going anywhere, *petite chouette*. I fear you are stuck with me."

Faith caught his face between hers. "And it is the only place I wish to be," she breathed against his lips.

"Forever?"

Faith smiled. "Forever."

And with a smile, Rex kissed her in return.

Epilogue

London, England

A near deafening cacophony of cries and shouts swelled around the parlor.

Faith clutched at her breast, staggered back, and then with all the grace she could manage, fell backward onto the pretty floral Aubusson carpet.

Opening her eyes, she stared up at her husband.

Her husband scowled. "I'm not amused."

"Oh, come. Even Cousin Rowan has gotten into the spirit of the game." Faith winked, and then promptly closed her eyes once more, throwing herself back fully into her role.

"You're dying," Rowan called out.

His sister Rose punched him in the arm. "She didn't die, you dunderhead."

Violet hopped up, clapping her hands. "I know. I know. *Rex* is dying."

"He didn't die, either," Faith's father pointed out. And where once he'd have sounded positively mournful at the thought of Rex surviving, since Faith's husband had saved her life days earlier, he'd proven generous in his respect and love for Rex.

"For which we are so very grateful," Faith's mother said from the sofa she occupied with Rex.

"Ooh-ooh," Aunt Caroline cried, to make herself heard over the din. "I have it! Faith falling in love with Rex!"

Faith sat up. "Huzzah! You have done it!"

Her aunt took a deep bow, welcoming the congratulations heaped on her by the rest of the Brookfield family and friends present.

Rex stood and helped Faith to her feet. Looping an arm about her waist, he drew her closer into his arms.

"Are you having a wonderful time, Mr. DuMond?" she murmured.

"Mr. DuMond?" he repeated. "Are you cross with me, *petite chouette?*"

"Never." Faith touched her lips to his. "I have since decided that I love being Mrs. DuMond so much, that I can never be cross when I hear it uttered."

"I want to go! I want to go!" Paddy cried, jumping up and down and waving his arms to earn everyone's attention.

As Faith's brother took the proverbial stage, Faith and Rex retreated from the center of the room. "Are you all right?" she asked softly.

He flashed a crooked grin. "Well, charades would have once horrified me. No longer."

She shook her head. "I meant…about Lord Malden."

"I don't want to talk about him," he said tersely, directing his focus to Paddy's latest antics.

It had been a week since the horror with Lord Somerville, and in that time, Rex had refused to speak with his partner. Instead, he'd had the apartments he'd kept cleared out and sent a man-of-affairs to discuss the purchase of the other man's holdings of the club.

"I know you don't want to talk about him, Rex, but you should."

"There is nothing to say. He put you in jeopardy. He allowed it to appear as though you were guilty of crimes he alone was guilty of. Such actions can never be forgiven."

"He cares about you and the club. He was attempting to help."

He growled. "Only you would attempt to make peace between me and a man who nearly got you killed."

"Yes." She smiled. "And you love me for it."

"And I love you for it," he allowed. He lowered his lips to hers, but Faith drew back slightly; denying him that kiss he sought.

"I do want you to promise to at least speak with him. And see if you can come to some kind of understanding."

"We can't. Even if he'd not almost gotten you killed, he also shared the name of a patron."

"I did, too," she pointed out. "And you forgave me."

A sound of frustration escaped him. "That is different."

"Why?"

"It just is, Faith."

She smoothed her hands down the front of his jacket. "Promise me you'll try."

Rex cursed. "Fine," he gritted out.

Faith patted him gently. "Very good."

A round of applause went up as Miles correctly hazarded Paddy's clue.

"Which means it is Papa's turn," Faith's brother called.

The marquess dropped his head into one hand and waved the other, begging off.

Paddy jumped up and down. "I'll go again!"

"Do behave," Violet gently chided. "You just went. It is Rex's turn."

All the occupants of the room looked as one to Rex and Faith.

Blushing, she stepped out of her husband's arms. "The floor is yours, dearest husband."

He placed his lips close to her ear. "I'd rather you were mine, *petite chouette*."

"I'm *always* yours."

The Marquess of Rutland's eldest son gagged. "This is *really* quite disgusting."

"You won't always feel that way, my boy," Lord Rutland drawled, ruffling the top of the boy's head.

Unresistingly, Rex took his place in the center of the floor, and all the guests fell quiet, waiting for him to begin his turn.

He looked across the room, his gaze locking with Faith's, and then pressing a hand to his chest, he staggered back in the same way Faith had moments ago.

"You're dying." Lord Rutland's youngest son, Garrick, ventured that ruthless guess.

His brother thumped him on the back of the head. "That was my guess."

"Last round it was with Lady Faith. This was my guess, *now*."

Faith's lips twitched. "I have it."

Her family and friends offered her their silence, and Faith made her way over to Rex. She stopped over him. "You are falling in love with me."

"Wrong," he murmured, pushing to his feet.

She wrinkled her nose, and he tweaked the end of it. "It's the moment I *fell* in love with you."

"And when was that, Mr. DuMond?" she murmured, twining her arms about his neck.

He touched his brow to hers. "The moment I first found you under my desk, *petite chouette*."

And to a chorus of laughter and sighs from the adults and groans from the children, Rex kissed her.

THE END

Want to know about Lady Caroline's scandal that brought Faith and Rex DuMond together? If you missed "Aunt Caroline's" happily-ever-after, be sure and order To Marry Her Marquess!

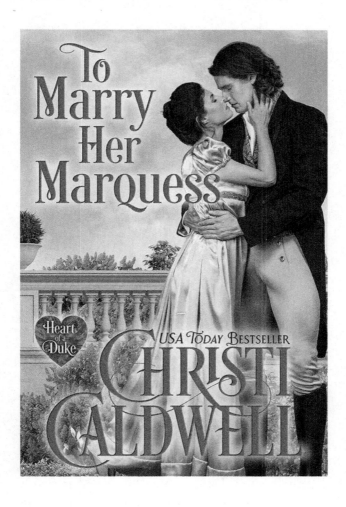

And if you missed Defying the Duke,
Lady Lettie Brookfield's book, you can order today!

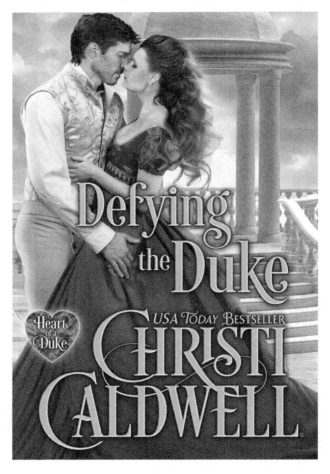

Bookish and spirited, Lady Lettie Brookfield is firmly on the shelf. The last thing she wants, however, is to spend the rest of her days as an unmarried sister, dependent upon her family's charity. Accepting she won't have a love match, she finds herself coming around to the idea of marrying the only suitor she's ever had… that is until she's suddenly reunited with her brother's former best friend, the brooding, formally charming, Anthony, Duke of Granville.

Years earlier, in an unselfish act intended to save his friend, Anthony committed an unforgivable betrayal; one that severed his friendship. Now he's a duke and must fulfill his obligations. The last woman he has any right to long for is his former best friend's younger sister, Lettie.

All grown-up Lettie is passionate, quick-witted, and desirable, and it isn't long before Anthony falls for her, the very last woman he should consider marrying. Will past betrayals keep them apart? Or is there a path to a new beginning with Anthony and the only woman he truly loves?

Be sure and check out the next installment coming from Christi
Caldwell's bestselling Heart of a Duke series!

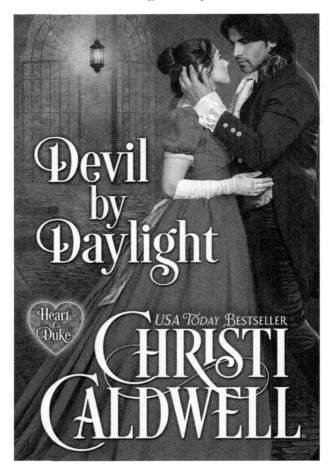

The Duke Alone

For an abandoned lady and a reclusive duke, the winter season brings a swirl of romance—and danger—in a bracing novel by *USA Today* bestselling author Christi Caldwell.

Lady Myrtle McQuoid has always felt a little forgotten, and this season is no exception. When her boisterous family vacates their London townhouse for the country, Myrtle finds she's been left behind. But she just needs to stay warm, keep her belly full, and distract herself until her relatives realize their mistake and turn back to collect her. Surely that won't take long.

Brooding widower Val Bancroft, the Duke of Aragon, has shut himself off from the world. He craves blessed solitude—a loyal dog, a silent house, and his own company are all he requires. Certainly not the nonstop chattering of the joyful, opinionated young woman next door.

But with a potential threat lurking in the winter shadows, Myrtle may need to pluck up the nerve to approach the reclusive duke. And Val is not one to turn his back on a vulnerable lady.

Amid the silent nights of London, beneath a blanket of snow, could the light of a new, warm love be kindling?

OTHER BOOKS IN THE
HEART OF A DUKE SERIES
BY CHRISTI CALDWELL

TO HOLD A LADY'S SECRET
Book 16 in the "Heart of a Duke" Series

Lady Gillian Farendale is in trouble. Her titled father has dragged her through one London Season after another, until the sheer monotony of the marriage mart and the last vestige of Gillian's once-independent spirit conspire to lead her into a single night of folly. When her adventure goes so very wrong, she has only one old friend to whom she can turn for help.

Colin Lockhart's youthful friendship with Lady Gillian cost him everything, and a duke's by-blow had little enough to start with. He's survived years on London's roughest streets to become a highly successful Bow Street Runner, and his dream of his own inquiry agency is almost within his grasp.

Then Gillian begs him to once again risk angering her powerful father. The ruthless logic of the street tells Colin that he dare not help Gillian, while his tender heart tempts him to once again risk everything for the only woman he'll ever love.

TO TEMPT A SCOUNDREL
Book 15 in the "Heart of a Duke" Series

Never trust a gentleman…

Once before, Lady Alice Winterbourne trusted her heart to an honorable, respectable man… only to be jilted in the scandal of the Season. Longing for an escape from all the whispers and humiliation, Alice eagerly accepts an invitation to her friend's house party. In the country, she hopes to find some peace from the embarrassment left in London… Unfortunately, she finds her former betrothed and his new bride in attendance.

Never love a lady…

Lord Rhys Brookfield has no interest in marriage. Ever. He's worked quite hard at building both his fortune and his reputation as a rogue—and intends to enjoy all that they can offer him. That is if his match-making mother will stop pairing him with prospective brides. When Rhys and Alice meet, sparks flare. But with every new encounter, their first impressions of one another are challenged and an unlikely friendship is forged.

Desperate, Rhys proposes a pretend courtship, one meant to spite Alice's former betrothed and prevent any matchmaking attempts toward Rhys. What neither expects is that a pretense can become so much more. Or that a burning passion can heal… and hurt.

Beguiled by a Baron
Book 14 in the "Heart of a Duke" Series

A Lady with a Secret… Partially deaf, with a birthmark marring her face, Bridget Hamilton is content with her life, even if she's been cast out of her family. But her peaceful existence—expanding her mind with her study of rare books—is threatened with an ultimatum from her evil brother—steal a valuable book or give up her son. Bridget has no choice; her son is her world.

A Lord with a Purpose… Vail Basingstoke, Baron Chilton is known throughout London as the Bastard Baron. After battling at Waterloo, he establishes himself as the foremost dealer in rare books and builds a fortune, determined to never be like the self-serving duke who sired him. He devotes his life to growing his fortune to care for his illegitimate siblings, also fathered by the duke. The chance to sell a highly coveted book for a financial windfall is his only thought.

Two Paths Collide… When Bridget masquerades as the baron's newest housekeeper, he's hopelessly intrigued by her quick wit and her skill with antique tomes. Wary from having his heart broken in the past, it should be easy enough to keep Bridget at arm's length, yet desire for her dogs his steps. As they spend time in each other's company, understanding for life grows as does love, but when Bridget's integrity is called into question, Vail's world is shattered—as is his heart again. Now Bridget and Vail will have to overcome the horrendous secrets and lies between them to grasp a love—and life—together.

TO ENCHANT A WICKED DUKE
Book 13 in the "Heart of a Duke" Series

A Devil in Disguise

Years ago, when Nick Tallings, the recent Duke of Huntly, watched his family destroyed at the hands of a merciless nobleman, he vowed revenge. But his efforts had been futile, as his enemy, Lord Rutland is without weakness.

Until now…

With his rival finally happily married, Nick is able to set his ruthless scheme into motion. His plot hinges upon Lord Rutland's innocent, empty-headed sister-in-law, Justina Barrett. Nick will ruin her, marry her, and then leave her brokenhearted.

A Lady Dreaming of Love

From the moment Justina Barrett makes her Come Out, she is labeled a Diamond. Even with her ruthless father determined to sell her off to the highest bidder, Justina never gives up on her hope for a good, honorable gentleman who values her wit more than her looks.

A Not-So-Chance Meeting

Nick's ploy to ensnare Justina falls neatly into place in the streets of London. With each carefully orchestrated encounter, he slips further and further inside the lady's heart, never anticipating that Justina, with her quick wit and strength, will break down his own defenses. As Nick's plans begins to unravel, he's left to determine which is more important—Justina's love or his vow for vengeance. But can Justina ever forgive the duke who deceived her?

One Winter with a Baron
Book 12 in the "Heart of a Duke" Series

A clever spinster:

Content with her spinster lifestyle, Miss Sybil Cunning wants to prove that a future as an unmarried woman is the only life for her. As a bluestocking who values hard, empirical data, Sybil needs help with her research. Nolan Pratt, Baron Webb, one of society's most scandalous rakes, is the perfect gentleman to help her. After all, he inspires fear in proper mothers and desire within their daughters.

A notorious rake:

Society may be aware of Nolan Pratt, Baron's Webb's wicked ways, but what he has carefully hidden is his miserable handling of his family's finances. When Sybil presents him the opportunity to earn much-needed funds, he can't refuse.

A winter to remember:

However, what begins as a business arrangement becomes something more and with every meeting, Sybil slips inside his heart. Can this clever woman look beneath the veneer of a coldhearted rake to see the man Nolan truly is?

To Redeem a Rake
Book 11 in the "Heart of a Duke" Series

He's spent years scandalizing society.

Now, this rake must change his ways.

Society's most infamous scoundrel, Daniel Winterbourne, the
Earl of Montfort, has been promised a small fortune if he can
relinquish his wayward, carousing lifestyle. And behaving means
he must also help find a respectable companion for his youngest
sister—someone who will guide her and whom she can emulate.
However, Daniel knows no such woman. But when he encounters
a childhood friend, Daniel believes she may just be the answer to
all of his problems.

Having been secretly humiliated by an unscrupulous blackguard
years earlier, Miss Daphne Smith dreams of finding work at Ladies
of Hope, an institution that provides an education for disabled
women. With her sordid past and a disfigured leg, few opportunities
arise for a woman such as she. Knowing Daniel's history, she wishes
to avoid him, but working for his sister is exactly the stepping
stone she needs.

Their attraction intensifies as Daniel and Daphne grow closer,
preparing his sister for the London Season. But Daniel must resist
his desire for a woman tarnished by scandal while Daphne is
reminded of the boy she once knew. Can society's most notorious
rake redeem his reputation and become the man Daphne deserves?

TO WOO A WIDOW
Book 10 in the "Heart of a Duke" Series

They see a brokenhearted widow.

She's far from shattered.

Lady Philippa Winston is never marrying again. After her late husband's cruelty that she kept so well hidden, she has no desire to search for love.

Years ago, Miles Brookfield, the Marquess of Guilford, made a frivolous vow he never thought would come to fruition—he promised to marry his mother's goddaughter if he was unwed by the age of thirty. Now, to his dismay, he's faced with honoring that pledge. But when he encounters the beautiful and intriguing Lady Philippa, Miles knows his true path in life. It's up to him to break down every belief Philippa carries about gentlemen, proving that not only is love real, but that he is the man deserving of her sheltered heart.

Will Philippa let down her guard and allow Miles to woo a widow in desperate need of his love?

THE LURE OF A RAKE
Book 9 in the "Heart of a Duke" Series

A Lady Dreaming of Love

Lady Genevieve Farendale has a scandalous past. Jilted at the altar years earlier and exiled by her family, she's now returned to London to prove she can be a proper lady. Even though she's not given up on the hope of marrying for love, she's wary of trusting again. Then she meets Cedric Falcot, the Marquess of St. Albans whose seductive ways set her heart aflutter. But with her sordid history, Genevieve knows a rake can also easily destroy her.

An Unlikely Pairing

What begins as a chance encounter between Cedric and Genevieve becomes something more. As they continue to meet, passions stir. But with Genevieve's hope for true love, she fears Cedric will be unable to give up his wayward lifestyle. After all, Cedric has spent years protecting his heart, and keeping everyone out. Slowly, she chips away at all the walls he's built, but when he falters, Genevieve can't offer him redemption. Now, it's up to Cedric to prove to Genevieve that the love of a man is far more powerful than the lure of a rake.

TO TRUST A ROGUE
Book 8 in the "Heart of a Duke" Series

A rogue

Marcus, the Viscount Wessex has carefully crafted the image of rogue and charmer for Polite Society. Under that façade, however, dwells a man whose dreams were shattered almost eight years earlier by a young lady who captured his heart, pledged her love, and then left him, with nothing more than a curt note.

A widow

Eight years earlier, faced with no other choice, Mrs. Eleanor Collins, fled London and the only man she ever loved, Marcus, Viscount Wessex. She has now returned to serve as a companion for her elderly aunt with a daughter in tow. Even though they're next door neighbors, there is little reason for her to move in the same circles as Marcus, just in case, she vows to avoid him, for he reminds her of all she lost when she left.

Reunited

As their paths continue to cross, Marcus finds his desire for Eleanor just as strong, but he learned long ago she's not to be trusted. He will offer her a place in his bed, but not anything more. Only, Eleanor has no interest in this new, roguish man. The more time they spend together, the protective wall they've constructed to keep the other out, begin to break. With all the betrayals and secrets between them, Marcus has to open his heart again. And Eleanor must decide if it's ever safe to trust a rogue.

To Wed His Christmas Lady
Book 7 in the "Heart of a Duke" Series

She's longing to be loved:

Lady Cara Falcot has only served one purpose to her loathsome father—to increase his power through a marriage to the future Duke of Billingsley. As such, she's built protective walls about her heart, and presents an icy facade to the world around her. Journeying home from her finishing school for the Christmas holidays, Cara's carriage is stranded during a winter storm. She's forced to tarry at a ramshackle inn, where she immediately antagonizes another patron—William.

He's avoiding his duty in favor of one last adventure:

William Hargrove, the Marquess of Grafton has wanted only one thing in life—to avoid the future match his parents would have him make to a cold, duke's daughter. He's returning home from a blissful eight years of traveling the world to see to his responsibilities. But when a winter storm interrupts his trip and lands him at a falling-down inn, he's forced to share company with a commanding Lady Cara who initially reminds him exactly of the woman he so desperately wants to avoid.

A Christmas snowstorm ushers in the spirit of the season:

At the holiday time, these two people who despise each other due to first perceptions are offered renewed beginnings and fresh starts. As this gruff stranger breaks down the walls she's built about herself, Cara has to determine whether she can truly open her heart to trusting that any man is capable of good and that she herself is capable of love. And William has to set aside all previous thoughts he's carried of the polished ladies like Cara, to be the man to show her that love.

THE HEART OF A SCOUNDREL
Book 6 in the "Heart of a Duke" Series

Ruthless, wicked, and dark, the Marquess of Rutland rouses terror in the breast of ladies and nobleman alike. All Edmund wants in life is power. After he was publically humiliated by his one love Lady Margaret, he vowed vengeance, using Margaret's niece, as his pawn. Except, he's thwarted by another, more enticing target—Miss Phoebe Barrett.

Miss Phoebe Barrett knows precisely the shame she's been born to. Because her father is a shocking letch she's learned to form her own opinions on a person's worth. After a chance meeting with the Marquess of Rutland, she is captivated by the mysterious man. He, too, is a victim of society's scorn, but the more encounters she has with Edmund, the more she knows there is powerful depth and emotion to the jaded marquess.

The lady wreaks havoc on Edmund's plans for revenge and he finds he wants Phoebe, at all costs. As she's drawn into the darkness of his world, Phoebe risks being destroyed by Edmund's ruthlessness. And Phoebe who desires love at all costs, has to determine if she can ever truly trust the heart of a scoundrel.

To Love a Lord
Book 5 in the "Heart of a Duke" Series

All she wants is security:

The last place finishing school instructor Mrs. Jane Munroe belongs, is in polite Society. Vowing to never wed, she's been scuttled around from post to post. Now she finds herself in the Marquess of Waverly's household. She's never met a nobleman she liked, and when she meets the pompous, arrogant marquess, she remembers why. But soon, she discovers Gabriel is unlike any gentleman she's ever known.

All he wants is a companion for his sister:

What Gabriel finds himself with instead, is a fiery spirited, bespectacled woman who entices him at every corner and challenges his age-old vow to never trust his heart to a woman. But...there is something suspicious about his sister's companion. And he is determined to find out just what it is.

All they need is each other:

As Gabriel and Jane confront the truth of their feelings, the lies and secrets between them begin to unravel. And Jane is left to decide whether or not it is ever truly safe to love a lord.

LOVED BY A DUKE
Book 4 in the "Heart of a Duke" Series

For ten years, Lady Daisy Meadows has been in love with Auric, the Duke of Crawford. Ever since his gallant rescue years earlier, Daisy knew she was destined to be his Duchess. Unfortunately, Auric sees her as his best friend's sister and nothing more. But perhaps, if she can manage to find the fabled heart of a duke pendant, she will win over the heart of her duke.

Auric, the Duke of Crawford enjoys Daisy's company. The last thing he is interested in however, is pursuing a romance with a woman he's known since she was in leading strings. This season, Daisy is turning up in the oddest places and he cannot help but notice that she is no longer a girl. But Auric wouldn't do something as foolhardy as to fall in love with Daisy. He couldn't. Not with the guilt he carries over his past sins… Not when he has no right to her heart…But perhaps, just perhaps, she can forgive the past and trust that he'd forever cherish her heart—but will she let him?

THE LOVE OF A ROGUE
Book 3 in the "Heart of a Duke" Series

Lady Imogen Moore hasn't had an easy time of it since she made her Come Out. With her betrothed, a powerful duke breaking it off to wed her sister, she's become the *tons* favorite piece of gossip. Never again wanting to experience the pain of a broken heart, she's resolved to make a match with a polite, respectable gentleman. The last thing she wants is another reckless rogue.

Lord Alex Edgerton has a problem. His brother, tired of Alex's carousing has charged him with chaperoning their remaining, unwed sister about *ton* events. Shopping? No, thank you. Attending the theatre? He'd rather be at Forbidden Pleasures with a scantily clad beauty upon his lap. The task of *chaperone* becomes even more of a bother when his sister drags along her dearest friend, Lady Imogen to social functions. The last thing he wants in his life is a young, innocent English miss.

Except, as Alex and Imogen are thrown together, passions flare and Alex comes to find he not only wants Imogen in his bed, but also in his heart. Yet now he must convince Imogen to risk all, on the heart of a rogue.

More Than a Duke
Book 2 in the "Heart of a Duke" Series

Polite Society doesn't take Lady Anne Adamson seriously. However, Anne isn't just another pretty young miss. When she discovers her father betrayed her mother's love and her family descended into poverty, Anne comes up with a plan to marry a respectable, powerful, and honorable gentleman—a man nothing like her philandering father.

Armed with the heart of a duke pendant, fabled to land the wearer a duke's heart, she decides to enlist the aid of the notorious Harry, 6th Earl of Stanhope. A scoundrel with a scandalous past, he is the last gentleman she'd ever wed…however, his reputation marks him the perfect man to school her in the art of seduction so she might ensnare the illustrious Duke of Crawford.

Harry, the Earl of Stanhope is a jaded, cynical rogue who lives for his own pleasures. Having been thrown over by the only woman he ever loved so she could wed a duke, he's not at all surprised when Lady Anne approaches him with her scheme to capture another duke's affection. He's come to appreciate that all women are in fact greedy, title-grasping, self-indulgent creatures. And with Anne's history of grating on his every last nerve, she is the last woman he'd ever agree to school in the art of seduction. Only his friendship with the lady's sister compels him to help.

What begins as a pretend courtship, born of lessons on seduction, becomes something more leaving Anne to decide if she can give her heart to a reckless rogue, and Harry must decide if he's willing to again trust in a lady's love.

FOR LOVE OF THE DUKE
Book 1 in the "Heart of a Duke" Series

After the tragic death of his wife, Jasper, the 8th Duke of Bainbridge buried himself away in the dark cold walls of his home, Castle Blackwood. When he's coaxed out of his self-imposed exile to attend the amusements of the Frost Fair, his life is irrevocably changed by his fateful meeting with Lady Katherine Adamson.

With her tight brown ringlets and silly white-ruffled gowns, Lady Katherine Adamson has found her dance card empty for two Seasons. After her father's passing, Katherine learned the unreliability of men, and is determined to depend on no one, except herself. Until she meets Jasper…

In a desperate bid to avoid a match arranged by her family, Katherine makes the Duke of Bainbridge a shocking proposition—one that he accepts.

Only, as Katherine begins to love Jasper, she finds the arrangement agreed upon is not enough. And Jasper is left to decide if protecting his heart is more important than fighting for Katherine's love.

In Need of a Duke
A Prequel Novella to "The Heart of a Duke" Series

In Need of a Duke: (Author's Note: This is a prequel novella to "The Heart of a Duke" series by Christi Caldwell. It was originally available in "The Heart of a Duke" Collection and is now being published as an individual novella.

It features a new prologue and epilogue.

Years earlier, a gypsy woman passed to Lady Aldora Adamson and her friends a heart pendant that promised them each the heart of a duke.

Now, a young lady, with her family facing ruin and scandal, Lady Aldora doesn't have time for mythical stories about cheap baubles. She needs to save her sisters and brother by marrying a titled gentleman with wealth and power to his name. She sets her bespectacled sights upon the Marquess of St. James.

Turned out by his father after a tragic scandal, Lord Michael Knightly has grown into a powerful, but self-made man. With the whispers and stares that still follow him, he would rather be anywhere but London…

Until he meets Lady Aldora, a young woman who mistakes him for his brother, the Marquess of St. James. The connection between Aldora and Michael is immediate and as they come to know one another, Aldora's feelings for Michael war with her sisterly responsibilities. With her family's dire situation, a man of Michael's scandalous past will never do.

Ultimately, Aldora must choose between her responsibilities as a sister and her love for Michael.

BIOGRAPHY

 is the *USA Today* bestselling author of the Sinful Brides series and the Heart of a Duke series. She blames novelist Judith McNaught for luring her into the world of historical romance. When Christi was at the University of Connecticut, she began writing her own tales of love—ones where even the most perfect heroes and heroines had imperfections. She learned to enjoy torturing her couples before they earned their well-deserved happily ever after. Christi lives in North Carolina where she spends her time writing, baking, and being a mommy to the most inspiring little boy and empathetic, spirited girls who, with their mischievous twin antics, offer an endless source of story ideas!

Visit www.christicaldwellauthor.com to learn more about what Christi is working on, or join her on Facebook at Christi Caldwell Author, and Twitter @ChristiCaldwell!

Printed in Great Britain
by Amazon

22592584R00165